This Is
How It Ends

This Is
How It Ends

KATHLEEN MACMAHON

sphere

SPHERE

First published in Great Britain in 2012 by Sphere

A CIP catalogue record for this book is available from the British Library.

HB ISBN 978-1-84744-546-9
C ISBN 978-1-84744-555-1

Typeset in Bembo by M Rules
Printed and bound in Great Britain by Clays Ltd, St Ives plc

Papers used by Sphere are from well-managed forests
and other responsible sources.

MIX
Paper from
responsible sources
FSC
www.fsc.org FSC® C104740

Sphere
An imprint of
Little, Brown Book Group
100 Victoria Embankment
London EC4Y 0DY

An Hachette UK Company
www.hachette.co.uk

www.littlebrown.co.uk

For Mark, for everything.

Acknowledgements

My heartfelt thanks to my agent Marianne Gunn O'Connor and to her sub-agent Vicki Satlow, to my editors Rebecca Saunders and Helen Atsma and to everyone else at Little, Brown and Grand Central for all their hard work on my behalf. Thanks to Cormac Kinsella who was there at the start. I'm very grateful for the assistance of Larry McDonald, formerly of Lehman Brothers, Andrew X Kopiak and Margot Collins from the American Embassy in Dublin, and Christine McDonnell of the National Library of Ireland. Thanks to Aoife Kavanagh and Pat Lynch for their guidance on all things Bruce Springsteen and to Kimberley Rogers, Valerie Bistany and Mema Byrne for their help with the manuscript. Thanks to Mary Reynolds for all her help and a special thank you to Margaret Dunne. Thanks to Niamh and Gerry Hurley for all their support. For their wise counsel, thanks to Sara Burke, Hilary McGouran, Ronan Browne and James Ryan. And to the much loved Caroline Walsh, who was a great champion of so many people, including me. Finally, thanks with all my heart to Lucy, Clara and Mark. To Meg, Kevin and Des, my endless love and gratitude. And to Valdi, I hope she knows.

Chapter 1

It was a wet Monday morning in mid autumn when Bruno Boylan finally set foot in the land of his forefathers.

He was travelling on a four-hundred-dollar return fare that he'd purchased just days beforehand from the comfort of his own home. A couple of clicks of the mouse and a sixteen-digit credit card number. No ticket, just an e-mail printout and a magic code. No delays, no stopovers, no adverse weather conditions for the crossing. He'd stayed awake through the drinks cart and the meal, he'd read his book for a while. Then he'd popped a Xanax, slicing hours off the flight time in one fell swoop. He was travelling light. All he had with him was a small backpack and a canvas bag in the hold. There was nothing whatsoever to suggest that this was anything in the nature of an epic journey.

The ping of the PA system woke him. He opened his eyes to find himself curled pathetically towards the wall of the plane for comfort, his face squashed against the window blind.

He hauled himself up to a sitting position, leaning his head back against the seat rest. Closing his eyes again, he sat there without moving, waiting for a voice to come.

He became aware of an overwhelming physical discomfort. His back ached, his knees were locked hard, they cracked when he tried to straighten them out. His butt hurt from sitting for so long. He needed to pee. The detritus of the journey was scattered around him. The thin blanket across his knees, the tangled earphones in his lap. His book was wedged somewhere underneath him, but he was so numb he couldn't even feel it. His shoes were under the seat. Soon he would have to find them and get his feet back into them. He allowed himself one more moment to savour the luxurious feeling of his socks on the carpeted floor.

Another ping and the pilot's voice spread over the cabin. Bruno could only hear him in snatches. But he could guess what he was saying, he could fill in the gaps. They would shortly be beginning their descent. Something about the weather in Dublin, Bruno couldn't catch it. He nudged up the blind and looked out at thick white cloud. All he could see was the wing of the plane, strangely still.

He turned his attention to the little blue screen on the back of the seat in front of him. A moving map, all it showed was a blunt outline of the east coast of America, the huge expanse of the Atlantic, and then the outline of Ireland and England up in the right-hand corner. A sweeping arc traced the trajectory of the flight, the dotted line ending in a virtual plane. The model plane was almost on top of Ireland now. It was so far out of scale that it was about to block out the entire country.

Bruno's mind shifted a gear. He experienced an unexpected moment of panic, a sickly feeling that he should have prepared himself for this arrival. He wasn't ready for it. He shouldn't have slept, he should have stayed awake the whole time. He should have been present for the journey. He remembered something he'd been told once: that American Indians sit in the airport after they arrive somewhere, that they like to give their spirit a chance to catch up with the body. Suddenly, that made complete sense to Bruno. His body was out of whack with his spirit, he needed time to catch up.

The screen in front of him changed. Now it was showing a list of statistics. Time to destination, 0:23 minutes.

He had to use the time. He had to straighten it all out in his head.

Three weeks since he'd lost his job, three weeks that seemed like three years. Or three days, or three hours. It made no sense, it seemed like a lifetime ago and yet it was all so fresh, the wounds still open and raw.

A month to go to the election. The wait was unbearable. You had to convince yourself that time was marching on like it always does, that any day now it would all be over and you would know the outcome. But the wait was still unbearable.

And here was Bruno, suspended in the air between these two points, 0:21 minutes to destination. He imagined himself as a little man on the moving map, a crude gingerbread cutout. He plotted his journey right along that sweeping arc across the ocean. He was just tracing the line with his finger when, without warning, the screen went black.

The PA system kicked into action again and the cabin lights came up. The seat-belt signs were turned on and the cabin crew started moving through the plane handing out immigration cards. Blinking in the vicious light, Bruno filled his card out carefully with the ballpoint pen they'd given him. Once he'd finished, he discovered he had nowhere to put the card. He tucked it into the inside cover of his book and held the book closed in his lap.

A slow descent through the clouds, there was Bruno hunched at the window, peering hopefully out at nothing. All he could see was the rain streaking the outside of the window, the grey expanse of the plane's wing ploughing on through dense white air. There was no way of knowing how close they were to the ground.

Suddenly, there was green outside the window, there was wet grass rushing by and a red-and-white-striped windsock and a low grey building and the terrible sound of the wheels briefly hitting the ground and then bouncing off it again. A messy landing, the body of the aircraft swung violently to the left and then to the right before finally steadying itself as the brakes took hold. Bruno held on to the back of the seat in front of him with his two hands to stop himself from falling forwards.

As the plane wheeled in towards the terminal building, he had a giddy sense of elation. After all these years, he had finally done it. Thirty years since that deathbed promise and it had been haunting him ever since. Now it was done. For a moment he imagined that he could just stay on the plane and go right back. Until it occurred to him, there was nothing to go back to.

His spine shuddered as he leaned over to grope for his shoes on the floor. He stuffed his earphones into the pouch on the back of the seat. Unclipped his seat belt. Sat there, longing to brush his teeth.

The plane jolted to a stop and there was a big exhale as the doors were opened. Immediately people were up and delving into the overhead compartments to retrieve their stuff. A moment or two waiting for the order to move, then they were shuffling along with their heads bowed like prisoners in a chain gang. Bruno shunted himself over to the aisle seat, heaved himself on to his feet and stretched up to get his cabin bag down. Then he moved with the line towards the door of the aircraft. He nodded at the stewardess and stepped out into the plastic tunnel connecting the plane to the terminal building. He began the gentle climb up the walkway, following the people ahead of him. There was a strange comfort in being part of this orderly procession, like being on a pilgrimage.

As he crossed over the elbow joint, it wobbled under him, as if it was a floating jetty. His stomach wobbled with it. He felt light as a balloon. He took his bag off his shoulder and let it hang down towards the floor, clutching it for ballast. Without it, he imagined he might just float up into the air.

The planes come in over Howth.

On a clear day you can see Dublin Bay laid out below you as you come in to land. Dun Laoghaire harbour way over to the left, Portmarnock to the right. Between them the vast empty stretch of Sandymount strand.

From the beach you can watch the planes arriving, a steady stream of them moving silently across the sky. They appear way out to sea, coming in on a gentle gradient above Howth

Head and gliding along the South Wall. Then they disappear noiselessly down into the city.

The planes are so much a feature of the landscape that Addie seldom notices them. The same with the smoke from the chimneys at Poolbeg, the same with the car ferries lunking their way along the horizon towards Dun Laoghaire. The clouds and the seabirds and the sea itself. Addie takes no notice of any of these things. She's so caught up in her own head, she doesn't notice anything else.

The beach is where she was born, pretty much.

She was five days old when they brought her home. She was carried out of the car in her mother's arms, a tiny bundle wrapped up in a purple angora blanket, a wool hat pulled down over her forehead and her ears. Her mother climbed the steps up to the front door, pausing at the top to turn back to face the sea.

Her father had the door open already, he had stepped into the hall and he was beckoning for her mother to follow. Come on in, woman, for God's sake, he said. You'll freeze out there.

But her mother stood on the steps for another moment with Addie in her arms, gulping in the cold sea air. It was heaven after the sticky heat of the hospital, she couldn't get her fill of it. It never occurred to her that her newborn daughter too was drinking in that salty air, that she was pulling it down into her spongy little lungs. Some of it must have made its way right down into her soul.

That's how Addie feels now, she feels as if the beach is a part of her. It's her special place, it's probably what's keeping her sane.

The beach is deserted at this hour of the morning, there's

6

nobody around but herself and the little dog. The tide is out and the clouds are hanging low over the sand, you can almost feel the pressure of them on your head. The forecast is for rain, but there's no sign of it yet.

Addie walks straight for the waterline. She's half a mile out and still the sea seems no closer, it must be a very low tide. There are some puddles now, more and more of them, so she doesn't go any further. She doesn't want to get her feet wet. It's starting to get cold, and she really should be wearing her boots. But she doesn't, she prefers to wear her runners. That way she can feel the ridges of the sand through the soles of her shoes. It makes her feel solid, the sensation of the hard sand under her feet.

All her life Addie has had the feeling that there's a black cloud following her around. These days she feels like that cloud has finally caught up with her. The beach is the only place where she has the sense that she can outwalk it.

Out on the beach she can talk to herself. She can sing along to her iPod and no one can hear her. She can scream if she wants to and sometimes she does. She screams and then she laughs at herself for screaming. Out on the beach, she can think about all the things that have happened, she can sift them, backwards and forwards in her head. She can cry hot tears of self-pity. She feels guilty about crying in front of the dog, but afterwards she feels much better, she feels almost content.

The dog is scrabbling in the sand for something that isn't there. She's shovelling wet sand with her front paws, tossing it back between her hind legs. A big pile is building up behind her and her whole underbelly is filthy, but she doesn't seem to notice. Addie stands there and watches the dog working away at her pointless task. Sure let her at it, she thinks, isn't she happy.

Addie throws her head back and looks up at the sky. She's studying it, as if she's looking for something up there. It occurs to her that she'd love to travel out into space, she'd love to look down at the world from out there. If she could see the world from the outside, maybe then she'd be able to gain a bit of perspective on her situation.

She turns and faces back towards the shore. Even from here, she's able to pick out the house. It's the putty-coloured one in the middle of a terrace of smudgy pastels. Three large windows looking out over the sea, two upstairs, one down.

He'll be sitting in the downstairs window. She can't see him from here, but she knows he's there. She knows he can see her, he's watching out for her. It makes her reluctant to go back in.

She takes her iPod out of her pocket and scrolls down through the menu. It takes her a moment to find what she's looking for. She selects the track and slides the lock over to stop it from slipping before she puts it back in her pocket. Then she pushes her shoulders back and raises her face to the wind as she waits for it to start.

A piece of music for a soprano, and Addie's voice is anything but. That doesn't stop her joining in. She sings along heartily, imagining herself to be in perfect harmony.

'*I know that my redeemer liveth . . .*'

She doesn't know all the words but it doesn't matter, it feels so good to sing. There's a lot of repetition of the bits she knows.

'*I know that my redeemer liveth . . .*'

She throws her head back and closes her eyes as she sings. There's no one around to hear her, and anyway, she wouldn't care if there was. The dog pays no heed to the singing. She's well used to it.

Addie's striding back towards the shore now, the little dog whirling around her feet as she goes. Behind her, the sky is black and angry, the rain only moments away. The line of the horizon is interrupted by an awkward cargo ship. It's just sitting there, blocking the view. The chimneys are still pouring smoke out into the air, the smoke pale against the darkness of the sky. The aircraft warning lights are blinking intermittently.

Out beyond Howth Head, another plane comes down out of the clouds and begins the gentle slide towards Dublin airport.

Coming through passport control, Bruno suddenly felt too old for all this.

So long since he'd done any travelling, he'd forgotten how physical it was. The rubbery legs, the parched throat. The creaking bowels.

'Reason for your visit?'

'Political refugee,' said Bruno in a moment of madness.

The guy looked up at him with raised eyebrows. Surely he wasn't old enough to be a policeman, he only looked about twelve. He had bright orange hair, hair the colour of a carrot. So that wasn't just a stereotype.

Bruno came to his senses.

'I'm only kidding,' he said. He tried to summon up some charm, leaning in towards the booth in a conspiratorial fashion. Aware now of the line forming behind him.

'I was stretching a point,' he said. 'I'm actually here on vacation. Until after the election. Look, November fifth.'

He held up the printout of his ticket but the guy didn't even bother to look at it. He was scrutinising Bruno's face.

'Fair enough,' he said.

He raised his stamp and brought it down with a little thump on the page. Closing the passport, he handed it back to Bruno. Slowly, as if he had all day.

'Tell you what,' he said. 'If that crowd are still in charge after the election, come back to me, and we'll give you asylum all right.'

Bruno wasn't sure if he'd heard him right.

'No offence now,' the young policeman added, worried all of a sudden that he'd gone too far.

'No offence taken.'

And Bruno was tempted to say something else but he didn't. He slipped the passport into the pocket of his jacket, picked up his carry-on bag and moved off.

He was still smiling to himself as he waited at the baggage carousel. Fancy that, he thought. Back home, joke with an immigration official and they start taking out the rubber gloves.

But it got him to thinking. By the time he'd spotted his bag snaking towards him, he'd made a pact with himself.

If the Republicans win, I'm not going back.

*

The rain started just as she was turning her key in the basement door. A spill of rain, sudden and violent. She dashed inside and slammed the door behind her. The dog only just managed to squeeze through the gap in time.

'We just about made it, Lola, we would have been drenched!'

She's been talking to the dog more and more lately. Sometimes she finds herself addressing full conversations to her. It can't be a good sign.

Lola was hovering at the empty water bowl, standing there with her tail swaying expectantly. Addie took the bowl and filled it up from the tap and Lola drank noisily, emptying the bowl in seconds.

Then Addie filled the kettle from the neck and switched it on, leaning back against the counter while she waited for it to boil.

She glanced over at the clock on the wall and saw that it wasn't even ten. She had the whole day ahead of her, the whole morning and then the whole afternoon and after that the evening. Suddenly, she couldn't face the thought of it, she couldn't for the life of her think how she would get through it.

As she stood there, leaning against the kitchen counter, a tiny puff of optimism took hold of her. She seized upon the possibility that she could visit Della. She could text her and suggest they meet for coffee. An upbeat text, she wouldn't want to come across as needy. But then she remembered that today was Della's library day, she had signed up to help in the school library. She wouldn't be free for coffee. Addie felt the tears rising up in her throat. She found herself yet again peering into a deep well of despair.

Do you ever feel like doing yourself harm? That was the

only thing that the counsellor had wanted to know. She was just covering herself. She was terrified Addie was going to kill herself and she'd be held responsible. So she kept asking, do you ever think about doing yourself harm and Addie said no even though it was a dirty lie.

How many times a day does Addie think about it? More than two, fewer than five, the fingers of one hand. She thinks about it and then she thinks about the reasons not to. Lola. Her dad. Della and the girls. The possibility that things will get better.

It flits across her mind and then it floats away again. She knows it's not an option. She's just turning the handle of a door she already knows is locked.

Lola was sitting on the ground in front of her, her head elegantly raised, her tragic spaniel eyes fixed on Addie's.

'Don't,' begged Addie, her voice cracking. 'You'll make me cry. Please don't make me cry.'

And she got down on her hunkers and wrapped her arms gently around the dog's wet little body, burying her face in the fur at the back of her neck. She closed her eyes and collapsed into the dog for comfort. Lola staggered and then steadied herself to take Addie's weight. A smell of damp sand, of salty shells and the creatures inside them, it was overpowering. Addie had to pull away. She got to her feet again just as the kettle reached boiling point and switched itself off.

A small victory, she had managed to regain her equilibrium. She made the coffee and heated some milk for it in the microwave. There was enough hot milk left over for another cup, that was as far as she would allow herself to plan ahead. She took her cup over to the table and sat down. She sipped the hot milky coffee, looking out through the patio doors at the rain falling on the back garden. Concentrating on just the coffee and the rain, she was determined not to think about anything else.

She was just about to get up and fill her cup again when she heard a pounding on the ceiling above her. One, two, three short thumps, the signal that he needed something.

She forced herself to sit there for another minute before she went up to him.

Outside the terminal building, there was a line for taxis. Groups of people in their summer clothes with sunburned skin were pushing trolleys piled high with big cases. Everybody seemed to be smoking. Bruno felt out of place and very alone.

When he got to the front of the line an usher waved him forward.

'How many?'

'Just one,' said Bruno apologetically.

He opened the door of the taxi and tossed his bags inside, then he climbed in after them. He leaned back against the seat, relieved that the trip was nearly over. It was a moment before he realised that the driver had turned around. He was looking back at Bruno expectantly.

The driver was saying something but Bruno couldn't understand him. He was having trouble with the accent.

'Pardon me?'

'I said I'm not a mind reader. You'll have to tell me where you're going.'

'Oh,' said Bruno cheerfully. 'I'm going to Sandymount, could you take me to Sandymount please.'

He hardly had the words out of his mouth before they were pulling away from the kerb.

Bruno leaned forward into the gap between the two front seats.

'Do you happen to know any hotels or bed and breakfasts in Sandymount?' he asked. 'I need a place to stay.'

The driver looked back at Bruno through the rear-view mirror.

'Anywhere in particular in Sandymount?'

'Is there a beach? Maybe we could find something near the beach.'

The driver was still looking at him. 'Fair enough,' he said. He sounded unconvinced.

'I have family there,' added Bruno. But the driver didn't seem interested.

Sandymount. That was all his sister had been able to remember. She'd written it down for him on a scrap of paper and he'd copied it into the inside cover of his guidebook. 'They lived right on the beach,' his sister had said. But that was all she could recall. There was no guarantee they'd still be living there.

He would look them up in the phone book, that was the first thing to do. And if they weren't listed, he could always start asking around. Somebody was bound to know them. Even if they'd moved house, maybe there would be a forwarding address, maybe someone would know where to find them. As the taxi sped through the city, Bruno worked through all the scenarios. He worked through them methodically and he came

14

up with solutions. The only thing he didn't contemplate was the possibility that they wouldn't want to see him. It never even occurred to him.

The taxi swung round a tight little traffic island. Then they drove over a wide ugly bridge. To Bruno's right, the river cut a path all the way through the city. Low grey buildings lined the quays on either side of the strip of quiet grey water. When he turned to the left he was looking at boats. Cruise liners and cargo ships leaned against the quay wall, little yachts moored precariously in the middle of the river. Beyond them, he imagined, must be the sea.

The taxi stopped in a line for a tollbooth. In the silence Bruno became aware of the car radio. The accent of the woman reading the news was delightful to him. He leaned forward in his seat to savour it. To Bruno, it was a voice from the past.

'The latest polls from the United States show the Democratic candidate Barack Obama gaining on his Republican rival John McCain in the key battleground states. In Ohio, where voters have chosen the winner in the last eleven elections, Senator Obama now holds a three per cent lead over Senator McCain. The two candidates are due to go head to head in a second televised debate tonight.'

Bruno smiled.

So much for getting away from it all.

Of course it's so obvious now, in retrospect. It's hard to imagine that it could have turned out any other way.

When you see this guy, sitting at his desk in the Oval

Office, his long arm draped in front of him to deliver that famous left-handed signature. When you see his lanky frame emerging from the entrails of Air Force One, his palms held up to the cameras, his lovely wife standing beside him, he looks like he belongs there. It's hard to imagine anyone else in his place.

When you turn on the news and you hear them say, for the hundredth time, that the property market is in freefall. When you hear them predict that the recession will be deeper than expected, that the bill for it will be bigger, you're not really surprised. Because it seems pretty clear that it was always going to turn out this way, it seems like things have reached their natural conclusion.

But what you have to remember is that back then, nobody knew how it was all going to end.

Chapter 2

The traffic was thinning out day by day. It was very noticeable, there were fewer cars on the road.

From his vantage point in the front window, Hugh was
perfectly placed to observe this.

'I'm conducting a study,' he said. 'I'm counting the cars for
a ten-minute period every morning. There are undoubtedly
less of them. You notice it in the evenings too.'

He looked like a big pathetic bear sitting there marooned
in his carver chair, his two paws set in Plaster of Paris, right
up to the elbows. The white casts resting on the gleaming
mahogany surface of the desk. His leather-bound diary open
in front of him, the fountain pen lying redundant in the crease
between the pages.

'Oh really?'

She was trying to sound interested. But she was tired this
evening. To tell the truth, she was tired most evenings. It
was getting dark earlier every day. You could feel the

evenings closing in. Addie was glad of this. Less daytime to fill.

Hugh was peering down at the string of headlights moving along the Strand Road.

'Less people going to work, I suppose.'

'Less work to go to.' And she should know.

'More joggers.'

'Yeah, there are more people in the pool these days too. They're trying to keep their spirits up, the poor things. It's not easy, you know, being unemployed.'

But he wasn't listening to her.

'I might write to the *Irish Times*,' he was saying. 'Get a piece of paper and a pen, will you? I'll have to dictate it to you.'

'Is this the right time for me to remind you that I'm your daughter, not your slave?'

'Is this the right time for me to remind you that you're the reason I'm in this bloody predicament in the first place?'

He fell over the dog, that's what happened to him.

He was coming out of the kitchen, carrying a glass of wine in each hand. He didn't even notice Lola sliding past him, her little body flattened against the wall. He was calling out to Addie, telling her to put some cashew nuts into a bowl and bring them up. He didn't see the dog crossing out in front of him until it was too late.

All his instincts told him to save the wine. When Addie came running to see what had happened he was on his knees on the hall floor, still clutching the two glasses by their stems.

Miraculously, they hadn't broken. The wine had spilled of course, it had been flung far and wide as he fell. There were burgundy splatters all over the walls. But the wine glasses themselves were unscathed. The stupid bloody glasses, they'd only cost one euro each in the hardware.

Both his wrists were broken, he knew that straight away. It was the wrists that had taken the full force of his fall.

Now he spends his days counting the things he can't do.

'I can't even wipe my own bloody arse,' he said. He was back at the hospital for his outpatient appointment. Looking for sympathy, looking at least for a laugh. Not that you'd get it from these people. Humourless bloody lot.

'Very unfortunate,' said the young orthopaedic fellow they'd sent in to him. 'What did Oscar Wilde say? To break one wrist . . . '

He'd have preferred somebody he knew.

'Better off with someone you don't know,' they'd said. 'Keep things simple.' Since when was that the way things were done?

Little did he know they'd passed his file along like a live hand grenade.

'I'm not paid to take that kind of grief,' said the surgical registrar. 'It's a job for a consultant.'

The nurses were all giggling and the matron had to step in. 'Professor Murphy is a patient like any other,' she said. 'Now can we show him some respect.' Which only made them snigger all the more.

They passed him right down the line. The last one in, a

self-important young Corkman, just back from a stint in Boston. He was the one left standing when the music stopped. Baptisms of fire were mentioned, there was talk of paying your dues.

'I'm happy enough with how this is mending,' the Corkman said, looking up at the X-rays on the wall.

He dragged out his vowels like an American, it made him sound silly.

'Very straightforward Colles fracture,' he was saying. 'Named after a Dublin doctor, the Colles fracture. But of course, you'd know that. Anyway we'll have another look at it in a fortnight, but for the moment I'm happy enough. Keep the fingers moving, easier said than done, I know. And come back to me in two weeks, you can make the appointment outside.'

But of course coming back to the hospital again was out of the question. It had been an exercise in humiliation from start to finish, from the moment Addie had stopped the car at the front door and rushed around to help him out. The looks from the hospital porters, he'd seen them smirking. And the nurse on duty at outpatients hadn't seemed to recognise him. She'd asked him for a referral letter. She'd actually called him dear.

'They seem to think I'm a patient,' he'd chuckled as he was ushered into the examination room. He was trying to be jovial, trying not to throw his weight around.

'Excuse me if I don't shake your hand,' he'd said to the young fellow. What was his name again? Impossible to keep track of all these chaps, there seemed to be new ones appearing every day. Some of them didn't look old enough to be in long trousers. But they had ideas about themselves, these guys, the way they spoke to you.

'Hugh,' the fellow had said. 'I hope you don't mind me calling you Hugh? The thing is, until those casts are off, you *are* a patient.'

He should have said he bloody well did mind. These fellows, where did they get the idea that everyone was their equal? They went off to Bristol or Brisbane or Bahrain for a few years and as soon as they came back they started calling everyone by their first name.

No, no. Coming back to the hospital was out of the question.

'I'm afraid you'll have to send somebody out to me next time,' he said. Trying to reassert his authority. 'It won't be possible for me to come in again.'

He had caught the look between the nurse and the young consultant. But they said nothing so he decided he'd won that round.

'How did you get on?' Addie asked when he came out.

'Oh, fine,' he said. 'Touch of the poacher turned gamekeeper. They're all on their guard.'

Five more weeks, they'd told him, before the casts would come off.

But he doesn't see how he can do five more weeks. He doesn't see how he can do five more days.

How do they put up with him?

That's what a lot of people ask themselves. Those girls, they say, they're good to him. How they put up with him, God

21

only knows! Just be glad you're not one of his daughters, that's what the nurses say. Can you imagine!

When they were children he would sometimes bring them to the hospital with him on Saturday mornings when he had nobody to mind them. He would deposit them at the nurses' station while he did his rounds. Addie remembers the way the nurses would crowd around to look at them as if they were animals in a zoo. The chocolates would come out and they'd be encouraged to have seconds.

Questions would be asked, innocent questions. Questions that wouldn't have seemed impertinent at the time. Addie would never have guessed they were prying.

Did your daddy pick out that dress for you? Isn't he a great daddy? And where do you go to school? And who minds you when your daddy's at work? And what's your favourite dinner? And your daddy cooks that for you, does he? Isn't he a great daddy?

Addie would have been too polite not to answer, she would have answered them eagerly. She would have sat there, swirling chocolate around in her mouth, her legs dangling off the swivel stool, and she would have sung like a canary.

Not Della, Della would not have been so easily led. Even now Addie remembers her refusing their chocolates, she has an image of her sitting there tight-lipped and glaring. Della was never one to let good manners get in the way of her principles.

The next thing they knew, their father would come flying back up the corridor and the questioning would stop as if he'd clapped his hands. God, he was handsome then, he was a matinee idol. The jet-black hair and the flashing eyes and the high colour. Patrician to his fingertips, the voice resonant with that innate authority he carried around with him.

Back then, Addie thought he was in charge of the whole hospital, she thought he was revered by all around him. A king in his kingdom, the way he would sweep through the corridors and people would nod respectfully and bend their heads as he passed. It's only now she knows that it was fear he instilled in them. Truth be told, it was hatred.

The strange thing is that none of this matters to Addie. He occupies a place in her heart that's beyond reason or logic. She remembers him plaiting her hair when she was a little girl. The smell of aftershave and soap, the smell of his freshly ironed shirt. The sportsmanlike way he would sit himself on the edge of a kitchen chair, his legs spread wide apart and her standing in between them. With his big doctor's hands, he would divide her hair into three strands and weave them into a perfectly acceptable plait, tying it off with a rubber band. Then he would take her shoulders and firmly swivel her a hundred and eighty degrees, beginning again on the other side. He never tugged, his plaits were almost as good as the other girls' plaits. Only now does she know, you're not meant to use rubber bands to tie up your hair. Rubber bands tear at the hair, you're meant to use bobbins. But how would Hugh have known that?

After her mother died Addie used to wake up lonely in the night. She would creep out on to the landing and sneak into his room, going around the base of the bed before climbing in on the far side. Without even waking he would pull her in closer to him. They would sleep together like spoons, his huge arm around her, her face nestled into the rough cotton sleeve of his pyjamas.

23

Addie remembers this of him, and she can forgive him pretty much anything.

It was only after dinner that she remembered to play his messages back for him.

They were sitting in the dark with their drinks. The TV screen spread a deep blue light over the room.

'We never checked your messages today.'

'No, indeed.'

'Do you want to listen to them?'

'Not particularly, but I suppose we had better do it anyway.'

There was no way he could use his mobile. It had taken Addie hours to work out how to forward his calls through to the landline.

She went over to the desk and hit the button on the answering machine.

A creepy computer voice filled the air, all synthetic waves.

'You have one new message in your mailbox.'

He winced as he waited. But what was about to come was worse than even he could have imagined.

'Hi there, this is a message for Hugh Murphy! I wasn't expecting to find you so easily.'

A big exuberant voice, unmistakably American.

'You don't know me but my name is Bruno Boylan, I'm an ambassador from the New Jersey wing of the family!'

They both froze, their eyes locked on each other in horror.

'My dad was Patrick Boylan, your mom's cousin. Which makes me your second cousin!'

He pronounced the surname with too much emphasis on each syllable, the way he said it, it sounded like BOY-LAN.

He had the tone all wrong too, he was frighteningly cheerful. It was having a terrible effect on his audience.

'You may remember one of my sisters came to stay with you once. That's going back a while . . . '

They remembered. Lord, did they remember. It was as if she was there in the room with them again, that dreadful girl. The frizzy hair, the train tracks. The unbearable accent.

'I was afraid you might have moved, it's been so long . . . '

There was an animal alertness in the room now, they were bracing themselves for what was coming next.

' . . . I've just arrived in Dublin and I was hoping I could stop by to say hi.'

He read out a long number, a cellphone number as he called it.

' . . . you may have to put a one in front of it. Look forward to catching up with you!'

A silence followed as Addie and Hugh stared at each other. It was so dark now, they could hardly make each other out.

Hugh was the first to speak.

'Good God.'

Addie gave a nervous little laugh, more like a splutter.

'Tell me we're going to wake up and realise this is all a bad dream.'

They were both looking at the answering machine as if it were a bomb.

'Quickly,' said Hugh, 'erase the message, we can pretend we never heard it.'

Addie jumped up and went over to turn on the floor lamp

behind the desk. The room was suddenly flooded with yellow light. She bent over and hit the erase button on the machine.

'What if he rings again? What if he leaves another message?'

'Let's cross that bridge when we come to it.'

He leaned forward to take another long sip of his whiskey, the straw spluttering indecently as he sucked.

'I've just had a horrible thought,' said Addie. 'You don't think he has the address, do you?'

'Highly possible. We mustn't take any chances. We mustn't answer the door.'

Addie giggled nervously. 'Listen to us, you'd swear we were under siege.'

But Hugh wasn't amused.

'This is no laughing matter,' he said. 'Under no account is that man to be entertained. I am in no humour for some fool American in search of his roots. I have more than enough to preoccupy me at the moment, thank you very much.'

And he was right of course. They were in no fit state to welcome a stranger into their wobbly little circle.

Chapter 3

It was hard to know what to do next.

He'd left a couple of messages for them. One the first day and two more yesterday. But he hadn't heard anything back, not a whisper. He didn't want to ring them again, that would make him out to be a stalker.

Maybe they weren't in the habit of checking their messages, there are people who don't check their messages regularly. Or maybe they'd tried to call and hadn't been able to get through, maybe there was a problem with the codes. Then again, there was always the possibility that they were away.

He knew so little about them. He had plundered his sister's memory and come up with almost nothing. That was nearly thirty years ago, Eileen had said in her defence. She was only twenty-two then, she's fifty-one now.

Two months Eileen had spent with them and all she could remember was this. There were two little girls, not much more than a year apart. They had storybook names, Imelda and Adeline. The mother had died, nobody had ever told Eileen what had happened to her. There was no trace of her around the house, nothing to suggest that she'd ever been there in the first place. The house was right on the beach, that she could remember clearly. You could see two big chimneys from the front windows.

Strand Road, that was it. Bruno had found the address in the phone book, he'd copied it down on to a piece of paper along with the phone number. He'd asked the lady in the guest house, was it far. Strand Road? she'd said, looking at him as if he was simple. Sure that's just around the corner. Left at the gate, she said, then left again.

He decided that he would walk past the house, just to look for signs of life. After breakfast, he would take a stroll down the beach and he would identify the house as he was passing. Just to get an idea of the lie of the land.

The beach is a city beach, forming the eastern border of the capital.

Tucked in beside it is one of the city's most exclusive suburbs, an expensive jumble of Victorian red-bricks and Regency villas, a lovely seaside hodge-podge of houses. During the boom, a garden shed in this area would cost you a million euro. It's the proximity to the sea, the estate agents would explain. Everyone wants to live beside the sea.

As Bruno strolled along the footpath, he took in the manicured driveways, he registered the multiple German cars squashed into the small front gardens. The fresh paintwork on the windows. Bruno grew up in a seaside town. He knows these windows would need to be painted every other year.

Some of the houses are numbered and some of them aren't. Some of them have names rather than numbers, names like Vista Mar and Rusheen. When Bruno comes upon a numbered house he takes it as his guide, he looks right and left to find out which way the numbers are going. Then he counts his way along, allocating a number to each unnumbered house he passes. He counts them down one at a time, there's only one side to this street. When he comes across another numbered house he has a little moment of satisfaction. He's right on track.

He must be getting close now, he's only a few houses away. He walks past a low bungalow set back a bit from the road. The next houses he comes to are laid out in a small terrace, four of them in a row. Tall and elegantly proportioned, each house has a wide flight of stone steps leading up to the hall door.

The first house in the terrace has been painted a pale pink, the next one a light dusky blue. Seaside colours, they look pretty up against each other, the contrast is nice. But the next house he comes to is unpainted, its façade a dull grey stone. It has none of the cheerfulness of its neighbours. It's a numbered house, there are peeling white numbers stuck inside the fanlight over the front door.

This is the house of his cousins.

Bruno stands for a moment at the gate. He notices the weeds sneaking through the gravel in the driveway, the battered little car parked over beside the basement drop. The chipped black paintwork on the railings and the lichen-clustered steps. He looks up at the impenetrable black windows, two upstairs and one down.

As he stands there he sees a movement in the downstairs window. He peers, trying to figure out if there's someone there or if it's just a trick of the light. But he can't make out anything at all. All he can see is opaque glass, the stubborn reflection of the sky glinting back at him.

Then he comes to his senses. He realises he's standing there on the sidewalk, staring into their house. He shouldn't be staring. There might be someone in there, they might be able to see him. He turns away quickly, rushing along the sidewalk, like someone escaping a crime scene. Only when he reaches the corner does he stop. He looks each way to check the traffic, then he crosses the road, slipping through the gap in the wall and out on to the promenade.

He's tired.

He realises this as he flops down on to a bench, he's tired to the bone. He's so tired he could lie down right here and fall asleep, like a vagrant. Nobody knows him here, nobody would care.

Even so, he can't do it. No matter how tempting it is, he forces himself to stay upright, sinking down into his padded jacket for comfort. One of the strangest times in his life, he's completely at sea. He doesn't know what to be doing with himself.

He's been sleeping during the day. He's been going back to his room in the bed and breakfast, with the purpose of reading for a few hours, with the purpose of resting. But the next minute he'll find himself in a kind of waking coma. Like he's been given an anaesthetic but he can still hear what the doctors are saying.

He sleeps, and yet he's aware of being asleep. How can that be? How can you be asleep and yet at the same time aware of the degrading sensation of the side of your face squashed against the pillow. Aware of the hard waistband of your jeans digging into your hip bones. Aware of being cold but still unable to climb under the bedspread. Somewhere, way down below him, he's aware of daily life going on. A vacuum starts and stops, a telephone rings and rings. Bruno lies there and hears and feels all of this but he can't move.

When he does manage to drag himself out of this strange non-sleep, he finds he's shivering, his circulation is sluggish. He's cold from the inside out, like someone who's been involved in a scientific experiment. He has to haul himself down to the village for another cup of coffee before he can even begin to feel normal again. He sleeps and when he wakes up he goes back for more coffee and then he wonders why he's having trouble sleeping at night.

It could be jet lag, he's thinking, it could be the time difference. He could be depressed, he could be suffering from post-traumatic stress disorder. Only he doesn't feel depressed. He doesn't feel anything except plain old tired.

A lot has happened, he tells himself.

Just three weeks ago he was walking out the door of the Lehman building with a cardboard box in his arms, all his stuff packed into it. Out on the sidewalk, the tourists were stopping to take photographs, the cops trying to keep them back behind the crash barriers. There's nothing to see here, they were saying, you're not gonna see anyone famous. Just folk who've lost their jobs.

Across the street, television reporters were lined up in a wide arc, their satellite vans humming. As he walked by, Bruno wondered to himself why they'd all arranged themselves in formation, like a flock of birds following some unspoken rule of the universe. It was only when he got home and surfed the networks that he worked it out. They were all positioned so you could see the bank's logo behind them, there it was, just over the reporter's shoulder. As they were talking they would move to the edge of the screen, angling themselves a little to the side. 'Behind me you can see the bank's employees leaving with their belongings. Many of them have spent most of the weekend inside the building, waiting for news. I've been talking to some of them this morning and they've described themselves as shell-shocked. What they're saying is, this is a financial tsunami.'

The others took themselves off to Bobby Van's to drown their sorrows. They tried to persuade him to come but Bruno had no stomach for it. He went home, sat on his couch and watched his life fall apart on live television. He hopped from channel to channel, digesting the soundbites, letting the stock phrases roll over him hour after hour. There was a script to this, maybe if he heard it often enough it would make some sense.

It wasn't just the job that was gone, most of his savings had disappeared with it. Half his pay going back almost six years, instantly and irretrievably gone. The funny thing was, he felt quite detached from it all. There was even a strange elation, an adrenaline rush. He was like a guy who comes home to find his house burning down, and all he can think is, I never wanted any of that stuff in the first place.

Hard to believe that it was only three weeks ago. Thinking about it now, it seems like someone else's life.

He sees himself through a stranger's eyes. A clean-shaven man in expensive clothes, he's walking up the steps from the subway. He's coming out on to Seventh Avenue, he's stopping to buy a coffee from the Iranian guy on the corner. He has the exact change ready. They toss a bit of loose banter back and forth. Then Bruno turns and disappears in through the doors of his office, coffee cup in hand.

Above his head, a map of the world is moving across the glass face of the building like a cloud across the sky. Islands and sea gliding silently over the surface, the Lehman Brothers logo crawling after them in a massive bold font. Magnificent, he used to think it was. It used to make his heart swell in his chest as he walked through the doors. Now it seems a lot like hubris, that gloating display of global supremacy.

He sees himself at his desk on the second floor, multiple screens in front of him. He's tracking airline shares, he's scanning those flickering rows of figures, looking out for anything unusual. Behind him, a wall of glass. If he swivels his chair around to the side he's looking right down the barrel of Seventh Avenue. Below him, the heaving traffic and the fumes and the people. At his eye level, constantly shifting billboards and neon signs. Rising up on the far side of the street, great tracts of concrete and steel and glass. And above it all, that vulnerable New York sky.

It occurs to him now what it is that he's been doing these past few years. He's been sitting there, waiting for another plane to appear on the horizon, heading straight for his office building.

And in a way it did.

Later in the day, Bruno will wander the streets looking for little bookstores but finding only big ones. He'll sit in a café and read all the local newspapers to catch up on the election. He'll be forced to order something he doesn't want to fulfil the minimum charge. After that he'll wander through a city square, standing for a while to watch pre-school children in quaint little uniforms collecting autumn leaves. He'll rest on a bench by a reedy canal, he'll smile at the drunks gathering on the opposite bank. And he'll wonder to himself, what am I doing here?

Later still, he'll go back to the guest house and shower in the tiny bathroom. He'll wander down to the village and eat supper alone in a bustling restaurant. He'll go back home and get into bed, only to discover that he's unable to sleep. And he'll find himself wondering all over again, what the hell am I doing here?

This is the day ahead of him, he can see it laid out like a path. But he's in no hurry to embark on it. Instead, he just sits there on the bench at the edge of the strand and stares out to sea. He's surveying his past, as if it's a field he's just crossed. He doesn't want to go back, but he's not ready to go forward either.

He's like a man who's been shipwrecked, he's been washed up on a desert island. He's letting his clothes dry off in the air and he's contemplating his new lease of life.

He's not sure yet what to do with it.

Chapter 4

'I fear our American friend is lurking.'

From where Addie was standing in the doorway, it looked like he was just a stencil. He was a black outline against the bright light of the window.

'What makes you think that?'

She was squinting through half-closed eyes, still half asleep.

'There was a strange-looking fellow out there this morning, I got the feeling he was spying on us.'

Addie walked over to the window. She peered out at the front drive but there was nobody there.

'How can you be so sure it was him?'

'There's no doubt in my mind. The beard, the blue jeans, the general demeanour. Straight out of central casting.'

He made a kind of clucking sound in his throat as she bent to kiss the top of his head. His hair was baby-thin now, a lick of it swept over his bald patch in a lame attempt at disguise. It made her tender towards him.

'Not much else I can do,' he was saying, 'but sit here and observe. If I sit here long enough, something interesting is bound to happen. Touch of the *Rear Window* about it all.'

This is his stock in trade, this habit of captioning every situation with a film title. He's well known for it, people joke about it behind his back. 'Nobody mention *My Left Foot*,' Addie's sister had whispered as they stood in his hospital room on the day of the accident, watching him trying to flip the page of his hospital chart with his chin.

'Do I get to be Grace Kelly?' Addie asked cheerfully as she bent down to scoop up his laundry from the basket beside the door.

'You're a dead ringer for her, my dear.'

It had been hard on him, the accident. Hard on her too. They were united by their helplessness in the face of what had to be done.

'I don't like it any more than you do,' she'd said, before he had a chance to complain. 'Anyway, it'll only be for a couple of weeks.'

They had worked it all out between them, herself and Della. A conversation almost without words, a quick conference in the hospital corridor. Addie had offered and Della had just nodded. It was the obvious thing to do, Addie was the obvious person, she had nobody to be looking after but herself. And besides, it would do her good to have something to occupy her, that's what Della was thinking. She'd been spending too much time by herself recently, she'd been moping. Looking after Hugh might be just the thing to take her mind off her troubles.

When they're together they refer to him by his first name, they always have done. Can't see Hugh making the easiest of patients, Della had said. And she wasn't wrong.

Addie had gone straight home to her apartment and thrown some things into a suitcase. She'd loaded Lola's bowl, her brush and her blanket into a supermarket carrier bag. Grabbed her own coat and scarf and stepped out into the street. A strange feeling, closing the door of the apartment behind her, leaving her carefully constructed life sealed away inside. Her milk-white walls and her white cotton sheets and her lily-of-the-valley soap. The little pots of fresh herbs on the kitchen windowsill and the espresso machine and the Nicholas Mosse mug with the violets on it that she liked to drink her coffee out of in the mornings. She had left the mug behind her on the shelf. She would not try to take her life with her. After all, it would only be for a couple of weeks.

Why then the sense of dread when she had opened the door of the basement flat? She had felt her throat contract and her shoulders hunch involuntarily as she had stepped inside. Straight away she had registered the smell of damp. It seemed to seep straight into your bones, making you shudder from the inside out. Even the dog had been reluctant to go inside. It's not for ever, Lola! That's what Addie had said. But her voice had sounded brittle and unsure. It was Addie who had needed convincing, not the dog. She had dumped her bags on to the bed and fled back upstairs.

Together Addie and Della had moved Hugh's bed down into the living room for him, shunting the couch back into the dining room and closing off the double doors. Of course he'd grumbled about it at first. But now Addie was beginning to think he quite liked it. There was something majestic about the whole set-up. To concentrate your life into one room, surrounded by all your favourite things. It had been clear he was coming to terms with the arrangement when he'd asked them to bring the Jack Yeats down from his bedroom and hang it over the sideboard.

A week since the accident and still no friends had come to visit. Addie was beginning to wonder if he had any. Hugh didn't seem to notice their absence.

'Did you get any breakfast?'

'Oh yes,' he said. 'The ever-helpful Hopewell made me some toast.'

Hopewell, the unfortunate nurse who had been hired to help him get up and dressed in the mornings. Naturally, he loathes Hopewell. But it has become a major focal point for him during his convalescence, this hating of Hopewell.

Hopewell is from Nigeria. Black as the ace of spades, as Hugh would say.

'I hope I don't detect a touch of racism in your attitude to Hopewell,' Addie had warned.

'On the contrary,' Hugh had replied. 'My position on Hopewell is quite the opposite of racism. I am assuming that there are very many highly capable nurses, right across the continent of Africa, so I am at a loss to understand how, with all those millions of possibilities open to us, we have ended up with one as singularly useless as Hopewell.'

What Hopewell makes of her father, Addie shudders to think.

*

39

Hopewell is tall. He must be well over six foot. He's black, black in the true sense of the word. His eyes are creamy white, his smile washing-powder blue. You could fit a one-euro coin through the gap between his two front teeth.

He takes his shoes off in the hall. Nobody knows if this is a habit he brings from home or if he thinks it's expected of him here. It's a little too intimate, the sight of him padding around in his socks, but nobody dares to say anything for fear of hurting his feelings.

He's from Lagos. When Addie asked him whereabouts he was from in Nigeria, he seemed baffled by the question. I am from Lagos, he said, as if there was nowhere else you could be from. He told them he was a nurse back home and they took him at face value. There was no way of checking.

He can be quite chatty when he's on his own with the patient, he doesn't seem to have noticed that he's so intensely disliked. Or maybe he doesn't care. When Addie shows up he goes silent.

He's punctual. He arrives every morning on the stroke of eight. Addie hears him ring the doorbell before he opens it with his own key. He embarks cheerfully on his morning routine, a series of duties that has been painfully negotiated down to the very last detail.

'He can unbutton my pyjama top for me but I'll take it off myself. He can turn on the bath water but he'll have to wait outside until I'm finished. He can pass me the towel but I insist on drying myself.'

Was it Della who said it was like dealing with a particularly demanding movie star?

Once Hopewell has guided him through what he refers to

as his 'ablutions', he helps him into clean underwear and a fresh pair of pyjamas. Then he assists him in putting on his clothes on top of the pyjamas. It's an eccentric scheme, but it seems to be working. He wears his normal clothes on the top half, tracksuit pants on the bottom. A hideous indignity but one that's unavoidable if he wants to be able to go to the toilet by himself.

Addie checks on him after breakfast. She collects the newspaper from the floor in the hall and brings it in to him, laying it out flat on the desk so he can scan the front page. Sometimes they have coffee together. Later in the day, Mrs Dunphy comes. Before the accident, he only needed her for a few hours a week, but now she comes every day. She does his shopping for him, posts any letters that need posting. She puts on a wash, does some ironing. Before she leaves, she makes lunch, serving it up to him on a tray at his desk. He looks out the window as he's eating.

'I could get used to this, Mrs Dunphy,' he says, without turning round. This is his idea of trying to be nice. But it's too late in their relationship for that now. She sticks her tongue out at him as she backs out of the room.

Come evening time, Addie arrives with the ingredients for dinner. Usually some kind of ready-made meal for two which she can throw into the oven, serve up on heated plates and pass off as home cooking.

While the food is warming she helps him to get undressed, in so far as he will allow her to. She unlaces his shoes so he can kick them off. She helps him pull his jumper over his head, trying not to knock his glasses off while she's doing it. She unbuttons his shirt but he manages to step out of his tracksuit bottoms by himself. As if by magic, he's back in his pyjamas again, his modesty undisturbed.

He climbs into bed as Addie lights the fire and gets the DVD lined up. When she has his clothes folded and draped over a chair, she goes to fetch the drinks. A glass of red wine for herself and three fingers of Tyrconnell for him. He has a cupboard bursting with unopened bottles of whiskey, all gifts from grateful patients.

Addie pours the whiskey into a cut-glass tumbler and drops a plastic straw into the glass. Given no other option, he has quickly come to terms with the notion of sipping whiskey through a straw.

They've been working their way through a Bette Davis box set. Already they've watched *Now Voyager* and *In This Our Life*.

'What about we throw on *The Old Maid* tonight?' she asks.

'Is that not a bit close to the bone?'

'You're very funny.'

He doesn't mean to be cruel to her, it's just his way. He loves Addie, she's his favourite child. She's probably his favourite person in the world.

Before she left to go back downstairs she filled up his water glass for him from the jug on the bedside table. She checked that his stick was where it should be, leaning against the desk.

'I have to go and walk the dog. But I'll check on you later. Be good now.'

He was glaring out the window.

'Be careful out there. He could be hanging about the place.'

She had the laundry slung over her shoulder like a bag of swag.

'This is ridiculous,' she said, as she backed out of the room. 'We're practically prisoners in our own home.'

He raised his voice. He had his eyes fixed on the road.

'I don't like your complacency. Not with the enemy in the vicinity.' He was enjoying himself now, the drama of it. He had nothing else to be doing.

He heard the door closing but he kept talking to her as if she was still in the room.

'That fellow,' he was saying, 'touch of *Deliverance* about him.'

Chapter 5

She spotted him as soon as she crossed the road, you couldn't help but notice him. A big man in a big padded jacket and a mad hat, he was sitting there on the last bench, the one right beside the steps.

People don't really sit on the benches at that hour of the morning. At that hour, they tend to be engaged in some kind of activity. They're either walking their dogs up and down the promenade, or they're jogging or they're speed-walking. Under-exposed figures that pass you by in the half-light. They tend to be hooked up to some kind of a personal stereo, or else they're obscured by a big scarf or something. Nobody pays any attention to anyone else at that hour of the morning, it's an unspoken agreement.

Maybe that's why he stood out. There was something strange about somebody who would just sit there on a bench at that hour of the morning. There was something not right about him.

She decided to take a closer look.

She crossed the road at the usual place. She stepped off the kerb, waiting for a break in the traffic. She couldn't be bothered to wait for the lights to go red. When she got to the far side, she picked the dog up and tossed her over the sea wall, then she climbed over herself, sitting on the wall side-saddle first, then swinging one leg over after the other.

To get to the steps she had to walk right past him. She made sure not to even look sideways at him, she just walked by and sat down on the top step just like she usually would. She made a play of unclipping the dog lead, talking to the dog while she was doing it.

Even with her back to him, she could feel his eyes on her.

'There we go now, that's my girl. Stay still now or I won't be able to unclip it, you silly thing. *Now*, off you go.'

And the dog was gone. Down the ramp and out on to the beach in a wide arc, her tail spinning with the wild joy of it all.

Addie hovered there for a minute on the step, her knees hugged into her chest, soaking up the sight of the happy little dog and the beach and the beautiful morning. There were patches of white frost here and there on the sand and the dog seemed confused by it. She was dashing back and forth, sniffing at the frost suspiciously. She looked up for guidance, a baffled expression on her face. You couldn't help but smile, she looked so funny.

From the bench, there was a noise that sounded like a laugh.

Addie turned round. The least little turn she could make,

she twisted her body from the waist, peering back over her shoulder. He was watching the dog with this familiar look on his face and he was chuckling away. You'd swear it was his own dog he was watching.

She didn't give him time to speak. She snapped her head back round to look at the beach. Jumped up and skipped down the ramp and out on to the sand. She raised the ball-thrower and gave the tennis ball an almighty whack, right out into the sky. Lola went tearing after it, her tail whirling round and round like a helicopter blade.

'Whoa, that's quite a throw,' he said cheerfully.

Addie pretended not to have heard him. She took her iPod out of her pocket and stood there at the bottom of the steps while she untangled the wires. Plugged herself in, wrapped her scarf twice around her neck and tucked the ends into the front of her coat, sealing out all the cold air. She selected a track and scrolled the volume up as high as it would go. Then she turned her face to the sea, closed her eyes and headed straight for the horizon.

They made a nice sight out there on the beach, the girl and the little dog. He felt happy just watching them.

It was a stunning day. The sky was clear as far as you could see, the water a shimmering blue. The frost on the beach was like shards of mirrored glass. Bruno could feel the heat of the sun on his face. He was almost too hot in his coat but he didn't want to take it off. It was a treat at this time of year.

The girl was so far out there now that she was just a

matchstick person, a black overcoat and two black sticks for her arms and her legs.

Bruno watched her as she raised her arm up in a backwards sweep over her head and whacked that ball-thrower thing she had with her, sending the tennis ball flying in a perfect arc, much further than you would think it would go. Every time she threw the ball the dog would go crashing through the shallows to fetch it back. She must have thrown that ball a hundred times but Bruno wasn't counting.

Behind her, streaks of deep fleshy pink cut swathes through the sky. The girl was just a shadow puppet against that blazing backdrop.

She was standing at the waterline now, still as a statue. She stood there for a long time. Bruno couldn't help but wonder why she was standing there.

He found himself longing for her to turn round.

It was cold down on the beach, a vicious wind sweeping the length of it. Addie's cheeks were smarting and her nose was numb. Her body was still warm though, the inside of her scarf a little clammy where she'd been breathing into it.

Tom Waits, she was listening to.

And those were the days of roses,
Poetry and prose. And Martha
All I had was you and all you had was me.

She was ready to go in now but she couldn't. She was waiting for him to leave. She figured he couldn't stay there all day.

Every so often she would turn to scan the promenade, expecting to find his bench empty. But he was still there. It was as if he was waiting for her.

Fuck it, she thought, I'll freeze if I stay out here much longer.

He sat and watched her as she walked back.

She was hopping from side to side. He guessed, wrongly as it happens, that she was avoiding the puddles.

At first he thought she was talking to herself. She had her head down and she was talking away as she walked. He wondered, was she talking to the dog? But the dog was nowhere near, the dog was racing round her in these huge loops, circling her wide. That's when it occurred to him. She wasn't talking, she was singing.

It came to him in little wisps, buffeted by the wind, as if you were turning the dial on a radio, trying to find the station. When he did get a clear signal, he didn't recognise what it was that she was singing, she was so far out of key.

You had to disconnect yourself from the tune, you had to concentrate on the words instead. When he did figure it out, he couldn't help but smile. He found himself singing along.

And a little rain never hurt no one.

With every step now, he could see her more clearly. She was wearing a heavy black overcoat, a huge brightly coloured scarf wrapped several times around her shoulders. She had a hat on now. A dark blue beret, he was sure she hadn't been wearing the hat before. There were licks of honey-coloured hair sticking out from behind her ears.

She had a cheerful face, a face a small child would draw. A perfect circle, huge round eyes and bright pink cheeks.

Bruno took an instant liking to her. Afterwards it would seem to him that he loved her from the moment he first saw her face.

She was aware that he was watching her. He wasn't even trying to hide it.

She was walking with her head down to avoid looking at him. She had her head down and she was looking at her runners as she walked.

She tried to concentrate on the music. She kept having to remind herself not to sing along. Even this far out, it wasn't safe. Sometimes the wind can carry sounds right in to the shore.

She was hopping from spot to spot on the sand, selecting her next move carefully so she would land on a razor-clam shell. She loved the satisfying crunch of them under her feet.

A hundred yards from the promenade, she glanced up quickly to check his position. Then she charted her course. She would walk right down to the far end of the beach. She would take the steps by the Martello tower, she would cross the road at the traffic lights and double back along the footpath. That way she wouldn't have to walk past him. She could avoid him entirely, she could slip back into the house without him ever having seen her.

It was a bit mean but it had to be done.

She slid the dog lead from where she had it draped around her neck, then she turned to see where Lola had got to. There was no sign of her. Addie whirled round full circle, scanning the beach to see if she was behind her but she wasn't. It was only when she turned back in towards the shore that she spotted her.

Wouldn't you know, she was right at the bottom of the steps. She was standing there with her tail wagging away as she waited for Addie to join her. There was no choice but to follow.

Addie walked with her head right down, her hands deep in her pockets. She was aware of him watching her but she was determined not to look up. She would hook the dog on to the lead and she would walk straight past him. Even at this late stage she was dead set on avoiding him.

Just as she approached the bottom of the steps, Lola began to spin round in a circle. The next thing she was squatting back on her hind legs, squeezing a big turd out on to the sand. Great, thought Addie, that's just fucking great. For a moment she thought about leaving it there. But she couldn't do that, not with him sitting there watching her.

She fished around in her pocket for a bag, coming across her keys instead. She pulled them out and transferred them to her left hand. Fished around again until she found the roll of bags. She held the loose end of the roll in her teeth and tore, leaving one bag hanging from her mouth. Out of the corner of her eye she was watching him.

Walking over to the spot where Lola had done her business, she bent down as gracefully as she could. Using the bag as a glove so she didn't have to make direct contact, she picked up

Lola's mess. She doubled the bag over itself and tied a knot in it. Then she held it away from her delicately with two fingers.

She looked up to see the steps right in front of her. A quick glance at the bench. She could see he was watching her intently.

With her keys still in one hand and the bag dangling from the other, she walked slowly up the steps, mustering as much dignity as she could under the circumstances.

When she got to the top, she straightened up. He was smiling at her with his eyes, as if she'd done something amusing. He raised his hand up to greet her in a familiar gesture, as if he knew her.

She smiled a wobbly little smile, inclining her head ever so slightly to acknowledge his greeting. Then she pulled her spine up tall and marched over to the poo bin to dump the bag. She let the lid fall back down with a clang. Without so much as looking at him again, she turned and swung her way along the promenade, calling to the little dog to follow her.

She couldn't believe it when she heard him shouting after her. She could not believe it. She didn't even have to look behind her. She knew it was him and she felt a sudden anger rising up inside her.

I don't need this, she hissed. I do not need this. And she started to walk even faster, pounding along towards the gap in the sea wall.

Hey!

Over the music and the sound of the traffic she could just about hear him.

As she stood at the edge of the footpath she could see him out of the corner of her eye. He was standing there beside the bench, a ridiculous figure in his beard and his daft-looking hat. He was holding one arm up in a kind of salute and he was shouting something at her.

'Wait!'

She pretended not to have seen him. She stood at the kerb, waiting for a break in the traffic.

A car stopped. The driver motioned for her to cross and she ran for it. Lola ran along beside her without questioning why.

She was aware now that he was following her, she heard a car horn beep and then she heard him shouting something at her but she was so agitated she couldn't hear what it was. He was just behind her now, there was no getting away from him.

She stopped suddenly and turned round, trying to feign surprise. She removed her earphones one by one, holding them in her open right hand, the way you would hold a pair of dice you were about to roll.

'I'm so sorry,' she said in her frostiest voice, 'I didn't hear you.'

He had come to a stop in front of her. He was bent over double, leaning on the fronts of his thighs and panting, the flaps of his hat hanging down on either side of his face like dog ears. He didn't speak, he just raised his right hand. He was dangling something between his thumb and his index finger.

A very familiar-looking set of keys.

She stared at them. Her mind was straining to catch up with what she was seeing. She looked down at her own hand where her keys should have been and there was the poo bag. Suddenly it dawned on her what had happened. She looked at him in absolute horror.

He looked so very unthreatening all of a sudden. Standing there, doubled up from the effort of chasing her, the brown eyes raised up to hers. The keys held aloft, like an offering.

She leaned back against the gatepost, threw her head back and laughed.

And that was how it started.

Afterwards, of course, he would joke about it.

What I had to go through, he would say, to get this woman's attention. I went through shit to get to her!

And Addie would laugh, she would smile with good grace every time he told that story.

'I kind of had to sleep with him,' she told her sister afterwards. 'I behaved very badly. I felt I had to make it up to him.'

Chapter 6

It's not like she slept with him right away. They actually spent the whole day together first.

'It's nice to meet you, Adeline Murphy, at long last!'

He was studying her face with this rapturous expression. He seemed genuinely delighted, his eyes shining.

They were sitting opposite each other at the battered old table in the basement. Two mugs of coffee set in front of them. The coffee was still too hot to drink.

Addie was in an agony of embarrassment. Even now she was trying to find the space in her head to go back over the excuses she'd made. She wasn't convinced she'd carried them off.

'We only just checked the messages last night,' she had said. 'We were going to ring you back today.' The dark red flush creeping up over her face gave away the lie. All her life, Addie had been a blusher. It was a constant source of mortification to her.

'I can't believe you're the cousin!' she had said in a desperate attempt to redeem herself. 'It never even occurred to me. I thought you were some stranger who was following me.'

The whole time she was making her excuses he was nodding politely. He was doing that thing of smiling at her with his eyes. He seemed amused by it all.

He was more handsome than you would have thought at first sight. The beard was a bit misleading. Salt and pepper hair, the hair in his beard darker than the hair on his head. Nice eyes, funny how you noticed the eyes more because of the beard. Ten years ago, he must have been really handsome. Now he looked like he was turning into a cartoon version of himself, his face all droopy and jowly.

She kept having to remind herself that he was her cousin. It didn't feel like they were from the same family. It didn't feel like they were from the same species.

New Jersey, he was from. He seemed surprised that she didn't know this about him.

'Springlake, New Jersey,' he said proudly. 'Most Irish town in America.'

And she winced.

He looked puzzled.

'You don't believe me!'

But it wasn't that Addie was finding it hard to believe him. It was something he would never be able to understand. She didn't want to believe him.

To Addie, Irish America was something you wanted nothing to do with. Irish Americans were fat people in check trousers and baseball hats who descended out of tour buses on to Nassau Street and waddled into Blarney Woollen Mills to buy Aran jumpers. They were red-faced people in sneakers who hung around the National Library trying to trace their family tree. They were people who attended fundraising dinners in hotel ballrooms in Boston and New York and talked nonsense about the North. They spoke too loud and they pronounced all the place names wrong. The very thought of an Irish American in search of his roots was enough to make you squirm.

Of course Bruno was oblivious to all the negative connotations he was arousing. He had no idea of all the prejudices and petty resentments he was stirring up. He was under the impression that he had nothing to be ashamed of.

'My sisters were all champion Irish dancers,' he said happily. 'My sister Megan still teaches at the Lynn Academy of Irish Dance in Audubon, New Jersey.'

And Addie cringed again, thinking, what have I got myself into?

'What are your plans for the day?'

'Do some work, I suppose.' God, she was a terrible liar.

'Seems a shame to be stuck inside while the sun is shining outdoors. Isn't there any chance you could take the day off?'

Americans and their sense of endless possibility, it caught Addie off guard, she couldn't think of a way out quickly enough. She didn't want to think of a way out.

'Listen,' she said, 'I'm an architect. I can probably take the whole year off.'

*

He thought she was joking about the swim.

'Yeah, nice day for a swim,' he had said, laughing.

She had left him waiting in the car while she ran up to check on her dad. She had started the engine, so the heat would come on while he was waiting. Thoughtful of her.

He leaned forward to turn the radio on again. They were talking about the election. They had some guy from NPR on the line and they were talking about Wednesday night's debate. Who won, who lost. CNN polls and CBS polls and they were saying Obama won, no question. McCain lost, he went over to the dark side and he lost. But that doesn't necessarily mean he'll lose the election, said the presenter. And the reporter came back in. No, ma'am, all it means is that he lost the debate. The election is still anybody's guess.

Bruno reached over and turned the radio off. He sat there in the buzzing silence and let the hot air blow over him. He breathed in through his nose, letting the air out again slowly. It was hard not to get upset about it. Even at this distance, it was hard not to get upset.

Why did Bruno care about it so much? Sometimes he hardly understood it himself. It had crept up on him, like everything else in his life. He wasn't a political animal, never had he thought of himself as politically engaged. He had been brought up Democrat, just like he'd been brought up Catholic. But the idea of getting involved in politics repelled him. Bruno was not a person to wear a badge on his lapel, he was not a bumper-sticker kind of guy. He was an observer, that's what he had always told himself. He was just an interested observer. But the more you observed the more you found yourself engaged, that was the problem. Especially these past few years, there seemed to be a lot of stuff to be engaged about.

There was the war in Iraq and there was the war in Afghanistan and there was nothing linking Iraq to Afganistan or to September 11. There was a failure of logic there that upset Bruno. There had been a deception and it offended his sense of order. Nobody seemed to have noticed it except for him. When he talked about it in the office they all looked uncomfortable, they laughed it off. Well, what would you expect? Republicans to a man, all they talked about was the tax implications. Then there was Sarah Palin and that was like a bad joke except that Bruno wasn't laughing. Even the thought of it made him crazy. Obama had to win, he just had to win.

Bruno was distracted by the sound of a door slamming. He turned to see Addie coming back down the steps, a bunch of towels rolled up under her arm.

So she wasn't joking about the swim.

The swimming is a religion to her. It's the thing at the very centre of her. She's a swimmer.

That's why she keeps her hair cut short, that's why she always smells of chlorine. She has swimsuits and towels perpetually draped over her radiators, multiple pairs of goggles in the glove compartment of her car. A huge framed David Hockney swimming pool on the wall over her bed. For Christmas one year Della gave her an Esther Williams box set. Addie has watched every one of those movies a hundred times.

In the wintertime she swims in the pool. But from June to October she swims in the sea too. She plans her life around the tides. She always knows what time is high water. She never has to check the paper.

She swims at Seapoint or the Forty Foot, she even swims at the Half Moon Swimming Club on the South Wall and nobody swims there any more. It's right next to the sewage plant, just under the power station, maybe that's what makes people squeamish about it. They prefer to swim on the other side of the bay. But the way Addie looks at it, it's all the same sea. People swim in the bloody Mediterranean, people swim in the Ganges, for God's sake.

From June to the end of August, there are lifeguards on duty, on the lookout for trespassing dogs. But they make an exception for Lola. Lola has earned their respect.

It's the elegant way she swims, with her neck stretched up to keep her head out of the water. It's the distance she covers, staying with Addie all the way. The only indication she gives that she's tiring is her heavy breathing. She makes these wide circles in the water, like a paddle boat, just for the pleasure of it.

'What an extraordinary dog!'

That was the nicest compliment Lola ever got. They were coming out of the water together after their swim. There were two old ladies sitting on the stone bench in their swimsuits and one of them said to the other, what an extraordinary dog. And Addie was so proud to be the owner of this extraordinary dog. Lola the swimming dog.

From the road, the sea had looked bright and blue and beckoning. But now that they were right down beside it, it was a horrible stony grey. Choppy and cold-looking and distinctly uninviting. Bruno was having second thoughts.

Of course Addie went straight in. She drew her clothes off and tossed them on the ground and she walked right down the ramp and into the sea as if there was no difference between the air and the water, as if they were all the same element.

They were out there right now, herself and the dog. Bruno could see the wet little head struggling along beside her. She was talking to the dog but he couldn't hear what she was saying, words of encouragement no doubt.

He registered a twinge of jealousy. I wish she'd encourage *me*, he was thinking.

He was finding it hard to believe he was doing this. Even as he was inching his way down the icy ramp, clinging for dear life to the handrail, he couldn't believe he was going to do this. His underwear was flapping in the wind, his chest hair was all rigid and petrified. His balls were clenched. He was worried about his heart.

Maybe this is how it ends, he was thinking, maybe this is it. Behaving like some damn fool teenager. Plunging my fifty-year-old body into the icy water to impress a girl. Now that would be a nice ending.

'Come on in,' she was shouting. Her voice rippling with laughter. She was floating on her back as if she was in the Caribbean. She was taking pleasure in taunting him.

'Don't tell me there's something stopping you?'

'Only the fear of death,' he roared back. He raised his arms over his head, took a big deep breath and in he went.

*

Three days he'd been in the country and now here he was, swimming in the freezing cold sea with his crazy cousin. The Martello tower, there it was, towering above him.

'I feel like I'm doing the *Ulysses* experience,' he shouted, once he'd recovered from the shock.

She was bobbing up and down beside him. Her hair was plastered to her head, her eyelashes long and spiky and her eyes big and bright. She looked like a seal.

'Never got past the first chapter,' she roared back, her voice bouncing off the surface of the water. 'Bit of a boys' book, isn't it?'

Bruno lay on his back. He kicked his legs furiously to warm himself up. The splash he made was hugely satisfying. He started to feel a warm glow seeping through his body.

The glow didn't last. Just a few minutes later he began to lose all sensation in his legs. He wanted to pee but he couldn't, his bladder seemed frozen solid. He ploughed a rough front crawl back to the shore. He had to tread water for a minute until he found the base of the ramp by stubbing his toe against it. Hauled himself out by the rusty railing and staggered up the slimy stone in his wet underpants, his skin burning as it came in contact with the air. He dried himself with the towel she'd given him and then he struggled into his jeans and sweater. The jeans kept snagging on his damp skin as he tried to pull them on.

He sat himself down on the ground and leaned back against the base of the tower. Closing his eyes he savoured the watery sun on his face. Every so often he opened one eye and scanned the sea for Addie.

'I'm not really your cousin, am I?' He could swear there was something flirtatious in the way she'd said it.

'Second cousin once removed.'

'Oh, we don't really count that stuff here,' she'd said.

And he'd smiled.

He could see her head now, dipping up out of the water and then disappearing down again. Lola's little head chugging alongside her. Behind them, sea and more grey sea. Above the sea, the thin horizon and above that again, the sky.

She was swimming a short raspy breaststroke parallel to the shore. Every so often she would turn round to encourage the dog. The sight of the loyal little creature swimming along beside her never failed to move her.

When she turned her head the other way she could see Bruno sitting up there in the sun. Without the hunting cap and the big coat he looked almost normal.

This was the start of a romance. That was very clear to her. As soon as she got out of the water she would have to pick it up where they had left off before the swim. She would almost definitely sleep with him, probably later this very day.

Suddenly she was exhausted by the thought of it all.

She didn't have the energy for someone new. She had no energy for all the questions she would have to ask and all the answers she would have to give. The enthusiasm and the self-belief to present herself one more time, to package herself and her history into something attractive and positive and lovable. She remembered that she hadn't shaved her bikini line for weeks and suddenly she had no energy for it all.

She rolled over on to her back and spread her arms out

wide either side of her. Then she let herself fall down into the sea, her bum and her hips and her tummy first, allowing the weight of her torso to pull her limbs down into the water.

She let herself sink like a rag doll. Bubbling the air out through her nostrils so she didn't float back up. She opened her eyes and saw her own legs wafting out in front of her. Her skin was white and eerie-looking, like the skin of a drowned person. She wondered for a moment if she might just let herself sink. Would she have the courage not to save herself? Would she change her mind when it was too late?

Part of her was curious to find out. But without ever making a decision, she found herself rolling over on to her tummy again. She was swimming back up towards the surface now, her face pointed forward like the prow of a ship, her arms pushing the sea down to either side of her.

The next thing she broke through into the air. Above the bobbing line of the water she could see Bruno standing up to look for her. He was scanning the water for her.

She found herself sticking her arm up and waving back at him.

They were both cold after the swim. They needed a pint to warm themselves up. As soon as the barman set it down on to the table, Bruno reached out to pick it up.

'Don't!' Addie yelped.

He looked up at her, confused.

'You don't drink it until it settles.' She pointed to the cloudy horizon between the black stout and the white head.

'It's part of the pleasure,' she said. 'The anticipation.'

And he caught her gaze across the table and held it, his dark eyes glinting. They sat there, the two of them, looking at each other and trying not to smile.

She drove fast on the way back.

She had the heating turned up high inside the car so they had to raise their voices to be heard. After a while they let the conversation fall off, there were longer and longer gaps, there didn't seem to be any need to talk. Outside, the day was gradually fading. The whole city looked like it had been dipped in deep blue ink.

By the time they crossed over the railway line and drove out on to the Strand Road it was really dark, the beach just a black space to the right of them. Addie let the car roll past the open gates of the driveway, bringing it to a stop out on the street. She turned the engine off and they sat there for a moment, registering the silence.

'So,' she said. 'Are you coming in or aren't you?'

He didn't hesitate.

'Oh, I'm coming in.'

He climbed out of the car. Closing the door quietly, he followed her over the crunchy gravel, down the side steps and in through the basement door.

And it was only then, only after they'd spent six hours straight in each other's company, only after they'd found out everything there was to be learned about each other in a single day, only then did they fall into bed together.

Chapter 7

It's an intimate thing to do, sleeping with someone.

Addie has been told this a hundred times, in a hundred different ways. It's what the nuns were getting at, all those years ago. And there was a central truth to what they said. Oh, how she wishes now that she'd listened to them.

Don't give yourself away lightly, that's what they used to say. Don't sell yourself cheap. Your body is a temple. Addie remembers the hilarity in the locker room, how they'd sniggered at the nuns behind their backs. How they'd imitated their accents, how they'd sneered at their saintly tones. Sixteen years old and they were already veterans of a world the nuns would never know.

They had a different vocabulary for it, the girls did. They had phrases that were especially constructed to take the intimacy out of it. They talked about getting off with people and when they were a bit older they were having it off with them and the next thing you knew you'd be giving him one and in the end all they talked about was riding. How Della revelled in all that unlovely language!

Even now, Della loves to reminisce about her colourful past. She delights in remembering all her conquests, the seedier the better. She remembers the roadies and the visiting businessmen and the college lecturers, she remembers the where and the what and the how and she laughs out loud at the memory. Her wild days, it does her good to remember them. Now that they're well and truly behind her.

How different it is for Addie. Addie remembers her past intimacies with horror. She's haunted by them, degraded by them. She has flashbacks. Things she said, things she never should have said. Oh, things she suggested in a moment of passion. Impulsive things, things you could never live down.

Like the time she went to meet a boyfriend at the airport. She wore a long winter coat with nothing on under it. No knickers, no bra, just a pair of high suede boots and the coat belted tightly around her waist. She'd been planning it for days. The whole time he was away she'd been imagining how she would whisper into his ear in the arrivals area. How he would slip his hand inside her coat, just to check. How she would let the coat fall open as she was driving, he wouldn't be able to stay in his seat. She would be forced to push him back over to his side of the car, just so they wouldn't crash.

Only it didn't work out that way. His bags never came through and they had to wait around the airport for hours and she kept worrying that her coat would open and by the time they finally got to the car they were squabbling and she was freezing cold and covered with goose pimples. She dropped him off in town. They kept seeing each other for a few more weeks after that but they both knew it was over. From time to time now she bumps into him in the supermarket and they make small talk while his two kids sit there in the trolley and Addie wants to die.

They bubble up, these memories, they simmer away in her mind like a toxic stew. A proposition that was turned down, a misunderstanding about a Valentine's card. A suggestive text message, sent to a client by mistake. Do these things happen to other people, or is it just Addie? Do other people get over these things?

It's a form of haemophilia that she has. The wounds just don't seem to heal.

It's always the distant past that she dwells on. It's the little things rather than the big things. Perhaps because the recent past is too painful, she can't even bring herself to talk about it yet.

Even the mention of it makes her feel queasy, as if she's standing on a ship and the ground is tilting up to meet her. She doesn't know what vocabulary to use to tell the story, nothing she tries to say tastes right in her mouth. Any words she does manage to produce seem too hard and too sharp, like pebbles on her tongue.

In her mind, it's still a silent movie.

There she is, lying straight as a mummy in the hospital bed, her head resting on a stack of pillows, her bare arms on top of the covers. She's pinned down by tubes, a thick plastic drain is feeding gunk out of the wound in her abdomen, a thin line pumping antibiotics into her through a needle they'd inserted in the back of her hand. An ugly bruise spreading up towards her wrist like a stain. The surgical tape that's holding the needle in place is stinging her, it's all puckered and uneven. She longs to peel it off but she's afraid of dislodging the needle. She doesn't want to be a nuisance. She tries to think about something else, anything to take her mind off it.

To the left of her bed, a wide rectangular window. A row of empty vases lined up on the sill. Outside the window, endless rain. If she turns her head to the right, she's facing her bedside locker. Crowded on top of it, the yellow roses Della had brought, the lilies from her dad, the homemade cards from the girls.

There had been no flowers from David, just a series of breathless voice messages, a litany of excuses and promises. I should be able to get away tomorrow, he'd said when she called him back, there's a flight first thing in the morning. Everybody loved the show, he told her. There was a gallery in New York interested.

Great, she'd said, that's brilliant. Good for you.

His art was shit, she'd always known that. But she'd never really admitted it to herself before. It didn't seem to matter, not until she was lying there in the hospital. The hospital was when, suddenly, everything seemed to matter.

A man is tested only a few times in his life, that's what Hugh said afterwards. He will seldom recognise the test when it comes along. And by the time he realises that it was a test, it will be too late. But how he behaves in that moment, that's what defines him. That's the mark of the man. Needless to say, David did not pass the test.

He did bring her to the hospital. In fairness he even went

68

as far as the waiting room with her. He waited with her until she was seen by a nurse. But he was late for his flight, and if he missed the flight he would miss the opening. He couldn't miss the opening, Addie understood that, didn't she? As she was being led in for the scan, he was already out on the street, wild-eyed, flagging down a taxi. When the doctor pointed to the screen and showed Addie the fluid flooding her abdominal cavity, as he pointed out where it was seeping right up towards her chest, which would explain the pain under her collar bones, when they showed her the extent of her internal bleeding, Dave was sitting in the taxi, barrelling through the port tunnel towards the airport. As she was being prepped for surgery, as the anaesthetist was being told to hurry, there was no time to waste here, he was trying her phone again while he stood in the queue for airport security. Let me know how you get on, he said to the answering service. Then he turned his phone off before putting it into a basket and sliding it on to the belt of the scanner.

He did try her once more before he boarded, but her phone rang out. He ordered a vodka and tonic when the drinks trolley came round. As soon as he'd finished the drink, he fell asleep. The stewardess had to wake him to tell him to straighten up his seat back for landing. When he called her again from baggage reclaim, it was Della who answered the phone, her tone distinctly chilly. They were able to save Addie, she said, but not the baby.

Ignorance is bliss. It never even dawned on David that this was a test. It never once occurred to him that he had anything to reproach himself for. Not even when he swung into the hospital three days later, a box of duty-free chocolates in his hand, the review from the London *Independent* rolled up in his pocket to show her.

His timing was unfortunate. As he came out of the lift, he walked slap bang into Hugh.

He went straight from the hospital to the nearest Garda station and claimed he'd been assaulted. The guards had no choice but to come to the hospital. After all, a complaint had been made. They had to question all the witnesses. They followed Hugh into his office for a chat, the soles of their big boots squeaking on the lino floor.

Hugh admitted everything straight away, he was quite unapologetic. 'I gave him a bit of a hiding, that's all,' he said. 'He had it coming to him.'

'The fellow's a cad,' he said, by way of explanation. 'A cad and a bounder.' And the Guards chuckled at that swashbuckling language. They were highly amused by the whole thing. This was light relief for them, a break from the drunks and the smackheads. They both leaned over to shake Hugh's hand before tucking their notebooks into their breast pockets and trundling off.

They wouldn't be taking this one any further. You never know when you might need a doctor.

That was the last they saw of David. He never dared to show his face again.

When Addie got home from the hospital, she gathered up his stuff and packed it into a cardboard box. There wasn't much to pack, a few T-shirts, a couple of pairs of black denims, some threadbare socks. There was a thin woollen scarf of his that she'd always liked so she hung on to that. A painting of his he'd given her one Christmas. She took it down, wrapped it up in bubble wrap and stuck it in the boot of her car. She was thinking she might return it to him. Or maybe it would be easier just to drop it off at a charity shop.

She drove around with the painting in the boot of the car for a few weeks. Then one day on the spur of the moment she pulled over and chucked it into a roadside skip. It wasn't anger that made her do it, or bitterness, or heartache. It was just that she'd never liked the painting in the first place, she'd only ever hung it on her wall out of politeness. She was absolutely certain it would never be worth anything.

'Good riddance to bad rubbish,' Della would say whenever he came up in conversation.

'David, who was David again?' That was Simon, trying to be sweet.

'I saw him off,' Hugh would say proudly, 'I put a stop to his gallop.'

And it wasn't that Addie was sorry he was gone, because she wasn't. She knew he was no good, she knew he'd failed the test. It was just that nobody had ever thought to ask her.

It never even occurred to any of them to ask.

Did she ever love David? In retrospect, she would think not. She certainly fancied him, he was her type, long-haired and lanky and unreliable-looking. She had been flattered when he had first asked her out. She had been unsure what it was that he had seen in her but it had been reassuring to think that there must have been something.

She fell easily into step with him. They slipped into a round of gallery openings and club nights. They went to dinner parties where people smoked joints openly at the table and drank copious amounts of red wine. At the weekends they lounged around nursing their hangovers. They ate a lot of takeaways and they watched a lot of TV. And in between the parties and the hangovers they managed to squeeze in some work. Neither of them had high expectations for the other and that was a nice safe feeling. But no, she had never for a moment been under any illusion that she was in love with him.

The worst of it was, she wasted six years of her life on him.

After she broke up with David, Addie threw herself into her work. That was her way of escaping it, she worked and she worked and she worked.

There was a craze out there for extensions, the world and his wife seemed to want an extension. They all wanted the same extension. They wanted light-filled American kitchens with worktop islands and glass doors opening on to what was left of their meagre gardens. They wanted Velux windows and chalky paint colours and designer tiles. So Addie gave them exactly what they wanted.

Then, almost overnight, the work dried up.

The first week in August, the phone stopped ringing. Addie thought maybe everyone had gone away on holidays, but then September came round and still nothing. Addie supervised the building work on her last few jobs and she signed off on the snag lists and then she had nothing left to be doing.

To her surprise, she found that she didn't mind in the

slightest. She would sit down at her drawing board every morning just like she always did, and the only difference was that she wasn't bothered by the phone. She was spared all those ghastly consultations, the bottomless pots of fresh coffee and the endless poring over Farrow and Ball paint charts and the interminable discussions about the suitability of travertine marble for a kitchen floor. It used to take all her self-control to keep her sitting there, nodding away as if she gave a shit. It was all she could do, to stop herself jumping up and screaming. It doesn't matter, you silly cow. That's what she always felt like saying, what does it fucking matter?

She didn't need their money. That made it all the harder to put up with them. Her flat was paid for, she had no mortgage on it. And there was still enough of her mum's money left to keep her going. She lived on practically nothing anyway.

So when the work dried up Addie didn't mind. She took all those paint charts out of her portfolio and she pasted them up on the wall above her desk. They were a thing of beauty, when you set them free of their purpose and allowed them to exist all on their own.

She placed her little jars of ink along the window sill next to her desk where they could catch the light. Now, in the early evening, when the sun comes round, they glow like stained glass, each colour shocking in its beauty. Hard to know which is her favourite. She can never decide. She sits there and tries to pick one. The Apple Green or the Cobalt Blue. The purple with the drawing of a plum on its label. Sunshine Yellow and Canary Yellow and Scarlet and Burnt Sienna. Some of them she loves for their names. The Carmine and the Viridian and the Vermilion. Others she loves for their labels. The long-legged spider on the front of the Black Indian ink and the frog on the Brilliant Green. She loves those inks, she only has to look at them and she's happy.

She enjoys sorting out her pencils, grouping the blues and the greens and the purples together in one jamjar. The sunny colours in another jar, the yellows and the reds and the oranges all bunched together in a gorgeous jumble.

She knows it's a silly way to spend your time but it gives her pleasure and it doesn't do anyone any harm. Harmless pleasures, that's what she tells herself. I'm finally discovering the joy of harmless pleasures.

Sometimes Della wonders, is Addie just a little bit autistic? Mild end of the spectrum, something that was never diagnosed. The way she lines her mugs up on the shelf, upside down, their handles all turned the same way. The way she laughs when the kids mess up her pencils, you just know she's going to spend the evening rearranging them.

'I love the way you use the word mild,' says Hugh with a snort.

Della teases her about it. 'Monica,' she says, 'you're being Monica again.' And Addie will laugh and pretend to be offended. But actually Addie doesn't mind being Monica. She's a tidy person, she always has been. Now it's verging on a pathology. Harmless pleasures, she tells herself, as she tucks shoe horns into all her shoes and lines them up on a rack at the bottom of her wardrobe.

Sometimes she feels like she's putting her affairs in order for some kind of a departure. She imagines her life is winding down. She's just filling time.

*

You know when you're at a wedding, or a dinner dance, and you're longing for it to be over so you can go home?

The champagne reception was enjoyable, the food was good. But now the meal is over and the tables have been cleared back to make space for the dancing. You're still nursing that last glass of wine, you were talking to someone during the meal but now they've gone outside to smoke and you've been left alone. It's too early to leave, it would be rude to leave now. But once the band gets started, once people are up on the dancefloor, you'll be able to slip away. You can whisper goodbye to the hosts. Or maybe you'll just get up to go to the bathroom and then keep on going, sure nobody will notice anyway.

The band is playing a Beach Boys medley and the men are throwing their jackets away, the women kicking off their shoes so they can dance in their stockinged feet.

You're standing at the door, your coat draped over your arm, and you're scanning the room to check if there's anyone you need to say goodbye to. But nobody seems to have even noticed you're leaving.

You're just about to slip off. But just at that moment, the band starts playing your favourite song. Not just a song you're fond of but your favourite song ever, the one that always makes you feel like dancing. The one that makes you forget all your troubles and makes you want to live. You stand there in the door and you don't know what to do. Do you stay or do you go?

That's where Addie was when she met Bruno.

Chapter 8

She was woken by an almighty racket, a ferocious banging on the door. It was more like a pummelling, an irregular drumming. She had a fair idea who it was.

She looked over at Bruno but he'd already pulled the duvet up and over his head and he was burrowing down under it. It was dark in the bedroom, the curtains were drawn. Impossible to tell what time it was. Addie laid her head back down on the pillow, closed her eyes and hoped they'd go away. But of course they didn't.

More banging. Little fists thumping, the hollow sound of a small pudgy palm slapping the door. She rolled over the edge of the bed and sat there for a minute trying to get her bearings before she grabbed her dresing gown and staggered out through the living room to the front hall. She opened the door just a chink, keeping her body behind it as she placed her face in the open crack.

'How did I guess it was you lot?'

They were all jumping up and down. They made a dizzying sight this early in the morning, all blinding pink and frenetic activity.

'We got a fish, we got a fish.'

Stella was the one holding the bowl. She was squealing at the others. '*Stop*, you're going to spill it. If you spill it, I'll kill you. He wants to meet Lola,' she said. 'Can we introduce him to Lola?'

'Lola will eat him,' said Elsa drily, her little voice husky.

'We're going to call him Lola.'

'No, we are *not*!' cried Stella. 'He's my fish and I'm going to name him.'

'We don't even know if he's a boy or a girl.'

'Guys. Your fish is lovely, but you can't come in,' said Addie. 'It's too early, I'm not dressed.'

They just stood there looking at her with their small bewildered faces. When they heard their mother coming up behind them, they all turned round.

'Hi, Ad,' said Della, sweeping down the steps, car keys still in her hand, her coat tails trailing after her.

'Hi, Dell,' said Addie.

'What's up?'

Addie answered in a slow whisper, spitting the words out carefully so she wouldn't have to repeat them. 'I had a sleepover last night.'

O. Della's mouth made a perfect circle and she responded in the same stilted tone. 'OK, girls. Auntie Addie had a sleepover last night.'

'That's right,' said Addie, echoing her words and nodding. 'A sleepover.'

'O-K,' said Della. 'What we're going to do, ladies, is we're going to take the fish upstairs and we'll introduce him to your grandfather. Lola can meet the fish another time.'

Addie watched through the crack in the door as Imelda herded them all back up the steps. When she got to the top she turned round and did a little mime act, sweeping her fingers under her eyes.

As soon as they were out of sight Addie shut the door softly and padded into the bathroom. Sure enough she had panda eyes, dry riverbeds of mascara streaking her face as far down as her cheekbones. As quietly as she could, she opened the tap up to a trickle of water. With a wet cotton pad, she swept the sludge away. Brushed her teeth and swished some mouthwash around her gums. She straightened her eyebrows with her wet toothbrush.

When she came back into the bedroom, she had the strangest feeling that she was seeing it for the first time. She took in the grubby paintwork on the walls and the flimsy old green curtains on the high basement window. Unlined curtains, they'd been hand-hemmed at the bottom, a loose tacking stitch that broke through to the other side, dimpling the fabric all the way along. Those curtains had been up in Della's bedroom once upon a time. But they'd ended up down here, along with everything else that wasn't wanted.

The armchair in the corner, the battered ottoman against the wall, the wooden floor lamp that somebody had tried to paint over with white emulsion: they were all sorry-looking things, the kind of things you'd expect to find in a holiday home. Even the sheets on the bed, the duvet cover and the pillowcases, nothing matched. The fitted sheet was navy blue and the duvet cover was blue-and-white gingham and the pillowcases were all bottle green. A faint smell of dry dust off them, the smell of a neglected hot press.

This is all he knows of me, she thought, as she slid back into the bed. This tatty basement. The little dog. The injured father lurking upstairs. She went through it like a list. And as she did so, she felt a weight lift off her. I don't ever have to tell him anything else about myself if I don't want to, we can stop right here.

When she turned towards him, she found him lying with his back to her, curled up towards the wall. The harsh winter light coming down through the window highlighted a wide expanse of freckly skin, a few dark hairs sprouting from his shoulders. She threaded her hand through the gap between his arm and his waist, resting her face against his back. She breathed in the smell of him, so familiar already.

She was asleep again within seconds.

It was nearly lunchtime by the time he left.

Poor Lola was dying to get out. Addie had to struggle to clip the lead on to her collar. She was skittering around in circles, trembling with the force of her desire to get going.

'OK, love, OK. We're going, I swear.'

The tide was in so they went all the way down as far as the park. She let Lola off the lead as soon as they got inside the gates. She had her iPod with her but she didn't even take it out of her pocket. She wanted to go over the memories of last night, she wanted to replay it all in her head. Already, it seemed like a dream. If it hadn't been for that delicious bruised feeling she had inside her, she might not have believed it had happened at all.

She spooled back and played it all out in her head like a movie sequence.

The awkward moment when they had closed the door behind them. Both of them afraid to make the first move in case they'd been reading the signals wrong.

Addie was so nervous she had started babbling. She didn't know what she was going to say until it was coming out of her mouth.

'Look,' she had said, holding her hands up in front of her to say stop. 'Before we go any further, I want to say something.'

The madness of it, she was cringing now as she remembered it.

'I have an announcement to make,' she'd said, her breath all raspy with nerves. 'I haven't been naked in front of a stranger for a while. I'm thirty-eight years old. I have a mark on my left breast where I had a lump removed last year. I have an appendix scar from when I was twelve. I'm not as skinny as I'd like to be. I'm riddled with cellulite and my pubic hair is going grey.'

Remembering it now, she was dying.

Already she could hear Della's voice booming in her ears. You said WHAT?

Fair play to him, he hadn't even appeared shocked. You'd think he would have been shocked but the look on his face, he was amused if anything.

He had smiled, that knowing smile that she was starting to find quite attractive. He had smiled and started to walk steadily towards her. And as he walked he had started to sing, in that low tuneful voice of his. It was his lack of embarrassment that she found the most astonishing.

He was so very uncool.

'Show a little faith, there's magic in the night
You ain't a beauty, but hey you're alright
Oh and that's alright with me.'

She couldn't help but laugh. It had been a long time since anyone had surprised her.

She walked round the park three times, rewinding that conversation and rewinding it again in her head. One minute she was smiling, the next minute she was wincing with shame. If anyone had been watching her, they would have thought her a mad woman.

Why the health warning?

Was this a normal thing for her to do? A lovely thirty-eight-year-old woman with half her life ahead of her. A girl with all her faculties and more besides. A talented person with a moral compass as sure as the stars in the sky. Why would she feel the need to issue a health warning before she offered herself up to a man? Why in God's name would she feel that way?

Because Addie, at this stage, feels like damaged goods. She feels old and jaded, she feels like she's been battered by life. She doesn't see herself as thirty-eight, she sees herself as nearly forty.

When she looks in the mirror these days she's shocked by what she sees. The pale face, she looks so dreadfully serious. Even when she makes herself smile, it's as if her eyes won't do what they're told. Those serious grey eyes, they just keep boring a hole in her, as if they're trying to tell her something.

She studies herself in the mirror and she notices new stray hairs appearing below her eyebrows. Now that she looks, there are dozens of them, they're stretching right down to the crease of her eyelid. She should pluck them but she can't be bothered. It seems so pointless, to pluck them. They'll only grow back again. It's a full-time job, keeping it all at bay. It makes her sad, this determination of the body to go on sprouting new growth, long after you've lost the energy to fight it off.

Addie remembers a French exchange Della had once upon a time. She was meant to be Della's exchange but of course Della would have nothing to do with her so Addie had to hang out with her instead. A beautiful golden creature, she used to stretch herself out on the couch in the breakfast room, wearing just a string top and these impossibly short shorts and she would pluck at the hairs on her legs with her tweezers. She would spend hours on end just plucking and plucking and after she finally dragged herself off the couch there would be a layer of fine little hairs all over the upholstery.

'It's disgusting,' Addie would say. 'It's absolutely disgusting, the way she does that.' And she would start brushing the hairs off the couch, slapping the fabric with the flat of her hand to make them jump.

Della would look up from her book. 'Nothing human disgusts me,' she would drawl, misquoting Tennessee Williams.

Sandrine the girl's name was, but she was always known as Madame Mao. A nickname Hugh had given her. Something about how Mao wanted to pluck all the blades of grass in China.

Addie wonders whatever happened to her, Madame Mao. Was she living in an apartment in some French city now, standing at the stove stirring hot chocolate for some caramel-skinned French children, waiting for a floppy-haired philandering French husband to come in the door? What would she think if Addie reminded her about that summer she spent lounging around on their couch, plucking at her legs with her tweezers? Would she even remember?

Nowadays Addie wouldn't mind spending her days plucking at her legs with tweezers. Now that she thinks about it, it seems like a grand way to spend your time. She just wishes she had the energy for it.

She has a tricky head, she knows that, she has a tendency to melancholy. That's why she has herself on a regime. The swimming, the walking, it works for her. She needs to give her head a workout, she needs to flush it out. It can be a full-time job, dealing with all the things that come bubbling up in her head. Sometimes she gets so tired of it all, she wonders if she can be bothered.

What doesn't kill you makes you stronger. Addie has been told that, but she doesn't believe it. Maybe that works for some people, but not for her. Everything that has ever happened to her has made her weaker, like someone has been kicking away at the scaffolding that was holding her up. So that now she's all rickety.

In her own mind, she's a fire sale of a person. She's a

battered relic of all the things that have ever happened to her.

And now here she is, sailing forth for another battering.

Bruno walked back to the B&B with a spring in his step. For the first time in weeks, he was wide awake.

All of a sudden the blood was racing through his veins, he felt limber and fit. He felt like he'd woken up from a bad dream and suddenly everything was OK in the world.

Forty-nine, he said to himself, forty-nine! He felt like punching the air. And as usual when he was feeling like this, as usual when he was feeling good about himself, he had Bruce Springsteen running through his head.

. . . *it ain't no sin, to be glad you're alive.*

Chapter 9

'Oh, to have your life,' said Della. 'Oh, to be free to hop into bed with a complete stranger!'

'He's not a complete stranger, Dell, isn't that the whole point? He's our cousin.'

'I thought you weren't allowed to sleep with your cousin, I thought you had to get a papal dispensation or something.'

'Second cousin once removed, I don't think the Pope's going to be too worried.'

Della snorted.

'Is he married? How many kids does he have?'

'None that I know of.' Addie heard the guarded tone in her own voice, the unsuccessful attempt not to sound naïve. 'I never asked.'

Della made another snorting noise which Addie chose to ignore.

'He's a banker.'

'Impressive,' said Della, trying not to sound too surprised.

'He's some kind of an expert in airline stocks. Actually, he's just lost his job. He used to work for Lehman Brothers.'

Now there's a surprise, Della was thinking. Addie's an expert at picking a dud and this guy is bound to be one too.

Addie could read her sister's mind. She jumped to make a joke out of it.

'Wouldn't you know my luck? Just when I meet a nice banker, the whole global financial system collapses.'

'Oh well,' sighed Della. 'We are in the middle of a recession, we can't afford to be too picky.'

Time was when a banker would have seemed like an even worse prospect to Addie than a serial killer. Bankers, accountants, solicitors, talk to the hand! She wouldn't have stopped to give them the time of day, not a girl like her.

How things change. These days a banker seems like love's young dream.

'There's one more thing,' said Addie. 'He's old.'

'Addie, we're all old.'

'I suppose.'

'How old exactly?'

'Forty-nine.'

'Sure Simon Sheridan's going to be forty-four this year.'

She has this habit of using her husband's second name when she talks about him. Anything to put a bit of distance between herself and her life.

'I know, I know,' said Addie. 'It's just forty-nine is only one year off fifty. I can't believe I'm shagging a fifty-year-old man. It's a bit weird, that's all.'

'It's the future is what it is,' said Della. 'Have you introduced him to Hugh yet?'

'Della, for God's sake. He's an American. He's a relation. And he has a beard. It's a recipe for disaster.'

'Ah yes, but don't forget, he's a banker.'

The trouble is, Bruno doesn't really see himself as a banker any more.

He's not sure he ever was one. It was just something that picked him up and carried him along with it. He was good at math in school and it all flowed from there. Now he feels like he was a passenger on a train that just crashed. He's walking away from the wreckage and he's thinking, how lucky was I to get thrown free?

If you saw him sitting there in Starbucks, with his notebook open on the table in front of him, you might think he was a writer, or a journalist. He's looking around him, his eyes shining with interest. Every so often he bends over his notebook and scribbles something down.

Saturday afternoon and the place is full of couples. Trendy young people dressed in jeans and cashmere. Cellphones and car keys strewn on the table tops among the mugs of steaming caffè latte and the expensive pastries. At each table, the Saturday papers are being divvied out, section by section. Bruno scans the headlines, the same phrases jumping out at him no matter where he looks. Budget deficit, global crisis, financial meltdown.

Funny, nobody looks too worried. They're all reading the papers and sipping their coffees and they're making plans for Saturday night. Bruno can hear them talking into their cellphones. Describing their hangovers. The detail they're going into, Bruno is intrigued. They have a special vocabulary for this. He can hear them making arrangements to meet in this pub or that pub, the next thing they're booking a restaurant table. 'I have to get my hair done, but I could meet you after that.' They're acting like none of this is going to affect them.

Bruno is interested in what's happening, how could you not be? He's an insider. He understands the way it works. Those banks that are falling down, he can take stock of them, he can measure their impact. Like a weatherman eyes a hurricane on a chart, like a mountaineer looks up at a rockfall. Bruno knows the weight of those boulders that are crashing down the mountainside, he knows their girth. He knows they're going to sweep away everything in their path.

He's watching it all the way you watch a movie, as if he has no stake in it.

Here he is, a man of forty-nine with no ties in the world. An unemployed, slightly unfashionable-looking man in casual clothing, sitting on a soft chair in a franchised coffee shop in Dublin, Ireland. As the world collapses around him, Bruno sits in Starbucks eating his Valencia Orange cake with a plastic fork. He's sipping his Americano and he's thinking to himself, how lucky was I to get thrown free!

The thing about Bruno is that he's interested in everything but himself. He can't imagine why anyone would find him interesting. It's a pathology that has been pointed out to him many times over.

'You're a closed book,' Laura used to tell him, 'you give nothing away.' And she would cry tears of frustration, begging him to reveal something of himself to her. Bruno always found this conversation baffling, unaware there was anything of him to reveal.

He had always thought of himself as an open person. Not so, apparently.

'Four years of marriage and still I don't feel I know you,' said Sara once. And she'd asked him, 'Do *you* consider this normal?'

Twice he'd been married, and twice he'd left the marriage behind him, like a snake slithers out of its skin. The third time round he had managed to avoid marrying, in case it was marriage itself that was the problem.

That relationship did last the longest, but its ending was by far the bloodiest.

'It's not like I was having an affair,' he had said.

'An affair I could understand!'

Even then he had tried to explain, doggedly refusing to acknowledge that he had done anything wrong.

'You know there is such a thing as a sin of omission.'

She was using her courtroom voice. That was when he knew it was over.

Three relationships, one per decade of his adult life. They all merge together now. It's hard to separate them out in his mind. There was a sameness to the relationships, if not to the women themselves. The same circular arguments, the same hellish impasse.

Relationships like an endless car trip, you kept missing the exit so in the end you just pulled over on to the verge and one of you got out and walked.

*

Bruno had failed to mention any of this to Addie. All day long they had talked, but he had failed to mention the central facts of his life.

He had told her about his father, about the dream of a return that was still on his lips even as he was sucking mints to take away the taste of death. He had spoken about his sisters and their children, relaying in the simplest of terms their achievements and their disappointments. He had told her about Bruce Springsteen, about Asbury Park and 'Darkness on the Edge of Town'. Even now, he had told her, he only had to hear Bruce's voice and he was filled with pride. The pride of belonging to something. He had told her all of these things, and yet he had failed to mention the two marriages, the last disastrous non-marrriage.

Then again, it occurred to him, she hadn't asked. There had been no forensic questions from her. In fact, she hadn't asked him a single question about his past. There had been none of the gentle probing, none of the leading questions, none of the clumsily disguised fishing expeditions that he had come to expect from women.

None of the bravado or the bluster, none of the tough talk that was used to distract you from the fact that scouts were being sent out to map your territory. They were charting your history, even now they were weighing up your baggage and measuring it against their own.

It was almost insulting to him, this lack of interest from her. Now that he thought about it, she seemed utterly incurious about his past. He was intrigued by this. She was so different from any of the women he'd ever met before.

In Addie, life seemed to have dealt Bruno the ultimate trump card.

Chapter 10

Addie was determined not to hang around waiting for the phone to ring. She would go for her swim. Her swim was sacrosanct.

She was just packing her things into the bag when there was a pounding on the ceiling.

Jesus, she thought. It's like living in a box. If they're not banging on the door, they're banging on the ceiling.

'*I'm coming,*' she roared, louder than she usually would. She stomped up the outside steps and let herself in the front door with her own key. That sour smell again, it always filled her with despair. She stood there for a moment in the hall, baffled by the smell, frustrated by it. She'd spoken to Mrs Dunphy about it, she'd even hung around to check up on her. The place was spotless. And yet there it was, the house was starting to smell like an old person's house, nothing they did seemed to make a difference. There just wasn't enough life in it, it smelled stale.

'Hi, Dad,' she called out, opening the door into the living room.

'Lazarus,' he said.

'Lie-in. It's Saturday.' And she bent down to kiss him. He smelled of soap and that lotion he used to comb his hair over his bald patch. A slimy smell.

'I need you to perform some secretarial duties for me.'

He thinks it's OK to talk to people like this. He's been doing it all his life.

'I was just about to go for a swim.'

Already she knew that she wouldn't go. She would give in to him, just like she always did.

He waved his bandaged right hand over the desk.

'Some documents came this morning by courier, I need you to open them for me. That one there. No, no, not that one. The one under it. The large brown one.'

Addie fished out the letter he was indicating, flipped it over and wiggled her little finger in under the flap. Ripped up and across, making a messy jagged tear in the brown paper. She slid her hand in and pulled out a single typewritten page.

'I merely asked you to open the letter. No need for you to read it.' A peevishness in his tone.

She only had time to register the headed notepaper, a firm of solicitors. She launched the page over to him through the air, watching it land neatly in front of him. He bent over it.

'I'm most obliged.'

He goes into character like this, talking to his daughters like they're staff. It drives Della insane. Addie just ignores it.

She began opening the rest of his post, stacking the letters up in a neat little pile on the desk. The envelopes she ripped and then ripped again, tossing the torn fragments into the waste-paper basket.

He was still bent over the letter, glaring at it.

'Well, if there's nothing else you need, I'll be off.'

She jumped up out of her chair. She checked her mobile, no missed calls. 'I won't be around later on so I've left your dinner all laid out in the kitchen. Is there anything else you require before I go?'

She stood up as tall as she could, raising her arms up over her head to stretch her spine. Her back was aching. Must be the way I was sitting, she thought. She reached over for the pack of Solpadeine on his desk, slid out a foil tray and cracked two pills out of their blisters. Popped them into her mouth and washed them down with a large swig from the open bottle of mineral water sitting on the desk.

'No, no,' he said in a distracted voice. 'That was all.'

Banging the front door behind her, she stood on the top step for a minute and gulped in the sea air. The tide was full in now and the sun was low in the sky, casting a cold light across the water. You could smell the salt in the air. She closed her eyes for a second and breathed in through her nose.

Suddenly she didn't know what to do. She should go for her swim, of course she should go for her swim. But he might ring her while she was in the water. Surely he would leave a message, but what if he didn't? She imagined herself swimming laps, trying not to think about the possibility that the phone might be ringing in her handbag.

She stood there on the top step, teetering between hope

and despair. The glorious promise of the morning was fading now. With every hour that passed she was less hopeful of hearing from him. She could still feel him on every inch of her body, her skin was still burning with the memory of him. But her optimism was waning.

This morning, as she'd walked the dog in the park, she had felt like a lover. She had felt like a blushing bride. It had seemed obvious that he would call, it had seemed clear that this was just the start of something. But now, now even this morning seemed like such a long time ago. Now she was starting to feel like a fool. It was nearly five o'clock. He wasn't going to call.

Suddenly, she couldn't bear to go back down to the flat to get her swimming bag, she couldn't bear the thought of knocking around down there all evening, just herself and the TV and the little dog. She couldn't stand the possibility that her life was about to go back to what it had been before she met him.

She dashed down the steps and opened the basement door, calling for Lola to come out. She didn't even put a foot inside, she didn't even reach in for her coat. She just kept the door open long enough for Lola to come bounding out and then she slammed it shut, as if there was something evil lurking inside. She tipped Lola into the back of the car, hopped into the driver's seat and turned the key in the ignition.

As she ground the gear lever into reverse, she glanced up at the window. And there he was, his neck stretched up like a mad giraffe so that he could peer down at her. She gave him a wave and he waved back, the big bandaged hand wobbling around on top of his arm. She eased the car back out of the drive, her eye fixed on the rear-view mirror, her heart weighed down with a heavy sludge of love and guilt.

He watched her pull away, following her little car as she inched it out on to the road. He watched as she waited for a break in the traffic. Then he saw her pull out. Swinging to the right, she joined the line of cars streaming off to the south.

Within seconds he had lost sight of her.

He let his head fall back against the chair and closed his eyes. He couldn't remember when he had last felt so disheartened.

The date had been set, that's what the letter said. The paperwork was all there, a thick clutch of photocopies, attached with a giant-sized paper clip. Hugh had been expecting it, he had known it was coming. But he'd been entertaining the vague hope that it might still be dropped, that they'd lose the energy for the fight, that they would finally see reason and call a halt to the whole thing.

Of course he should have known, there was no chance of that happening. This one was going to go all the way.

He was overcome by a wave of weariness.

He sat there slumped over his desk, his shoulders falling forward in a gesture of defeat. His head felt huge and heavy, the weight of it too much for his neck. He let his forehead drop forward, his chin fell in towards his chest and he closed his eyes for a moment. He felt like a Christian martyr, waiting to be thrown to the lions.

The papers would lap it up, he knew that. It had all the elements. A young mother, dead before she turned thirty. Two

95

small children left with no one to care for them. A heartbroken husband struggling to earn a living, a pair of angry parents out for revenge. A routine procedure, that's how the papers would describe it, a needless death. They would refer to Hugh as the eminent professor. And in the careful phrasing of their copy they would imply that there was plenty more that they couldn't say about him for legal reasons.

When the details of the case came out, there would be a debate. There would be talk of the need for new standards, people would say this kind of behaviour just isn't acceptable any more. They would call on the Medical Council to publish industry standards, they would demand new guidelines on dealing with patients and junior staff. They would talk about the importance of a good bedside manner, they would suggest that this be included in the syllabus.

They would say it was time for a changing of the guard.

The most difficult time in his life.

Not that there haven't been difficult times before, of course there have. But he was always equal to the challenge, he always put his shoulder to the wheel. That's what he's done his whole life, he's always been a worker.

Sixty-four years old, which means it's forty-six years since he embarked on a career in medicine. There's a symmetry to that, he can't help but think. There's something neat about it. If he keeps on going to his retirement date, that much will be lost. In his heart he knows he won't make it to his retirement date.

That's all the thanks you get. Forty years working at it,

fifty weeks a year. Twelve-hour days, fourteen-hour days. Saturdays and bank holidays, he even made his rounds on Christmas Day. He made a point of it, he used to bring the girls with him. Phone calls in the middle of the night, patients with all sorts of complications. Conferences and bloody case conferences. He never once complained about the workload. Whatever had to be done, he did it. He loved being a doctor, he still thrilled to the sound of the word.

If only they'd just let you *be* a doctor, if only they'd let you practise your trade. But no, you had to be a bloody psychologist now as well. You had to be a social worker too, you had to submit yourself to interrogation. They'd all been watching too much *ER*, these people, they'd all been looking things up on the internet. They wanted to know about all the available options.

There are always options, that's what he liked to say to them. The options are these. We can treat your mother as best we can, in which case there's a good chance she will survive. Or she can choose not to receive treatment, in which case she will almost certainly die.

Very few people appreciated his frankness. There was even the odd complaint. People had no bloody sense of humour any more, they couldn't take a joke.

He doesn't understand the language people use, he doesn't know where they're getting it from. They talk about consultant cover 24/7 and they talk about thinking outside the box and they talk about face time. They've started calling patients 'clients', for Christ's sake. They talk about service providers and patient journeys. It all sounds like nonsense of the highest order but as soon as you say that all you get is the raised eyebrows. They're all playing the game, all afraid to say boo.

They don't even seem capable of keeping the hospitals clean these days, they're riddled with MRSA, the nurses won't so much as change a bedpan. Well, what do you expect, letting accountants run the hospitals, bloody bean counters. Bring back the nuns, that's what he's been saying for years. The nuns knew how to run a bloody hospital.

He knows he sounds like an outdated, antiquated old fart. He's past his sell-by date, he's aware of that. Still, he'd been hoping to limp over the finish line.

It's been on his mind for a while, the dreaded retirement. Lately, he's found himself thinking about it more and more. Part of him has been thinking, no dinner, no fuss. But the next thing he'll find himself rehearsing his speech, he'll be picturing himself struggling to his feet, tapping a spoon against a glass. A hush falling on the room. He glances down the table and sees . . . who does he see?

Who would come to his retirement? Who would he even want to have there? In his mind, he scans the faces of his colleagues and it occurs to him, he couldn't count a single one of them as a friend. Not a single one who he would ever meet up with for a drink. He's never been invited to any of their homes and it never occurred to him to invite any of them to his. There was no wife to make friends with their wives, no wife to throw dinner parties that would further his career. And of course he never went to any of those medical functions. God, how he hates those ghastly functions.

He should have played golf. But how could he have played golf? He had two little girls to rear, he wasn't free to bugger off and spend his weekend on a bloody golf course. And anyway, it was far from golf he was reared. Still, he should have played the odd game of golf, it might have been the saving of him now. He never played the game, he can see that now. You have to play the game.

Would any of them stick up for him? That's what it came down to. If none of them would speak up in his defence, he was done for. He was as good as finished.

An outsider all his life, the herd had never allowed him in. Their instincts were infallible, they could smell it off him. A good doctor he may have been, but he wasn't one of them.

He was never lonely until now.

He mustered all his courage and raised his head, opening his eyes on to the harsh daylight. He used his elbows to push himself up off the armchair, stumbling like an old man as he got to his feet. He shuffled over to the music cabinet, maybe some music would save him from himself.

He didn't know very much about music. He'd like to know more about it, he really would, it's something he's always been meaning to get around to. Opera, that's what he likes, he sees himself as an opera buff. But all he has in his repertoire is a few compilation CDs, Christmas presents and the like. He's ashamed of his ignorance, he regrets it. It would be such a comfort to him now, to be a music lover.

He remembers his first tantalising taste of opera. He'd been given a wireless for Christmas, he had it in pride of place on his bedside table. He was studying for his exams, it must have been his Leaving Cert. He can still remember the frigid cold of his feet under the desk, the ache in his neck as he bent over his books. The merciless damp of the winter morning, you were hungry for any morsel of comfort. The radio was on low, he wasn't even aware it was on until the music started. He lifted his head from his books, pricked up his ears and listened.

A heavenly sound. He didn't even know what it was they were singing, all he knew was that it was beautiful. And in that moment he felt his mind open up, like a parcel falls open when you remove the twine. He sat there in a spell.

Suddenly he was aware of the world outside his window, a world of infinite possibility. He imagined all the people sitting in great opera houses around the world, decked out in all their finery, listening to this same beautiful music. He imagined people in large-windowed apartments looking out over glittering cities, they would be listening to this music too, it would be a part of the fabric of their lives. And he realised that he would leave this place soon and he would go out into the world and he would be a part of it all. Maybe it occurred to him then that he would never come back.

'The Chorus of the Hebrew Slaves' it was, that first piece of music. He recognised it when he heard it again years later. And every time he has heard it since, it's as if he's back in that cold bedroom in that cold house, the richness of the world revealing itself to him for the first time.

It should have been the start of a great journey, it should have been the beginning of a lifelong love affair with music. He should have made it his business to go to La Scala, to Covent Garden. He should have gone to Verona. He could have been a regular at Wexford. By now he would have explored all the great recordings, he would have been qualified to say who was the greatest Norma, who was his favourite Madam Butterfly.

Instead of which he's still back where he started, with the *Great Opera Choruses* collection. Well, so be it, he would listen to the Slaves' Chorus again and to hell with being an opera buff. The Slaves' Chorus never failed to lift his spirits.

He swept the disc over to the edge of the cabinet with his sleeve, then picked it up with the tips of his fingers. Slowly, he bent from the knees until he was down on his hunkers, his back creaking as he went. Then he dropped the disc into the open tray. It fell perfectly into place and he grunted with satisfaction. With his middle finger, he nudged the button to close the tray, then he hit play.

He got to his feet with the feeling of a job well done. The first strains of music filled the room and he was flooded with hope again.

Only a matter of weeks before his casts would be off. Then he would be fit to fight the case, and there was no reason on this earth why he couldn't win. He would be vindicated, he would see out his career on a high note. He might even do some teaching again. You can't beat experience, at the end of the day it's experience that matters.

He could still go to La Scala, if he wanted to, there was nothing stopping him. He would take Addie with him. He would treat her, they could make a weekend of it. He felt buoyant. There was life in him yet, he could see that now.

There was life in him yet.

Chapter 11

Della answered the door in evening dress. A full-length black satin gown with short scalloped sleeves and a deep scoop neckline. She had no make-up on and her feet were bare.

Addie's heart sank when she saw her.

'Are you getting ready to go out?'

'God, no,' said Della, turning and walking back through the hall. 'I'm just cleaning out the hot press.' She started up the stairs, the train of her dress slithering after her.

Addie traipsed up in her wake. Lola was too polite to follow. She stood watching them from the hall, her tail wagging slowly. Then she flopped down on to the tiles, her chin resting on her front paws, her eyes fixed on the stairs.

The landing was scattered with storage boxes and canvas bags.

'Sit there and talk to me while I'm doing this,' said Della. 'I've started so I have to finish.'

Addie selected a clear space against the wall. She sat down

on the carpet, her knees pulled up to her chest, her back resting against the scalding radiator.

Della was climbing up on to a shelf inside the press. She yanked the hem of her dress out of the way with one hand as she climbed.

'I'm looking for the ski gear,' she shouted. 'Can't remember where I would have put it, it must be up here somewhere.'

A child's slipper came flying out and landed on the ground beside Addie.

'The things you find!'

There were terrible noises coming from one of the upstairs bedrooms. The sound of a large number of little girls making a horrible mess. Screeching sounds and thumping and a general kerfuffle. Every so often somebody would wail.

'How many of them have you got up there?'

'Oh, God knows,' came the muffled voice from inside the hot press. 'Well,' she said, 'did he call?'

'No,' said Addie softly.

'Well, that doesn't mean he won't,' said Della. She swung round to face out. She was hanging from the top shelf, her feet perched precariously on the bottom shelf, her head bent sideways to avoid the lampshade.

'He's not going to call,' said Addie despondently. 'I can feel it in my bones.'

But Della didn't answer. Now she was groping along the top shelf, her body hanging out into the void.

'I might as well face facts,' said Addie, her voice slightly louder this time. 'He's not going to call.'

Della was holding on to the shelf with one hand now, using the other to tug at a huge plastic storage bag.

'Here, Ad, help me take this down. Wait, it's coming, watch out!'

Addie hugged her knees in closer to her chest, flattening her back up against the radiator as the bag came crashing down. Della hopped down after it. Now she was standing triumphantly inside the hot press, her hands on her hips, her face all flushed. She bent down to unzip the bag.

An overpowering smell of fermented urine wafted out.

'Oh, please no,' Della was saying, her face in her hands. 'This can't be happening to me.'

Addie was holding her nose, her voice came out all distorted. 'How long have they been in there? Don't tell me. Not since last January?'

'Muck savages,' Della was muttering. 'They're nothing but muck savages.'

She started pulling the suits out one by one, holding them up to her nose and sniffing at them suspiciously.

'I can't figure out which one is the guilty party.'

At that moment, the door of the upstairs bedroom burst open and they came thundering out like a herd of elephant. Six of them, seven, Addie counted as they swept by, hopping over her feet as they negotiated the return. They were dressed in fairy outfits mainly, lots of cheap polyester and netting in ghastly shades of pink.

Lisa was the last to appear, mincing her way along the upper landing. Addie noticed that she had both legs squeezed into one leg of a pink velour tracksuit.

'Hey, Lisa old girl,' said Addie, 'I think you've got your knickers in a twist there, do you want a hand?'

The child stood at the top of the little flight of stairs,

looking at Addie with disdain. Her eyes were almost white, they were so pale. Simon's eyes.

'I'm a mermaid,' she said.

'Well, obviously you're a mermaid!' said Addie. 'I was just checking. Do you need any help getting down the stairs, love?'

Lisa just ignored her. She sat down on the top step and pushed herself off, bumping down the six steps and struggling to her feet again on the return. She shuffled around to the top of the main flight, sat herself down and pushed off again. Bump, bump, bump, twelve times until she got to the bottom. By the time she'd reached the foot of the stairs, the others were already on their way up again.

'Say hi to your auntie Addie,' Della roared.

'Hi, Auntie Addie,' they all said as they trundled past.

'Who's that one?' Addie asked, pointing at a child she'd never seen before. 'I'm not your aunt,' she shouted after her.

'I give up,' Della was saying, staring helplessly at the pile of ski suits. 'It seems to have kind of permeated them all.'

'Delightful,' said Addie.

'I'll have to wash the whole lot.' She piled them all up in her arms and side-stepped over Addie's feet. 'Come on, we'll have a cup of tea.'

So Addie traipsed downstairs after her, feeling utterly at sea.

'I think Dad might be depressed,' she said as she followed Della into the kitchen.

'What makes you think that?'

'Oh, I don't know, he's gone very quiet. He seems preoccupied.'

'Of course he's preoccupied, Addie! He should be preoccupied. He's being sued, for God's sake. It's very serious for him. It will all be in the papers. It will affect his reputation, it could be the end of him.'

'You sound as if you already know he's going to lose.'

Della was down on her hunkers, stuffing the ski suits into the washing machine. She paused for a minute.

'Simon says they have a strong case.'

'Dad told me they don't have a leg to stand on!'

'Well, of course he would say that! He never admits he's wrong, you know that.'

Addie filled the kettle and turned it on. She knew Della was right, of course she was right. And yet there was that gulf between them, the same gulf that always appeared whenever they got to talking about their father. Addie didn't like to say anything bad about him. Della seemed to relish it. For Addie, the truth was always less important than the love.

The kids came coursing through the kitchen again, a rowdy crocodile of them. Elsa was out front. '*Runaway Bride*,' she was screaming as she ran out into the back garden.

'Della. I can't face the thought of being on my own any more.'

Della was moving around the room, it wasn't clear if she was listening. Did Della ever sit down any more?

Addie kept on talking.

'I thought I was cool with it, I really did. I thought I was cool with the idea of being single, what with the dog and the swimming and everything. But now I realise I'm not.'

She had tears in her eyes. She started blinking them away. 'I don't want to be on my own.'

Della had her back to her. She was standing at the kitchen counter making the tea. But it turned out she was listening after all.

'Being married isn't that great either, you know,' she was saying. 'I envy you your life, I really do. Do you know what I feel like sometimes? I feel like an office worker, I'm like someone in a dead-end civil service job. I'm just pushing paper around on my desk, nobody even notices what I do.'

Addie was already opening her mouth to reply, but Della hadn't finished.

'Nobody seems to care as long as I don't complain.'

This is something Della does, she's constantly coming up with new similes to describe her life. Sometimes she's a factory worker, she's a worker in a chicken factory, she's working on the assembly line day in, day out. Other times she's a tennis player, she's a tennis player with nobody on the other side of the court, she's hitting balls all day long that nobody returns.

Addie has heard it all a million times before. But she also has to consider the fact that Della and Simon slow-dance together in the kitchen late at night when the kids have gone to bed. She knows they have sex on the kitchen table after their dinner guests have gone home. So it's hard for her to have too much sympathy.

Anyway, thought Addie, weren't we talking about me?

She looked out the window into the back garden.

'Della,' she said, in a disjointed voice, 'Elsa's wearing your wedding dress.'

'Oh, don't worry about that, I let them have it. It's not like I'm ever going to use it again.' She came over to the table and turned a chair sideways so she could kneel down on it.

107

'But she has it out in the garden, Dell, she's getting it all muddy! Lola's eating the veil!'

'Who cares?'

Della dumped a heaped spoon of sugar into her mug of tea. 'That's my new catchphrase, I find it applies to almost every situation I find myself in. You should try it. Who cares?'

And she looked so pretty kneeling there at the kitchen table in her mad evening dress, the mug of tea held between her two tiny hands. Addie couldn't help but smile.

'You should dress like that all the time, it suits you.'

'I think I might. Who cares!'

'That's it, who cares.'

So there they were again, two sisters against the world.

They're alike, the two of them. You'd know they were sisters. The same round face, the same wide-open grey eyes. The same neat little nose. Even their hair would be the same shade, somewhere between brown and blonde, if they didn't colour it.

Nowadays Addie's hair hovers around a dark honey colour. Number 78 is the number on the box she buys in the supermarket, whenever she can be bothered. Della's hair is lighter, she goes to an expensive hairdresser every four weeks to have it highlighted, her one concession to respectability.

If Addie ever became famous and they made a doll of her, it would look like Della. The head just a little bit larger in proportion to the body. The boobs smaller and neater. The cheekbones a little higher, the eyes a little wider. She's the image of Addie, only better-looking. There's something more perfect about Della, it's as if the mould got slightly out of shape when it came to making Addie.

They weren't at all alike as children. People used to remark on how different they were. People used to say that Addie looked like her dad while Della took after her mum.

'You got one of each.' Addie remembers someone saying that, but she can't remember who.

They weren't close when they were growing up. They grew up side by side of course, they spent every day in each other's company, but they weren't close.

Each of them alone in her bedroom for hours on end. Those hours must have attached themselves to each other, they must have turned into weeks and months and years. But Addie remembers them as just one moment.

She's crouched down on the floor over a huge piece of white card, mapping out lines with a pencil and a wooden ruler. Her back is aching, her knees and the fronts of her calves a raw red from the rough pile of the carpet. She's listening to Radio Nova, she can almost hear the song they're playing, it's hovering at the edge of her memory. If you hear a certain three songs played in a row you have to ring them, she can't remember what it is you win.

She's mapping out make-believe houses on these huge sheets of paper. Elaborate mansions with interior courtyards surrounded by wooden balconies. Bedrooms with spiral staircases that lead to secret gardens. Rooftops with full orchards planted on them and hammocks slung from tree to tree, so you can sleep under the stars.

That's where Addie spent her childhood, in those beautiful, fantastical houses of her own imagining. It was only her shadow that was lunking around that big cold house on the Strand Road. In Addie's head, she was floating through a series of interconnecting rooms, each one painted a paler blue than the last, floor-to-ceiling French doors opening out on a deep dark lake, her white dress billowing in the breeze. She was sitting perched on the edge of a shallow pool in a tiled courtyard crowded with tropical plants, her toes dipped in the still green water, her back resting against a cool stone pillar.

In her memory, Addie is aware of Della's presence in the room next door. She knows that Della is stretched out on her bed, reading. Every so often you can hear the whispery sound of the pages turning.

'Jesus, child, your eyes will go square.' That's what their childminder used to say, as she reached in to turn on the light switch. She would have tried calling up to them from way down in the basement kitchen but neither of them would have replied. So she would have traipsed up one flight of stairs, calling as she went. Hauling herself up another flight when she got no answer, until at last she found herself on the upstairs landing, panting and exasperated.

'You girls need to get out into the air,' she would say. 'Get some colour into those cheeks.' And they would look up at her with ghostly eyes, as if to prove her point. They were easy children though, she had to admit that. They were easy children to mind, they never gave her any trouble. Poor motherless mites, she would say, he has them well brought up.

Looking back now, Addie realises they were eccentric children. They were allowed to be eccentric. There was nobody to put a stop to it.

For a while there they seemed to grow out of it. When they were teenagers, they hung around with other girls, and talked a lot on the phone. Right through their twenties, they seemed to be going along just fine. By the time she'd turned thirty, Imelda was married to a doctor and she was pregnant with her first child. Addie was qualified as an architect and she had her own apartment. On the face of it, they had come good.

'They've turned out grand, those girls, you have to hand it to him.'

Only recently has it begun to dawn on Addie that those middle years might have been a blip, a brief flirtation with conventionality. What song is that from? *Conventionality belongs to yesterday*. These days Della is every bit as eccentric as she ever was as a child, maybe even more so.

'I'm trying to stand out from the other doctors' wives,' she'll say in defence of her outfits. 'It's a sea of Burberry and designer jeans out there, the poor kids have a hard time picking out their own mother.'

It's as if she's reverting. She's turning back into the girl she was thirty years ago, the girl who didn't care what anyone else thought of her, the girl who just wanted to read her book and be left alone. The 'everybody-else-can-fuck-off-club', that's what Della used to call it. Membership of one.

Addie has her own exclusive club these days too. Herself and Lola are the only members. Sure who else would join? Her friends are all married, most of them have kids. She doesn't see them as much as she used to and even when she does, it feels like there's a noisy road between them. They're shouting, but they still can't hear each other properly.

These days, Addie is closer to Della than she is to anyone. It's as if everyone else has fallen away and all that's left is family.

She misses her mother like never before.

Della was on her feet again, clearing away the mugs.

'Will you stay for dinner?' she was asking. 'Shepherd's pie. Glass of wine. Good comfort food. Come on, stay and save us from each other.'

They were in the middle of the meal when Addie's phone rang. She'd just eaten her first helping of shepherd's pie and was about to offer her plate up for seconds. The kids hadn't touched theirs of course, they were all moaning that there was onion in it and Simon was roaring at them and Della was saying you can starve for all I care. With all the ruckus, Addie only just about heard the phone ringing. She delved into the pocket of her cardigan, checked the screen and saw the American dialling code. Ran out of the room to answer it.

'Hi,' she said. Her heart was beating so hard, she was afraid he would hear it.

'Hi,' he said. 'I'm not sure what the local customs are around here but is it considered appropriate for a guy to ask a girl out to dinner?'

Chapter 12

As soon as Della closed the front door she felt a wave of self-pity break over her. She had to stand there for a minute in the hall to steady herself. She knew it was shitty of her. She was pleased for Addie, of course she was pleased. She'd even managed to act pleased. She'd sent her off with strict instructions to get home and put some make-up on, she'd stood there in the doorway smiling as her sister tore off down the path with the dog tearing after her. She'd waved as Addie drove away, she'd shouted after her, have a great time!

But as soon as she'd closed the door behind her, she had felt utterly abandoned.

Now she leaned back against the closed door and looked around her. Simon's coat had fallen off the hall stand and was lying in a pool on the tiles beside her. There were muddy wellies strewn around the floor, among them a pair of damp-looking knickers and tights still intertwined. From the living room she could hear the telly. She could picture Simon tucked up in the corner of the couch, the bottle of beer and the remote control sitting on the armrest.

Upstairs, another TV was on, something unsuitable probably. It was bound to be unsuitable, for Lisa at the very least. Della had been forced to ban *The Simpsons* recently after Lisa asked, what are edible underpants? It was a token ban, they were all still watching it anyway. Poor Lisa, she was named after the bloody programme, so what do you expect?

Della bent down to pick up Simon's coat, feeling weary and worn out. My life is like something out of a country and western song, she thought.

She made her way down to the kitchen, shoving the pile of wellies aside with her foot as she passed. Crept by the open door of the living room, and down the three steps into the kitchen. She made a beeline for her reading chair, the white wicker chair she'd bought when she first moved out of home. The paint on it was all chipped now, the wickerwork loosening up. It was sagging, like herself. She pulled her book out from behind the cushion and sank down into the chair, drawing her feet up under her. She started reading where she'd left off that morning, wondering already how long she'd get before someone came looking for her.

When Della was a child she could spend an entire day stretched out on her bed, reading. She would read for hours on end, she would read until she had lost all feeling in her body, until her tummy was rumbling with hunger. She would break for dinner and then she would go straight back up to her bedroom and read until it was dark.

It's like a dream to her now, the memory of all that time she had on her hands and no one to disturb her.

Sometimes now she tries to sneak away. She slides up to her bedroom in the middle of the afternoon without telling any of them where she's going. She lies down guiltily on top of the covers, she grabs the book from her bedside table and opens it greedily, devouring it like pornography. She reads with both ears open, listening out for loud bumps or wails, for fights and people falling out of trees. She seldom gets through a single chapter.

Mum.

A voice moving up the stairs.

Mum! Where are you?

That's the word she hears all day. Mum, they shout and somehow they manage to squeeze five syllables into it. Mum, do you know where my runners are? Mum, can we watch TV? Mum, Stella never asked if she could play with my Nintendo. A plaintive Mum, an outraged *Mum.*

Mum, *Mum, Mum!*

Do you remember when you were a kid and you used to practise writing your name down on a piece of paper over and over again? And after a while the letters would start to make no sense, they would begin to seem like a random construction of marks on paper, a thing with no meaning. You would start to wonder was that your name at all, you would begin to feel like you were falling through the air and there was no one to catch you.

That's what Della feels like when they call her Mum, it makes no sense to her.

The last straw was when Simon called her Mum. Mum, he said, do you know where the tennis rackets are?

Simon, she said, I am not your mother. Call me that one more time, and I'll never sleep with you again.

She doesn't take any prisoners, Della.

When their mother died, Della took her place. She became the mother in the house. The way a new president is sworn in as soon as the old one dies.

She's so like her mum, people still say it. The same lovely face, the same wild air about her. She's a reader, just like her mum was.

Addie has no memory of the night their mother died, she has no recollection of that time at all. Della remembers but she wishes she didn't. She remembers them coming back to the house after the hospital, she remembers the loneliness of it being just the three of them. She remembers taking some soup out of the fridge and heating it up. She remembers how they all sat around the table with the bowls steaming in front of them. Addie was the only one who managed to eat anything. After all, she was still only a child. After supper, they all changed into their pyjamas and Hugh and Addie tossed their dirty clothes into the washing basket in the bathroom, just like they always did. The next day, Della took the washing out and stuffed it into the machine. And that was how it started. She was ten years old.

A lady was hired, there was always a lady. But Della was in charge. She made the school lunches for the two of them. She wrote the sick notes. She made sure there were wrapped presents for Addie to take to birthday parties. She always remembered to include a card. Part of her is still waiting for somebody to thank her.

Overnight, a family of four became a family of three. A couple with two little girls became a couple with one little girl. Della moved up a rung, taking her place alongside Hugh as the other adult in the house. And Addie became the treasured only child.

Now Della is a mother again. Sometimes she feels like she's a mother to them all. She's the wild one with the settled life, her house is home to all of them, even if they don't all live here. And the truth is, much as she might grumble about it, that's the way she likes it.

When Addie lost the baby, Della was heartbroken for her and for the little niece or nephew she'd already started to love. Already, she'd begun to imagine their circle widening, another family apart from her own. Another home with Addie at the centre of it. Addie as a mother herself. It would change things between them, no question. It would change the whole structure of the family.

In a dark dirty corner of her heart, Della is glad that change never came about.

Chapter 13

Thirty-eight years old and Addie had never been asked out to dinner before.

She tried to explain this to Bruno but he couldn't get his head round it.

'What it means for you is all good,' she said. She wasn't looking at him, she was pretending to read the menu.

'What does it mean for me?' He was intrigued.

She still didn't look up. 'Oh, there are certain sexual favours I always promised myself I'd award to the first guy to ask me out on a proper date.' She couldn't believe she was hearing herself say this.

'Well, what are we waiting for?' He put down his menu and reached for his jacket, raising himself slightly off his chair.

'Without the dinner?' she laughed. 'You must be joking.'

They'd wandered into about six restaurants looking for a table. Nine o'clock on a Saturday night and everywhere was heaving, they were putting people on waiting lists. In the end they just went to Danny's place. Addie rang ahead and somehow Danny figured out it was a date and by the time they got there he had the little table at the back all set for two, a lonely rose sticking out of a milk jug.

Bruno insisted on pulling Addie's chair out for her. As she sat down she could see Danny hovering there behind him clutching their coats. The look on his face, she could see him getting all excited for her. She glared at him, but he just smiled back sweetly and wiggled his head like a pantomime genie.

'I'm so hungry I could eat a horse,' said Bruno.

'Farmer's arse through a hedge.' Addie opened up her menu and pretended to study it. She'd already decided not to mention the shepherd's pie.

'I thought there was supposed to be a recession,' said Bruno. He was looking around at all the packed tables.

'Penny hasn't dropped yet,' said Addie.

'Penny dropped for me a while ago.'

'Is that why you came? Because you lost your job?'

'That,' he said, 'and the election. I was getting upset about the election, I needed some perspective. So I told myself, book a round trip, Bruno. Book a round trip, come back when it's over. If Obama wins, I can make a triumphant return. If McCain wins ...' He leaned in over the table for extra emphasis. 'If he wins, I'm tearing up my return ticket. If he wins, I'll *eat* my ticket.'

She laughed, that bubbly laugh that burst out of her with no warning. But silently she was thinking, that's less than a month away.

119

The food arrived, big blackened fillets of beef and a small bowl heaped high with skinny chips.

'The plan was to spend a month driving across the country. That's still the plan, I suppose. I just haven't got going yet.'

'A month?' She opened her eyes wide in an exaggerated expression of surprise. 'Sure you can drive across the country in a day. Less than a day. It only takes about four hours to get to the other side.'

He didn't look convinced.

'I'm finding it a bit hard to get my head around that. It's hard to imagine anywhere so small when you come from somewhere so big.'

'You'd have to do a loop,' said Addie. She was trying to work it out in her head, squeezing one eye shut as she drew a line in her mind right round the island. 'You'd have to go right round the edge, slowly, for it to take a month. I wonder, even then, would it take you a month?'

'Maybe we should try it.'

She said nothing, concentrating on cutting into her steak.

'This trip has been in my head for such a long time,' he said. 'I made a solemn promise to my father that I would come. That was thirty years ago. I can't believe I'm only keeping my promise now.'

'What took you so long?'

He had to stop and think.

'You know, I've been asking myself that very question. Ever since I got here, I've been asking myself, where did all that time go? It's been thirty years since my father died, thirty years next summer. And all that time I've been wanting to make this trip, I've had this need to make the trip. It's been there all along, like a little voice in my head.' He cupped his hand over his mouth and whispered into it. He was making fun of himself a little. 'Go to Ireland, Bruno. Go to Ireland . . . '

'But you didn't.'

'No. I didn't. Not until now.'

He looked puzzled. He was frowning, as if he was searching his memory for something.

'In the beginning I think it was too soon. To come here, to my father's country. I wasn't ready for that, I was too young. And by the time I was ready to come, I was too busy. I was working a lot and I was travelling a lot and the last thing I wanted to do when I wasn't working was more travelling. I vacationed in Mexico. I like Mexico. Mexico is close, it's easy.'

'Mexico,' said Addie. He had her thinking now of all the places she'd never been.

'Yeah, Mexico. Also, there was my mother to think about. She was sick for a long time, she was in a retirement home. I was afraid to make the trip. In case something would happen to her while I was gone.'

'That's a reason not to make the trip. A good reason.'

'Yeah, well. There were always reasons not to. Plus there was this weird thing, after September eleven, you felt like you had to stay close, it would have felt . . . '

He paused to find the right word. She had noticed this about him, how carefully he chose his words. You had the feeling he was searching his soul for every single one.

' . . . it would have felt disloyal to leave.'

'So what changed?'

He looked startled by the question.

'What changed?'

He leaned in over the table.

'Everything changed.' He raised his hand in the air and snapped his fingers. 'Just like that, everything changed.'

He was looking straight into Addie's eyes as he spoke. He was boring a hole in her.

'All those reasons not to, I went through them one by one. I was laying awake in my bed, it was just after I lost my job and I couldn't sleep, and I lay there trying to think of all the reasons why I couldn't leave. And none of them were there any more. And I thought, now, Bruno, there's nothing stopping you. The moment of truth.'

'That must have felt good.'

He paused, thought about it for a moment before he answered.

'No,' he said. 'It felt fucking terrifying!'

And he burst out laughing, his laughter so unexpected and so infectious that Addie laughed along with him. Her laugh was like an outboard engine, it started deep down in her throat, coming out of her mouth as a noisy splutter.

'Reinventing yourself,' he was shaking his head, as if he was seeing something he didn't quite believe, 'it's scary at my age.'

'At least you weren't too afraid to do it,' said Addie.

And she was thinking, I would never have the courage to do that, to start over. Correcting herself in her mind as she went. I don't have the courage, she thought. I haven't had the courage. But at the same time, somewhere inside her, a tiny spark had been lit, a tiny spark that said maybe.

It was as if he could read her mind.

'What would you be, if you could reinvent yourself?'

She didn't hesitate, not for one second.

'I'd be a swimming pool designer.'

'A swimming pool designer . . . ' He turned it over in his mind, smiling to himself as he examined it. It was as if she'd just handed him a peculiar object.

'Why a swimming pool designer?'

'That's what I always wanted to be, when I was a kid. I used to tell everybody I was going to be a famous swimming pool designer, I would design these amazing swimming pools and then I would travel the world testing them out.'

She was uncomfortable under his scrutiny, she felt suddenly shy. She reached for her wine glass.

'So why didn't you?'

He was looking at her expectantly, waiting for an answer. She choked on her wine, a sip of it went down the wrong way and her eyes started watering and she could feel her face going purple. She pounded herself on the chest with the flat of her hand and reached for her glass of water.

She took a big gulp, her eyes started to clear and she began to breathe easy again. He was watching her, still waiting for an answer.

'I can't believe you just asked me that.'

'Asked you what?'

'I can't believe you asked me why I never became a swimming pool designer. It's just funny, that's all.'

'Why is it funny?'

'Because it's ridiculous. You can't be a swimming pool designer.'

He looked genuinely puzzled.

'Why not? I don't understand. Don't they need people to

design swimming pools? Surely there are people out there who design swimming pools.'

Now she was the one watching him. He was utterly serious, she realised. He was absolutely and completely serious. He was asking her a question and he wanted to know the answer.

'It's just a childish notion,' she said. 'Like my niece, she wants to track lions in Africa. That's what she wants to do when she grows up. Kids come up with these things, Bruno, they're not realistic career choices.'

'But why not?' he asked. 'I have a friend from college who tracks tigers in Cambodia, she works for the World Wildlife Fund. I'm sure they track lions in Africa, I'm sure there's somebody who does that for a living. I'm sure there are people who design swimming pools for a living, there have to be. I don't see why it shouldn't be you.'

And he raised his glass to her. He was almost smirking.

He's interesting, she thought, he's actually interesting. And it was a revelation to her. She hadn't expected him to be interesting.

She kept her eyes on his, holding on to his gaze longer than was comfortable. Then she raised her own glass to him for a moment before taking a long sip.

'So what are you going to be, in your new life?'

He answered her very slowly and with great dignity.

'What I'd like to be is a writer.'

It had a bad effect on her. She found herself suddenly irritated. A moment ago she had been fascinated by him. Now she was bored. She didn't want him to be a writer, she was happy with him being a banker. A writer was the last thing she wanted him to be. She forced herself to raise her eyebrows, trying to look interested.

Oblivious to the nasty thoughts she was having, he leaned in to confide in her.

'... all my life I've wanted to be a writer, I've always believed I would be one. It's just that I never got around to writing anything.'

She had a sudden urge to be mean to him, she couldn't stop herself. Even as she was saying it, she was ashamed.

'Doesn't everyone think that? I mean isn't that what they say, that everyone thinks they have a book in them?'

'So they say.'

'So,' she said. 'What's yours going to be about?'

'Well,' he said carefully. 'I'm working on an idea. It's just the start of an idea.'

He looked at her for a minute, scrutinising her face. He might have been weighing up whether to tell her or not.

Don't, she was tempted to say. Don't feel you have to.

But it was too late.

'OK, I'll tell you.'

He folded his napkin on the table in front of him, smoothing his hand across the surface of it to work out the creases.

'It's about this guy. He's American obviously, like me, from New Jersey.'

Addie was struggling to control her face.

'When the book starts he's just arrived in Ireland, the land of his forefathers. He's on a voyage of self-discovery, he's looking for his backstory.'

He was still working his hand across the face of the napkin. Every so often he would glance up at her.

'That's something I've been thinking a lot about lately. There comes a point in your life when you have to discover your backstory before you can go forward.'

She had to suppress an urge to roll her eyes.

He closed the napkin over as if it were a book. He patted it shut.

'Anyway. As soon as he arrives in Ireland he meets this beautiful Irish girl. A lovely, lost Irish girl. And he falls madly in love with her.'

In a flash, she was interested again. He kept turning out to be cleverer than she expected.

She smiled. 'I think I can see where this is going.'

He put his index finger to his mouth, he indicated to her to shush.

'He meets this woman. And right away he knows, this is the woman of his life.'

She cocked her head, smiling at him knowingly.

'He's just trying to get her into bed.'

But he held his hand up in the air to quiet her, a priestly gesture, as if he was about to scatter holy water over her.

'You're cheapening it, you shouldn't cheapen it. This is a great love affair I'm talking about.'

Addie shook her head, interrupting him.

'There's no future in it. He's a foreigner, he'll go back home and forget all about her.'

'How do you know? How can you be so sure that's how it ends?'

She was horrified to find that her heart was pounding in her breast. She tried to make her voice sound flippant.

'Why don't you tell me how it ends, you're the writer.'

'I can't,' he said.

He shook his head apologetically.

'I don't know how it ends, not yet. And even if I did, I wouldn't tell you. A good writer would never reveal his ending.'

By the end of the night, the waiters had pushed the tables back against the wall and everyone was up dancing. Harry Belafonte, *oh island in the sun,* and they were all dancing and singing along as they danced, and it was very strange but everybody was having such a good time. It was as if they'd all left their troubles at the door and there was nothing in the world to be worrying about.

If this is what recession is like, Addie was thinking, then bring it on. But she was misreading the signs. This wasn't recession, this was the bit that comes beforehand. This was suspension of reality, this was denial.

'This isn't your usual Saturday night in Dublin,' Addie was shouting to Bruno. Her face was all amazement. Nothing like this had ever happened before, it was most unusual.

'You're getting a very misleading impression of us,' she roared into his ear, not sure if he could hear her or not.

'This is not what we're like.'

Afterwards Bruno would often think back to that night when they danced with strangers in Danny's place into the small hours of the morning. He would think back to that night, and in his mind he would always have an image, of the band playing on deck as the *Titanic* slipped down into the sea.

Afterwards, people would argue about the precise moment when the bubble actually burst. Some people would say it was Waterford Crystal, they would say that when they heard Waterford Crystal was gone, that was when they knew it was all over. Other people would say Dell, they would say it was the thought of Dell pulling out, that was the death knell. One guy rang in to a radio station to say his orange tree had just grown a lemon.

But back when Addie and Bruno first met, back when they went on their first date, all that was still to come. The signs were all there, but nobody wanted to know. Every day there were new reports of job losses, declining house prices, banks in trouble. Everyone was saying it was inevitable, but they just didn't believe it yet.

In those blinkered weeks in the run-up to Christmas, it was still just a train coming down the tracks. Already you could see its lights, you could hear the whizzing sound it made as it came towards you. But still you stood there in its path and you wondered was it absolutely certain it was coming your way, was it possible that it would stop before it reached you, maybe it would curve off onto another siding and sweep by you alto-gether.

Until it actually came and ran you over, there was still some hope.

Chapter 14

From the very beginning, it was a romance.

There was a lot of kissing, a lot of hand-holding. Endless talking. And laughter, God, they made each other laugh. There was an innocence to it, almost like a playground romance. If you'd seen them together that first week, the two of them and Lola, you would have thought they were a family. The way they moved, they were in step with each other. They looked like they'd been together for ever.

Every night they would fall asleep all tangled up in one another. And when they woke up the next morning they would find themselves still entwined. Nobody pretended it was just about the sex.

The most complicated things, the things that had been live minefields in other relationships, they were topics for discussion here. They were things you could talk about.

'Were you ever pregnant?' he asked her.

Even at the time Addie thought it was the most extraordinary thing to ask. And yet the most fundamental, if you wanted to understand a woman.

Their third night together, a Sunday night, they'd stayed in to nurse their hangovers. They'd sparked up the gas fire and settled themselves on to the couch. They had the telly on, but they were only half watching it. A movie about a pregnant detective. They'd both seen it before.

'Were you ever pregnant?' he asked. Like you'd ask someone if they'd ever been to France.

'Yes,' she said, answering straight away.

She kept her eyes fixed on the TV. She was conscious all of a sudden of the way she was sitting, one foot propped up on the couch, the other tucked under her. She felt the need to stay very still, as if a dangerous animal had just crept into the room.

'No baby?' he asked.

'No baby.'

'Me either,' he said. 'No babies.' And in that way, he closed it off for her.

She could have left it there, but she didn't want to.

'It's not what you're thinking,' she said, turning her head slowly to face him.

'I'm not thinking anything.'

'It was an ectopic. Do you know what that is?'

'Kind of,' he said, meaning no.

'It's when the baby gets stuck in the tube. It doesn't end well.' She took a deep breath and carried on. 'I probably can't have children.'

She tried to make it sound like it didn't matter so much,

like it wasn't anything to do with him. But the way he looked at her when she said it made her want to weep.

She snapped her head away. Looking at the TV instead, she blinked her eyes to clear away the tears. She'd been blocking it out for so long, she'd been telling herself it wasn't a big deal. Sure she hadn't found anyone she wanted to have babies with, that's what she'd been saying to herself. But now that she'd said it out loud, now that she'd seen his reaction, suddenly it did seem like a big deal.

That was why she was getting all this pain, she was sure of it.

It was all because she should have had a baby by now. In the natural order of things, she should have had six. The back pain and the cramps and the bloated tummy, you could sense the source of it all, it felt like a blockage. She'd researched it on the internet, she'd come across words she never even knew existed. Gruesome words like fibroids and endometriosis, words like cyst. Of course she'd heard of cysts before but she never knew what they were. When she googled the word she found it was exactly what it suggested. A disgusting, fluid-filled thing. She couldn't even think about it, she couldn't bear the thought that she had one of those things floating around inside her.

My insides are a mess, that's what she told Della, that's the way she described it. And Della had been a bit concerned. Shouldn't you see someone about it, she had said. Oh, no, Addie had responded, I know what it is, it's because I haven't had any babies. It's going against nature is what it is.

After the self-diagnosis came the self-medication. The

131

swimming helped, so did the walking. She tried acupuncture, she went for the odd shiatsu massage, she took a lot of vitamin supplements. She put herself on a regime of oil of evening primrose and starflower oil and calcium and multivitamins. She drank cranberry juice. And she took Solpadeine, lots of it. Nurofen too if necessary, you could double them up without damaging your organs, that's what it said on the internet.

At the hospital they'd told her to come back and have a probe done, some kind of keyhole surgery. They'd told her to wait six months and then make an appointment. But she never did. In her heart, she knew. And really, for a long time she didn't mind. She believed in fate. She believed that what's for you won't go past you. She looked at Della's life and she wasn't at all sure that was what she wanted, so she told herself that she really didn't mind.

Strange, the way you manage to block things out. The way you convince yourself about something one way or the other, the way you manage to convince yourself so convincingly. Until the moment you realise you were never convinced at all.

Addie is fond of her sister's children, she loves them like they're her own. She knows their birthdays. She keeps photographs of them on her phone.

She's more like a big sister to them than an aunt. She takes them clothes shopping, letting them buy whatever it is they want. When she brings them swimming she always treats them to hot chocolate afterwards. She invites them for sleepovers and they watch telly together on the couch. They feed popcorn to the dog.

She likes the programmes they like. She likes *The Simpsons*, she even likes *Friends*.

'I'm Rachel,' says Stella.

'No, I'm Rachel!' says Tess.

Why do they all want to be Rachel? wonders Addie. I don't want to be Rachel, if I could be anyone, I'd be Phoebe. That's the thing about getting older, she thinks. You don't want to be Rachel any more, you want to be Phoebe. But Addie knows Della is right, if she's anyone she's Monica.

The kids have accents they've picked up from the TV. 'Omigod that is so phew,' they say. They call Della Mom. They say 'I'm done' when they've finished their dinner.

Della blames Addie. 'You encourage them to watch this rubbish,' she says. 'And then you walk away. I'm the one who has to listen to them.'

The not having children thing, it changes. That's what Addie's discovering about it now, it evolves. A few years ago it was all about the baby, it was all about being pregnant, and seeing other people being pregnant and yearning for it to be you. It was about the tiny baby, the smell of it. It was about holding that tiny baby in your arms and watching it fall asleep and placing it into the Moses basket and kissing it good night and standing there in the dark listening to its breathing.

Addie doesn't really think about that stuff any more. Maybe it's because she's single again now, maybe it's because she's given up hope of ever *not* being single again. Maybe it's because Della's girls are growing up and they're not babies any more, they're just people now. Addie enjoys their company, she likes hanging out with them. Her own life seems very quiet by comparison.

'You have to think about the future,' Della says. 'There's nothing good about having children,' she says. 'It's hell. But it's an investment in the future, you have to believe it will be worth it in the years to come.'

How many times have they had this conversation? Della is well versed in it, she has it all thought out.

'I like to have people around me,' she will say. 'If you have enough children, you're bound to have people around you. Even if it's just their ghastly boyfriends and their ghastly husbands or their lesbian lovers. There'll be people in and out. Otherwise it would be just me and Simon. And it's hard to see how that would work.'

And on it goes.

'We didn't have enough people around us. When we were growing up, it was too quiet in the house. I want to have people around me.'

She has such a clear vision of the future. She often talks about it.

'When they're teenagers,' she says. 'That's when I'll go back to work. I'll get a job and you won't see me for a cloud of dust. Simon can deal with all those hormones. He's a doctor, after all, he should be well qualified to deal with it.'

Addie finds it strange, this planning thing her sister does. The way she has it all worked out.

'We'll buy a house in France,' she says. 'When the girls are older, the plan is to buy a house in France and I'll go there for the whole summer and Simon will come back and forth and the girls can learn French and I'll sit in the garden and read.'

She can see it all in her mind.

'Where do *you* see yourself in ten years?' she says to Addie. 'What do you see yourself doing?'

'Jesus, Dell, I don't know where I see myself in ten days.' And that way she kicks it into touch.

But she does worry about it. When she's on her own, she worries about it. She tries to imagine herself at fifty, but she can't see it. She simply cannot see it.

And this frightens her.

Bruno came back to it later. They were in bed, she was lying with her face nuzzled into the hot curve between his shoulder and his neck. She was just about to drift off to sleep when he asked her a question.

'When did that happen, the baby thing?'

'At the end of last year.'

'So the baby would have been born by now. If it had lived, the baby would be here by now.'

He had worked it out, just like that.

She couldn't bring herself to answer, the words wouldn't come out. And before she even knew what was happening, she was crying, silent tears pouring out of her. She cried into his shoulder, the tears pooling into sticky puddles on his skin.

He didn't say a thing. He just pulled her in closer to him and he bent his face down to kiss the top of her head as she cried. He let her cry and cry and when she was all cried out she was tired to the bone. Her whole body felt like it had been cast in lead. But for the first time in the guts of a year, her head was clear.

Never had she imagined that anyone would care that much about her. To guess what she was thinking, to keep her company in her most private thoughts. It had a powerful effect on her.

For the first time since her mum died, she had the feeling that she wasn't alone.

Chapter 15

She's not really talked about, Addie's mum. Oh, she was mentioned over the years, of course she was mentioned. Your mother would have been able to make a much better job of this than me, he would say as he struggled to sew a button back on to a school blouse. Your mother was a great woman for the sewing.

Or when one of them would be struggling with the maths homework. That's your mother coming out in you, he would say, I never had any trouble with maths when I was a youngster.

But he never remembered her to them, he never told stories about her. So Addie and Della know nothing of the person she was.

Whenever they take out old photographs, which isn't often, their dad does this thing of skipping over her. He'll say, 'That's me on the left there, and that's a fella who was in medical school with me. What in God's name was he called?

I'll remember it in a minute. There on the right, that's Maura. You'd hardly recognise her, she wasn't bad-looking back then.'

And he will have skipped over her in the photograph. He does it seamlessly, he doesn't even mention her, it's as if she was never there. It's an extremely odd thing to do.

'You have to understand,' says Maura. 'Your father is a very odd man. But that doesn't mean he didn't love her. He loved her all right. He just has no way of showing it.'

Maura knew him well then, she was in college with him. He went on to specialise in surgery, she did psychiatry. 'Mad as a bunch of frogs,' says Hugh, 'like all those head doctors.'

But she's not a bit mad of course, she's eminently sane. To Addie and Della, she's an endless source of wisdom.

'Your mother decided to marry your father because she liked the way he dried between his toes.'

That's what Maura has told them. It's a story she's told them umpteen times over the years. They never get tired of hearing it.

'We all went swimming one day, a glorious summer day, the exams were just finished. We went out to Portmarnock Strand. And your dad sat down after his swim and he dried between his toes. Your mother was very impressed by that, she always said that was the moment she decided to marry him. She realised he would always do things properly.'

Now Addie's waiting for a sign like that from Bruno, she's hoping for a moment of clarity.

The fact that he's a foreigner, she's not sure if that makes it easier or more difficult. His pronunciation is problematic for her, she doesn't like the way he pronounces things. Like the way he says Ca-*ribb*-ean, that's not good. But you could hardly call it a thing of substance, it's not exactly a firing offence.

In other ways, he's eloquent. She's starting to notice that. He doesn't stutter or stammer, he chooses his words carefully. He's precise in his use of language, and she likes that. He takes care to pick the right word.

'Obama has grace,' he says. 'It's my favourite characteristic in a person. All the best people have grace.'

Now Addie is beginning to think that Bruno has grace. It's in the way he leans his torso forward as he walks, the way he drags his feet behind him like a teenager. His head is too big for his body, but there's an honesty about his movements, a humility to him. Courtesy too, the way he holds his hand out just behind her back to guide her ahead of him as they cross the road. It's in the way he speaks, the thoughtful way he composes his sentences. The way he listens to you, he tilts his head a little and he listens, it's the most flattering thing.

Are these the signs she's looking for? Addie doesn't know, she doesn't trust her own judgement any more.

'First impression,' said Della.

'Oh, let's not do this.'

'Come on, just tell me the first thing that came into your head?'

'I'm not sure I want to tell you, it will colour your opinion of him for ever.'

'No, it won't. First impression is just first impression.'

Addie was making the tea. She'd poured out two mugs of boiling water and she was dangling teabags over the mugs, dunking them up and down by their strings. The smell of peppermint rose up in thick clouds between them.

Della was leaning in over the table. She had a tight white T-shirt on her. Across the front of it was written in bold black letters: *HOW WOULD I KNOW?*

'What's the story with the T-shirt?' asked Addie.

'Oh, I ordered it over the internet. So I don't have to keep on saying it. The questions they ask me, Jesus wept.'

Impatiently, she brought the conversation back to where they were before.

'Come on now,' she said. 'First impression, spit it out.'

'OK, OK. I thought *Confederacy of Dunces*, that's what I thought. I thought he looked like the guy out of *Confederacy of Dunces*. Promise you won't ever tell him.'

Della gave a little scream and slapped the palms of her hands on the front of her thighs in a kind of drumbeat.

'Oh Jesus, Ad, are you sure you know what you're doing? Oh, I can't wait to meet him now.'

She was actually rubbing her hands together, this was all entertainment to her.

'*Confederacy of Dunces*! Didn't he have special needs or something, the guy from *Confederacy of Dunces*? I can't believe you're sleeping with the guy from *Confederacy of Dunces*.'

'He's not the guy from *Confederacy of Dunces*! That was just my first impression. It was the hat. You know, he was wearing one of those hats with the earflaps, what do you call them? And the beard of course, the beard was a bit off-putting. But actually, he doesn't look anything like the guy from *Confederacy of Dunces*. He's actually quite good-looking. Now that I know him, he reminds me more of George Clooney.'

'Oh Jesus, I'd forgotten about the beard.'

Addie was struggling to defend him, she felt disloyal talking about him like this.

'He didn't always have a beard, it's not like it's an intrinsic part of him or anything, but yes, at the moment he has a beard. I actually find it quite handsome, it draws your attention to his eyes. He has nice eyes.'

Della's brow was furrowed, she was thinking.

'I don't know if I've ever kissed a man with a beard. Hang on, I must have kissed a man with a beard ... surely I've kissed a man with a beard.' Her face was all scrunched up as she tried to remember.

Addie blew on the surface of her tea to cool it.

'It's a bit like kissing a hedgehog. But in a good way.'

'I wonder, could I persuade Simon Sheridan to grow a beard.'

Della was sipping at her tea, her lips puckered as she sipped.

'What does Hugh make of him?'

Addie put her face in her hands.

'I haven't been able to bring myself to introduce them yet.'

'Still!'

'I know, I know ...'

She was peering at Della through her fingers, her voice muffled by her cupped hands.

'I'm afraid he'll ruin it for me, I'm afraid he'll say mean things about him and it'll ruin it. I don't have to introduce them, do I?'

When she took her hands away she had a pleading look on her face.

Della was shaking her head.

'I'm the wrong person to ask. I don't think you should have to do anything you don't want to.'

'Della,' said Addie nervously. 'I think this one might be a good one.'

Della just raised one eyebrow.

'I know what you're thinking,' said Addie. 'But I really think this one might be a good one.'

Addie was expecting Della to give her a diatribe. She was steeling herself for Della's analysis, waiting for her to divide him up into bullet points. She was fully expecting her to write him off. But to her surprise she didn't.

All she said was, 'I hope so, Ad, I really hope so.'

But what she was thinking was, I'll believe it when I see it.

'Is that your sister, the kid with her hands over her face?'

He was standing outside the bathroom, peering at a framed photograph on the wall. It had been there for so long that Addie didn't even notice it any more, she'd been walking by it ten times a day for weeks now but she had never actually looked at it.

She came up behind him and leaned her chin on his shoulder. A vivid colour photograph, it had been professionally framed but somehow water had got in behind the glass and now the mounting board was all stained.

You've seen the photo, you've seen a hundred like it. A little girl on the beach, she's eating an ice cream, she's wearing a summer dress. Her sister is sitting on the rocks behind her. It's the first good day of summer.

Addie was studying the picture, trying to remember.

'I don't know where that came from. It's one of the only ones we have of the two of us together after our mum died. My mum was the one who took all the photographs.'

'You look exactly the same! You haven't changed at all. How old were you then?'

That's what Addie was trying to figure out. How old would she have been? Eight, maybe nine?

She's wearing a yellow cotton dress with white daisies on it. The dress had come with a matching scarf but she's not wearing the scarf in the photograph, it probably got lost somewhere. Anyway, in the photo Addie's wading through the shallows on Sandymount strand, just in front of the house, and she's holding her dress up out of the water very daintily as she's splashing along and the thing you can't help but notice about the photo is that she looks so content. She's in a world all of her own.

These days Addie feels closer to that little girl than she has done for years. She feels the water lapping around her ankles. She remembers the damp sensation of her knickers where she'd peed in them. The scalding feeling of the pee and the salt water where the tops of your thighs rubbed together. She remembers how the wet hem of your dress clung to your calves, the exotic vanilla taste of the ice cream and the way the cone went all soggy from the drips running down the side. She remembers with surprise how happy you felt to be on your own.

'I love you in that photograph.'

He announced it happily, in the lightest, easiest tone you could imagine. Then he went on into the bathroom, closing the door behind him.

And Addie was left standing out in the hall, a grin on her face.

She knew what he meant by it, she understood the context. But it was the first time a man had said he loved her, in any context at all.

That photo, the one with the yellow dress, it was taken on the day of their mother's funeral. Addie doesn't know this, but Della does, she remembers. Sometimes it seems to Della that she remembers everything. It's something she's been cursed with, this constant remembering.

It wasn't considered proper for children to go to funerals back then, it wasn't considered appropriate. So a neighbour looked after them instead, someone they hardly knew. She took them to the beach. To this day, Della remembers being furious that she wasn't allowed to go to the funeral. She doesn't remember being sad that her mother had died, she just remembers how much she wanted to go to the funeral.

She remembers sulking. She remembers an ice cream being bought and she remembers that she refused to eat it, even though she wanted to. She remembers where she was sitting when the photographs were taken. She was sitting back on the rocks, watching Addie play with the neighbour's children in the puddles. When the neighbour tried to take her photograph, she put her hands over her face.

That neighbour, Della can't for the life of her remember her name. She probably meant well, taking them to the beach. But Della wonders now, what possessed her to take those photographs? Was it to remind them of the day of their mother's funeral? Or did she just take the photograph because she happened to have a camera with her, because it was a sunny day and they were two sweet little girls in pretty dresses, playing on the beach. Della would like to know.

She's a reader, she's always searching out the story.

Chapter 16

Bruno had started working on his family tree.

When you looked at it on paper it was a winter tree. It was a naked-looking thing, all bare branches ending in blank spaces. There was no foliage and no colour, no life in it yet. Only on the far left-hand side of the page was there any indication of growth. Starting with his grandfather, Bruno had constructed a system of straight lines and neat boxes dropping down through the generations. Inside the boxes, in tiny meticulous letters, he had inscribed the names of his father and mother, his sisters and their various husbands. All his nieces and nephews. Below their names he had printed the year of their birth and, where appropriate, the year of their death. In his father's case he had also included the year he emigrated. His aunt Nora too, she had followed his father out two years later. Born 1926, he wrote below Nora's name. Emigrated 1950. Died 1990.

It filled him with emotion, to see it written there on the

page. 'I come from pioneer stock!' he told Addie. 'I'm very proud of that.'

'Oh God,' she said, a jaded tone to her voice as she leaned over his shoulder and surveyed his work. 'It reminds me of those novels that have a family tree at the start. You have to keep flicking back to the beginning to check who's who. I always find that a total bore. I always give up on it when it gets too complicated.'

Addie was proving less than helpful with the family tree. She didn't even know the name of her paternal grandfather. 'He was a ship's doctor, I think. I'm not sure I ever met him.'

'But you must know his name?'

'He'd be Murphy, wouldn't he? Something Murphy, I suppose.'

So Bruno wrote Murphy down, with a question mark beside it.

'We could ask your dad, he would surely know.'

Addie's eyes narrowed at the thought of it.

'He's not very keen on talking about the past. I'm not sure it would be safe to broach the subject with him.'

'All I need are some names,' said Bruno stubbornly. 'Once I have the names, I can take it from there.'

'By all means,' said Addie. 'I'll ask him. But I wouldn't hold out too much hope.'

Only now is it dawning on Bruno that he has come unprepared.

He should have done some foundation work. Before he left New York, he should have questioned his sisters, he should

147

have got them all round a table and purged their memories. But of course he didn't, it never even occurred to him to do that. For some reason he had imagined that his search would only start when he got here.

'I always tell people to start with old family stories,' said the genealogist in the National Library. 'It's amazing what people remember once they start to think about it. If you trawl through your memory you'll probably find you already have the bones of your family history.'

A tiny man in a perfectly ironed shirt, the genealogist had welcomed Bruno like an old friend. He had gestured for him to sit down at a large table in a room halfway up the sweeping stairs. The hush of the library was all around them but the genealogist didn't lower his voice, moving through the silence as if he didn't even notice it. He was like a doctor in a hospital ward, going about his business.

'Any little snippets you can think of,' he said. 'They're like gold dust. Things your father would have mentioned about his family. Maybe he talked about what his ancestor did for a living, maybe he said where they were from, that kind of thing. If you can piece them together, you'll find that one clue leads to another.'

Bruno was writing all this down. He had brought a leather-bound notebook with him for this very purpose. This was the first time he'd used it.

'Once you have the bones of the story you can start going through the public records. The births, the marriages, the deaths. Of course if you have the dates it will make your task all the easier. When was it that your ancestor emigrated?'

'The late forties,' he said.

'Assuming they were Catholic you'll be looking at church records. Civil registration didn't come in here until 1864 ... '

Bruno interrupted him. 'The *nineteen* forties. My father left in the nineteen forties.'

The genealogist looked surprised. 'Sure that's within living memory,' he said. 'You should be able to make a good start on it from memory.'

Bruno was overtaken by a moment from the past. His recollection of it was so nebulous that he was afraid it would leave him again before he was finished with it, like a burst of song heard through the open window of a passing car.

In his memory, Bruno is painting someone's porch. He's dipping the paintbrush into the can, sweeping the brush against the inside rim to take off the excess, otherwise you would get drips. It wasn't a good brush he was using. He kept having to stop to pick loose hairs out of the wet paintwork. When that happened you had to give the woodwork another sweep, to get it even again. He remembers how anxious he was to get it even. He knew his dad would be coming round later to check his work.

The next thing his sister was standing behind him. She was telling him he had to come home. Our grandmother died, she said. Dad says we have to go to the church to pray for her. What year would that have been? 1972, Bruno was guessing, it would have been his first summer working for his dad. He wrote the date down in his notebook with a question mark after it.

The genealogist was still talking, Bruno snapped himself back into the present.

'Do you have any old family photographs with you? The

photographs can be invaluable, especially if they've been dated. Often people used to inscribe the names on the back of them, that's the kind of lucky break you're looking for!'

Bruno took the photograph out of his notebook and passed it across the table.

His father was at the centre of the picture, squinting at the camera. His sister Nora was standing beside him. There were three other women in the picture. Two of them were standing alongside Bruno's father, the other one on the far side of Nora. They all had their arms around each other's waists, perhaps they'd been told to do that so they would fit into the picture. The women were wearing summer dresses, their expressions solemn. You could see they weren't used to having their photograph taken. There was a strong family resemblance between them, they all had the same pale eyes, the same honest round face. They all shared the same awkward stance, their shoulders hunched up in their shyness.

The genealogist didn't even look at the photo. He flipped it over straight away and studied the back.

Someone had written down the date on the reverse. It was inscribed carefully in watery blue ink, the colour faded with time. Bruno wondered who it was that had written it. He wished they'd written the names down as well.

They were cousins of his father's, that much Bruno knew. A family of girl cousins. One of them would have been Hugh's mother but Bruno wasn't sure which one.

'Kitty was the looker,' that's what Nora used to say. 'She was the beauty of the family. She was the one all the lads were after.'

And that in turn reminded him of an old song his father

150

used to sing. *She is handsome, she is pretty, she is the belle of Belfast city.* Bruno had always thought of Kitty as the girl in that song. But peering at the photograph now, he couldn't figure out which one she might be, they were all good-looking women as far as he could see.

'What I suggest is that you write down everything you can remember,' the genealogist was saying. He handed back the photo. 'Write everything down and then take it from there.'

Bruno passed out of the sanctity of the library into a barrage of noise.

There was a crowd outside, some kind of a protest. They were spread out in front of the parliament building, spilling off the pavement on to the street. As Bruno stood there looking around him someone came up and handed him a flier. He glanced down to read it.

NO BANK BAILOUT! A list of questions followed in smaller print. Why should we pay for a decade of greed? Was it for this our forefathers died?

Bruno looked around him again.

Some of the protesters were carrying placards. They all bore a similar message. There was a surprisingly amiable atmosphere, the protesters clustered in little groups chatting companionably. Some of them were talking to the policemen on sentry duty at the gates. Passing motorists were honking their horns. A woman with a briefcase made her way through the crowd and they stood by to let her pass. She slipped in through a side gate.

Bruno became aware of himself again. He realised he was

still standing there holding the flier in his hand. The noise of the traffic and the thick air were swirling around him and he felt like he'd been drinking. He spotted a hotel across the street and made a dash for it. He pushed his way through the doors and collapsed into an armchair in the lounge area. Ordering himself a pot of coffee and a ham sandwich, he took his notebook out of his backpack and opened it on the table in front of him.

He had so many things coursing through his head, there was no order to them. He was afraid he'd lose them if he didn't write them down. He couldn't get his pen to write fast enough, his hand was racing to keep up.

Slices of conversation, disjointed phrases, Bruno was as sure as he could be that he was remembering them word for word. His father's unique turn of phrase, Bruno would never have been able to replicate that for himself.

Get thee behind me devil and push, that's what his father used to say every time he unscrewed the lid off the bottle of whiskey. Not that he did it that often, he was a careful drinker. But he took great pleasure in the drinking, he took pleasure in everything he did. The cackle of laughter he would let out of him, Bruno could still hear it. Get thee behind me and push.

The sigh of disapproval from his mother, it would only have encouraged him all the more. Would you relax, woman, he would say. Come here and sit on my knee, for God's sake. 'Tis little enough attention I get in this house. And he would pull his wife on to his lap. She would wriggle to get free and the girls would all shriek with laughter.

He was larger than life, Bruno's father. A big man, with a

big presence in their house. He could be a rough man sometimes, he could be uncouth. On a summer evening, he would walk out into the back yard, unzip his fly and piss into the flower beds. Oh Patrick, Bruno's mother would sigh. She used to make this clicking sound with her tongue when she disapproved of something.

What's the world coming to, his father would say, if a man can't piss in his own garden. Sure it's good for the roses. And he would swagger back into the kitchen, bowing his legs like a cowboy so he could yank his fly up. A mischievous glint in his eye, he always got a great kick out of winding her up.

Thirty years since his father had died and suddenly Bruno could hear his voice again, as if he was listening to a recording that had been dug out of an old radio archive. The rhythm of his father's voice, the way the words bellowed out from deep within his chest.

He was some man for one man. That's what his father used to say about his own father. A bear of a man. Bruno remembers stories from his father's childhood, stories of swimming in a swollen river, stories of stolen oranges during the war. They descended on Bruno like a flood, these stories. An uncle who had the loan of a car, a trip to the beach at Bettystown. A baby cousin who fell into a slurry pit and died.

Bruno scribbled all these snippets down. He poured them out on to the page. He had the sense he was only just starting. All those stories his father had told them as children, if you'd asked him last week, Bruno would have said he'd forgotten them. He was amazed now to find that they were all still there.

Three decades his father had been gone and suddenly it was

as if a door had been opened into the past. This man he thought he'd forgotten, he was all around him now.

Bruno would be walking along the street and up ahead of him he would see his father. Even from the back, he knows him, the thick neck rising out of the shirt collar, the tight haircut, the stocky set of the shoulders in the heavy overcoat. Merrion Square on a sunny afternoon and he's chasing after a man who's been dead for thirty years. He has to stop himself from shouting out.

Bruno is standing at the bar in the pub in Sandymount and the bartender is pouring his pint. The man looks over the taps at him, he looks at him with those watery blue eyes and the flushed cheeks and for a moment Bruno thinks he's going to call him son.

This is where my dad was from, he has to tell himself. These are his people, of course they remind me of him.

It wasn't something he had expected to find here, this connection with his father. But it's as welcome as it is strange. All his life, Bruno has been told he's Irish. Now, for the first time, he's starting to understand what that means.

Needless to say Hugh wasn't jumping over himself to help with the photograph.

'As I predicted,' said Addie, 'he wasn't hugely forthcoming.'

'Oh,' said Bruno, taking the photograph back from her and studying it again.

'I warned you, he's not crazy about talking about the past.'

Bruno nodded. He was finding all of this difficult to understand.

'He did tell me which of them is which.'

'Oh,' said Bruno again, 'well, that's a help.'

Addie moved in behind him, leaning over his shoulder to point them out.

'On the right of your father, that's Margaret, she was always known as May. Next to her, that's Patricia.'

Addie burrowed her chin down into the cradle of his collar bone.

'And on the left, that's the other sister. Hugh's mother.'

'Your grandmother,' said Bruno.

'Yes,' said Addie in a detached voice. 'My grandmother. Her name was Catherine but they all called her Kitty.'

She looked into the photograph. She searched her grandmother's face, finding nothing in it. It was just a stranger looking back at her. For the first time Addie was flooded with curiosity. This was her grandmother. Surely she had the right to know something about her?

'Did he happen to mention their surnames?'

'Wouldn't they all have been Boylans?'

'Sure. But what I really need are their married names. If I knew their married names I could look them up, maybe some of them are still alive.'

'Hardly.'

'It's possible. At least if I knew their names I would have somewhere to start.'

'I'm not sure it would be a good idea to broach the subject with Hugh again, I'm a bit scared of what he might say.'

Even now, she could hear his voice booming in her ears.

What does that fellow want, raking over the past. I told you that's what he came for, don't say I didn't warn you. The bloody family tree. Firewood, that's all it's good for, our family tree.

Bruno didn't seem to grasp the hopelessness of the situation.

'Maybe I could ask him,' he said cheerfully. 'If you don't want to get involved, I could always ask.'

Maybe if she'd given him a clearer picture of Hugh's reaction he wouldn't have pursued it. She only had herself to blame. Diluting him always, softening him. Smoothing over his ravings.

'Honestly, Bruno, I don't think that's a good idea.'

'I don't know what you're so concerned about. I can be quite charming when I want to be.'

'Oh, believe me,' said Addie, 'it's not you I'm worried about.'

Chapter 17

In many ways Bruno and Addie are highly incompatible. And never more so than in the mornings.

'Do all American men talk like this?'

He'd been awake since before seven, which meant that she'd been awake since before seven. He'd moved her radio out of the kitchen and into the bedroom and he'd turned on *Morning Ireland*. All the talk was of Colin Powell's endorsement and Bruno was lapping it up. Every time they read out the headlines he told her to shush. Already they'd heard it three times.

'Shush,' he said, as the presenter cued the eight o'clock bulletin.

'I wasn't the one talking.' She rolled over on to her front and buried her face in the pillow.

'Listen, this is important.'

'The former US Secretary of State Colin Powell has formally endorsed Barack Obama for President. Speaking on NBC's Meet the Press yesterday, General Powell said that

Senator Obama was a "transformational figure" and he criticised his own Republican Party's use of personal attacks during the campaign. General Powell also said that the choice of Sarah Palin as vice-presidential candidate raised questions about John McCain's judgement.'

'Yes!' said Bruno, clenching his fists as he said it.

She spoke into the pillow. 'That's exactly what they said at half seven. And seven.'

'I know, I know. I just can't hear it often enough. This has to be good for us, no way it can't be good.'

She rolled on to her side.

'Bruno, can I ask you a question? Do all American men talk like this in the mornings?'

'Sure, do Irish men not?'

'Oh, most definitely not,' she said. 'Irish men only talk to women when they're drunk. Never in the morning, not under any circumstances.'

Bruno was taking all this in, his head cocked to the side while he listened.

'The thing is,' said Addie, 'about the not talking in the mornings. That's what I'm used to. I'm finding this morning chat thing a bit weird. I'm not used to talking to anyone before I've had my cup of coffee.'

'Well, how about I try not to talk to you until you've had your coffee?'

So from then on he started to bring her coffee into the bedroom for her and he would sit there and watch her as she sat up in bed drinking it and then he would ask her if she was finished and she would say yes and he would say great, now we can talk.

'There was me wondering why you're still single at fifty. Now I know.'

'Oh yeah?'

'Did nobody ever explain to you about personal space?'

He was unperturbed by her question. Impossible to offend.

'Hey. I live in New York. What would I know about personal space?'

'My point exactly. The thing is,' she said gently, 'I have a routine. There's the walk and then there's the coffee. I don't speak to anybody until I've had the coffee.'

'So we don't speak on the walk?'

'That's what I'm trying to tell you. You don't go on the walk.'

'OK,' he said cheerfully. 'I don't go on the walk.'

'You're not hurt?'

'I'm not hurt.'

And really, he didn't seem to be. He was remarkably resilient.

On the days when the tide is in, the walk takes Addie along the Strand Road, across the edge of the park and out on to the Shelley Banks. A beautiful name, the Shelley Banks, the name is much prettier than the place itself.

All it is really is a path, a tatty path snaking along the shoreline. On one side of the path is a low hill. On the other side is the sea. It's supposed to be a nature reserve, but all Addie can see are weeds. Some wild roses, some seabirds. Occasionally she wonders what kind of birds they are, she keeps meaning to look them up but she never does.

It's prime Lola territory, the Shelley Banks, it's all tall reeds and grasses and rocky places. Lola is in her element out here, she races up the hills and comes bounding back down, her coat full of burrs. She scrambles down the rocks and plunges into the sea. Then she appears in front of Addie again, muddy and bedraggled, her tail whirling wildly with the joy of it all.

Other dogs pass them by but Lola pays no heed to them. She has no interest in her own kind, she's like her owner in this.

Of course Addie knows all the other dog owners by sight, she greets them every morning.

There's the man with the two black Labradors, he has to walk ten miles a day because of his bypass. Another man brings his baby grandchild along with him while he walks the dog. He trawls the baby buggy behind him like a golf cart, he says it's better for his back that way. There's the mums in their tracksuits, they talk as they walk, their dogs tumbling along together. There's a very old lady with eyes as blue as the sky. She sings to her dogs in a sweet low voice. She wears open sandals all year round. She's Addie's favourite.

There's an etiquette among the dog owners, there's a routine that Addie observes. They acknowledge each other with a nod, they ask after each other's dogs.

'How's Rambo this morning?' 'How's Lola?' 'Did Rambo get a haircut?' 'Oh he did. But Lola's hair is too nice to cut, you couldn't be cutting Lola's hair.' 'It's true, all the ladies admire Lola's hair.'

They never address each other by name, they speak only through their dogs. They don't even stop walking, they just toss a few pleasantries back and forth as they pass. No greetings and no goodbyes.

It always seems to Addie an ideal way to conduct a relationship.

'What a morning.'

'Amazing.'

'Compensation for the summer we've had.'

'Let's just hope it lasts.'

Addie turned in through the entrance to the park. Lola was out in front, pulling on the lead, with Addie leaning back on it like a waterskier.

The whole park was awash with light, like one of those Hare Krishna posters you see on the wall in health food shops. A strange landscape, an other-worldly light, you could almost make out the separate rays spreading out from the sun. From the corner of her eye Addie noticed a dense flock of birds gathered on the grass in the middle of the park. They were sad-looking creatures, their necks an elegant flourish, their bodies strangely bottom-heavy. They were huddled together like immigrants just off the boat. Lola was facing towards them, her whole body poised to charge. Addie wound the lead tighter round her hand and dragged her past them.

The day was unseasonably warm and Addie was getting sticky. She took off her jumper and wrapped it round her waist. Too late, she realised she'd never bothered to put on a bra, her breasts were clearly visible through her T-shirt, her nipples indecently upright. She unwrapped her jumper again and draped it over her shoulders so the sleeves were hanging down over her chest. They went some way towards preserving her modesty.

161

A cyclist came along and Lola tumbled across the path in front of him. The cyclist swerved out on to the grass verge to avoid the little dog, only just about regaining his balance as he straightened up. Addie watched it all in slow motion. She called out a pointless rebuke, for the benefit of the cyclist. She was resigned to the fact that Lola was going to take a cyclist down one of these days. It was only a matter of time.

She was finding the walking heavy going this morning. She was dragging herself along. Her back was aching and her pelvis was weighing her down, she felt like she was carrying rocks around in her belly. She set her sights on the bench just up ahead. She would stop there and let Lola run wild while she rested. Already she was feeling guilty about cutting short the walk.

By the time she made it to the bench she was sagging under the weight of the pain, holding on to her lower back with both hands as if to bear herself up. She sank down on to the bench oh so carefully, supporting her spine like it was a glass column. She closed her eyes and slowly, ever so slowly, she leaned herself forward.

She concentrated on her breathing for a moment, drawing the air in noisily through her nostrils and letting it out slowly again through almost closed lips. She had her teeth clenched the whole time. She felt like a wounded horse. She thought for a moment about how inelegant she must look, but then she told herself there was no one around to see.

The pain scared her, the unholy inconvenience of it. Not now, she told herself, please not now.

*

162

'Have you been doing anything particularly strenuous recently?' That's what the massage therapist at the pool had asked her. Addie had been meaning to go for a massage for weeks, she'd been putting it off.

'Have you been getting up to anything out of the ordinary?'

'Well, I've been having a lot of sex,' Addie had mumbled. 'That's out of the ordinary for me.'

She was lying on her tummy with her face buried in that face-shaped hole they have in the massage bench. She was talking to the floor.

'Are we talking anything particularly physical?' asked Jessica.

'Lord no,' said Addie. She could feel the blood pooling under her skin, her eyes were bulging. 'He's nearly fifty,' she said, in an effort to clarify things.

The masseuse was applying gentle pressure to the small of Addie's back. With the flat of her hand, she was feeling her way along.

'Nothing would surprise me,' she said cheerily.

She pressed and she prodded but she couldn't really find anything wrong, nothing that would explain the pain.

'Watch your posture,' she said. 'Keep the shoulders well back. And do those exercises I showed you, I think they'll help.'

And Addie nodded obligingly. Already she knew that she wouldn't do the exercises.

'Whatever you do, don't stop having sex, it's good for you!'

Was it possible to be more embarrassed? I'll never be able to face her again, thought Addie.

But she didn't really mind.

She was so happy.

She was smiling now, just remembering it.

The pain was receding, it was only the aura of it that was left, a blurry residue. When the pain went away, the fear went with it. It couldn't be anything too serious if it went away again like that. It couldn't be anything to worry about. It was all part and parcel of being a woman, that was Addie's theory.

She got to her feet. She crossed the path and peered down on to the rocks but there was no sign of Lola.

She stood there and looked out across the bay. On a clear day like this you could pick out the houses along the Strand Road one by one, they were like a row of neat teeth. Even from here, Hugh's house looked discoloured and decayed. It made Addie sad to see it.

There was a time when that house had seemed to Addie a magical place to live. It had seemed to her as fine and grand a house as there could be. She had believed herself the luckiest girl in the world to live there.

The house was full of antiques, Hugh loved antiques. He was always browsing through auction catalogues, turning down the corner of the page when he spotted something he was interested in. After the auction there would be numbers scribbled in blue biro next to the lot.

'Poor Hugh,' said Auntie Maura once. 'Not an iota of taste.'

Maura always took a poor view of Hugh. 'All that rubbish he buys, it's all completely worthless. The dealers must see him coming. But don't tell him I said that, for God's sake, it keeps him busy.'

She's not really their aunt, Maura. She was their mother's best friend, her bridesmaid. She's Della's godmother. In practice she plays godmother to them both.

'The fairy godmother,' says Hugh with a snort. He was the one who coined the phrase and he never ceases to be amused by it. Now the girls even call her that to her face.

'Cranky old lesbian,' says Hugh. 'That sharp tongue on her, sure no man would have her.'

After their mother died, Hugh used to bring the girls with him on his antiques trail. On Sunday mornings, when everyone else was at Mass, the three of them would troop down Francis Street, going into one poky shop after another. Addie can still remember the sweet smell of furniture wax, how your eyes strained to adjust to the darkness inside after the bright light of the street. She remembers the sharp pain in your shin when you tripped over something in a cluttered basement.

The memory of it made her heart hurt. How Hugh had tried to make that house a home, how he had tried to involve Addie and Della in the homemaking.

Those were happy times, the three of them together. They bought old glass-fronted chemist's cabinets that Addie and Della filled with shells and stones they found on the beach. They bought roll-top desks with cubby holes and secret compartments, a globe that opened up to reveal a drinks cabinet. A stuffed mouse in a sealed glass dome.

But the thing Addie loved most of all, the thing she set her heart on as soon as she spotted it, was a giant wooden mermaid.

Addie fell in love with that mermaid, the minute she saw it she just had to have it.

'She came from the prow of a ship,' said the man in the shop. Which made Addie love her all the more, already she was imagining the mermaid looking down at her from the wall of her bedroom.

'She's far too big,' said Hugh, 'sure where would we put her?'

'In my room,' said Addie, as if it was the most obvious thing in the world. 'We'd put her up on the wall in my room.'

They were both craning their heads to look up at her.

'She's a monster,' said Hugh. 'She'd pull all the plasterwork down off the wall.'

But there was no talking Addie out of it, she was dead set on acquiring that mermaid.

'Let's sleep on it,' he had said, in an effort to put her off.

She had tried bargaining with him. She pleaded and cajoled. She sulked and she begged. She kept it up for days, until eventually he relented. But when they went back for the mermaid she was gone, somebody else had bought her. Addie never let Hugh forget it.

Poor Hugh, she couldn't help feeling sorry for him now. He was marooned in that big old house, stranded among all those curious treasures. He was a curio himself now, the old boy. A human anachronism, sitting there fossilising in the window while the rest of the world carried on without him.

That's how it seemed to Addie as she stood there looking out over the stretch of still water at the drab old house across the bay. Funny how clear it all seemed from a distance.

*

166

'*Lola.*'

Addie shouted out her name and waited for her to appear.
'*Lola!*'

There was still no sign of her. Addie turned to look back up the hill. Her attention settled on a large noticeboard right in front of her. A Dublin City Council notice, it was the photograph that caught her attention, a picture of a flock of birds grazing on the grass.

She took a few steps closer, leaning in to study the birds. They had the same black swirl of a neck and chest, the same waddling grey bottom, the same awkward stance. The light-bellied Brent geese, it said on the notice (*Branta bernicla hrota*).

There was a map showing their migration route. A jagged yellow line traced their journey from north-western Canada, through Greenland and Iceland, ending up in Ireland.

THE LIGHT-BELLIED BRENT GEESE BREED IN CANADA DURING THE SHORT ARCTIC SUMMER. THEY SPEND THEIR WINTER IN THE BAYS AND ESTUARIES OF THE EAST COAST OF IRELAND. THEN THEY MAKE THE EIGHT THOUSAND KILOMETRE RETURN JOURNEY IN SPRING, STOPPING BRIEFLY IN ICELAND ON THEIR WAY HOME.

Addie stared at the sign. How many times had she walked this path, how many times had she stopped to sit on this bench? And she'd never noticed it before!

She stood there and read the short piece of text again very slowly, thinking carefully about every word. She studied the map. Then she read the text again. She took in the information about migration paths, her mind registering the notion of seasonal movements. She absorbed the certainty of the homeward journey. And it seemed to Addie that there was a message for her in all of this.

Bruno was bound to go home.

Back in his room in the bed and breakfast, Bruno was taking the e-mail confirming his flight details out of his backpack.

A clutch of paper that he had printed up himself on the inkjet printer in his apartment, it didn't seem like an airline ticket at all. He was finding it hard to take it seriously. There was a ridiculous code printed on it, a magic combination of numbers and letters that you had to quote to the check-in clerk in order to travel. There was a list of baggage restrictions and prohibitions running to four pages of dense type.

Bruno checked the return date, even though he knew it already. He checked the time, even though it was too soon to worry about that kind of detail. Then he folded up the pages and tucked them back into the inside pocket of his backpack.

He had a sudden burst of nostalgia for those airline tickets they used to issue in the old days, those chequebook-style tickets with the airline logo on the front and a sheaf of carbon paper counterfoils underneath in increasingly faded type, going from black to pink to grey.

You were a voyager with one of those tickets, you were an airline passenger. You could turn up at the airline's offices in any city in the world, and they would call you sir. You could discuss a change in your travel plans, you could have them issue you with a new ticket. Afterwards, you were left with a record of your journey, you had something to be tossed into a box and discovered again years later.

There was a time when Bruno used to travel a lot. Back in a previous job, his work used to bring him to China regularly. Japan, Korea, Malaysia, Thailand, that was his beat. He learned a little Mandarin Chinese. A few words of Japanese, just enough to exchange pleasantries. He had lightweight suits made especially. A frequent flier account. He had a passport crammed with stamps.

'Is it true that only one per cent of Americans have passports?'

Bruno looked up from his newspaper with interest. He seemed interested in everything she had to say.

'I've never heard that before.'

'Oh, don't take my word for it,' said Addie. 'I don't know where I got it from. There's probably no truth to it.'

Probably not. Most likely it was just one of those toxic little facts about Americans that you hear tossed around in pub conversations. Luckily Bruno didn't take it personally.

'It's possible,' he said thoughtfully. 'A lot of Americans have never even seen the ocean.'

And Addie narrowed her eyes trying to imagine it. But she couldn't.

'Have you ever been to Berlin?' he asked her. 'We can go to Berlin for nine euros!'

He'd discovered Ryanair. He was feasting his eyes on the full-page ad in the paper, drunk on the idea of all that cheap travel. The cities of Europe, all of them within easy reach.

'What about Venice?' he suggested. 'We could go to Venice for the weekend. Nineteen euros, it says here.'

'I thought Venice was flooded. I saw a picture in the paper. It's sinking down into the water.'

'Even more reason to go! We should go before it disappears altogether!'

'The ads are a bit misleading, you know. It costs way more once you add in the taxes.'

But all her arguments fell on deaf ears.

'Paris is only ninety-nine cents!'

She hated to dent his enthusiasm.

'The thing is,' she said gently, 'I don't really like to leave Lola.'

He closed the newspaper and laid it down on his knees. Now that the ad was out of sight the idea of all that air travel was suddenly less tempting.

'To be honest with you I'm not that crazy about flying any more,' said Bruno. 'I find it increasingly unpleasant. It never really bothered me before. But it does now. Must be something to do with getting older.'

'And anyway,' he said, 'I haven't seen anything of Ireland yet. I'd like to see a bit of Ireland first, before I think about going anywhere else.'

And in that way he talked himself out of it again.

It wasn't a time for going anywhere, they both knew that. It was a waiting time. A time filled with the fragile magic of possibility, a time equally fraught with danger. It was as if they had met in the transit lounge of an airport. Each of them caught between two worlds, they were just sharing this moment in time.

Chapter 18

Every morning, Hugh watches them leave the house together.

The same routine every day. They emerge from the basement, he hears the door slam shut and the sound of their feet on the steps. Then they come into view, they appear on the gravel down below his window. He sees the tops of their heads, their bodies foreshortened.

Addie is dressed for the beach, she has her overcoat on and her wellington boots. She's checking her pockets to make sure she has everything she needs. He has on that enormous jacket and the ludicrous hat. He seems on very good terms with the dog, he bends to attach the lead to her collar before handing it over to Addie. When they get to the gate they stop and turn to each other without speaking. They kiss. Then he turns right and walks along the footpath. Hugh can see his head bobbing along above the next-door neighbour's hedge. A moment later, he's gone.

Addie and Lola drift across the road. Hugh watches as

Addie throws the dog over the sea wall, then climbs over herself. He watches them skip down the steps and out on to the beach.

She has a spring in her step these days, even Hugh can see that. When she comes in the door her cheeks are pink, her eyes are bright, she's smiling for no reason. It's slightly ridiculous, he thinks, her happiness.

Neither of them refers to it, not a word is spoken.

At first it was easy not to mention it. It would have seemed impossible to broach the subject, what on earth would you say? But as the days wore on, as they turned into weeks, it was becoming more and more difficult for Hugh not to say something.

They were conducting their romance right under his nose, for God's sake. The least he could expect was an introduction.

'Have you and Simon met him yet?' he asked Della tentatively. He was bracing himself for the answer, he had visions of them all sitting around Della's kitchen table together, laughter filling the air.

But no, they hadn't been introduced. He had to drag that out of her, she was reluctant to admit it, he got the sense she was a bit miffed herself. Hugh imagined that, for once, he and Della could be allies in something, they could support each other, they could make common cause.

'I see him leaving every morning,' he said. 'But I never see him arrive, it's very curious.'

'Mmm,' said Della. She slid out of her coat and threw it over a chair.

He was sitting at his desk by the window. An air of melancholy hung over him. He was wearing his Saturday-morning rounds outfit. A grey brushed-cotton shirt, a sleeveless lambs-wool V-neck. The shirt was rolled up past his wrists to accommodate the plaster casts.

'How's the English Patient?' she had said brusquely when she arrived.

He grunted to acknowledge the joke.

'Oh, you know, slowly festering.'

As she bent down to kiss him she noticed a speck of shaving foam that had dried and crusted near his earlobe. She scraped it off with her fingernail. He swatted her hand away with his cast.

'You could go out, you know.'

She was using her ward sister voice, just to annoy him.

'You could go down to the village. Bit of air would do you good. It's a gorgeous day.'

She looked at him, all innocence, waiting for a reply. He just glared at her. He continued on with his own conversation.

'The only explanation I can think of is that he arrives under the cover of darkness.'

Della stood there surveying him. He'd got heavier, that's what she was thinking. There was an overhang that hadn't been there before, spilling over the waistband of the tracksuit bottoms. All that sitting around, she thought. All that whiskey.

The stack of documents on the floor beside his desk was growing by the day. Say nothing, thought Della. Say nothing.

'The thing is,' he tried explaining to her, 'I'm curious about him now, I wouldn't mind meeting him.'

But Della was unsympathetic.

'Well, Hugh,' she said. 'You only have yourself to blame.'

In the absence of a meeting, he finds himself imagining one. He will sit there all day long in the window, looking blindly out to sea, rehearsing heated conversations with an absent adversary.

He has him for an Obama supporter. You can tell just by looking at him.

'I'm a McCain man myself,' he will find himself saying. 'That Obama fellow is completely untried, he's an unknown quantity. The situation is too serious for that now, this is no time for amateurs.'

If the American was any good he would be up for the cut and thrust, he would enjoy a robust debate.

'He's photogenic, I'll give you that, he looks good on television. But where we come from, that's not a reason enough to be elected. Here in Europe, we select our leaders for something other than their looks.'

He would be nice to him, he would be convivial. But he would leave him in no doubt as to where he stood on things.

'America,' he said. 'I blame America.'

The solicitor and the barrister looked at each other nervously.

'That's where this is all coming from.' A flush had spread up over his face and his hair was standing on end. He was leaning forward in his chair, his two plaster-casts resting on the highly polished boardroom table.

'This whole bloody culture of litigation, it's an American import. It's a deadly bloody cocktail of political correctness and litigiousness and rampant greed. It's dangerous! Believe you me, it's going to paralyse the ability of doctors to go about their bloody job!'

He paused for breath. The solicitor ventured to step in. He had a faltering delivery, not quite a stutter.

'I appreciate where you're coming from, Professor Murphy. And I must, I must confess that I have some sympathy for your standpoint. But I'm afraid that the ... the reality of the situation is that we will not be able to defend this case with an argument about the prevailing culture. Specific allegations have been made against you. We, we will be forced to defend them in some detail.'

Hugh waved his hand dismissively.

'Medicine is an imperfect science,' he said. 'That's what you people refuse to accept. Life is an imperfect bloody science!'

The blue eyes were hot and bloodshot. He shook his bandaged right hand at them.

'I've got some news for you people,' he said. 'Patients die on us sometimes! Old people die, young people die. Children die, for God's sake. And sometimes there's not a lot we can do about it!'

The solicitor was doodling on the front of his affidavit. He glanced up despairingly at the barrister. He gave a barely perceptible shrug of the shoulders. Hugh didn't even seem to notice. He was in full flight.

'I'm a doctor! I've spent my life trying to stop people dying.

175

But it's not a perfect science. And I won't be held up as some kind of a monster because I had the misfortune to lose a patient and the rabble are baying for a scalp.'

He sat back in his chair, crossing his arms over each other in defiance.

'I refuse to be made a bloody scapegoat of.'

He paused for dramatic effect and the solicitor jumped on the opportunity to come in. He stammered a little as he got going.

'There is also . . . em, I think it might be worth mentioning at this juncture, there is also the complicating factor of the aggravated damages. You are aware, I assume, that the plaintiffs are seeking aggravated damages. They claim to have been frightened by your behaviour.'

He was wincing slightly as he proceeded, bracing himself for another outburst.

'They say they were in some fear that they might be in harm's way.'

Hugh gave another dismissive wave of the hand.

'That old chestnut,' he said. 'They always say that, par for the course. Terrified by the insensitive approach of the doctor, and so on and so forth. Unable to ever so much as darken the door of a hospital again, unable to watch an episode of *ER* on the television . . .'

And so on it went. An hour-long consultation and by the end of it, despite the exorbitant fees the two lawyers would mark up for the session, they had both well and truly earned their money.

As they stood up to bring the proceedings to an end, it seemed their pinstriped suits were more than usually crumpled, the carefully oiled kinks in their hair were slipping out of place, their normally tight faces sagging.

They both stuck their arms out automatically to shake hands before realising that it wouldn't be possible. Hugh stood there with his bandaged hands at his sides and gave a funny little bow. Then he swivelled round and stormed off, head down, towards the door.

The solicitor rushed to open it for him. Half hiding behind it, he waited for Hugh to pass through.

They could still hear him ranting to himself as he disappeared down into the darkness of the stairwell.

A pint was called for.

The light was streaming in through the stained-glass windows of the snug. It picked out the water marks on the wooden table, the torn leather vents in the banquette seats, the yellowed foam peeping out. The sun highlighted the dandruff on the barrister's shoulders, the red veins on the solicitor's nose. The ten colours lurking in the black depths of the Guinness, the bubbles climbing up to settle in the creamy head.

The two men waited, even though they were in need of the drink.

'I don't see how we can put him on the stand.'

'It's not as if he's going to agree to settle.'

'He may not have any choice. The insurance company won't want this to get to court.'

'We could drag out the discovery, perhaps?'

'It would buy us some time.'

'Maybe something will happen in the meantime.'

'A bolt of lightning could strike him down.'

'Fingers crossed.'

And they lifted their pints and toasted to that.

It was only when Hugh was settling into the back of the taxi that he realised he had failed to mention the hospital inquiry. No doubt they were aware of it already, they would have to be aware of it. But he had intended to warn them all the same.

The hospital couldn't be trusted.

The hospital had its own agenda, it had even appointed its own team of lawyers. They would be seeking to avoid publicity, they would be engaged in damage limitation. They would be prepared to do anything to stay out of the headlines.

That's what Hugh wanted to say to his lawyers, he wanted to warn them. Never mind the forty years of experience, he would say. Never mind the professorship and the fellowship of the Royal College of Surgeons, never mind antiquated concepts like loyalty and collegiality. The hospital was run by bureaucrats now. It was run by little men in Marks and Spencer's suits. They wouldn't hesitate to cut him loose.

That's what he wanted to say to his legal team, he wanted to mark their card for them. He needed them to understand. This was a battle they had on their hands. This was one man against the world.

Chapter 19

Two weeks to go now to the election and everywhere people were talking about it. It was like a world election.

There was Bruno thinking he was getting away from it all by coming here. He'd wondered would he be able to follow it properly, he'd thought maybe there wouldn't be much coverage in the local press.

He needn't have worried.

Everybody seemed to be up for Obama, Obama was the home team. Already, they were claiming him as one of their own. A band no one had ever heard of had recorded a song about him. 'There's No One as Irish as Barack O'Bama.' It was a surprise hit on YouTube.

'It's embarrassing,' said Addie. 'You'd think we'd have the decency to let this one go.'

But Bruno thought it was great. 'If only you all had a vote.'

Every shop he went into, every bar, every restaurant, all the talk was of Obama. As soon as Bruno opened his mouth, he'd be asked what he thought. He gave them what they were looking for and more besides.

'What do I think of Obama?' he would say. He would draw it out a bit, he would work up a momentum.

'I'll tell you what I think of Obama. I think he embodies the hopes of our nation. I think he may deliver us from the disrepute that has dragged us down in the eyes of the world. I think all we have to do now is elect him. So pray for us, please.'

'He won't make it that far,' said the barman as he poured Bruno's pint. He poured it three-quarters of the way up and then he set it down on the draining board and stood back to wait for it to settle. 'They'll get to him first, how much do you want to bet?'

But Bruno didn't want to bet anything on that, he didn't want any part of that kind of wager.

The Bradley effect, that was another thing everyone was talking about. Impossible to predict the power of the Bradley effect, that's what all the pundits were saying. It could be enough to lose him the election. Forget the polls, they were saying. What we won't know until election day is, how many Americans won't be able to bring themselves to vote for a black man? How many people will go into that booth and look at that name, Barack Hussein Obama, and at the very last moment choose the other guy.

Bruno was reading Obama's *Dreams from My Father* again, reading it over slowly and letting himself revel in the possibility, however outlandish it might seem, that a man of this talent might actually get elected to the highest office in the land.

Bruno sat in a corner of the pub, with his pint in front of him, and he read Obama's book, letting those honeyed cadences cast their magic over him. And he got to a passage he didn't remember reading before, a passage that had an eerie prescience about it. A passage about some advice the young Obama received from one of the few older black men he knew when he was growing up.

As Bruno read it, he got a hollow feeling in the pit of his stomach.

They'll give you a corner office and invite you to fancy dinners, and tell you you're a credit to your race. Until you want to actually start running things, and then they'll yank on your chain and let you know that you may be a well-trained, well-paid nigger, but you're a nigger just the same.

Bruno got shivers down his spine just thinking about it. Just thinking that maybe, just maybe, that rule was about to be broken.

Bruno is a Bruce Springsteen fan.

You already know this about him, it's one of the first things he tells you.

'Bruce is the man,' he says, without a trace of self-con-sciousness. 'I live by Bruce.'

'Never got it myself,' says Addie.

To Addie, Bruce is 'Born in the USA', Bruce is the Stars and Stripes and those lumberjack shirts with the sleeves rolled up over the biceps. Bruce is not something you would ever have considered liking.

'You see, to me, that sounds a lot like a challenge,' said Bruno. 'I think I've just found my purpose here. Now I know why I've been sent.'

181

'No way!' She was shaking her head. 'Absolutely no way are you evangelising me. I'm actually happy with the music I listen to. I happen to like my music. I don't feel the need for Bruce Springsteen in my life.'

He had grabbed her iPod off the table where it had been lying, he was flicking through it.

'Jesus Christ,' he was saying, 'you can't be serious. You listen to this stuff? This is what you listen to every day? How do you manage to get out of bed in the morning?'

'I happen to like depressing music,' she said. 'I find it cheers me up. It makes me feel quite cheerful. By comparison.'

'This makes no sense. This makes no sense whatsoever. You need to be on the Bruce programme, baby. You might actually start enjoying your life.'

Don't quote, she was thinking, please don't quote. But he was off.

'*Roll down the window and let the wind blow back your hair,* babe.'

She put her head in her hands in mock despair.

'I can't believe I'm hearing this.'

He calls me baby, she was thinking. He calls me babe and he's trying to make me listen to Bruce Springsteen and I'm still prepared to go out with him. I must be out of my mind.

'Let's do the loop,' he said to her.

A freezing cold night, they were wrapped up together for warmth. Addie had her pyjamas on, she even had her socks on.

'Winter sex,' he said. 'There's nothing like it. I always think

182

there's something very sexy about making love to a woman with your socks on.'

Addie wasn't keeping up. What loop, she was thinking. Is this another sexual favour I promised him?

'You and me and Lola,' he said, 'we should do the loop. We should go on a road trip, just the three of us. Discover this fine country of yours.'

'Jesus, I'd better let her in,' said Addie, hopping out of the bed. She'd thrown Lola out of the bedroom, she couldn't have sex with her in the room, she just couldn't do it. She's a dog, Bruno had said, she won't understand what's going on. She will, Addie insisted, she won't like it.

'I can't do the loop,' she said, as she climbed back into the bed. 'I'd love to, but I can't. I have to be here for my dad, I have to cook his dinner for him. He can't be left alone in the house. In case he needs something during the night, I need to be here. And anyway, what would we do with Lola? Most places don't allow dogs.'

But Bruno wasn't that easily put off. He came up with another plan instantly.

'What about the spokes of the wheel?' he said. 'We could do the spokes of the wheel. We could pick places within reach of here, we could do day trips. That way we would be back here every night.'

Addie was thinking about it.

'Lola would like that,' he said, and at the mention of her name Lola jumped up and came over to the bed, resting her chin on the duvet and narrowing her eyes at them.

'You'd swear she knows what we're talking about,' said Addie.

'Of course she knows what we're talking about!' said Bruno. 'We're talking about *trips*, we're talking about *walks*, in the *countryside*.'

'Stop it,' said Addie. 'I know what you're doing, you're trying to get her on side. You're ganging up on me.'

'I have a guidebook back in my room,' he said. 'I can do some research.' (He broke it up into two words, he called it re-search.) 'I can identify suitable destinations. I can rent a car, I'll be your chauffeur. You won't have to do anything. Just come along for the ride.'

'Do you know what kind of places are within reach of here?' she asked doubtfully. 'You're talking about the midlands,' she said, watching his blank expression. 'You obviously don't know about the midlands.'

'We could go up the coast,' he said cheerfully.

'Louth,' she answered. As if that was all you needed to know.

'Down the coast?' he ventured.

'Wicklow, Wexford. The Irish Sea.'

'OK, OK,' he said, bowing to her superior knowledge. 'But there must be somewhere within reach of here that's worth visiting. Let that be my quest, I'll find us somewhere worth visiting.'

So she bowed to his blissful ignorance, to his endless enthusiasm.

'OK,' she said. 'At the weekends, if I can persuade my sister to check on my dad, we'll do the spokes of the wheel.'

*

Bruno got cracking on his plan straight away.

He started compiling playlists from iTunes, he started downloading them from his laptop on to blank CDs.

He delved through the back catalogue, choosing oh so carefully, tunes that would reel her in. Old Bruce, new Bruce. Obscure Bruce and less obscure. He knew his way around this. He was confident she would not be able to resist.

Bruno was a missionary now. He was a man on a mission. He had checked out the soundtrack of her life, he had taken it in with one glance down her iPod directory. The way she had her life story set up, it was a weepie. It was a fucking tragedy, sad beginning, sad middle, sad end.

One look through her iPod and Bruno had made a decision. I am going to turn this into a feel-good movie.

Chapter 20

'Aren't you going to tell me where it is we're going?'

'Nope.'

'Come on, you have to tell me where we're going.'

'No, ma'am. It's a mystery destination. You'll find out when we get there.' He sounded like a US Marine.

The route he was taking was ominous. Along the quays and through the Phoenix Park, he had Bruce Springsteen blaring out from the car stereo.

He wouldn't let Addie speak.

'This is extraordinary rendition, you know. I feel like I'm being taken to a secret prison in Cavan.'

'Just listen,' he said. 'You've got to give it a chance to work on you.' As if it was a pill.

So she sat there like a prisoner. There was nothing for it but to listen.

'I know this music,' she roared. 'I just don't like it very much.'

But Bruno ignored her. He was singing along silently,

bobbing his head from side to side as he drove, mouthing the words.

Coming up to the roundabout in the middle of the park, Bruno spotted the Stars and Stripes ahead of them. The flag was flying high in the sky above the gates to the American ambassador's residence, stunning against the blue sky. The Irish tricolour was flying from the opposite gatepost, the dear old dowdy tricolour.

With Bruce Springsteen's husky voice blaring out from the car radio, Addie couldn't deny it, it was a moment.

Bruno smashed the heel of his hand down on the horn and started to sing along at the top of his voice.

'*Come on up for the rising,*' he sang. '*Come on up for the rising tonight.*'

His voice was hoarse with emotion, it was almost contagious. If Addie had known the words, she might even have been tempted to sing along.

Instead she leaned her head back against the seat and looked out the window. A weird strip of mist was hanging over the ground, just a few feet high. It was hovering over the grass without actually touching it, like a band of static. Rising out of it, the antlers of hundreds of deer, their bodies lost in the mist. They looked like creatures materialising out of a time warp.

She would have liked to say that to Bruno but she couldn't hear herself think.

Forty minutes later, twenty miles inside the County Meath boundary and another ten tracks into the Bruce Springsteen introduction CD, Bruno pulled the car over.

'This is our first stop.'

'What? But there's nothing here.'

'Oh, but there is.' He gestured to the house right beside them, a pebble-dashed bungalow painted a sickly mint green. 'The home of our country cousins. We're invited for tea.'

Addie's eyes widened in horror.

'Oh Jesus. This *is* extraordinary rendition. This is torture. I don't want to visit any of my cousins, you know I don't want to visit my cousins.'

She was repeating it because she couldn't quite believe it. She felt trapped, she felt like she'd been outwitted, out-smarted, boxed into a corner. How to explain how little she wanted to call on her long-lost cousins in a pebble-dashed bungalow outside Navan? For a moment, she considered refusing to go in. She thought about waiting in the car, she thought about walking back to the nearest town. She wanted to be a child again. She wanted to have a tantrum, cry and wail, beat her fists so as not to have to go.

'I should never have helped you,' she said. 'I should never have shown Hugh that bloody photograph, I should never have pestered him for their names.'

She was sitting in the passenger seat, her arms crossed stub-bornly over her chest. She felt like locking all the doors, she wanted to barricade herself in.

But Bruno was already getting out of the car. He was open-ing the hatchback to let the dog out.

'I'm sure they won't mind if Lola comes too.'

*

Afterwards, of course, Addie would feel so guilty.

They were so nice. They'd gone to a lot of trouble. There was homemade brown bread and a fruit cake. The best china was out, there was a freshly ironed tablecloth on the kitchen table. When you went to the loo you could tell it had been scrubbed. A brand new bar of soap on the sink. The Hoover marks were still visible on the carpet in the hall. They'd had a busy morning, preparing for their American visitor.

When they arrived Addie had hung back. She had imagined herself as peripheral to the whole situation. The way she looked at it she was just coming along for the ride. But Bruno introduced her to them and they fell on her. They were so glad to see her! They hugged her and they held on to her like she was one of their own. They stood back and studied her face.

'She has a look of Auntie May, doesn't she? There's no denying her, she's definitely one of ours.'

'I can't believe it, where have the years gone? The last time you were here you can't have been more than six or seven. We brought you out to show you the puppies. The dog had just had puppies. Do you remember that?'

Addie didn't have the heart to tell them that she had no recollection of them at all. She never even knew they existed. She looked desperately over at Bruno for help. He was hovering down on the ground, delving in his bag for something, a gift he'd brought with him. Addie's head was spinning with it all, the rush of their emotion. She asked for directions to the bathroom.

I'm a snooty cow, she thought to herself as she washed her hands. I didn't want to meet these people. I think I'm better than them. I deserved to be put in my box.

She dried her hands slowly on the pristine white hand towel before venturing back out.

There were two of them. Two sisters, Mary and Theresa. Addie wasn't concentrating properly when they introduced themselves and she forgot immediately which one was which. One of them actually lived in Navan, she explained, but she'd come over especially. She made it sound like the trip was four hundred miles rather than just four.

They were daughters of one of the women in the photo. Which would make them first cousins of Hugh's, could that be right? How come Addie had never heard of them? It didn't make any sense.

'Of course you're the only Boylan left,' said one of the cousins to Bruno. 'It was all girls on our side of the family, after our brother died. There was no one left to carry on the name.'

'That never occurred to me,' said Bruno. 'You're right, I'm the last of the Boylans!'

He had this rapturous expression on his face.

'We're relying on you now,' said one of them, 'to keep the name alive.' They nudged each other and nodded at him.

'Now,' said the other one.

Addie cringed. But Bruno was lapping it up. Leaning forward over the table, he was making no attempt to conceal his delight.

Addie looked over his shoulder to see where Lola was.

'She might like to go out into the garden,' they'd said as soon as they saw Lola.

The two of them agreeing with each other.

'Oh yes, I'm sure she'd prefer to be outside.'

Meaning they didn't want her in the house. Which was a relief to Addie, because as soon as you looked around the living room, as soon as you took in the delicate tallboy stacked with china ornaments, and the lace doilies on the side tables, and the antimacassars on the backs of the couch and the chairs, you *knew* it was not a good idea for Lola to be in the house.

Addie could see her now, she had a clear view of her out through the glass kitchen door. She was cruising around the garden, sniffing wildly at the flower beds. She was circling, like a circus horse in the ring. Round and round in ever-decreasing circles, which only ever meant one thing. Now she was whirling, round and round three times and then she was squatting, squeezing out an endless turd, right there in the middle of their lawn.

Addie leaned forward to help herself to another piece of cake. She pretended not to have noticed. She tried to concentrate on what it was they were saying.

They were all peering over the photo Bruno had brought with him.

'That would have been taken just before he went to America,' said the older one.

'They were heartbroken he never came back. Mammy and Auntie May. They doted on him, you know.'

'Yes,' said the younger one. 'There was always the hope that he would come back.'

Bruno reassured them.

'He always wanted to come, you know, it was a dream of his to come.'

'Well, it wasn't to be, I suppose. Still it's sad all the same, that they never got to see each other again.'

'Sure they thought they'd have all the time in the world. Doesn't everyone think that?'

'Well, they're all together now, please God.'

There was a reverent silence as they contemplated this. Then one of the cousins perked up. She gave a little squeak of excitement.

'Nora came! Do you remember that, Mary? That was a big thing for them. The presents she brought! When would that have been?'

'God now, I'm trying to think. Wait now . . .'

'I've letters from her somewhere, she used to write to Mammy. I must try to dig them out for you . . .'

Addie's attention was wandering. She was studying the pictures on the wall. An uneven clutch of framed photographs, each one showed a different young person in a cap and gown standing in front of a mottled studio backdrop. The roll of parchment held awkwardly in the two hands. They were proudly displayed, those photographs, hung in the kitchen for maximum exposure. It occurred to Addie that her own graduation photograph was lying in a box somewhere. Hugh didn't set much store by architecture as a qualification.

The family tree was spread out on the table now, they were all poring over it.

God, this is boring, Addie was thinking. She felt like she was in Mass. She felt like she was in a Latin Mass, the boredom was almost physical.

Out of the corner of her eye, she could see Lola digging up the grass, scrabbling like a cartoon dog to cover her tracks, sending clumps of grass and earth flying backwards between her rear legs.

'That's right,' one of them was saying. 'Your grandfather would have been James. He would have been a brother of our grandfather's. John Boylan, that was our grandfather. You have it right.' She tapped the page with her index finger.

'There's a few things I need your help with,' said Bruno. He was squinting down at his notes. 'Your father was Michael, isn't that right?'

They both nodded enthusiastically.

'Daddy's name was Michael Daly,' said one of them eagerly. 'And May's husband was a Lynch, Seamus Lynch.'

Bruno was scribbling it all down in his notebook.

'And Kitty's husband, what was his first name do you happen to know?'

A look between the two sisters, Addie caught it immediately.

'Kitty's husband,' said one of them mechanically.

'Yes. Murphy was his surname. Hugh's father.'

They had both of them glanced over nervously at Addie, now they were staring back down at the family tree. From where Addie was sitting she could make out the upside-down question mark that Bruno had inscribed beside her grandfather's surname.

'The first name escapes me, can you remember it, Theresa?'

'Not for the life of me.'

Bruno's pen was hovering over the page. As they were talking, he found himself tracing over the question mark again. Now it appeared to have been written in bold. It stood out like a sore thumb.

'He's gone a long time.'

'I'm not sure we ever met him.'

Bruno looked up at the two sisters.

'My father talked about them all, you know. He often spoke of them.'

'They were so proud of him. They were always telling people, our cousin Patrick went to America. Did very well for himself over there.'

She turned to Addie.

'They were proud of your father too. A doctor in the family, isn't that what everyone wants?'

There was something in the air again. Some tension, Addie couldn't put her finger on it.

'It meant a lot to Mammy, that he came back for the funeral.'

Addie was lost now, she didn't know who they were talking about. They must have noticed her confusion.

'Auntie May's funeral. It meant a lot to everyone that your father came back.'

The other one was nodding.

'She was a mother to him, she was the only mother he ever knew.'

And Addie nodded as if she understood. She nodded and she smiled, even as the questions were forming in her mind.

'Your mother was very good about visiting her. She used to be very good about coming back, she always brought you girls with her. It meant so much to Auntie May, to see you girls growing up.'

A wisp of a memory, dancing around the edges of Addie's mind. Boiled sweets, a round tin of them. A clip being placed in her hair. Face powder, the soft pink smell of it when you leaned in for the kiss.

'She was a lovely woman, your mother, we were all very fond of her.'

To her horror, Addie found the tears welling up in her eyes. She was overcome by everything she didn't know, by all the things these women seemed to know about her. She didn't remember any of it. She felt as if she'd walked into a room and suddenly people were jumping out from behind the couches and the curtains and they were shouting, surprise! She wanted to cut and run.

Bruno must have noticed her distress. He came to her rescue.

'While I'm here, I'd very much like to go visit the grave-yard. I'd like to see the family plot.'

The two cousins went into a flap.

'Oh yes,' they said, 'you must go to the graveyard. We can give you the directions.'

'It's hard enough to find, unless you know where to look, we'll have to write it down for you.'

Bruno opened the notebook again.

'Please God there are no weeds, it's weeks since we were out there.'

There followed an endless series of directions, they were still issuing clarifications as Addie and Bruno stood up to leave.

'Make sure to come back now, next time you're here,' said the older one to Bruno as they were saying goodbye.

'There will be a next time,' said the other one decisively.

They kissed Addie and held her close as they said goodbye. But they didn't pass on their regards to her father. And they didn't urge her to come back. She only realised that as she climbed into the car.

Bruno started up the engine and Addie waved and the two ladies stood at the gate waving back. As soon as they were around the corner Addie leaned back against her seat and let out a long breath. Her head was spinning, her mind struggling to grasp something that remained just out of sight.

'Look at those trees!' he said. 'Have you ever seen anything like them?'

The trees were so tall and dense they formed a roof over the road. Driving under them, you had a restful feeling. It was like walking down the central aisle of a great cathedral. A feeling that something bigger was in charge.

Addie hadn't spoken since they'd pulled away from the house. Bruno didn't seem to have noticed her silence.

'I never knew this was such gorgeous country,' he was saying, looking hungrily out of the window. 'Such land! I don't know why, but I always imagined it to be more barren.'

Addie looked out across the rolling fields, hot tears pricking her eyes.

She was irritated with him, but she wasn't even sure why. She was annoyed with herself too, she was writhing with a discomfort that was close to pain. A witch's brew of teenage emotions, a stubborn vein of petulance wrapping itself tighter and tighter around her heart. The more irritated she became, the more clueless Bruno appeared to be, the more infuriating his delight in the trip.

'Imagine!' he was saying. 'My father and your father, they would have travelled these very roads as young men, they would have known this route so well.'

God, he sounded so American.

He had stopped the car at a gap in the hedgerow. He was leaning over the steering wheel, gazing eagerly out across the fields towards the fast-moving river below them.

'How my father would have loved to be here with us,' he said wistfully.

And she felt guilty all of a sudden for grudging him his history. Now that she could see how much it meant to him. But it was different for her. It was difficult and complicated and now here he was, making her feel bad about herself again.

She closed her eyes to conceal the tears that were in danger of slipping down her face. Hot angry tears, and with them a wave of resentment.

She should have listened to Hugh. There was nothing to be gained from all this. No good would come of it.

She had been happy before he came. She grabbed that thought and tried to hang on to it. As if it were a branch over a swollen river. But it was no use, she had to admit she was lying to herself. OK then, so she hadn't been happy. She had been safe, at least. She had been secure in her own misery, before he came.

Bruno was shocked by the gaps in Addie's knowledge. It was hard not to be shocked. He had asked her about her family, all innocence.

'What part of the country was your mother from?'

A simple enough question, you would have thought. Only Addie didn't seem to know the answer.

They were wandering around the gravestones in Navan

cemetery. They were the only people on foot. The other visitors all seemed to come by car. Turning slowly in at the gates, they would cruise down the pathways, coming to a stop at a particular spot. A minute's pause, or two minutes, the arm resting on the open car window. Enough time to smoke a cigarette. The next thing they would drive on at a snail's pace, crawling back out through the open gates and on to the road.

'The drive-by visit,' said Bruno, fascinated. There was something Mafioso about it, he thought, something stylish and sinister.

Addie had Lola on the lead, it didn't seem right to let her run wild among the graves. She was pulling on Addie's arm, creeping along the ground like a platypus, her ears scraping against the gravel.

Addie was still puzzling over Bruno's question.

'I think she was from Wexford, I have an idea they were from somewhere near New Ross. She was an only child, she came to college in Dublin when she left school.'

'But don't you ever go down there, to New Ross? Don't you ever visit?'

'I don't think there's anyone to visit, as far as I know they're all dead. My grandparents died before I was born. I think it was New Ross they were from but I'm not sure. Maybe it was Enniscorthy. Somewhere in Wexford anyway.'

She could see that Bruno was taken aback by her vagueness. He didn't seem to know what to do with it.

'Where did your parents meet?' He was walking along a row of headstones, leaning in to peer at the names. He was holding his notebook in his hands, studying the directions.

Addie realised she was shocked herself now.

'Do you know, I don't have a clue. Not a clue. My dad doesn't really talk about her very much.'

That did seem strange to her. Looking at it through Bruno's eyes, it seemed positively weird.

'Here we are!' said Bruno triumphantly.

He was standing in front of a large square plot. There was a low iron fence around the perimeter, the fence buckled in places. The plot was covered with threadbare gravel, a rippled layer of refuse-sack plastic peeping through in places. A plain headstone, the surface blurry with moss and lichen. Etched on the stone was a long list of names, it was hard to make them out. Boylans and more Boylans, James and John and another John after him, that was the little baby who died. You could work it out from the dates, he was only two, the poor little mite. There was a Catherine too, could that be her grandmother? But surely she would have been buried with her husband? Addie didn't know, she didn't have any of the answers. It did seem strange to her now that she had never been here before.

Bruno was writing in his notebook. He was balancing on the balls of his feet, the notebook resting on one raised knee, meticulously copying down everything that was written on the headstone.

Addie stood at the edge of the grave and studied what was written there, waiting for some emotion to take hold of her but none did. She could feel nothing, there was nothing she was thinking except that she should be thinking something.

I'll say a prayer, she thought. She felt an awful fraud, but she had to do something. Hail Mary, she said, going through the words silently in her head. The prayer was over very quickly, she had a feeling she'd missed a bit in the middle. So long since she'd said it. They'd learned it in Irish too, and in French. *Sainte Marie, Mère de Dieu. Priez pour nous, pauvres pécheurs.* She was amazed that she could remember that. She waited a moment or two with her head solemnly bowed, then she moved on along the row. She found she was just as interested in the other headstones as she was in theirs.

She came to the end of the row and found herself standing in front of a small white marble cross. The engraved letters had been filled out in bold black ink.

Phelan, it said, *Angela. Born Robinstown 27 April 1911. Died 11 May 1989.*

A Life Lived.

'I love that,' said Addie, and her heart swelled with new-found cheer as she walked on. She repeated the inscription to herself, savouring the poetry of it.

'A life lived.'

They drove over to Tara, but Addie couldn't tell Bruno why it was so special. Something about the High Kings, she said.

They climbed the mound.

'You can see thirteen counties from here.' Bruno was reading from his guidebook.

'They all look the same to me,' said Addie. 'It's not exactly the hanging gardens of Babylon, is it?'

And she turned to go back to the car.

They stopped at Bective Abbey on the way back and Addie told him the monks had been banned and had to go into hiding. When, he wanted to know, what century?

'God,' she said. 'I don't have a clue. I don't remember doing much Irish history in school.'

He was standing behind her, his arms wrapped tightly around her. He was kissing her ear.

'I do remember learning about the wives of Henry the Eighth. We had to learn them all off by heart. The Spanish Inquisition, that kind of stuff. But I don't remember much of my Irish history.'

The Boyne, she knew there was a Battle of the Boyne, she knew it was a watershed. But standing in a muddy field, looking down at the river's choppy waters, she couldn't for the life of her remember why it was so important.

'I know it's historic, this river, I just can't remember why.'

'Don't worry,' he said, 'I'll google it.'

It was a bit embarrassing all the same. Up until now, she had never thought of herself as an ignorant person.

Lola, untroubled by her own ignorance, was swimming away happily in the historic river.

Chapter 21

From the very beginning, it has been clear that Lola has a beautiful heart.

The signs are there for everyone to see. It's in the way she holds her head, so shy and yet so dignified. The way she looks at you, humble and yet still looking for love. It's in the hopeful swish of her tail. The non-barking dog, Della's children call her, because she hardly ever barks.

She's a rescue dog, a damaged dog. She steers clear of people she doesn't know, she's even wary of other animals. If someone she doesn't know comes along and pets her, she goes to ground. She splays her legs and presses her body down towards the floor and she does this thing with her head as if she's trying to burrow under a duvet. Sometimes she shakes.

Addie doesn't have any information about what happened in Lola's past. She arrived like a refugee, dropping down out of the boot of the rescue lady's car one summer evening. All she had with her was a battered red collar and a sleeping mat.

'You can change her name if you like,' said the lady, 'but it's probably better not to.'

She warned Addie that Lola might cry during the night. But she didn't cry, she didn't make a sound. Of course Addie didn't sleep a wink, she kept creeping into the kitchen to see if Lola was sleeping. Kept finding herself standing there in the doorway in her nightdress, a pair of shining eyes coming out of the darkness at her.

She's a nervous creature, Lola, she jumps when she hears a loud noise. All you have to do is drop a saucepan lid on the floor and she's under the table, peering out from beneath her fringe with frightened eyes. She seems to be waiting for something bad to happen to her.

Addie reckons she was a gundog in her past life. She reckons they got rid of her because she was gun-shy.

'They tie them up,' the vet had said casually. 'The ones that are gun-shy. They try to beat it out of them.'

Addie had put her hand up straight away to stop him. 'Please don't,' she had said, 'I can't bear it.'

But there was no unhearing those words. Once you'd heard them, there was no getting them out of your head again. Addie had this image now, of Lola tied up somewhere, strapped to a fence in a dirty yard with cruel men hovering around her.

At least they didn't put her down, that's what Addie tells herself. At least they gave her to the rescue lady who put her photograph on the internet and that's where Addie found her. As soon as she saw the photograph she knew. It was the way Lola had her head half turned away from the camera, the way she was looking back expectantly. Addie knew this was the right dog for her, it was as if she recognised her from somewhere.

'I'll never let anything bad happen to you again.' That's what Addie whispers to Lola last thing at night as she crouches down beside her on the bedroom floor and fiddles with her crimpy ears. She smoothes down Lola's spiky fringe and she kisses her in the hollow dip on top of her velvety head.

The gentlest dog, the most ladylike of dogs. Lola understands personal space, she respects boundaries. An affectionate dog, she nudges Addie's elbow with her nose when she wants to be petted. A clever dog, she lies in the patch of sun under the window. When the sun moves, she moves. And she never cries. Not when she gets whole branches of thorn bush caught in her tail, not even when glass gets lodged in the pad of her paw.

Three months Addie has had Lola, she arrived at the end of July. But it didn't take three months, it didn't take three days to get the measure of her. One look at her and you can tell, she's good through and through, she's good and loyal and true.

If only it were so easy to read a human being.

'Can we bring Lola to the blessing of the pets?'

It was Elsa on the phone. She was ringing from Della's mobile so at first Addie thought it was Della ringing her.

'When's the blessing of the pets?'

'On Sunday. Mum says will you come for lunch here afterwards.'

'Put your mum on to me.'

There was a muffled transfer and the next thing Della was on the line.

'I'm driving so I can't talk for long.'

'Is she for real, the blessing of the pets?'

'Oh, they're desperate to get people in. They even have a blessing of the Christmas presents. Anything to draw a crowd. We're bringing the fish, but we think Lola should come too.'

'Are you sure it's OK to bring a dog?'

'Last year someone brought a horse.'

'Fair enough. And lunch?'

'. . . we thought we'd give you lunch afterwards. Wait a minute, there's a Guard, I'm putting the phone down . . .'

'Lunch would be lovely,' said Addie with an air of resignation, talking into the phone even as it lay in Della's lap. Bruno would be delighted, he was all for meeting them.

'One other thing,' Della said, when she came back on.

Addie could hear the kids fighting in the background. 'Would you shut up!' roared Della. 'I'm trying to drive *and* have a conversation on the phone.'

Silence.

'The hospital has completed its inquiry,' said Della. 'Simon heard it on the grapevine in there. The word is, it's not pretty.'

'Oh Jesus. Does Hugh know?'

'I suppose he must know, they must have told him.'

'He didn't mention anything to you?'

'No.'

Instantly Addie felt bad, she felt that she should have known. Maybe if she had been spending more time with him, maybe then he would have told her. But she'd been spending all her evenings with Bruno. She'd been dropping his dinner up to him, leaving him to eat it alone.

'I'll talk to him,' said Addie, 'I'll sound him out.'

'Do you want the good news or the bad news?' That's what she said to Della when she phoned her back later that night.

She had put Bruno off for the night. She had explained to him, she'd been all apologies.

'I've been neglecting him,' she said. 'I think he's in a huff. He's a very jealous old boy.'

'That's OK,' Bruno replied. 'I'll wash my hair or some-thing.'

So then Addie felt guilty about Bruno. You couldn't win. For one crazy moment she thought about inviting him but she ruled it out again straight away.

She went alone, her bag of ingredients with her. She made a cheese soufflé to butter him up. His favourite meal, she had learned to cook it as a birthday present for him once. It's the only complicated thing she has ever learned to cook. She pro-duces it whenever he's in need of cheering up, it's something of a tradition between them.

They ate it at the kitchen table with a green salad and a bottle of Bordeaux. Hugh drank his wine through a straw, but he insisted on managing his food by himself. It was pathetic, watching him trying to grasp the fork between the ends of his fingers. It took him an eternity to get each forkful to his mouth. The soufflé must have been stone cold by the time he got to the end of it.

'You wouldn't get it in a restaurant.' That's what he always said when she made him cheese soufflé. 'You wouldn't get it in the Shelbourne.'

Only after they'd opened the second bottle of wine did she succeed in getting him around to talking about the case.

'Do you have any idea when it will be?' She was all innocence.

'Oh, some time in the New Year,' he said. 'The wheels of justice turn very slowly. But you're not to be worrying about that now.' He was at his very sweetest, the soufflé had done the trick. 'I have every confidence that we'll win.

'They're just looking for someone to blame,' he said. 'They can't bring her back so they want someone to blame. I wouldn't mind, but I did my damnedest to save the bloody woman.'

'Who's they?'

'The parents.'

'I thought it was the husband taking the case.'

'Yes, but it's the father pushing it, he's the driving force. He's a taxi driver.'

As if that explained everything.

'Money. That's what it all comes down to. That's what this whole bloody business is about, getting as much money as possible out of the insurance company. The more claims they throw in, the more they stand to gain.'

He was quite forthcoming. He talked about it at length, right through the second bottle.

'She was the size of a house. I don't know how they can object to me mentioning that. It's not as if it's a matter of debate, it was on her chart, for God's sake. Clinically obese. It contributed to her death, the obesity. If she hadn't been so bloody fat, she wouldn't have died. I warned her about that, I told her she should lose some weight first, but she wouldn't hear of it. She wanted the operation over and done with in time for some damn family wedding. *You* try operating on somebody with more blubber than a whale, you can't even find their bloody gall bladder.'

A shadow of doubt passed over Addie. She felt it moving silently across her world like a cloud.

'But you didn't put it like that.'

He was coiled in his carver chair like a big snake, there was menace in the way he unfurled himself.

'Pardon me?'

Addie was wincing.

'Tell me you didn't say that to the family.'

'Of course not, what kind of a person do you take me for?'

So then she felt bad for doubting him. If his own daughter didn't believe him, who else would?

She leaned across and poured out the last of the wine. She thought maybe they were over the worst of it. But still Hugh kept talking.

'Naturally the hospital are running for cover. They seem to be seizing the opportunity to put me out to pasture. Nothing more than what you would expect. They seem to have signed up some of the younger members of staff to do their dirty work for them. All to be expected, I'm afraid, my dear, they love nothing better than to kick a man when he's down.'

He was frightening her. The whole thing was taking on new proportions, like a sinister shadow moving across a wall.

She was beginning to regret having asked about it at all. But she couldn't stop now.

'What do you mean?' she said. The words wobbled as they came out of her.

He answered her with gusto, his voice rolling along with a musical flourish.

'Oh, from what I hear they've cooked up a complaint against me. A little conspiracy. This is what they do, they put their heads together and they come up with a story to protect themselves.'

He held up his bandaged hands in front of him like a boxer.

'It's unfortunate, this business. The fact that I'm not there to fight my corner, it's very unfortunate.'

Addie stared at him in horror, her mind struggling to take in what he was saying.

'This could be the big one,' he was saying, his eyes sharp and gleaming behind his glasses. 'This could be my last stand.'

As soon as she got back down to the basement, she rang Della.

'I was only joking,' she said, 'there is no good news. There's an accusation of bullying against him.'

'What! On top of the negligence thing?'

'Apparently. It surfaced during the inquiry, according to Hugh. They went around interviewing everyone who was there that day and apparently one of the junior doctors has accused Hugh of bullying him. The nurses are backing it up. Hugh says it's all a conspiracy to get rid of him.'

'Oh, sweet Jesus.'

'I know, it's ridiculous!'

'Well, hang on a minute, is it?'

'Of course it is! He's direct, he doesn't mince his words. But that's not a crime, is it?'

'Addie, you know what he's like. He says the first thing that comes into his head. He says nasty things. He can be cruel, you know he can.'

'But he doesn't mean it. When he says those things, he doesn't mean them.'

'It doesn't matter whether he means them or not, you're not allowed to behave like that any more.'

'The family are seeking aggravated damages,' said Addie in a voice that wasn't much more than a whimper. 'The family of the woman who died. They're saying he frightened them. They're saying he lost his temper and they were afraid he was going to get violent.'

'I can just picture it.' Della's voice was hard and thin.

'Oh Della.' Addie was whispering into the phone now. 'You don't think Dad could be a baddie, do you?'

Della paused before answering, which said it all.

'I think he's old style, Ad. And these days, that means you're a baddie. People expect a good bedside manner, they expect sensitivity. They expect you to adhere to best practice. They should expect it, for God's sake.'

'I know, Dell, but he's a good doctor, you know he's a good doctor.'

'It's not enough to be a good doctor. You have to be a good person too.'

'But he is a good person.'

'You and I know that, Ad. But not everyone else does. And you have to admit, all appearances are to the contrary.'

After Addie hung up the phone she padded into the bathroom to brush her teeth, the silence of the flat swirling around her.

The conversation with Della was running wild in her head. She had no control over it. It was trying to rearrange itself in her mind, snippets of her voice and Della's voice fighting to get out on top.

In her head, she was trying to fight back, she was trying to butt in with a defence. But opening up beneath her was a loss of faith so huge and so terrifying that it was making her physically sick.

All her life Addie had held unwaveringly to the belief that Hugh was a good person, refusing to contemplate the alternative. She had taken his part against the world. She had shaped her whole world view with Hugh at the centre of it. Now she felt like a fool.

She climbed into bed, turning over on to her side and curling up into a ball. She felt like she was huddled on a ledge halfway down a steep cliff. If she moved an inch she would fall into the void. She was rigid with fear. She didn't know how she was going to get through the night.

Chapter 22

In his little room in the B&B, Bruno woke up in the grip of a nightmare. His heart was thumping so hard in his chest, he could almost hear it. He could barely breathe, he had to swallow hard to drive the rising fear back down his throat.

The curtains were drawn and the room was pitch black. Bruno leaned over and turned on the bedside light. Falling heavily back on to the pillows, he looked around the room warily, as if he'd never seen it before. He had the sense that he had spent the past few hours wandering the house of his childhood. He was still in the fog of the dream.

A dream he has had before. He remembers it now, it's a recurring nightmare. It comes maybe once a year, and every time it comes he recognises it from before. But within an hour or two he will have forgotten it again, he will forget it utterly. The dream seems to possess this strange power, it can draw a cloak over itself. A dream that's not like a dream at all, there's no script to it. An insidious dream, it's so lifelike that it always takes him a while to work out that it's not real.

In the dream, his mother is still alive, she's living in the nursing home. Bruno hasn't been to visit her for years, nobody from the family has been to visit her. The staff at the nursing home wonder why no one ever comes to see her. His mother asks for them but still no one comes.

Bruno wakes up with a wave of horror breaking over him. Not since he used to wet the bed as a child has he had that feeling. The feeling that you've done something awful, something you weren't even aware of doing, something you'll never be able to fix.

When Bruno would wet the bed his mother would take him down to the bathroom and strip off his soaking pyjamas. She would sponge him and pat him dry with a towel. He can still remember the clammy feeling of his skin as she dried him off. The comfort of the clean pyjamas as he climbed into them. The relief of getting back into bed, a folded-up towel strategically placed to soak up the wet patch, a fresh sheet spread out over it. The joy of going back to sleep with a problem solved.

It's that same feeling he has now when he finally convinces himself that the dream is not real. It takes him a while to work the argument through in his head, he has to think it through logically. His mother is dead, she's been dead for five years now. When she was alive he went to see her every week, he visited her right up to the end.

He is not a bad person.

*

He visited her every week, he just didn't tell anyone about it. Not even his girlfriend. Something she found impossible to understand. In Bruno's opinion she refused to understand.

They weren't married, they weren't even living together. This was something they had decided at the very beginning, that there was to be no talk of marriage. They'd both been stung before.

He hadn't intended to hide his mother's existence from her. He just hadn't told her about it. By the time she eventually found out it had become a big thing. It wasn't personal, that's what he had tried to make her understand. It wasn't about excluding anyone. It was an act of gallantry on his part. It was hard to explain.

'It's not like I've been having an affair,' he had said.

But for some reason she seemed to think this was worse.

'I assumed she was dead! A reasonable assumption considering you only ever talked about her in the past tense. When you never mentioned visiting her, I think it was reasonable of me to assume that she was dead.'

He had been afraid that she would want to meet her, that's why he hadn't told her. He hadn't wanted anyone to see her like that. The frightened eyes peeping out of the pale little face. The long wizened hands clutching at the bed sheets. The outsized knuckles, the surgical tape holding her wedding ring on to her long bony fingers. He didn't want to talk about that to anyone.

It wouldn't be fair to her, bringing a stranger in to see her. Going through the fiction of an introduction, making an attempt at conversation around the bedside. He couldn't bear to contemplate it.

He hadn't actually intended to lie to her, but he could see that it amounted to the same thing. She took it personally, she thought it was about her. White with outrage, she stood up and walked out.

Bruno was shocked to find that he wasn't even sorry.

Bruno's mother was German. Her family had moved to America before the war.

Bruno and his sisters were hardly aware of this side of them. Everybody they knew was Irish and they were Irish too. It always seemed as if their German blood held less sway than the Irish. It was as if the Irish genes were dominant. There was only one thing Bruno and his sisters got from their mother and that was her soft brown eyes.

A quiet woman, people generally assumed that she was Irish too. Actually I'm from Germany, she would say. And people would express surprise. They would say they would never have guessed.

She didn't speak German at home. It was only when they were brought to visit their grandparents that Bruno would hear German spoken. He remembers sitting on a footstool in that dark living room of theirs, watching his mother as she conversed. He remembers how he studied her face in the hope that he would be able to understand her, just by watching her. He remembers his horror when he realised that he had no idea what she was saying. He remembers the feeling of panic, the urge to jump up and scream at her. It was as if she had become another person, she wasn't his mother any more. It was only when they were safely back in the car and she was conversing exclusively in English again, only then would Bruno feel safe.

In her later years she reverted to the language of her birth. By the end it was all she spoke.

Every Monday evening after work Bruno would sit for an hour in the high-backed chair by her bed and he would listen to her speak in a whisper about people and places from long ago. He would sit there and listen to her without understanding, just as he used to listen as a little boy. But this time there was no anger, only amazement at the beautiful sounds coming out of her. He would close his eyes and listen to that lilting voice, those lovely sounds that made no sense. He would sit there and listen like it was music. And people say German is an ugly language! Bruno has never been able to understand that.

It was Schwäbisch that she spoke, strictly speaking. A beautiful sibilant dialect, the soft rhythms of it seeped into her English, giving her voice little upturns where you would least expect them. It was an accent that lent itself to a gentle certainty, which suited his mother's personality perfectly.

All his life Bruno's mother had told him that he would know love when he found it. And Bruno took that to mean that love would find him, that it would strike him down and there would be no mistaking it. For years, he went about his life expecting a bolt from the blue that never came.

As the years wore on, as one marriage after the other went to the wall, his mother's certainty on the subject persisted. 'You just haven't met her yet,' she would say. When his mother spoke, the end of every sentence turned back on itself, as if words held no sway against eternal truths. 'When you meet her, you will know her.'

Now at last Bruno thinks he understands what she meant.

The very first time he saw Addie, she was familiar to him. Even though he'd never seen her before, he felt like he knew her. It was as if he recognised her from before. Even now, when he looks at her face he feels that strange sense of familiarity. Her face is a face he knows.

Maybe it's because we're related, he thinks, taking the family photo out of his notebook and studying it again. Maybe that would explain it. He scans the faces for a resemblance to Addie but he can't see it, there's nothing of her in these women.

The familiarity that he feels, it comes from the future, not from the past.

Funny how quickly you got used to sleeping with someone.

He kept reaching out to her in the bed, he kept waking up when he found that she wasn't there.

The third time this happened he made a decision. He got up and threw on his clothes. Crept down the dark, creaking stairs of the B&B like a thief and slid back the latch on the front door, letting himself out into the freezing cold night.

The sky was clear, with a crescent moon straight out of a fairy tale. The silvery sea creeping in over the beach. Bruno made a romantic figure, he was aware of that. Making his way up the street in the dead of night, driven by love.

He didn't want to knock on her door, afraid he would give her a fright. He was worried she wouldn't wake up and he would wake her dad instead. So he crept around the side of the house to the bedroom window. Leaned up and tapped on it with a coin he happened to have in his pocket. No response. Tap, tap, tap. Suddenly, her face appeared behind the glass, pale and confused-looking. She was squinting, she must have had trouble seeing him out there in the dark.

'It's me,' he hissed. 'Let me in, will you, it's freezin' out here.'

He went back round the front to wait for her. When she opened the door he saw that she was wearing his Bruce Springsteen T-shirt. He was just about to tease her about it when she launched herself at him. She threw her arms around his neck, falling against him with all her weight. He had to take a step back to steady himself. He was touched that she was so glad to see him. Usually she was more reserved than this. He put his arms around her and hugged her to him.

She raised her face to whisper into his ear.

'I can't remember the last time a boy threw stones at my window.'

'I missed you,' he said simply. 'I couldn't sleep.'

Taking his hand, she turned and led him into the flat.

Hovering on the edge of sleep, he confided his worst fear in her.

'Addie,' he said. 'I need you to talk me off the ledge. I'm afraid McCain is going to win.'

'He's not going to win,' said Addie, her voice slurred with sleep. 'Obama's going to win. I can feel it in my bones.'

Already the next sentence was forming in her head, but she didn't say it.

Obama's going to win, she was thinking. And you're going to go back home.

With his arms wrapped tightly around her, and with that one thought in her head, she fell asleep.

Chapter 23

'He's not going to win,' said Della with absolute certainty. 'Obama's going to win.'

They were sitting around Della's kitchen table, they'd just finished eating. The clocks had gone back that morning and outside the light was already fading. It was only four o'clock.

'I wish I shared your confidence,' said Bruno. 'Maybe I'm just afraid to hope.'

'Well, take it from me,' said Della as she moved around the table clearing away the plates. She was wearing a gingham apron over a tight black dress. High heels, hair up, she was in fifties housewife mode. She had insisted on cooking a leg of lamb, roast potatoes, all the trimmings. 'We'd better put the best foot forward,' she'd told Simon. 'You know, him being an American and all.'

All day she'd been excited about meeting him, her mind had been racing. She had wanted to know did he read Philip

Roth, Annie Proulx, Anne Tyler? What did he think of Joyce Carol Oates? She was dying to talk about the election.

'Obama has history on his side,' she was saying. 'It's Hillary I feel sorry for. It's never going to happen for her.'

'How can you be so sure?' asked Bruno. 'She might get a chance again, if McCain wins she can try in 2012.'

'No,' said Della, a note of exasperation in her voice, like a teacher trying to explain something to a child who just won't understand. 'McCain's not going to win. Obama's going to win. And Chelsea's going to be the first woman president, I'll bet you any amount of money. And poor Hillary will have been the wife of a president and the mother of a president. But never one herself.'

Bruno turned to Addie, smiling. 'How does she know all this?'

'She doesn't.'

'Often wrong, seldom in doubt,' said Simon in a slow drawl.

'Don't mind them,' said Della, pulling a cigarette out of its box. 'I'm a reader. It's all about understanding narrative.'

They were different to how he'd expected them to be, they were more vivid. Della, with her dark red lipstick and her honey-coloured hair and Simon with his neatly ironed shirt and his gold-rimmed glasses, they were clearly defined people, the two of them.

Even the house was distinctive. It made an impression on you, from the glossy black door with the stained-glass panels to the chessboard tiles in the hall. The bright white of the

221

woodwork and the deep yellow of the walls. As Bruno was led into the kitchen he noticed framed prints lining the passageway. He would have liked to study them but Della was leading him through and he had no choice but to follow.

'Watch your head,' she called back to him. He ducked just in time.

The kitchen was at the back of the house, a big open space with sliding doors on to the garden. It was Addie who had designed this extension. Bruno stood for a moment and looked around him, registering with respect the results of her work. What a wonderful thing it must be, he thought, to see your ideas turned into reality.

Framed paintings by the children covered one wall of the room, a large laminated map of the world covered another. There were small plastic pegs sticking out of some of the countries. Bruno noticed one sticking out of New York and wondered, was that for him.

Below the map, a long wooden table was set for dinner. There were bright pink napkins twisted into the glasses, a wide bowl of pink and red roses set in the centre of the table. Butter dishes, the surface of the butter smoothed over with a knife.

The girls had made place names, they'd decorated Bruno's with the Stars and Stripes. Addie's was adorned with love hearts. They were all giggling as they showed it to her, putting their hands up to their mouths and wriggling with suppressed laughter.

'You rats,' said Addie. 'Just wait until you're teenagers, I'll get my own back on you.'

Even Lola had a place setting. They'd decorated it with paw

prints and propped it beside a pudding bowl of water that had been placed on the floor.

Addie was proud of them as she made the introductions. Polite kids, for all their high spirits, they knew how to behave. 'Nice to meet you, Bruno,' said Elsa very formally, her shoulders bunching in her shyness.

Bruno replied with equal formality. 'Nice to meet you, Elsa.'

Once they'd all told him their names he wanted to see if he could remember them. They crowded around him expectantly.

'Now let me see,' he said, pointing at the nearest one. 'You're Tess.'

She blushed, shaking her head.

'No!' said her sister. 'I'm Tess!'

'Forgive me, Tess.' He turned to the first one again. 'That means you must be Stella.'

She nodded vigorously. 'We all got our names from books,' she said. 'My real name's Estella, it's from *Great Expectations*.'

'What a wonderful book to get your name from,' said Bruno. And Stella looked so pleased, she blushed again.

'I got my name from *Born Free*,' said Elsa. 'Elsa the lioness.'

Bruno made a little bow with his head in respectful acknowledgement.

'Lisa's the only one who didn't get her name from a book,' said Stella excitedly. 'She got her name from *The Simpsons*.'

'A sure sign that the culture is in decline,' muttered Simon.

But Bruno nodded reverently, his face very serious. It was only his eyes that were smiling.

Lisa was standing in front of him wearing a swimsuit over a pair of wool tights, her stubby little legs planted apart on the

223

floor. She had a cloth swimming cap on her head, a pair of goggles strapped across her forehead. The goggles were so tight they were pulling her eyebrows out of shape. She was standing there staring at Bruno, and he realised she was waiting for him to say something.

Bruno took a deep breath.

'Lisa Simpson,' he said, 'is one of the great characters of modern fiction. A truly heroic figure, you should consider yourself very lucky to be named after her.'

Lisa stared at him for a second, then turned and ran out of the kitchen.

'We let the kids choose her name,' said Della, setting a glass of wine down on the table in front of Bruno. 'I don't know what we were thinking.'

'Four kids in five years,' said Simon, pushing his glasses back up the bridge of his nose. 'Clearly, we weren't thinking.'

Della raised her eyes up to heaven.

'Don't mind him,' she said. 'He's exaggerating.'

Della stood out in the garden while she smoked her cigarette. Through the open doors she could see them all sitting round the table. Simon had his back to her. He was tipping back in his chair, God she wished he wouldn't do that. Addie and Bruno were sitting side by side, he was leaning forward and speaking to Simon. He had his hand on Addie's thigh.

She couldn't hear what it was that he was saying. But she could see his face, the honest enthusiasm of him. She liked him already, she liked him very much. She was so relieved.

She pulled hard on her cigarette, drawing the smoke right

down into her lungs. She was a bit over-revved, she was aware of that. She'd been talking too much. She was just anxious for it to go off OK, anxious for him to like her.

She turned and faced down towards the back of the garden. She needed this moment alone. Raising her face to the sky, she blew the smoke out in a slow stream. The trees against the back wall were in shadow, the evening was closing in. The garden was a living thing in the darkness.

'Do you mind if I join you?'

She turned round and found Bruno standing at the open door, framed by the light in the kitchen.

'I thought I might take a cigarette from you, if you don't mind.'

'Of course,' she said, rushing back towards the house. 'I should have offered you one. How rude of me, it didn't occur to me that you would be a smoker. Racial stereotyping, I apologise.'

'I gave up years ago,' he said. 'Haven't smoked in more than ten years.'

She was already taking two cigarettes out of the box. She was just about to hand him one, when she paused in mid-air.

'Are you sure you want to?' She felt suddenly responsible for him.

'Absolutely,' he said. 'I'm on vacation. It doesn't count.'

A click in Della's mind, a silent tutting. I hope that's not your attitude towards Addie, she was thinking. She struck up the lighter. Bruno leaned forward to take the light and she studied his face in the glow of the flame.

'I feel like a crack dealer.' She watched him pull on the cigarette. He had his eyes closed to savour the hit.

'Don't worry,' he said, 'I take full responsibility.'

I hope you do, she thought, I hope you do.

They stood there for a moment, smoking away without saying anything. Della was just starting to worry that it was turning into an awkward silence when Bruno spoke.

'You know Obama is a smoker,' he said.

'You're joking me!'

'They've managed to keep it pretty quiet. No photographs. But he's a smoker all right, Marlboro Red. Apparently he's promised Michelle he'll give up if he wins.'

'I can't believe it! How could they keep that a secret?'

'He must smoke in the men's room, no cameras. They're afraid it will get out.'

'They're right to be afraid. It's bad enough that he's black. If it gets out that he's a smoker, he'll never get elected.'

'I know,' said Bruno ruefully. He was holding the cigarette out in front of him, studying it as he exhaled.

'Personally,' he was saying, 'I think it's a good quality in a president, being a smoker. He might pause for a cigarette break before he presses the button.'

'Plus,' said Della, 'I hope you don't mind me saying so but he was just a little too virtuous for my liking. I much prefer him now I know he's a smoker. Now he's perfect.'

She was holding her cigarette right out to the side, as if it had nothing to do with her.

Bruno took one last, delicious pull on his. Then he bent down to the patio floor and stubbed it out in the grouting between the tiles. He straightened up, holding the squashed butt carefully between his thumb and index finger.

Della was watching him, smiling.

'Just throw it into the bushes,' she said. She tossed her own butt up and out with a flourish, then she turned to go back into the house.

'You're getting very skinny,' she said to Addie as they were making the coffee. 'You bitch,' she whispered, 'it must be all that sex.'

Addie looked quickly over her shoulder to see if Bruno had heard but he was deep in conversation with Simon.

'Well,' said Addie, sliding her glance back to Della. 'What do you think?'

Della looked over at him for a minute as if she was seeing him for the first time. Then she turned back to her sister. Putting her arm around her, she leaned in close.

'I think he's gorgeous, Ad, I think he's really gorgeous.'

And she meant it. For the first time ever, she was able to say it and mean it.

Watching them together, you couldn't quibble with it, they were perfect for each other. There was something innocent about them, their joy in each other, like childhood sweethearts. The way he looked at her, he was in love with her, no doubt in Della's mind. And Addie was glowing. Della had never seen her like this before. She looked like she'd spent the whole day in the sun.

There's no reason to worry, that's what Della had to keep telling herself. There's no reason why anything should go wrong. It's just because she's so happy, that's why I'm nervous. I don't want to see her disappointed again. I'm being over-protective, I'm worrying too much. But no matter how much she reasoned with herself, Della couldn't escape the sick feeling she had in the pit of her stomach. Something was telling her, this was all going to end badly.

The next time they went out for a fag, she decided she would say something.

The kids had all gone up to change into their pyjamas and Simon had cracked open another bottle of wine. Sunday night, it was most unlike him to let his hair down like this. But he'd taken a great shine to Bruno, they'd bonded over Bruce Springsteen.

'Not you too,' Addie had said, groaning.

'Did you not know I was a Bruce fan?' asked Simon, amazed. 'Slane Castle, 1985, been there, bought the T-shirt.'

Della was throwing her eyes up to heaven. 'The only concert he's ever been to.' She drew the shape of a square in the air with her two index fingers.

'I met him at a wedding,' she explained to Bruno as she handed him a cigarette outside. 'I gave him half an ecstasy tablet and we ended up having sex in a broom closet. I came away with the mistaken impression that he was a bit of a wild man.' She laughed. 'It's the only wild thing he's ever done in his life, apart from marrying me.'

She could just about make out that he was smiling.

They were sitting at the patio table, the tips of their cigarettes glowing in the darkness of the garden. The windows were big yellow squares of light against the black house.

'Bruno,' said Della, with sudden urgency. 'I want you to be careful with her.'

She stopped for a moment to take a drag on her cigarette, blowing the smoke out again before going on. She knew she was out of order but she ploughed on regardless.

'She's fragile, you know. She's been through a lot lately, I presume she told you?'

Bruno hesitated before answering. He felt disloyal talking out of school like this. He turned to look back through the glass doors into the house. He could see Addie sitting there at the kitchen table with one of Della's kids on her lap. She was twirling the child's hair in her hand. The other children were all sitting down at the table again, bathed in yellow light, their little faces glowing. A burst of laughter carried out through the open door.

Bruno had the sense that he and Della were out at sea, bobbing up and down on a boat in the darkness, looking in at the lights of the shore.

He turned back to face her.

'The baby thing,' he said. 'She told me—'

Della cut him off as he was still speaking, she was anxious to get this said.

'It took a lot out of her, you know. She's still a bit wobbly.'

'Of course she would be. To lose a baby . . . '

But Bruno couldn't finish the sentence. Fifty years old and all he could think was how little he knew about life. He felt young and green, he felt like an explorer who has wandered into the midst of a tribe whose customs he knows nothing about.

'To lose a baby . . .' he said. And the unfinished sentence was left hanging there. For a moment Bruno thought they could just leave it at that.

But Della wasn't the kind of person to leave anything unsaid.

Without taking her eye off him she tossed her cigarette end into the bushes.

'Addie's nearly forty, you know. In another eighteen months, she'll be forty.'

She was starting to get up from her chair now, there was something businesslike about the way she did it. She stood and smoothed her hands down the front of her dress, stretching her back as if she was yawning.

'*Not* having a baby,' she said, standing there beside the table for a moment, her head slightly tilted to the side as she spoke. 'For a woman Addie's age, not having a baby, it's a much bigger thing than having one.'

And with that she turned and walked back into the house, leaving Bruno sitting alone in the dark garden.

Della was definitely drunk.

Bruno realised that when she started smoking at the table. She lit herself another cigarette before she'd finished the one she was smoking. The old one was still burning away in the ashtray but she didn't seem to have noticed. Without saying anything, Simon picked it up and stubbed it out. Della reached for the bottle of wine and started filling up everyone's glasses, even though they were all half full. Addie shot a hand out and covered her own glass but Della was already pouring.

A few drops sloshed on to the back of Addie's hand and she licked them off.

She laid her hand back down on Bruno's leg. Straight away he covered it with his own.

'So, Bruno,' said Della with a dangerous edge to her voice. 'How much longer are you here for?'

Addie tried to remain impassive as she waited for Bruno to answer. She could have killed Della for doing this. But Bruno was the essence of good manners.

'My return ticket is for November fifth,' he said. 'The day after the election.'

Addie couldn't help but notice the way he'd phrased it. Despite herself, she found she was clinging to that little chink of hope.

'If Obama wins,' he was saying, 'I'm planning a triumphant return.'

'And if he doesn't?' asked Simon.

Addie was waiting for the answer when Della barged in.

'Would you *stop*! How many times do I have to tell you, Obama is going to win. Obama *is going to win*.'

Addie could have choked her.

But Della was right of course. There was an inevitability to it now, there was a sense of history on the march. Addie felt helpless in the face of it, like as if she was sitting on a rock, watching the tide come in. And when that tide went out again, it would take Bruno away with it. Leaving her back where she started. She could see herself already, alone on the beach with the little dog. She couldn't bear to contemplate it.

She snapped her head up and looked around her to see who was talking.

Bruno was explaining something about his job to Simon.

'What I do is kind of specific,' he was saying. 'I'm a bit like a guy trying to sell sandbags after the flood. I'm not sure there's much of a market for what I do any more.'

'That's the great thing about being a doctor,' said Simon. 'People are always going to get sick.'

Chapter 24

The whole world fell in love that autumn.

The air was crisp and cold, the sky blue. The trees every colour from brown through to gold. American weather, it was as if the glorious East Coast fall was blowing across the Atlantic along with everything else.

Della had a simile for it, of course. She had a whole collection of them.

'Poor old Sarkozy,' she said. 'Poor Angela Merkel. They all seem so dowdy now, by comparison. It's like we all went to the movies in the middle of the afternoon and spent two hours swooning over George Clooney. Then we came home and found the husband sitting on the couch with his beer belly.'

It was like the world had found a new lover. All of a sudden poor smug old Europe seemed so very down at heel. And America, the butt of the world's jokes for so long, was shiny and new.

But for once in her life, Addie had backed the right horse.

*

Never had Bruno wanted anything so much, never in his whole life had it seemed to him that one thing would make everything OK. That Christmas Eve feeling, the heart pumping with hope. And along with it, the dread of disappointment.

There was this one Christmas, he must have been nine or ten. He'd asked Santa Claus for a bow and arrow. It was his heart's desire, to possess a bow and arrow. And Christmas morning arrived and Bruno found a long thin package under the tree. His name carefully printed on the label. But inside the wrapping he found not a bow and arrow but a hockey stick. There was a handwritten letter explaining why it had not been possible to get a bow and arrow, why a hockey stick was better. The letter had been signed by Santa Claus.

Even then Bruno realised there was something familiar about the handwriting. The notepaper was exactly the same kind his mother kept tucked away in the kitchen drawer.

Bruno can still remember that feeling. A horrible grown-up sensation, the realisation that disappointment is an inevitable part of life. And the lesson he learned from it, that there's no such thing as magic.

Forty years later and here was Bruno, bracing himself for that feeling again.

'How about we go on a trip?' suggested Addie. 'It might be a way of putting in the day.'

And Bruno jumped at the suggestion, anything to fill some time.

'What about Glendalough?' he asked. 'I've been reading about Glendalough in the guidebooks.'

'Glendalough it is.'

They threw the dog in the car. As they drove, Bruno read out bits from the *Lonely Planet*.

'. . . the epitome of rugged and romantic Ireland,' he read. 'A deeply tranquil and spiritual place.'

'I'm not sure I've ever been there,' said Addie. She couldn't picture it in her mind. But when they arrived it did seem a bit familiar. The round tower and the elevated graveyard, she had a vague memory of running around among the headstones, a school trip maybe?

The familiarity increased as they drove through the village. The cramped hotel on a tight corner, the metal sign for the tearooms, the sign swinging in the breeze. The vast car park, almost empty today. A few hawkers selling leprechaun T-shirts and keyrings with sheep on them.

Addie felt a rising discomfort as they drove along the narrow tree-lined lane towards the lakes. She had a sudden desire to turn back, she was worried that this had been a bad choice, she was afraid it wouldn't be right. On this day of all days, it had to be right. If it wasn't right, it would be a bad omen.

As she swung the car reluctantly into the car park, all her energy was focused on fighting off this sense of impending disaster. Like a teenager introducing a new boyfriend to her embarrassing parents, she was possessed by a horrible, disloyal shame.

She stopped to take a ticket at the barrier, protesting silently at having to pay to park here, in her own bloody country. Her sense of outrage was compounded by the presence of a chip van in the middle of the car park, its striped awning propped open, a few forlorn wooden benches set out on the tarmac in front of it. As soon as Addie stepped out of the car she was assailed by a smell of rancid cooking oil.

'Looks like we have the place to ourselves,' said Bruno cheerfully as he set his backpack on the bonnet of the car and started pulling a jumper out of it.

Addie stood and watched him in horror.

'Tell me that's not an Aran jumper.' It wasn't clear if she was talking to herself or to him.

He couldn't hear her anyway. He was halfway into the jumper already, he had his two arms through, the next minute his head popped out the top.

'Nice jumper,' she said sarcastically.

But the irony was lost on Bruno.

'Do you like it?' he asked, looking down at his own chest.

And he looked so handsome in the jumper, with his wide open face and the beard and the glowing eyes, he looked so happy and so entirely unashamed of himself, that Addie hadn't the heart to pursue it.

'I do,' she said, smiling. 'I do like it.' She went round the back of the car to let Lola out.

As soon as the hatchback swung open Lola dropped down on to the ground. She spun around like a compass finding its bearings. Then she was gone, tearing off in a straight line towards the gap in the trees. She must have been able to smell the lake.

Addie locked the car and then she and Bruno set off after her, bumping against each other as they made their way up the narrow path.

*

They took the path along the edge of the lake, walking in the dark shade under the trees. Pine cones and needles underfoot. A light breeze whipped ripples on the surface of the black peaty water.

They were holding hands as they walked. There was so much between them today, all of it unspoken. Addie could think of nothing but the return ticket, she kept having to chase it out of her mind. She would have died rather than mention it. And Bruno was preoccupied too, a decision lurking around the edges of his mind, a decision he had yet to make.

Lola was weaving along the path ahead of them, her nose to the ground like a hoover.

All of a sudden Bruno stopped walking. He stood and watched her.

'Have you noticed her limping?'

'No.'

The way she said it, it was a question to herself, already there was a defensive note. Have I noticed her limping? Maybe she's been limping and I haven't noticed.

Bruno called Lola over to him. He crouched down and put his arm around her. Then he rolled her over on to her side, cradling her front paw in his hand as he bent down to examine it.

Addie was standing behind them, peering over them, trying to see what was going on. But her view was blocked by Bruno's back and shoulders.

He was hugging the dog's little body to him with one arm. With his free hand he was cradling her paw. She had her head turned to the side, her eyes wide and desperate. Bruno was bending right down over her, it looked like he was licking her. Addie was baffled.

The next thing Bruno let go of the dog, taking his hands away suddenly as if he was dropping something that was sure to shatter when it hit the ground.

Lola leapt up. She righted herself, standing there for a second to take stock of her situation. She was tilting a little on her four legs. Then she was off, scrambling up an embankment, sending a small avalanche of dusty clay down in her wake. Bruno raised himself up to full height, and as he did so he plucked something out from between his teeth, holding it up in front of him with pincer fingers for Addie to see.

'Oh shit! Did she really have that in her paw?'

Addie reached out to take it from him, placing it in the palm of her hand so she could study it. It was a giant copper-coloured staple, one of those things they use to seal cardboard packaging. It had Lola's blood on it.

Addie felt sick to the stomach just looking at it.

'Oh Bruno, the poor little thing, I wonder how long it was there?'

And Bruno put his woolly arm around her and told her not to worry. The dog was fine, just look at her, she was absolutely fine.

But Addie couldn't shrug it off like that. She was sorry for the dog, she really was, she couldn't bear to think of her in pain. But she was troubled too, she was upset that she hadn't noticed anything. I'm so bloody self-absorbed, she was think-ing. Thanks be to God Bruno noticed. And she couldn't help but think, he's a better person than me.

If there was a moment of revelation, maybe that was it.

This was a good man she had stumbled across. This was a man who would prise a staple out of a dog's paw using only his teeth. She took hold of his hand, leaning her head against his shoulder as they walked. She tried to clear her mind of everything but this one moment.

They came out from under the trees into a harsh light.

Towering over them on either side were mountains, Addie and Bruno were just two tiny creatures at the bottom of the steep valley, the little dog so much tinier still. They stood for a moment, their heads reeling as they took stock of their place in the grand scale of things.

Bruno surveyed the stony path that snaked up the valley. Alongside the path a stream of silvery water made its way downhill.

'Do we go up?'

Addie lifted her head, tracing the path up the rocky mountain. It seemed a daunting climb from here. She spotted a bench up ahead. It was much more tempting.

'Let's sit for a while first,' she suggested. 'My back is giving me a bit of trouble, I'm not sure how far I'll be able to go.'

Bruno whirled round to study her face.

'Again?' he said. He was all concern. 'I didn't know that was still happening. You need to go see someone about that.'

'I know,' she said. The colour was draining from her face, she felt clammy. But she was resentful of his concern. It had nothing to do with him now. Afterwards, she was thinking. I'll worry about it after you're gone.

They sat down on the bench. Around them the mountains made a huge deep bowl. It was a strange sensation, sitting there at the bottom, you felt surrounded. It was like sitting in the orchestra pit of a huge theatre. There was a feeling of being watched. Even though there was nobody else there.

Addie swivelled herself so she was lying down lengthways, her head resting in Bruno's lap.

This could be our last day together, she was thinking. I should be giving him something to remember. If I was Della I'd be leading him back into the woods, I'd be laying my coat down on the moss. If I was Della I would have thought ahead and worn a skirt, I would have taken off my knickers before I left the house.

Just thinking about it, Addie was imagining the sharp stones under her back. She was thinking about the awkward fumbling with buttons, the indignity of his bare bum with his trousers around his ankles. She was hearing voices approaching, imagining strangers stumbling across them in the act. She would never be able to do that, she was too shy. She was too tired.

She closed her eyes and savoured the hard wood of the bench against her lower back, the gentle pressure of Bruno's hand as he stroked her hair. She opened her eyes again and watched the clouds roll endlessly by. The beauty of the place was a roaring noise around them.

'The polls are opening on the East Coast now.' His voice cut through the air like a knife.

His own ballot had already been cast. He thought about it now, one little vote in a vast sea of votes, he had cast it out from the post office in Ballsbridge. He had prevailed upon the

240

lady at the counter to notarise the envelope. Just in case. No more could he do.

'I feel like I'm on death row,' he said. 'I feel like I'm waiting for an eleventh-hour pardon.'

A conversation like a dream, you could say anything you wanted to say, it didn't have to make sense.

'What's your death row meal?'

Bruno didn't even stop to think.

'Huevos rancheros, black coffee. And a cigarette.'

'Where?'

'I thought I was on death row.'

'No, you're allowed to say where.'

'Oh. Cabanas Zamas in Tulum, overlooking the ocean. After a swim.'

For once, she said what she was thinking. It flowed straight from her head and out through her mouth.

'I want to go there with you.'

There was a wistfulness to the way she said it, as if she knew it was never going to happen.

And she liked the way he didn't say anything in reply. This was one of the things she liked most about him, the way he never said things unless he meant them. He never said things unless he knew them to be true.

'You haven't told me yours,' he said.

'Oh, that's easy. Pint of Guinness and a pack of pub crisps. Sweeney's bar in Claddaghduff. After a swim.

'You see,' she said as he leaned down to kiss her, 'I'm a cheap date.'

*

They stayed up late to watch the election results. They made a big pot of coffee and they settled into opposite corners of the couch, their feet fighting with each other in the middle. They had a quilt to keep them warm, the dog nestled on the floor below them.

Addie was fighting to stay awake. Two cups of coffee but still her eyelids were so heavy, she could feel them shuddering down. She kept having to raise her eyebrows right up into her hairline to winch her eyes open again.

She was so comfortable, that was part of the problem. With her shoes off, she had her stockinged toes nuzzled under the rough denim of Bruno's leg, she had a cushion doubled up under her face to smooth out the gradient from the arm of the couch. It was hopeless, she could feel herself falling. She had no power to stop herself.

Bruno was surfing the channels, frantic not to miss anything. He was frantic for Addie not to miss anything, every time she dozed off he would poke her awake again.

'I'm not sure it's entirely necessary for me to know which way Maine voted,' she said, her voice slurred with sleep.

But Bruno wanted her to witness every second of this. Already it was clear which way it was going.

He woke her up to tell her about Pennsylvania but she fell asleep again straight away. He woke her again to tell her about Ohio. She opened one eye, she took in the on-screen graphics showing blocks of red and blue across a map of America. Red for Republicans, Democrats blue. It seemed to Addie that there was more red than blue. She fell asleep again.

When Iowa was called, she opened one eye. Bruno was perched on the edge of the couch. Like a guy watching a

242

football match, he had the remote control in his hands, he was leaning out over his knees as if he could throw his weight behind what was happening.

Addie was feeling shivery. She felt like she'd been taking drugs and they'd worn off and the hangover was setting in. She swung herself round and sat up straight. Bruno looked over at her as if he'd never seen her before. Then he looked back at the TV.

South Dakota, Nebraska, they were both called for McCain. More big red squares appeared on the map, they cut a swathe across the bottom of the country. The blue states looked small and higgledy-piggledy, they were all bunched together. It looked to Addie like the reds were going to win, but everyone on the telly was saying the opposite. There's a realization in the McCain camp, they were saying. It's only a matter of time.

Bruno's phone started going like a pot of popcorn, hopping with dozens of incoming texts. Until now it hadn't occurred to Addie that he had friends. She knew he had sisters, if she'd thought about it at all she would have realised that he must have had other people in his life apart from his family. She had never given it any thought but here they were now. With every beep, with every shudder of his phone on the coffee table, they were making their presence felt. They wanted to share this moment with Bruno, he was one of the people they felt they had to share it with. It made Addie feel like she had lost him already.

At four in the morning, the networks called it for Obama.

Immediately the screen switched to Chicago, you could see the crowd going wild. Everyone was crying and hugging each other and they were waving these little American flags against the night sky, it was the most beautiful sight.

Bruno sat on the couch with his eyes fixed on the screen, oblivious to anything else. He just sat there and watched with the tears pouring down his face.

Addie had her arm around his waist, she was hugging him to her, her face squashed up against his shoulder. You couldn't help but be caught up in the emotion of it, you'd have had to have a heart of stone not to rejoice in it. She had tears in her own eyes, a gaspy feeling in her throat. But in her head, there was confusion, she didn't know whether to be happy or sad.

She felt like an executioner hearing that the death penalty had been abolished. She knew it was a good thing, she just wasn't sure it was a good thing for her.

It was six in the morning before they finally slept.

After the celebrations. After they'd watched the Obamas come out on to the stage to the roar of the crowd, their four shadows falling long and dark behind them. After they'd watched the speeches and then the highlights over and over again. After Bruno had called everybody he knew, after everybody he knew had called him. Only then did they go to bed.

Exhausted and exhilarated, they had slow careful sex. Neither of them said a word. Addie kept wondering if this was goodbye. She was still wondering that as she fell asleep.

She woke before he did. She tried to work out what time it was from the light coming into the bedroom, from the sounds outside. She reckoned it must be mid-morning.

She knew she had to wake him. She lay there thinking about it. She started practising the words silently in her head.

Wake up, lazybones, she would say, in her most cheerful voice. Even in her head it sounded flippant, there was a defensive tone to it. Isn't it time you were up, she would say, you've got a plane waiting for you. She was still lying there rehearsing it when an alarm went off in the room.

The sound shocked her. It was a sound she didn't recognise, an unfamiliar tone, she'd never heard it before. She realised it must be the alarm on his phone. She couldn't figure out where it was coming from, she couldn't see it anywhere. There was nothing on the bedside table, just a glass of water she'd brought to bed with her.

The noise seemed to be getting louder. Bruno was lying with his back to her, curled towards the wall. There was no sign he'd heard the alarm. But then his shoulders moved, his head jerked back.

'Shit,' he said, 'is that the time?' And he scrambled out of the bed, climbing up and over her, like a soldier tumbling out of the trenches.

Addie turned over on to her side and lay there watching him. She was aware of the seconds passing, there was nothing she could do to stop this.

Bruno was bent over the chair where he'd dumped his clothes, fumbling in the pockets of his jeans. At last he found the phone, took it out and started stabbing at the keypad. Eventually, the noise stopped.

He looked up at Addie and saw that she was awake. She smiled at him, the very bravest smile she could muster. She tried to make sure that her eyes were smiling along with her face. He stared at her for what seemed like a long time. Then, without ever saying a word, he came back round to the bottom of the bed. He climbed up on top of it, scrambling over the covers and settling into the space he'd just left. Turning over on his side to face Addie's back, he pulled her in close to him.

Within moments they were both asleep again.

Chapter 25

Hugh's casts came off towards the middle of November.

His hands emerged all pink and flabby, like big ugly slabs of offal. The skin on them was dry and flaky, the hair thick and matted. Staring down at them in horror, Hugh was reminded of some ghastly fish that roams the seabed, a horrible thing with pink eyes and clammy scales. He removed his hands from his eyeline, tucking them in under his thighs. He couldn't stomach the sight of them.

He had always been so proud of his hands.

'Doctor's hands,' Helen used to say reverently, and she would bend down to kiss them, one by one.

The girls were all mad for a doctor in those days. It gave you a great head start, being a medical student, you were never short of a date. And it wasn't just the nurses, all the girls went mad for a medical student.

Of course the engineers used to try to get in on the act. At the dances, they used to put TCP behind their ears. By the time they were caught out, they might have made some headway, they might already have a foot in the door.

Hugh sniggered at the memory.

'You're a medic,' Helen's father had said, gesturing towards an armchair by the fire in his study. A delicious aroma of roast beef filled the house, a velvety smell of pan juices. You could smell all the different elements of it, the seared surface of the meat and the red blood trickling out into the hot oily gravy. Hugh's stomach was rumbling, he had to shift noisily in his seat to disguise the sound, afraid Helen's father would hear it.

To this day, he can remember every detail of that first meeting.

In the car, on the way to New Ross, they had passed through places Hugh had never seen before. Tidy towns with humpbacked bridges, red-brick houses with carefully tended gardens. They didn't look Irish to Hugh, some of these places, they had a look of England to him. Not that he'd ever been to England, but this was what he imagined England might look like.

He remembers now how young and poor he felt beside her. But he felt deserving too, he felt almost greedy.

She had a car of her own, that was most unusual. Some of the lads had the use of their parents' car, but for a girl to have her own car was unheard of. The only child of a country solicitor, she was doted on by her parents. She'd been to Paris and Vienna. She spoke a little Italian.

Her parents were both in their forties when she was born, they'd long ago given up any hope of having a child. Her mother didn't even realise she was pregnant until she was six months gone. When she did finally go to the doctor, it was because she thought she was dying. A tumour, that's what she thought it was, her belly all swollen up with it. But the doctor began to smile as he examined her, you could have knocked her over with a feather when he told her. She ran up the street to Eddie's office and he took the rest of the day off. First time in his life he'd left the office early, he treated her to a slap-up lunch in the hotel in Wexford.

Hugh had heard Helen tell that story so many times. Her face shining with the knowledge of a happy ending. That guileless certainty she had, the security of an adored child. She had brought such joy into their lives, she knew that and she accepted it without question. As long as they both lived, they only had to look at her and they were happy.

Gentle people. Genteel and kind, they welcomed Hugh into their home like he was one of their own. The son they never had. Helen's mother clucked over him and mothered him. Her father spoke to him man to man.

Amazing how clear that memory still was. Among all the things he'd forgotten. He could still remember his awkwardness in the face of their gracious hospitality. The luxury of the house after his student digs. The rich smell of furniture wax in the dark hall, the unfamiliar taste of expensive whiskey. The sharp edges of the cut glass in his hand. The silence when you set the glass down on the leather-topped side table.

He had decided then and there, sitting in front of that roaring fire with Helen's father sitting opposite him. The whiskey burning its way down his throat, he had decided, this is what I want for myself.

Never again would he go back to that dank farmhouse in Navan. Never again would he breathe in that stale air. The endless cups of tea and the snide questions they asked him, the barbed responses they made out of their slack mouths. He was tired of it all, he wanted nothing more to do with it.

This was the life he wanted. The quiet assumption that this was the way things were meant to be.

The memory ended abruptly and he looked around the room.

It was as if he was at the cinema. The film was over and the lights had come up again. He found himself sitting there surveying his surroundings. He was blinking away the memories, slowly coming back to the present.

A fine room.

That's what he was thinking as he looked around him, it had everything in it that he had set out to acquire. The mahogany furniture and the antique gilt mirrors, the worn oriental rugs. The bed jarred with him, it was time to get the bed out of here. High time we got things back to normal. His eyes wandered around to the far corner of the room. The sideboard and on top of it a silver tray, set with a crystal decanter of whiskey and a clutch of crystal glasses.

I got what I wanted, he thought. I got everything I wanted. Now it's me who's the old fart sitting in my study drinking whiskey out of a cut glass.

And yet.

There were shadows forming in his mind, a nebulous presence lurking around the edges of his consciousness. Something that was stopping him from taking any satisfaction in his achievements. A brooding thing, like a bad spirit. He had the sense it wanted to say something to him.

He was just about to grapple with it. He was sitting there with his head cocked to one side, his eyes watery with questions, when he was distracted by a noise from outside.

It was Addie coming back in from the beach, the noise he'd heard was the gate clanging shut after her. She came bounding up the steps, taking them two at a time. Her dark coat was flying open, her legs taking great lunging leaps at the steps. The little dog was scrambling awkwardly after her, climbing steps was a different affair with four legs.

Hugh felt his heart surge, just watching them. He was aware of an abrupt change in his mood. In an instant, the shadows were gone. She always had this effect on him, every time he set eyes on her his troubles vanished.

He could hear her turning the key in the lock, then there was a gasp as the door fell open. The scattery sound of the dog's toenails on the tiled floor of the hall.

Hugh sat up straight and turned to face the door. Shoulders back, he settled his face into an expression of bonhomie, a mask of defensive humour. Without even realising what he was doing, he was drawing a veil over his love.

'Your casts are off!'

He was sitting at his desk in the window, clenching and unclenching his fists. He had the fingers splayed out, he looked like he was counting something up in tens.

'Oh yes, they took them off this morning. Did I not tell you?'

251

She shook her head. But already she was wondering, maybe he had told her. Maybe she hadn't been listening, maybe she'd heard him and forgotten.

He was rotating his hands on his wrists now, drawing circles with them in the air. As he did so he kept turning his head from side to side to watch what his hands were doing. As if he were watching a tennis match. As if the rotations his hands were performing had nothing to do with him.

'Surprisingly hard to do, these exercises they gave me. Like standing on one leg and putting your finger on your nose.'

He kept having to start the exercise over again, his hands kept going out of kilter with each other. One would be going faster than the other, or he would notice that one had started to go in the opposite direction. He was determined to co-ordinate them. Good exercise for the brain.

'Let me see,' she said, throwing herself into the chair beside his desk. She held her own hands out, palms up, to receive his.

Reluctantly he placed his hands on hers.

She studied them for a moment, stroking them with her thumbs. Then she bent down to kiss them.

'Poor hands,' she said, her voice full of tenderness.

He had to resist the urge to snatch them back.

'So,' she said, still holding on. 'When can you go back to work?'

She was looking up at him, her face open and bright. He noticed, for the hundredth time, how beautiful her eyes were. The whites were perfectly white, the irises a deep grey, like the sea on a stormy day. He loved her eyes, not that he'd ever dream of telling her that.

Gently, he pulled his hands away from her and placed them

on his thighs. He rubbed them up and down a bit on the front of his trousers, savouring the feeling of repossession.

'Oh, I think it will be some time yet,' he said lightly. 'I'm only just starting on the physio.'

He began shunting some papers around on his desk, pretending to look for something.

'How long do you reckon?'

'For the physio?'

He still didn't look at her.

'No. Until you go back to work.'

He assumed a distracted tone as he answered.

'Oh, I should think it will only be a matter of weeks. It's entirely up to me to decide.'

And he started to hum a little tune to himself, anything to fill the silence. He was like a little boy when he lied.

Chapter 26

'He's been suspended,' said Della. 'Pending a hearing at the Medical Council.'

'No.' That was all Addie said. 'Please no.'

'Oh yes,' said Della. 'Apparently it's the talk of the hospital. The place is in uproar, if you listen to Simon Sheridan.'

'Ah no, Della, don't tell me this.'

Addie's eyes were welling up with tears, she had one hand cupped over her mouth.

But Della just kept on talking. The things she was saying were terrible things, Addie couldn't believe she was hearing them.

'There was a row in the operating theatre. Hugh wanted one of the junior doctors to do the procedure. But the guy didn't speak English properly, he says he couldn't understand what Hugh was saying to him.'

'Oh Jesus,' said Addie.

She could hear Hugh's voice in her head. Sink or swim, he

254

was saying. That's how it was in our day. How are they going to learn if they don't get their hands dirty? They expect to be spoon-fed these young fellas. Well, I'm not running a bloody crèche.

'He could be sacked, you know. He could even be struck off.'

Addie just nodded. She was sitting up very straight, her head held high, but there were tears streaming down her face. She felt sick to her stomach. She felt like she was standing on a rug that had just been pulled out from under her. She was falling backwards through the air and what she was thinking was, I was happy! For a minute there, I was beginning to think I could be happy.

'Oh Della,' she said. 'I can't believe this is happening to us.'

Della came over and she put her arms around her. Pulling her sister's tawny head down into the crook of her neck, she brushed the top of Addie's hair with her lips.

'I know, love,' she said, 'I know.'

But even as she was saying it she felt like a fraud. Her eyes were dry, her voice steady. She felt numb to it all.

She was stroking Addie's hair. Standing above her, she could see that Addie's roots were showing. A full centimetre of muddy brown growth before the honey colour of the dye set in. A single wiry white stalk sticking straight up out of her scalp, Della longed to pluck it out.

Addie was sobbing now, her shoulders rocking.

'I know,' said Della, resting the side of her face on Addie's head. 'I know.'

She could feel her sister's grief, it was like a wave of heat coming off her. Della envied her, that she was capable of feeling such pure sorrow.

Della felt nothing, just a dull ache in her heart.

She was just wondering how she would pull away when Tess came thundering into the room. It was inevitable that this would happen. Every conversation they've had for the last ten years has been interrupted by one or other of the kids.

'Mum?'

Tess was standing there staring at them, she'd forgotten whatever it was she had come down for.

Sometimes Della thinks there's an invisible thread connecting her to Tess, the most intuitive of all her children. When Della first opens her eyes in the morning the child is always there, standing right beside the bed waiting for her to wake up. It can be quite eerie.

'What's wrong with Addie?'

It was Della she asked, even though Addie was right there. That was Della's job, to interpret the world for them. To act as their intermediary.

'Oh, nothing's wrong with her, sweetheart, she's just premenstrual.'

A blank expression.

'Believe me, darling, you don't want to know.'

Addie gave a spluttery little laugh. She had picked up her tea, she was gulping at it. Her face was all blotchy.

Tess was still standing there studying her, scrutinising Addie's face for a clue.

Addie smiled weakly at her. Tess didn't smile back.

'I'm hungry,' she said. She had just remembered why she'd come down.

Della went over to the counter and started slapping butter on to cream crackers. She made a sandwich out of them, then another one.

'Here, one for each hand.'

The child took them and whirled towards the door.

'Wait, take the packet with you. Otherwise they'll all be down.'

Tess took the packet of cream crackers in her teeth and went crashing out the door. A thump as she tripped and fell on the stairs, the two sisters cocked their heads and waited for a wail that didn't come. Instead they heard her pick herself up and carry on.

'She's getting so big,' said Addie.

'More and more eccentric every day. She wants a cat now.'

The way Della said it, she might as well have been talking about a rat.

'Oh no,' said Addie. Her dismay was genuine. 'Not a cat.'

Della sighed.

'I know. She's been bringing home books from the school library. Facts about cats. All you need to know about looking after a cat.'

'Oh Jesus, Dell. Could you not get a dog instead? A rabbit?'

Della was shaking her head helplessly.

Addie's mouth was turned upside down in her distaste. 'Even a hamster would be preferable.'

'No. It seems it has to be a cat. It's OK. I'm resigned to the inevitable. My life is not my own, I know that. It can't be helped.'

'What about the fish? Won't the cat eat the fish?'

'There's always that hope.'

Addie glanced over at the fish tank. The water was a bit murky but she could see the fish lolling around in there. He was getting bigger all the time, it was a bit weird the way he just kept on growing.

'Do you think it makes me a bad person?' said Della in a thin voice. 'That I hate the fish so much?'

They were both looking over at the tank now.

'I really hate that fish.'

It was hard to feel sorry for him. Looking at him now, even Addie couldn't find it in her heart to feel sorry for him.

She shrugged her shoulders.

'When does the cat arrive?'

'Christmas?'

'I thought you were going skiing for Christmas.'

'We are. Maybe the cat could be here when we get back?'

Addie was dubious.

'It's not that far away, you know. Christmas.'

'Oh, don't say that, it's still only November.'

Della dreaded Christmas. All that effort. All those presents to think of, the false cheer. It made her tired just thinking about it.

'Have you thought about what to get Bruno?'

'For Christmas?'

'He is going to be here for Christmas, isn't he?'

'Oh, I think so. There's no talk of him going home.'

'Well then. You'll have to get him a present.'

It wasn't that Addie hadn't thought about it because she had. She'd already started worrying about it.

'I hardly know him,' she said. 'I only realised how little I know him when I started thinking about what to give him for Christmas.'

'Give him a voucher,' said Della. 'You can't go wrong with a voucher.' And she gave Addie a big wink. She took a wicked satisfaction in making Addie blush.

Della gives Simon a voucher for a blow job every Christmas. Sure what else can you give someone who earns half a million a year?

'What does Simon think?'

Funny how the tempo of a conversation can change. They were all businesslike now. They were talking about it calmly. The emotion was over and done with for the moment. Much to Della's relief.

'Simon thinks he should take early retirement. He only has a few months before he'll have to go anyway. Simon thinks he's mad to stick it out, they obviously have it in for him.'

Della was over at the kitchen counter again, switching the kettle on.

'And what do you think?'

Addie was wincing as she waited for her sister to answer, her heart in her boots.

Della had turned round again, leaning back against the counter while she waited for the kettle to boil. She was re-adjusting the hair grip holding her fringe back. Addie noticed it was a Hello Kitty clip.

'Oh, I think fuck them,' said Della casually. 'That's what I think. Fuck the bastards.'

Addie's heart surged with love for her.

'I don't see why he should admit defeat. He's a cantankerous old bugger and he's rude to people and he's got a nasty temper but that doesn't mean he deserves to be struck off. If he takes early retirement it will look like he's admitting he was wrong. And I don't think he should. I think he should fight the fuckers all the way.'

She had picked up a plastic tumbler and was watering the plants on the window sill. She seemed to have forgotten that she was waiting for the kettle. She started cleaning out the children's lunchboxes, leaving them upside down on the rack beside the sink to dry. It seemed to Addie that Della was always doing five things at a time these days.

'Here,' she said, setting some leftover grapes on the table in front of Addie. 'Fulfil a public service and eat these for me. They never eat the fruit I give them.'

Without even thinking about it, Addie started picking at the grapes one by one and popping them into her mouth. They were a bit bitter but she kept on eating them anyway.

'I thought you said he was in the wrong.'

'Maybe,' said Della. 'But that doesn't mean he should admit it. Anyway, he's too old to admit he's wrong. If he started, where would he stop?'

'Bruno says Irish people are always apologising, he finds it quite noticeable.'

'Well, Bruno's right, we spend our whole lives saying sorry. If we bump into someone in the street we say sorry. If we interrupt someone we say sorry, we're falling over ourselves to apologise. I've had enough of it. Hugh's right. Why should he apologise? He didn't *set out* to do anything wrong. It's not like he's an axe murderer or something. Like I said, he's just a cranky old bollox.'

Della does this sometimes. A complete turnaround. It's what makes her so exciting to be with, you never know what she's going to say next.

Tentatively, Addie gave her a little poke.

'You've had a bit of a change of heart.'

Della shrugged. 'Maybe I'm just bored giving out about him. I think I'm going to take his side from now on.'

There was a fierce expression on her face. She had her hands pressed flat on the table, bearing down on them as she leaned over towards Addie.

'We were brought up to be afraid of everything, Ad, we were brought up bowing and scraping and apologising to the world for everything under the sun. Well, I've had enough of it.'

She was on a roll now, there was no stopping her.

'I don't want my kids to live their lives like that, Addie. I want them to go out there in the world and believe in themselves. I want them to believe they can do anything. Fearlessness, that's what I'm trying to breed in them. If I can do that, there'll be no stopping them.'

'Della.'

'I know I'm ranting. Just indulge me.'

'It's not that, Dell. Look.'

Della turned her head round, just in time to see a small girl dangling in the air outside the kitchen window.

She leapt out of her chair.

'Jesus Christ!'

She dashed for the back door, Addie right behind her.

261

By the time they got outside the child had landed. She was standing with her feet firmly planted on the patio, and was busy untangling herself from a twisted bed sheet.

An unfamiliar child, Addie had never seen her before.

The sheet she'd descended on was hanging down the side of the house. Addie and Della craned their necks to follow it back up the wall. One, two, three sheets tied together, covering the three storeys of the house. And at the top, where the sheet disappeared in through a window, a little face was peering anxiously down at them.

'*Elsa!*'

Della's voice was a bark. She had her hands out to her sides, rigid with rage.

'GET DOWN HERE NOW!'

The face disappeared from the window.

A minute later they all appeared down in the kitchen. Their breathing heavy and uneven, their faces flushed with fear. There were six of them, including the two visiting children.

They tried to put up some resistance. 'We were just practising a fire drill,' ventured Tess. 'In case the house ever goes on fire.'

Della yelped. She held up her hand.

They stood there in a ragged little line and they took the scolding. Six serious sets of eyes fixed on Della.

Chastened, they scurried back upstairs to haul in the sheets.

Della waited until she was sure they were gone. Then she turned to Addie.

'Oh Jesus,' she said, 'what have I gone and created?'

*

When Addie left, Della followed her out to the car. She didn't bother putting her shoes on, she just came out in her stockinged feet.

Addie was turning the key in the ignition when she saw her sister bending down to peer in through the passenger window at her. Della rapped on the glass. Addie leaned over and wound down the window.

'I meant what I said, Ad.'

Della was leaning right into the car, her two hands gripping the open window frame.

'We have to stop being so afraid, Addie, we have to stop all that now. What happens with Hugh will happen, it's not the end of the world. There's none of us is perfect.'

Addie had tears in her eyes as she nodded.

'You're right,' she said. 'I know you're right.'

Della drew her head back out of the window. She straightened up again. Slapping the roof of the car with the palm of her hand, she turned and headed back up the path into the house.

Addie drove off slowly, tears clouding her vision. She blinked a few times to clear them but she was still having trouble seeing. She stopped the car at the corner for a moment to compose herself, then she turned out on to the main road. The steering wheel felt light in her hands, it was as if she was floating above the ground. She knew she should pull over but she didn't, she kept the car going towards home.

Everything looked different to her all of a sudden. The whole scene outside her window, she was looking at it with new eyes. It was the same but different in some way she couldn't identify. As if the world was a painting and somebody had just picked it up and turned it upside down. She couldn't tell yet if she liked it better this way or if she wanted it to go back to the way it was before.

She got stuck at the traffic lights on the canal. It was rush hour and there was a steady stream of people pushing their way home along the towpaths. People in dark coats carrying briefcases and laptop bags, people on bikes with reflector bands slung across their chests to light them up in the darkness. She watched their faces as they went by, registering a pang in her heart for each and every one of them. She felt their weariness after the long day, she felt their desire to be home. And it occurred to her, they were all of them only doing their best.

Suddenly it seemed to Addie that Hugh was just one person among all the other people in this busy city. He was just another face in the crowd, a stubborn old man in an endlessly moving world.

A dizzying experience, she felt light-headed just thinking about it. But for the first time in a long time her heart was light too. It took her a moment to identify the emotion. And when she did she was taken by surprise.

She felt sorry for him.

Chapter 27

Now that the casts were off, there was no need for Addie to stay in the house with him any more. He was well able to manage on his own.

'What about Hopewell?' asked Addie. 'Will we keep him on for a while?'

'God, no,' said Hugh. 'Hopewell is a thing of the past, I'm happy to say.'

'Do you mean he's gone already?'

'Terminated,' said Hugh. 'I rang the agency on Friday.'

Addie stopped in her tracks and stared at him. He was sitting there in the window, peering over his glasses at some papers that were lying on his desk. He had a sleeveless jumper on, a newly ironed striped shirt underneath it. He was doing his hand exercises as he read the document, opening and closing his fists in sharp spasms.

In the past Hugh had sometimes irritated Addie. He had provoked resentment in her, he had made her sad. He had tired her out with his rantings and his ravings and his endless rage against the world. But this was the first time Addie had ever found herself actually disliking him.

Was this how it was going to be now, she wondered. Now that her eyes had been opened to him, was she going to start noticing more and more things to dislike?

'I'm sorry to hear that,' she said. She found herself using a tone she'd never used with him before. He must have noticed it because he looked up from what he was doing, he stared over at her, waiting to hear what she was going to say.

'I'd like to have said goodbye to him. He did a good job for us, I'd like to have had a chance to thank him.'

'For putting up with me? Oh, you needn't worry. He did quite nicely out of the whole thing, old Hopewell. He was nicely rewarded for his efforts.'

It infuriated her, the way he said it, it made her so angry that she had to turn her back on him.

That man had cared for him for six weeks. He'd been paid for his work, of course he'd been paid. But there was more to it than that. He'd been kind to Hugh, he'd put up with a lot of abuse. Surely he deserved better.

'Well, you won't be needing me now either,' she announced. She turned to face him. 'I'll be moving back into the apartment now.'

'Naturally,' he said, and he didn't even look up. 'You mustn't worry about me, Adeline, I'll be well able to manage by myself.'

And that was it.

If Addie was expecting any thanks from him, she wasn't getting it. It would have been impossible for him to thank her.

*

Bruno gave up his room in the B&B. There was no point in him paying for it any more, he was never there.

'You might as well stay with me,' said Addie, careful in the words she was employing. There was no talk of them moving in together, they weren't living with each other or anything. He was just staying with her, that was all.

'Is this really where you live?'

He was standing in the living room, looking around him with wide eyes.

She'd been nervous about bringing him here, she'd felt self-conscious about it. As if she was taking her clothes off in front of him again for the first time. As long as they were camping in Hugh's basement, they were in a neutral space. But this was her place. It said things about her in a way that Hugh's basement didn't. This apartment was like a scrapbook of her life, now she was inviting him to look through it.

She looked over at him anxiously.

'I don't know what to say,' he said. 'It's amazing.'

You weren't expecting it, when you came in off the street.

You came in through the front door into a dark windowless hall, a long corridor with four doors off it. The most ordinary apartment corridor you could imagine, wall-to-wall carpeting and light switches and recessed ceiling lights. A half-open door to the right revealed a galley kitchen. Down the corridor to the left you would expect to find a bathroom and a bedroom. So the living room must be straight ahead.

But when you stepped through the living-room door it was like walking out on to a ledge over a great canyon. You found yourself standing in a huge white room, floor-to-ceiling glass windows running the whole length of the apartment. Outside the windows, a dizzying quantity of water and air.

Bruno walked over and stood at the glass, looking out.

'You can go outside. Over there to the right. Look, there's a door.'

She went over and opened it for him and together they stepped out on to the narrow balcony.

Opposite them, an old mill rose up out of the water, the painted name of the bakery still legible on the grey stone. There were other buildings too, smaller ones. Stone ware-houses, old grain stores.

'What is this place?' asked Bruno.

Addie laughed. 'It's the Grand Canal Basin.' She pointed to a low bridge on the right-hand side. 'That's the canal down there.'

Turning to the left she pointed to a bigger bridge. 'And that's where it flows out into the sea.'

A bright yellow boat appeared from under the bridge, packed with people. Most of them seemed to be wearing Viking hats. You could just about make out the commentary, a tour guide in a brown monk's habit talking to them over a PA system. His voice was being thrown about by the wind.

The boat passed in front of Addie's balcony and all the heads turned. The tour guide said something and the next thing they all gave a big Viking roar, some of them shook their fists at Addie and Bruno.

Addie and Bruno roared back, waving their fists furiously.

Bruno was still laughing as the boat made a slow turn in the water and ploughed on across the far side of the basin.

'I love it! When do they come by again?'

'Oh, every hour,' she said. 'Sometimes twice an hour. The novelty of it wears off.'

He bent down. She thought he was going to kiss her but instead he leaned in and whispered in her ear.

'I'm not so sure it does.'

'Is there enough room, do you think?'

When she came into the room he was standing in front of the open wardrobe, staring inside. He looked puzzled.

There was a lot of empty space. He'd never met a woman before who had empty space in her wardrobe.

Addie came and stood beside him, both of them peering in.

He had a whole half a wall to work with, five empty shelves and a twelve-inch hanging rail. He looked down at the rucksack at his feet, then he looked back up at Addie.

'OK,' she said. 'There's enough room.'

She was as nervous as a cat, she couldn't stay still.

'I think I might go for a swim if you don't mind, let you settle in by yourself.'

Already she was grabbing her swimming bag. She was out of the room before he could answer. He threw his rucksack into the bottom of the wardrobe and closed the door. As he sat down on the bed he heard the latch of the front door clicking shut.

A static silence in her wake.

*

The swimming pool is Addie's refuge, it's the place where she's always been happiest.

She loves the artificial blue of the water and the wobble of the mosaic floor. She loves the way the sunlight falls in sloping oblong blocks through the windows, the way it lights up the particles of dust under the water. She loves the booming silence under there.

When she arrives she allows herself to sit for a moment on the edge, her toes clenching the bar, her knees drawn up to her chest. She pulls her swimming hat down over her ears. She wears one of those old-fashioned hats with the plastic flowers on them. She has a whole collection of them. You have to buy them in the chemist, the sports shops don't stock them any more. They're more comfortable than the modern cloth hats, they don't slip and slide all over the place as you're swimming, they stay firmly in place. The only problem is that the rubber seal leaves an imprint across your forehead that lasts for hours. Addie ends up walking around looking like a freak but she doesn't care.

She lowers herself into the water, shuddering as she dips her shoulders below the surface. This end of the pool is in shadow and it feels chilly. She adjusts her goggles and bobs her head under to test if they're keeping the water out. Then she launches herself off the wall. Gliding under the surface in a deep breaststroke, she keeps her eyes open the whole time, making the stroke as long and strong as she can, prolonging the moment until she's forced to come up for air.

Then she dips down again, coursing through the water, kicking out with her legs like a frog. Charlie Chaplin feet, that's what her swimming teacher told them. Addie has never

forgotten it. Funny the way those things stay with you for
ever.

By the third stroke she's in the light, swimming through
liquid sunshine, the shafts of golden sun illuminating the particles of dust suspended in the water. She pushes her hands
through the light-drenched water, turning her head to the
side as she swims so she can watch her arms moving through
the illumination and back into the shadows. She passes one
more window, swimming through one more magical block of
sunshine before she reaches the far wall. Then she turns and
swims back. She does this over and over again.

It used to be that she could swim forty lengths no bother,
some days she would find herself doing fifty without a
thought. These days she's struggling after twenty. It's because
I haven't been coming often enough, she tells herself, it's
because I've been swimming so much in the sea. Old age, she
thinks, I'm going to be thirty-nine in a few weeks. Maybe my
stamina isn't what it used to be.

She stops to rest after twenty laps, drapes her arms over the
bar and pushes her chest forward, savouring the stretch in her
spine.

Slowly, she labours her way through another ten lengths.

The old ladies in the changing room were all talking about
books. From what Addie could tell, they were all in the same
book club.

'Did you not find the sexual violence a bit distressing?' one
old lady was saying, her head bent over to towel-dry her hair.

'Funny, that didn't bother me,' said another one. She was

standing in front of the hand dryer, holding her towel wide open and letting the warm air blow-dry her body. 'I liked the girl in it,' she was saying, her thin voice rising over the noise of the dryer. 'She had a bit of spunk.'

Addie loves these old ladies, she loves their ways.

She loves their lumpy old-lady swimsuits and their chicken-flesh legs. Their leathery chests and their freckled arms. She loves to watch the way they rub body lotion all over their skin. The way they painstakingly style their flyaway hair. They're brave women, Addie admires them. She aims to be like them when she's old.

'I don't know why I bother,' one old lady was saying. She was sitting at the mirror, carefully applying a coral shade of lipstick to her vanished lips. 'I'm going straight home, I don't know who I think is going to see me.'

'Oh, you always feel better with the lipstick on,' said another one as she pulled up her tights. 'It never fails.'

Addie was still smiling as she made her way out to the car.

Pool or sea, he asked, when she came back in the door, her hair wet and scraggly. She had two deep ridges across her fore-head from the cap, an imprint around her eyes from the goggles. She looked like an owl who'd been caught out in the rain.

She held her arm out for him to sniff. Instead, he licked her, wincing at the sharp taste of the chlorine.

He was standing at the cooker, stirring a little pot with a metal spoon. A sweet smell of tomatoes, something salty in there too.

'Pasta puttanesca,' he said, 'one of my specialities.'

She settled herself on to the high stool in the kitchen. She liked to keep him company while he cooked.

It was getting dark so early now, the water of the basin was black outside the window, the buildings huge dark slabs against the dark sky. The kitchen was like a TV in a darkened room. The yellow light over the cooker, the radio turned on low, a man with a beautiful voice talking about Chinese art. Addie's wet towel was steaming on the hot radiator. The dog was curled up on her mat at the window, her belly rising and falling in her sleep.

Bruno turned to say something to her. He was holding the wooden spoon in mid-air, drops of hot red sauce falling on to the tiled floor. Addie had her eyes wide open as she listened to him, then she threw her head back and laughed.

Anyone looking in at them from the outside would think, what a happy home.

Chapter 28

During the daytime, Addie was working on her swimming pools.

Using huge sheets of graph paper she would map out the pool from every angle. She would make 3D drawings and cross sections showing depth and width. Bird's-eye views to show the outline. Photographs of tiles and ink drawings of the colour of the water.

More than anything, it was the colour of the water that fascinated her. You could play around with it, you could make the water any colour you wanted, just by changing the colour of the tiles. Why are pools always blue, she wondered? And she couldn't think of an answer. So she designed pools that were red and pink and deep purple, their tiles the colour of tropical flowers. She imagined what it would feel like to swim in one of those pools. It would be like swimming in a sunset.

She made green pools too. Cool pools like caves, their outlines rough and irregular, their edges overhung with ferns and drooping fronds. Those were pools to swim naked in.

Pools like ice bowls, with leaves trapped inside them. Pools with steaming water like those lagoons in Iceland. Night-time pools and deep dark industrial pools like the basin outside her window.

'They're beautiful,' said Bruno when she finally let him look at them. A note of wonder in his voice. 'They're so beautiful!'

He had taken them out of her portfolio one by one, laying them out side by side on the floor. Then he had climbed up on to the couch to look down on them from above. He had looked at them for a long time without saying another word. Then he had turned round to look at Addie. That unsettling look again, he was studying her as if she was a stranger.

'You should be doing something with these,' he said. 'You have to do something with them.'

She blushed.

She turned away and started tidying up the loose sheets of paper on her desk. Her heart was swelling in her chest. Behind her she could hear flapping noises as Bruno gathered up her drawings. She took them from him without a word. She tucked them all carefully back into her portfolio, trying to hide her face from him. She was embarrassed by his attention, she didn't know what to do with it.

It was only afterwards that she came back to it. When they were sitting down with their dinner, she looked across at him with her big round eyes, her voice thin and brittle.

'Do you really think they're any good?'

*

The return ticket was never mentioned again, not directly at least.

'It's still George Bush's America,' said Bruno. 'Until January it's still in the hands of the enemy. It wouldn't be safe for me to go back there yet.'

The truth was that he was in no rush to go back. He was enjoying his exile status. The distance he'd put between himself and his country, there was a clarity that came with it. It was as if a wind had blown right through him, a dry wind that had cleared out all the dust and the doubt in his head.

'I like it here,' he said to his sister when he talked to her on the phone. 'I'm starting to feel at home.'

He had a little routine going. Every morning after breakfast, he would set off for the library. Strolling down the canal, he would hang a right at Mount Street Bridge, walking down the side of Merrion Square. Through the bustle of Nassau Street, Bruno would step off the sidewalk to avoid the clumps of Americans trundling into the gift shops. Up Kildare Street and through the doors of the National Library. The guy at the front desk knew him by now, when Bruno arrived he would always linger to talk. He made friends easily, he always had done.

Upstairs in the reading room he would settle himself down at an empty desk. As he untangled his laptop cables and assembled his workspace, he would glance around, nodding at some of the regulars, the same faces day after day. Bruno began to be familiar with their habits. He found himself wondering about the nature of their work.

There was a straight-backed woman with a twist of dark red hair that tumbled down her spine into a smooth pool on the seat of her chair. A very old gentleman in tweeds who tapped furiously with one finger on a laptop all day. There was an acne-scarred teenager with fair spiked hair who was always hunched over his desk, making careful notes in a large hard-backed notebook. Bruno noticed with interest that he wrote in landscape orientation rather than portrait. Another guy had a scraggly goatee and a ring in his nose. He did nothing but read all day. Bruno never saw him write anything down.

These were Bruno's colleagues now, they were all part of the same silent community.

Before he turned his attention to his work, Bruno would sit for a moment and savour the smell of leather and old wood. He would allow his eyes to wander over the naked cherubs that adorned the base of the domed ceiling, his gaze resting on the golden roman numerals that marked out the bookcases. The pale blue of the paintwork, the hue of a bygone era.

It always took him a while to get used to the hum of the generator. The creaking chairs, the occasional coughs and yawning stretches from his companions. The scratching sound of pencil nibs on paper. The library was a silent haven of lead and wood and leather and paper. To be here was a miracle to Bruno, he was happy just to be here.

He would unfold the family tree, spreading it out flat on the desk and allowing his eyes to wander over the page.

There was an alchemy involved in this work, there was the potential for some magic. If you collected enough facts, there was the possibility of conjuring some life out of them. All of a sudden a story would rise up, like a vaporous cloud that has been produced by mixing two chemicals together in a laboratory. And Bruno was the magician, he was the one bringing his ancestors back to life.

He had tripped across his great-grandmother's story by accident. He had discovered her name on his grandfather's birth certificate, he had hunted down the date of her marriage. Nora Boylan, that was her name, she had been born a Maguire. Her birth date was given as 1850. But try as he would he wasn't able to locate it in the church records, there was no trace of her.

The birth dates are unreliable, he was told. 'Women regularly lied about their age. When she was getting married, she might have told a little white lie. If she said she was thirty the chances are she was probably a bit older.'

It was pleasing to Bruno, the thought of that lie. It brought a smile to his face. He had an image of Nora, closer to forty than she was to thirty. She was standing before the altar, her intended husband next to her. She was holding her breath as the priest read out the vows, another moment and her spinsterhood would be safely behind her. That little white lie was the only price she would have to pay. She wouldn't even bother to mention it in confession.

Over a century later, her chivalrous great-grandson made a decision to protect her secret. He wrote her name down carefully in black ink on his tree, inscribing her dates faithfully below. Born 1850. Died 1898. He drew a frame around her name, connecting it up with double lines to John Boylan's name. Dropping down out of their union, three sons.

James, John and Patrick. She died the year Patrick was born, maybe she died in childbirth. Maybe she was too old to be having another baby.

He stared down at what he had achieved so far, trying to imagine the lives concealed behind all those names and dates. There were more stories there, he knew there had to be countless more stories.

He just didn't know where to find them.

'Hugh would die if he thought you had him on your family tree.'

He hadn't even noticed that she was standing behind him, he'd been so lost in his work. He was holding a tiny oval picture of Hugh between his fingers, pasting it carefully on to the page.

'He'd have a fit if he could see it!'

Bruno didn't even look up.

'That may be,' he said calmly. 'But it doesn't change anything. He belongs here whether he likes it or not.'

Using his middle finger he pressed the photograph down on to the paper.

He had assembled a lot of the names by now, he had most of the dates. He'd spent hours trawling the register of births, working painstakingly back through the years generation by generation. Chasing down birth certificates and marriage records. Plucking facts from the air like late-season fruit.

He had borrowed some photographs from Addie and brought them down to the newsagent's in the village to have them colour-copied. Then he'd trimmed them until they were just a little cameo of the face, like those photographs Italians put on their headstones. It gave the tree life, to see the faces on it. There they were, looking back out at you.

'Oh, I can't look at it,' said Addie, walking back over to her own desk and plonking herself down heavily. She gave an exaggerated shiver. 'It gives me the creeps. All those dead people.'

A cloud passed over Bruno's face. He was staring down at his work, his expression troubled.

There were still gaps in the tree and they were niggling at him. The more information he hunted down, the more glaring the omissions. He kept coming back to them, the way you can't help worrying away at a cracked tooth with your tongue.

'I don't know why he's so reluctant to help,' he said. 'All I'm looking for is his father's name. When he was born. Surely he would know that?'

'Bruno, would you just drop it?'

He shook his head in frustration.

'I don't understand you people.'

There was a note of irritation in his voice that had not been there before.

Addie picked up a thin paintbrush, carefully dipping it into a pot of turquoise ink. She ran the brush across the page, her head bent low in concentration.

Bruno was looking at her, waiting for her to answer.

She could feel an anger rising in her. Slowly, she brought her head up.

'What are you looking at me like that for?'

Silence from him, he was studying her face.

She could feel her jaw tightening.

'Would you stop looking at me like that! You're looking at me as if I'm an animal in the bloody zoo.'

'Well,' he said gently. 'Sometimes it seems to me you might as well be. For all the interest you take in where you came from.'

So there it was, it had reared its head. What she had feared all along. He was going to challenge her. She was not prepared to be challenged, she would turn him away if she had to.

She swivelled round in her chair, the hand with the brush held up in the air. She was pale with rage.

'Are you actually trying to be offensive?'

He seemed genuinely surprised that she would think that.

'Of course not!'

'Well, do me a favour and try to bear one thing in mind. You're not from here, and you don't understand what it's like. You're a tourist, Bruno. I'm sorry but all you are is a fucking tourist.'

He was listening to her very intently. That slow listen of his, he kept looking at you long after you'd finished talking, as if he was still taking in what you'd said. It was quite disconcerting. Even after all this time, Addie still couldn't decide. Was he very stupid or was he actually very, very clever?

'I bet you had this really happy childhood,' she said. 'That's why you're so keen on talking about the past. People who had happy childhoods always love to talk about the past.'

She couldn't keep the bitterness out of her voice. She was shocked by it herself.

Bruno paused to think. He was spooling his memories in his mind. And he couldn't deny it, they were all happy ones.

'Wait a minute,' he said, a confused look on his face. 'Did you not have a happy childhood?'

He sounded so innocent, it was ridiculous.

'No!' she said. 'I didn't have a happy childhood. My mum died, it was shit! Maybe that's why we don't like talking about the past, has that never occurred to you? We don't like talking about the past because it was sad.'

He waited a long time before he answered her.

'Addie,' he said. 'You're the people who survived the famine! Where I come from, that would be something to be proud of.'

She couldn't bring herself to speak.

She stared at him for a moment in stunned silence. Then she turned back to her work, bending right down over the page with her eyes narrowed and her teeth clenched shut. She sat there and listened, frozen to the spot, as he got up and walked into the kitchen.

At that moment, really and truly, she hated him.

That was their first fight.

Once they got safely beyond it, they seemed to be in a different place. Like when you're playing a computer game and you move on to the next level. There was more bickering between them now than there had been before, but the tension was gone. Addie felt more like herself. She felt more like herself than ever before.

Every weekend, they drove out into the country. No

graveyards, she said, no long-lost relations. And he agreed to that, it was all out in the open between them now.

It was quiet, once you got outside the city, everything was slowing down for the winter. The pale wheatfields with their back-to-school haircuts, the colour of them a cool gold. The hedgerows were monochrome now, all the colour of the summer gone out of them. The trees were shedding their leaves late this year, it seemed to Addie. As if they were loitering to take full advantage of the thin winter sun.

Bruno insisted on using the GPS on his iPhone for directions. He saw himself as the navigator. He would sit there in the passenger seat hunched over his phone. Every two minutes he would call out directions that seemed to fly in the face of all reason.

'Left,' he would shout, just after they'd passed a crossroads. He wouldn't have even seen the turn, he was so busy looking down at the phone.

'I'm an architect,' she would say. 'I actually have a pretty good sense of direction.'

'It's definitely left,' he would say, in direct contravention of all the road signs.

And Addie would humour him. She would reverse and take the turn, ploughing down another narrow lane that she knew full well would lead nowhere but to another winding lane and another one after that.

They covered miles and miles of country, they saw places they never would have seen otherwise. They got lost over and over again, they spent whole days working their way through the back roads. A blind corner in the middle of the fields, a potholed road up and over a quiet hill, below them more narrow tree-lined country lanes. Until eventually they would chance upon the main road again.

As they drove they listened endlessly to Bruce Springsteen, Bruce was the soundtrack of their car journeys.

The lakes of County Cavan, the lonely hills of Laois. The woods of west Wicklow. All of those unremarkable inland places Addie had been so quick to write off, she had to admit to him now, they had been well worth the visit. The midlands and the heartlands and the badlands, in Addie's mind, they all blended into one. She was thinking like Bruce Springsteen now, sometimes she would even join Bruno in singing along.

If you'd told Addie just three months ago that she'd be spending her weekends driving around the midlands with her new love, singing along to Bruce Springsteen on the car stereo, she would have told you that you were cracked in the head.

'Well I've tried so hard baby
but I just can't see
What a woman like you
is doing with me.'

The three of them were singing together now. It was Bruno, herself and Bruce, in perfect harmony. Addie looked out the window at the wet fields as she sang.

'. . . the gypsy swore our future was right
But come the wee wee hours,
Well maybe baby the gypsy lied.'

Just weeks to Christmas, and they were both of them alive with a sense of possibility. The possibility that Addie might put all that fear and doubt behind her, that she might show her swimming pools to someone, that they might hang in a gallery somewhere, that some day somebody might even buy one of them. The possibility that Bruno might be a writer after all, that he might start by putting one word in front of another on a page. That together those words might weave themselves into a story. All of those things seemed possible now. More than anything, in those in-between winter weeks, there existed for both of them the possibility of happiness.

Chapter 29

Every Christmas, Simon and Hugh have a few pints together. It's an annual ritual that's quietly encouraged by Della. And never more so than this year.

'It would do him good to have a chat.'

'About what?'

'About whatever it is that you two talk about.'

'Grand,' said Simon. 'But I know what you're up to. Just so you know that I'm not thick. I know what you're at.'

'He trusts you, Simon, he might even confide in you.'

'You think?'

'He has to be worried. He'd be too proud to admit it to me, of course. But he wouldn't be human if he wasn't worried. Everything he's worked for is on the line. His whole life, it's hanging in the balance.'

'I don't see how I can help.'

'You're his only friend,' said Della.

'Ah, don't say that.'

'But you are. Sure who else would he have to go for a pint with?'

'You were sent,' said Hugh.

He sat down heavily into the corner seat. He paused for a moment to catch his breath before he started to wrestle his way out of his jacket. Unwrapping the scarf from around his neck, he deposited it on the seat beside him.

Simon was untangling himself from his own scarf and hat, stuffing his gloves into the pocket of his coat.

'Well,' he said, 'I wouldn't put it quite like that.'

Hugh gave an impatient snort.

They sat in silence for a moment until the barman arrived with the pints. Hugh delved into the pocket of his cords and pulled out a fifty-euro note. He always insisted on paying and Simon always conceded to him after a slight protest. A gesture of kindness on Simon's part, he knew it would only make Hugh feel old if he wasn't allowed to pay.

Hugh picked up his glass and took a long gulp. The head of the pint left a thick white moustache across his upper lip.

'That Guinness has been refrigerated,' he said, wiping his mouth with the back of his hand.

'The barman swore to me it wasn't.'

'Well, he's lying.'

'I think a lot of people prefer it cold nowadays.'

'Everyone except old farts like me. It's America is what it is, it's not Ireland any more. I should just accept it for what it is.'

Chance would be a fine thing, Simon was thinking.

'So,' said Hugh, looking Simon straight in the eye. 'I've a court date for January. And a Medical Council Inquiry as the icing on the cake.'

'So I hear.'

'My reward for a lifetime of service.'

Hugh even mustered a little laugh, he was trying to be jovial.

'No good deed ever goes unpunished,' said Simon companionably. 'Sure we both know that.'

They each of them reached for their pints.

Hugh tried out a more general opener.

'I don't know what to make of it all any more.'

Simon didn't attempt to say anything. He just raised one eyebrow to show he was interested in what was coming next.

'I've had a bit of time on my hands lately, Simon, I've been giving it all a bit of thought.'

He paused for a sip of his pint.

'The more advances we make in medicine, the further we seem to be moving away from any kind of an understanding of life. It's as if the science of it is taking over, there's no room for philosophy any more. Religion is long gone of course.'

He was shaking his head, his forehead furrowed, feigning an air of confusion.

'It worries me, Simon. It's a worrying development.'

Simon knew exactly where this was going. But he lied a little, out of politeness.

'I'm not sure I follow you.'

'What I mean, Simon, is that death is no longer a natural part of life. There's no such thing as death by natural causes any more. If someone dies, someone else must be to blame, someone has to be sued. And in our game, that's very bad news.'

He shook his head in despair.

Simon gestured to the barman to put on another round before turning his attention back to Hugh.

'My fear is that death is becoming a bit of an aberration. Every death now is a death that could have been prevented. I don't know where it's all going to end.'

'We're becoming victims of our own success,' said Simon. 'They think we can fix everything. They get angry with us when we can't. I agree with you, Hugh, it makes things very difficult.'

And he did agree with Hugh, to a certain extent. Everything Hugh was saying, you couldn't argue with it. He was right. And yet at the same time he was wrong. How could you even begin to explain it to him? At a fundamental level, Hugh was so utterly and completely wrong.

Simon didn't interrupt him, there was no point in even trying.

'Delaying the inevitable, that's all we do. That's what people can't accept, Simon, they don't want to accept it. But we know, we know because we deal with it every day. We know that death is just a natural consequence of life.'

Simon nodded in agreement.

'This kingdom of ours,' Hugh was saying. 'It is not eternal. And yet. People are starting to get the notion that it is.'

'No,' said Simon. 'None of us is here for ever.'

'Do you understand it, Simon? The anger! It's a rage they have, and it's directed straight at us.'

'It certainly feels that way sometimes.'

'Where does it come from, all that anger?'

'Denial,' said Simon quietly.

But Hugh wasn't listening to him.

'Grief,' said Simon, his voice tapering off until he was barely talking out loud.

He was looking Hugh straight in the eye. And Hugh was looking back at him. But you could tell that he wasn't listening. His expression was glassy.

'Love,' said Simon softly, just for his own benefit.

'You needn't have worried,' he said when he was alone with Della again that evening. 'He's not even contemplating defeat.'

Chapter 30

With Della, Simon and the girls away, it was just the three of them for Christmas.

Bruno had suggested that they cook dinner in the apartment but Hugh wanted them to come to the house. In Hugh's mind an apartment was not somewhere you could have a Christmas dinner. An apartment was somewhere you served cocktails maybe, but not proper food. 'Let's humour him,' said Addie, for the umpteenth time in her life. 'That way we can escape whenever we want.

'We'd better order the turkey,' said Addie. 'Do they even make turkeys that small?'

Hugh looked at her over the rim of his glasses.

'Oh, I think a chicken will suffice.'

They were all of them nervous. They'd left it too long, the meeting. It was crazy to have left it so long. A head of steam had built up behind it. And now it had all the emotional weight of Christmas with it too.

'Do I buy him a gift?' Bruno had asked.

'Oh Lord no,' said Addie. 'Sure you've never even met him.'

She had visions of Bruno browsing the menswear department in Brown Thomas. She imagined him holding up scarves, the salesperson helpfully sliding open drawers of leather gloves. Outside it was snowing, like Christmas in the movies. Bruno was walking down the street, his face obscured by the stack of gift boxes he was carrying.

'But I can't go to his house at Christmas without bringing him a gift,' said Bruno. He seemed shocked at the thought.

A bottle of wine was settled upon. Addie even allowed Bruno to gift-wrap it.

'I wish we didn't have to go. If only we could stay in bed all day, we could have cereal for our Christmas dinner and not get dressed and not see anyone.'

'But we could do that any day,' said Bruno. 'This is Christmas.'

There was something childlike about the way he said it. She was sad for him that she couldn't offer him more. For Bruno's sake, she found herself wishing that she was the kind of girl who had a Christmas outfit all planned. She imagined herself in a cream lace blouse and a black velvet skirt with a cummerbund and black tights and high heels. She pictured a traditional family reunion, a big gaggle of old people and young people and children, all of them going to Mass together. Afterwards there would be a ritual present-giving around the tree, champagne in flutes and the smell of turkey roasting in the oven.

'We couldn't leave him alone at Christmas,' said Bruno.

'And anyway,' he said, 'I've been waiting to meet him for months. I wouldn't miss it for the world.'

Needless to say they got on like a house on fire.

Despite all of Addie's worst fears, despite all of Hugh's prejudices, they hit it off right from the start.

Addie and Bruno had arrived a little early. She gave a ring on the doorbell, just to warn him they were there. Then she leaned in to open the door with her key.

He must have been waiting for them. Just as she stuck the key into the lock, the door swung open and Hugh emerged out of the shadows. Addie nearly lost her balance. Lola shot past her through the open door.

'Good God,' said Hugh. 'That bloody dog! Hold on a minute,' he said, his voice coming out of the darkness. 'Let me throw some light on the situation.'

He delved behind the door and found the switch. Then he swung back around to face them, like a sumo wrestler preparing for a fight.

Bruno stepped forward, holding his hand straight out in front of him. 'It's very nice to meet you,' he said. 'Sir.'

And that was all it took. Just that one little three-letter word and, as if by magic, Hugh was defused.

All his life, he'd been waiting for someone to call him sir.

He wasn't at all what Bruno had been expecting.

He was taller, for one thing. For some reason Bruno had assumed he would be small and solid. Perhaps because Addie and Della were both so tiny, Bruno had assumed he would be a stocky little man.

He was younger too, in his demeanour he was young and vibrant. All those weeks Addie had been caring for him, Bruno had pictured an invalid. He had imagined him as an elderly person. But there was nothing elderly about Hugh. He was almost boyish.

He had a spring in his step, a bounce about him that spoke of youthful energy. He was self-possessed, an air of certainty emanated from him, an aura of innate authority. This was a man who liked to be in command of things.

But it was the eyes that disarmed Bruno the most. As he stood on the doorstep holding out his hand to Hugh for that first handshake, Bruno was taken by surprise. He hadn't been expecting to see his own father's eyes looking right back at him.

'I must say I'm delighted to meet you, Bruno. At long last.'

He had settled into his wing-backed chair, his whiskey glass balanced nonchalantly on his corduroy knee.

'For some reason Adeline has been determined to keep us apart.'

He was at his most devilishly charming. It was quite unnerving.

'Revisionism,' muttered Addie, narrowing her eyes at him. But he didn't see her, he had his face resolutely turned towards his guest.

'Addie tells me you're a banker. So you come to us from the eye of the storm.'

'Yes, sir, I'm afraid you could say that.'

'You don't have to call him sir,' said Addie testily. 'You can just call him Hugh.'

And she looked to Hugh for agreement. But he just gave her a gloating smile before turning his attention to Bruno again.

'Is it New York you're from, Bruno?'

He seemed determined not to acknowledge the family connection, intent on treating Bruno like a stranger.

'No, sir, I grew up in New Jersey. Springlake, New Jersey. The Irish Riviera, they used to call it. All the Irish used to vacation in Springlake. A lot of them had holiday homes there. In the old days, it was the place all the rich Irish used to go.'

Hugh didn't say anything. But Addie knew exactly what he was thinking. Maybe Bruno guessed it too, because he answered the question without being asked.

'My dad worked for them. He looked after their homes for them. You know, painting and general maintenance, keeping an eye on things when they weren't there. That's how he made a living. He turned it into a pretty good business.'

Addie noticed the unabashed pride in his voice. She cringed a little for him. He sounded so American, even the way he was telling the story was so unashamedly American. She was worried for him, dreading a backlash from Hugh.

But Bruno sailed on, oblivious to the danger.

'Actually, it was a guy from home that gave him his break. When my dad first came to the States, he let him stay in his house in Springlake that first winter. All he had to do was paint the place and fix it up a bit. That's where he got the

295

idea. All those guys, they needed someone to fix up their homes for them. And my dad was one of their own, they trusted him.'

Hugh was listening with interest.

'What a very American story,' he said, his tone a little scathing.

Addie was on the edge of her seat now, on red alert. She was about to jump in when Bruno answered. Either he hadn't noticed the edge to Hugh's voice or he had chosen to ignore it.

'Yes,' said Bruno cheerfully, 'a very American tale.'

Hugh seemed fascinated by Bruno. Addie had never seen him show so much interest in anyone.

'I understand you were the only son,' he said convivially. 'There must have been some pressure on you to join the family business?'

'Oh, there was, sir, there most certainly was. But Springlake is a pretty small town. To be honest with you, I couldn't get out of there fast enough.'

'Ha,' said Hugh with a chuckle. 'I know how that feels.'

Addie left Bruno sitting in the front room with a glass of wine while she went down to the kitchen to check on Hugh.

He was standing in front of the oven, a tea towel slung over his shoulder. He was peering in through the glass panel in the oven door. 'I parboiled the potatoes before I put them in to roast,' he said, 'a little tip from your sister.'

The way he was standing, she could see the bald patch at the back of his head. His shirt had slipped out over the waistband of his cords, probably because of his exertions. It gave Addie a pang, to think that he'd sought out Della's advice. Her heart suffered a little jolt, as if she'd been hit from behind, memory after memory piling up on top of each other.

He never used to cook. Before their mother died, he never had to. And even after she was gone, the housekeeper used to prepare the supper before she left for the day. She would leave the potatoes all peeled and sitting in a saucepan full of cold water. Three lamb chops set out on a plate, or maybe three pieces of salmon, with clingfilm laid carefully over them. Simple fare, it was all he could manage.

How Addie and Della had longed for a mother's cooking. God forgive them, that was the thing they missed the most about her. Sometimes they would come home from a friend's house, talking about some hearty meal they'd had. A casserole, perhaps, prepared by a stay-at-home mum whose heart broke to see those brave little motherless girls, how they enjoyed her food. Sure they probably never get a decent dinner, she would say to her husband that evening. He can't have much time to be cooking, when he gets home.

Hugh tried, he really did try. He would get the girls to describe those motherly meals in minute detail. He would try to work out the component parts, uncracking the recipe like a secret code. Addie remembers him standing at the cooker in his pinstripe suit, a confused look on his face as he struggled to reproduce a chicken and broccoli bake the girls had eaten at someone's house. Of course it was never the same. But Addie and Della would eat it anyway, for fear of hurting his feelings.

'Anything I can do for you, Dad?'

'Let me see. Yes, you could set out some of that brown bread. I have a platter ready for it.'

And he pointed at an ornate china plate, one of his auction house finds no doubt. Beside the plate was a packet of supermarket brown bread, ready sliced. Addie took a handful of slices and fanned them out.

Hugh was behind her now, they were back to back. He was stooped over the kitchen table, trying to extricate slivers of smoked salmon from a plastic pack. The slivers kept tearing as he lifted them out, he was forced to prise them away from each other with a knife.

He motioned with his head towards the kitchen door.

'I thought I'd better put up something traditional for our transatlantic friend.'

'Bruno?'

He'd disappeared. The chair she'd left him sitting in was empty. Addie looked all around in a panic. It was hard to get used to the room without Hugh's bed in it, it was disorienting. The couch had been moved back in and the double doors were open again on to the dining room. Addie walked through and found Bruno standing at the back window, looking out into the garden.

'There you are.'

The dining-room table had been set, a linen tablecloth spread out. Places had been laid for three. The silver salt and pepper cellars were out, there was a battered silver coaster ready to receive the wine bottle.

'Just like America,' Addie said, and Bruno turned round. 'What?'

'Oh, it's an old family joke. My dad used to say it apparently, when my mum would put a tablecloth out. He would say it was just like America. She used to tease him about it. It became a bit of a catchphrase.'

'Why America?'

'Oh, you know, sophisticated. Don't tell me you don't use tablecloths in America?'

'Oh we do, we most certainly do.'

'Oh good,' she said, 'you had me worried there for a second.'

'So,' said Bruno. 'You're a small-town boy yourself, sir.'

Addie snapped her head up to catch Hugh's reaction.

She held her breath, expecting at the very least a withering silence. But she couldn't have been more wrong. Hugh was smiling, beginning to unfurl under the warm glow of Bruno's attention.

'Yes,' he said. 'Except that the use of the word "town" implies there was some form of civilisation.'

They were sitting at the table now, eating the smoked salmon. Hugh had produced a bottle of white wine from the fridge, a crisp Sancerre. It was delicious.

'You're looking after us very well, Dad,' said Addie. But he hardly looked at her. All his attention was focused on Bruno, like a child with a new friend.

Addie felt the first stirrings of jealousy. They were both of them ignoring her. She might as well not be here.

'I've been there,' said Bruno enthusiastically. 'With Addie. We paid a visit.'

Hugh swung round to look at Addie. On his face, an expression of surprise. Why had she never mentioned the trip?

Addie was incredulous. The cheek of him.

'And what did you make of it?'

Bruno paused before he answered, searching his mind for the precise words he wanted to use.

'It's hard to say,' he said. 'I think I was looking at it through my father's eyes. Everywhere we went, I was imagining what it must have looked like to him. My father spoke of it so fondly. I suppose I was looking for something that would explain why he left.'

Hugh was listening intently, his attention almost aggressive.

'Maybe you can explain it to me, sir. Maybe you under-stand why he might have left?'

Hugh's expression was a mixture of contempt and pity.

'Jesus, son,' he said, spitting out the words. 'You wouldn't ask me that. If you'd seen the place fifty years ago, you wouldn't ask that question. Why anyone stayed, that's the bloody mystery.'

Bruno nodded, drinking it all in. And Addie should have been pleased that they were getting along so well, she should have been relieved.

Instead she felt betrayed by both of them.

'Do you think this is cooked?'

Hugh was stooped over the kitchen counter. He was peering

300

down at the serving plate, a carving fork in one hand, the knife in the other. The chicken was laid out already in slices on the plate, the legs and the wings arranged to one side. It did look a bit pink to Addie, but it was clearly too late to do anything about it now.

She summoned some false cheer.

'Looks perfect to me.'

Pray we don't all get food poisoning, she was thinking. She followed him back up the stairs, holding the gravy boat carefully in the palm of her hand. Instant gravy, from the smell wafting up off it.

'Help yourself to some chicken, Bruno.'

Hugh passed the platter across the table. They'd moved on to the red wine now. Hugh had uncorked a bottle of Bordeaux earlier, leaving it on the sideboard to breathe. There were carrots as well as peas. He'd pulled out all the stops.

'College was my escape route,' he said. 'That was my ticket out.'

It was Hugh doing all the talking now. Bruno seemed happy just to listen.

'It took me ten years to get through. I had to take every second year off to earn my fees. Medicine was the preserve of the upper echelons in my day. Still is, for all I know.'

And he stopped to eat a slice of chicken. Reaching out for his glass, he took a long gulp of wine.

'They'd never seen the likes of me. I still had the mud on my wellies when I arrived. They used to take pity on me, they used to invite me home for dinner, the lads from Dublin. I must have looked like I needed a good feeding.'

Addie was watching him in amazement. She couldn't have

301

been more surprised if Hugh had suddenly revealed that he could speak Serbo-Croat. This was a side to him that she'd never seen before. He was talking about himself.

'They were all sons of doctors,' he said, 'most of them were grandsons of doctors.'

He paused for another mouthful of chicken.

'I'd never even seen a doctor before, the one time I was sick as a child it was the vet was called out to me.'

And Bruno laughed. But Addie wasn't so sure it was a joke.

Touch of the *Angela's Ashes*, she was tempted to say, but she didn't. Instead she found herself asking a question. Even as she was saying it, she wished she could take it back.

'I always thought your father was a ship's doctor?'

She could hear her own voice vibrating from inside her ears.

'My dear,' he said, a dismissive snort in his voice. 'Have you not worked it out by now? There was no ship's doctor. How many ships do you think sail into Navan?'

By the end of the evening Hugh had the whiskey decanter out and he and Bruno were talking poetry. Bruno was talking about Robert Frost and Wallace Stevens. He was asking Hugh about Yeats.

'Forget about Yeats,' said Hugh dismissively. 'It's Kavanagh you need to read if you want to understand Ireland. Or Padraic Colum, even better.'

And he began to quote. Watching him, Addie was struck by how theatrical he was, he could have been an actor.

'O! Strong men with your best,
I would strive breast to breast
I could quiet your herds,
With my words, with my words.'

Well I'll be damned, thought Addie. I never knew he was
interested in poetry.

Chapter 31

'His mother wasn't married, did you know that?'

'I didn't. But I'm not surprised, if that's what you mean. It makes complete sense.'

They were sitting at Della's kitchen table, a pot of chamomile tea in front of them. Della picked the pot up with two hands and began pouring the steaming yellow liquid into their mugs.

'New mugs?' asked Addie.

'Christmas present from Simon's mother. She heard the company was going bust so she went tearing into town to buy up everything they had.'

'And we think our family is weird.'

'I know.'

'Well?'

'Well what?'

'I can't believe you're not surprised.'

'Oh Addie, come on. It's always been obvious he has

some kind of a secret in his past. He's ashamed of his background. Why do you think he never talks about his family, why do you think he never brought us down there to visit them?'

That voice Della uses sometimes, it's like she's explaining things to a simpleton.

'It never even occurred to me,' said Addie, her voice full of wonder.

'He has a chip on his shoulder the size of a house.'

Listening to her, Addie felt dizzy. How did Della know all of this?

Addie thought back to a summer she once spent Inter-Railing. With a few friends from college, she'd spent a month taking trains around Europe, that was what everybody did back then. An over-ambitious itinerary, you tried to see too much, you ended up seeing nothing. Addie got so tired from all the travelling that she kept falling asleep on the train. One day she woke up in the late afternoon to find she'd slept her way through Belgium. A whole country had gone by without her even noticing.

She had that exact same feeling again now.

'Why did he never tell us, Della? I can't understand why he never told us.'

Della threw her eyes up to heaven.

'I suspect you'd never get to the bottom of it.'

Why had he never told them?

That wasn't really the point, it occurred to Hugh. The why of it was obvious. It was what he had never told them, that was the heart of the matter. The what of it was too nebulous to tell anybody.

He was frightened of the dark. He'd never told anyone that. He used to creep into their bedroom in the middle of the night, he can still remember standing there on the creaking boards, pleading with them in a whisper. But they would never let him stay, they would always send him right back. They wouldn't let him have the light on either, they said it was too dear.

He can remember lying stock still in his little single bed, afraid to breathe. Outside his window, creeping country noises. The trees rustling and the cows breathing. Something falling over in the yard, a clatter as it crashed to the ground. An animal cry, something in pain. In the morning, the shame of having appeared to them, the wounded pride.

He didn't even like them.

He had always been made to feel like a stranger in that house. He had never understood why. The way she always made sure he knew how much she'd spent on his clothes, the way she grumbled as she darned his socks. When she baked a cake he always had to ask her before he could cut himself a slice.

The farm repelled him, he wanted nothing to do with it. His chores, he did them under sufferance and badly. The marks he got in school, they were further proof of his unwillingness to work on the farm. As if he earned those marks out of spite.

'Well, I only hope it serves you well.'

That's what she'd said when he got his Leaving Cert results. She'd stuffed the precious slip of paper into the envelope and handed it back to him. He'd been expecting no more from her.

That was when she had told him, that summer. She'd been worrying that he might need his birth certificate to register for college.

'There's something I should tell you,' she said.

Her glance was shifty. She was foostering about with some cutlery, making a play of polishing it. She couldn't meet his eye, she only looked up at him after she'd told him. His surname, he would find a different surname written on his birth cert. His name wasn't Lynch, it was Murphy. It had always been Murphy. She told him why.

Something righted itself inside him, like a stone settling on to the bed of a river. He was glad, that was his immediate reaction. He was glad she wasn't his mother. He needn't feel so guilty now for not loving her.

He thought of the English stamps on the letters that had come from her sister every month for as long as he could remember. He'd never bothered to read any of those letters, he'd just steamed the stamps off them for his collection. Most of the time they were just plain old stamps with the Queen's head on them. But sometimes around Christmas time they would be more decorative. Sometimes there would be a special edition issued for some royal anniversary or other.

Hugh had pasted all of those stamps into his album, never knowing what it was that they represented. He'd examined the postmarks on them. They were always posted in Reading.

An absent aunt, she was seldom talked about. Kitty was her name, she'd been in England for years. She worked in a hospital, that was all he knew. He'd never had any reason to show

307

any interest in her. He'd only met her once, when she came home for her father's funeral. Hugh would have been twelve then. She had hugged him outside the church. He had been embarrassed by the hug, she had held on to him for such a long time. All he had wanted was to get free of her.

'Is she a nurse?' he'd asked them afterwards.

And they'd laughed at him, the two of them. No, she wasn't a nurse, they'd said, she was just a cleaning lady. Had they meant to be so cruel? Whether they'd meant it or not, the memory of it was cruel.

She had died when Hugh was in his fourth year of secondary school. They'd brought her home to be buried, that was what she would have wanted apparently. It was only afterwards that he was able to make sense of the pitying looks people had given him at the funeral.

At the time of course he hadn't understood.

He never went back to visit them.

It seems unbelievable to him now. He searches in his mind for a reason for his behaviour but he can't find one. He tries to pinpoint what it was that they did to him that was so awful. But he can't for the life of him think of anything.

They took him in, they gave him a home. A childless couple, they must have hoped for children of their own. They would have imagined that this foundling nephew could fill the void, they would have been disappointed when it didn't work out that way. Even the lie they'd told him, it was probably meant well. It would have seemed like a solution that worked for everybody. You could imagine them sitting around the kitchen table and working it all out. May and Seamus would get the child they yearned for. Kitty would get a new life, free of the disgrace that she had brought upon herself. And her child would be reared within matrimony. His murky origins would be whispered about for miles around but never spoken of out loud. The child himself would be none the wiser. The road to hell, it's paved with good intentions.

Helen had tried to persuade him to go back. After they were married, she had suggested it to him several times. Gently at first. But after Della was born she brought it up more often, she was more insistent. In the end she gave up on him and went on her own, bringing the girls with her. It was never spoken of between them after that.

Helen had figured it out, he was sure of that, she had figured it out before he did. She understood him so well. It wasn't anger that was holding him back, it wasn't hurt. It was snobbery, pure snobbery that kept him away.

Chapter 32

On New Year's Eve they walked over to Della's house.

Lola was sniffing her way along the ground ahead of them. In the front windows of all the houses, gloomy-looking Christmas trees loitered in the dark. Nobody could be bothered to turn on the fairy lights any more. The pavements were littered with broken glass and Addie was worried that Lola was going to get some stuck in her paw, it was hard to see how it could be avoided. The street cleaners weren't back at work yet. Nobody was going back to work until after the weekend.

It was Della who answered the door. She was wearing a black sequinned dress that hardly covered her knickers. Black tights, black stiletto heels.

Bruno leaned forward to kiss her on both cheeks. He handed her the bottle of champagne they'd brought with them and stepped inside. Addie followed him in. She took off her coat reluctantly. Underneath it she was wearing her usual V-neck jumper over a T-shirt and black leggings. She felt like the babysitter.

The kids all came crashing down the stairs, one after the other.

'Addie! Addie!'

Tess was holding something in her arms, her shoulders hunched into her chest to protect it.

'We got a kitten!'

Lisa looked like she was about to burst. She couldn't keep still, she was jumping up and down on the spot.

'I love your outfit, Lisa.'

She was wearing her ballet leotard over woolly tights, her little legs rattling around in a pair of wellies. A tiara perched skew-ways on her head.

Addie crept forward to take a peek at the cat.

Tess offered her up for viewing.

'Do you want to hold her?'

'No offence, darling, but I'm not wild about cats.'

'I hate cats too,' said Elsa in her slow husky voice, her eyes sliding over to meet Addie's, her mouth twitching into a reluctant smile.

'Dad's allergic to her!'

'That's not good.'

'He says she has to go.'

'I don't think Lola likes her much either.'

Lola had gone slinking into the living room, her tail between her legs. She was sitting under the coffee table now, peering out.

'Don't tell me Lola is afraid of the cat,' said Simon, a dry laugh in his throat.

'Simon,' said Addie, 'Lola is afraid of her own shadow.'

*

'Well, did you go to the doctor?'

Della had been nagging her to go. 'You're in pain,' she kept saying. 'You need to find out why. There must be a reason.'

But pain, as far as Addie was concerned, was something to be ignored. If you ignored it, it would eventually go away.

'It's probably just wear and tear,' that was Addie's view. 'You know, the human condition.'

But Della was sceptical.

'I'm not convinced it works that way. Will you just go to the bloody doctor?'

And Addie had promised, she had sworn that she would.

Della brought it up again as soon as they were alone. The boys were in the living room at the fire, the kids parked upstairs in front of the telly. Della and Addie had come down to the kitchen to get some glasses.

'Well,' said Della, 'did you go to the doctor?'

'I did, but she didn't really say very much.'

'She must have said something.'

Della had kicked off her shoes. She was climbing up on to a chair, trying to reach the champagne glasses on the top shelf of the press.

'She said my blood pressure was a bit high.'

'Oh?'

'She took some bloods.'

'Did she say why?'

'She said it might help her figure out what's going on.'

Della handed the glasses down to Addie, one by one. She was climbing back off the chair now. Her dress was so tight on her that she was having some difficulty getting down.

She hitched the skirt up over her hips and hopped off the chair.

'OK,' she said with a sigh. It wasn't clear if the sigh was about the blood tests or the climb for the glasses.

'She said it would be a week or two before she gets the results back.'

Della shimmied the dress back down and climbed into her shoes again.

'Do you want me to ask Simon about it?'

'God, no!'

'OK. Well, I'm sure it's nothing to be worrying about. But it's no harm getting it checked out anyway.'

'Absolutely. You're absolutely right.'

'Do we need an ice bucket?'

'No, no. It just came out of the fridge. It should be cold enough.'

'We'll have it drunk so quickly, it wouldn't be worth it.'

Addie was just following her out the kitchen door when Della turned round.

'Try not to worry,' she said tenderly. 'They always say it's probably nothing but it doesn't stop you worrying.'

And Addie nodded, she brushed off Della's concern. But she was left thinking. Even as they were standing in front of the fire, even as Simon was unwrapping the foil on the champagne, there was something that had got snagged in her mind.

They didn't say it was probably nothing. Most definitely, the doctor did not say it was probably nothing.

The pop of the cork gave her a fright. She held her hands up in front of her, leaning away instinctively.

The others were all laughing. 'Happy New Year,' they chimed, and they leaned in and clinked their glasses together.

Addie got a bit pissed that night.

Della had put together an extravagant meal: six courses, each of them small and delicious. But there was a lot of drinking time in between and not much soakage. Addie could feel herself getting drunk but she didn't want to stop. Something in her wanted to let go of herself tonight, just to see what would happen.

Simon was in flying form, telling amusing stories from the hospital.

'Oh, we get all human life coming through our doors,' he was saying. 'You can't imagine, Bruno.'

He liked Bruno, you could tell. You could always tell if Simon liked someone, he was easy to read.

'The vast majority of people are hypochondriacs, Bruno, they're just time wasters. Ninety per cent of the people I see, there's nothing whatsoever wrong with them. And then there's the other ten per cent. The ones who come in with a lump the size of a football growing out of their head. And they're saying, sorry to trouble you, doctor, the wife made me come. But sure I'm grand.'

They were all laughing, Simon was the only one with a straight face.

'It's very depressing,' he said, in an effort to convince them. But they all just laughed.

*

For a long time nobody realised Tess was standing at the kitchen door. She was standing in the doorway, looking about her with wild eyes. Her hair was matted with sweat.

It was Della who spotted her. She went over and heaved her up into her arms. The child was so big now, her skinny legs dangled down past Della's knees. Returning to the table, Della flopped down heavily into her chair. She turned Tess round so she was sitting on her lap facing out. Della stroked the child's sticky hair, pushing it back off her face.

'Did you have a bad dream, doll?'

Simon leaned in towards her and blew gently on her face to cool her down.

Tess stared at him as if she hadn't heard him.

'Can you remember what it was in your dream? If you tell somebody right away, then it won't ever come back.'

She had her eyes fixed on a point straight ahead of her. When she spoke, it was a surprise to everyone. They all fell quiet and listened to her.

'We were in school,' she said. 'And the teacher was giving around these pieces of paper.'

Her voice was fractured.

'There was one for everyone in the class, it had your name written on it.'

She faltered, as if she wasn't sure if she was going to remember what came next.

There was silence at the table.

'You had to open up your piece of paper.'

Her eyes were wide open and staring. She was looking from one to the other but it wasn't clear if she was seeing them.

'The piece of paper,' she said, her voice wavering. She looked like she was about to cry. 'It had the date of your death written on it.'

Everyone's reaction was different.

Simon laughed, a yelp of a laugh. He was impressed by the dream, he was amused by it.

Della gasped. 'Oh,' she said, 'oh, sweetheart.' And she pulled the little body into her chest. 'Oh, you poor baby, that's so scary.'

Bruno was gazing at Tess, fascinated by the dream. That such a small person would come up with such a thing, he was amazed. He was remembering himself at that age, he'd forgotten how wide open your head was, the whole universe passing through it.

Addie was watching Bruno, she wanted to see his reaction. She wanted to see if he was as spooked by it as she was.

Maybe because it was New Year's Eve, maybe everybody was alert to the idea of the future, what the future holds. Maybe it was the unsettling lucidity of the child, the other-worldly voice that came out of her. Maybe it awakened their own worst fears. Whatever it was, they were all rattled by it. They were at that point of the evening, they'd already had too much to drink. They would either get drunker now or they would sober up. Everything seemed very serious all of a sudden.

Simon started to fill everyone's glasses and Addie jumped up and started passing around the cheese. Della made soothing noises to Tess. The child was curled in against her mother's body but her eyes were still wandering around the table, following the conversation. Addie watched as her eyelids began to shudder, within moments she was asleep.

Addie motioned to Della, keeping her voice low.

'I think she's gone.'

Della peered down at her daughter's face. Looking back up at Addie she nodded without speaking. Using her legs to push herself up, she struggled to stand, staggering under the weight of the sleeping child. She sailed out of the room, Tess's long legs dangling down either side of her like empty stirrups.

'Would you want to know?'

Della's face was thin and peaky-looking under the low-hanging light. The shadows under her eyes were accentuated, the hollows in her cheeks cavernous.

Nobody had to ask what she was talking about, it had been hovering in all of their minds.

'No,' said Simon. He was the first to answer.

'Are you sure? Think about it. You'd get a chance to do all the things you've always wanted to do.'

'I've already done everything I want to do,' said Simon decisively. That was the kind of mind he had, clean as a whistle. 'For this stage in my life, I'm exactly where I want to be.'

'Seriously?'

That was Bruno. He was looking at Simon in disbelief, his eyes searching Simon's face for an answer.

'Sure. I'm married to the woman I love, I have four beautiful children, I'm doing the work I always wanted to be doing. Nice home, nice car. Nice holidays. I'd like to have some more holidays, I suppose. Many more holidays hopefully.'

His glasses had slipped down the bridge of his nose. He

pushed them back up with his middle finger. A habit of his that Bruno had noticed.

Della kept up the interrogation.

'So you wouldn't change anything! If you found out tomorrow that you only had months to live, you'd carry on exactly as normal. You'd go into work on Monday morning, same as usual?'

Simon thought about it for a moment. He answered very carefully, putting thought into every word.

'Yes. I honestly believe I would.'

'Bruno?'

Bruno didn't hesitate, he'd been waiting for his turn to be asked.

'I'd go see the Northern Lights. All my life, I've wanted to see the Northern Lights.'

They had all turned to Bruno now.

'Where can you go to see them?'

Bruno had thought about this, he had researched it.

'Well,' he said, 'you can see them in Canada or Alaska. Norway is another place. But I'd go to Iceland. I've always wanted to go to Iceland.'

'I thought it was impossible to predict when they're going to happen.'

Bruno shook his head.

'Not impossible. But you have to be prepared to wait around.'

'But if you knew you were dying you wouldn't mind waiting, you'd have nothing else to be worrying about.'

'That's exactly right.'

Addie smiled at him. She was imagining him all wrapped

up in his padded coat and his hunting cap. He was perched on a little stool in the middle of a vast stretch of ice, staring patiently up at the sky.

It was Simon who broke her train of thought.

'And yet,' he said, 'we all know we're dying. It's the only absolute certainty we have. But still we don't do these things. Not until it's too late.'

Della started stacking their coffee cups up in front of her on the table.

'This is starting to freak me out a bit.'

She stood up.

'All I can think about is the kids. Maybe if they were a bit older I'd feel comfortable talking about it. But I can't think about it now, it gives me the creeps. I think we should change the subject.'

'I seem to remember you were the one who started it.'

'Well, let me be the one to end it then.'

'But what about me?'

They all turned their heads to look at Addie. She was sitting bolt upright, her eyes shining.

'I'd swim in more swimming pools,' she said happily. 'I'd sell my flat and I'd travel the world from pool to pool. I'd track down the most exotic pools on the planet. I'd make a list of them and I'd swim my way through them.'

She was picturing herself already. In her mind she was looking at an aerial shot of a grand hotel in Naples perhaps, or Capri. One of those pictures they take for the postcards they sell at reception. Beyond the hotel terrace, a row of railings gives way to a steep cliff, far below that again you can see the deep blue sea. The pool is a long turquoise oblong surrounded by striped umbrellas. Addie can see herself, a frog-shaped creature in a dark red swimsuit, moving through the pool at a slow breaststroke.

Even as she's thinking about it, there are other pools lining up in her head. An infinity pool in Cabo San Lucas, the Pacific Ocean melting into it. A pool on a blazing rooftop in Cairo, the sound of Friday prayers reverberating in the air. A cavernous pool in a Paris basement, what was that movie? *Three Colours Blue.*

It was Della who interrupted her.

'Yeah, yeah,' she said impatiently. 'But would you want to know? That was the question.'

'No,' said Addie with a sigh. 'I suppose not. But it's a nice thought all the same.'

Chapter 33

The morning of Addie's birthday, the post fell from the letter box on to the floor with an unusually loud thud. A lovely sound, Addie registered it from where she lay in her warm bed. The bedroom door was standing ajar and she could almost see the heap of letters on the floor. Her heart gave a little jump, she could feel the love.

She had woken early, thinking of her mum, as she always did on her birthday. Imagining that morning, thirty-nine years ago now, when her mum would have opened her eyes with a start, her sleepy brain suddenly waking to the fact that this was the day. Outside it would have been still dark, her mum would have rolled over to wake Hugh, the cramps racking her bursting belly. Or maybe the pains would have come upon her as she was making the breakfast for Della, or as she was walking up to the shops with the buggy. Maybe she had rushed home to phone Hugh at the hospital, stopping to ask a neighbour to babysit for her while she was gone.

Addie has never been told the story, so she has to imagine it for herself.

'What time of the day was I born? I need to know what time I was born so I can work out my astrological chart.'

'Good Lord, child, I don't have a notion. How on earth would I remember that?'

But Addie remembers thinking, how on earth would you not?

As she lay in the bed, she could hear Bruno clattering around in the kitchen. From the sound of it he was making her breakfast. She had to resist the temptation to jump up to collect the post. If she got up it would spoil the surprise. She needed to pee as well but it would have to wait. Already she could smell the coffee, she could hear a ping as the microwave finished heating the milk.

'Happy birthday to you. Happy birthday to you. Happy birthday, dear Addie. Happy birthday to you . . .'

His timing was perfect, he set the tray down on her knees just as he sounded the last note. She tilted her face up as he lowered his, closing her eyes to savour the kiss. The creamy smell of the steaming coffee, the thin sun filtering through the window, the grizzly scratch of his beard against her chin as he kissed her.

He had brought the post in with him, the letters stacked up on the edge of the tray. She started to open them hungrily.

A card from Hugh, *To a Wonderful Daughter*. There was a picture of a teenage girl on the front, standing proudly beside her pony. Hugh still picks these cards out for Addie as if he hasn't noticed that she's turned into an adult now. *To my darling Addie*, he had written inside. *A very happy birthday. Love, your old dad*. The nib of his fountain pen was so thick that the ink pooled in the loops of the letters. His cartridge was running out on him, the handwriting was getting more and more watery as he went along. *PS*, he had written at the bottom of the page, the letters so faint they were barely legible. *I must get myself some new ink*.

Addie smiled as she laid the card down on the tray. She reached out for the next envelope in the pile. A card from Della, it had a photograph on the front of two old ladies sitting in deck chairs wearing their swimsuits. There was a sheaf of homemade vouchers tucked inside. A voucher for a hug from Lisa. A nail-painting voucher from Elsa, another for dog-brushing from Tess, a back massage from Stella.

Bruno was perched on the edge of the bed. Addie passed the vouchers over for him to see.

The little parcel she kept until last. A padded brown envelope, it didn't look like there was an awful lot inside. Addie tested the weight of it on her open palm, it felt like it was empty. She recognised the writing on the front, the familiar upright character of Maura's hand.

'Open it,' said Bruno, 'I'm intrigued.'

But Addie set the parcel back down on the tray. Picking up her coffee cup, she leaned back against her pillows.

'I always wait a while before I open a parcel. Once you open it, the magic is gone.'

'I bet you even did that when you were a kid.'

Addie nodded. 'It used to drive Della crazy.'

In a businesslike fashion, she put her coffee cup back down on the tray and picked up the parcel again. She began to slide her finger under the seal, flipping it open and slipping her hand inside. She pulled out a small folded page of notepaper, then a square paper sleeve housing an unmarked DVD.

'Curiouser and curiouser.' She opened up the letter.

Bruno sat and waited while she read.

'She's in Rome, she won't be back until next weekend.'

She began to read the letter out loud. She was imitating Maura's voice for Bruno, her tone brusque and businesslike.

'At last I found somebody to put this on to a DVD. We have the technology!'

She looked up at Bruno.

'She doesn't say what it is. Oh Jesus. I hope she's not going batty, she's the only sane person I have.'

She tucked the letter and the DVD back into the envelope. Only then did she realise Bruno was waiting for her to say something.

'Oh Bruno! Apart from you of course.'

Good old Maura, she never fails to remember Addie's birthday. For Helen's sake, more than for Addie's even, it's a date that is forever etched on her mind. She always feels Helen's death sorely on this day, the tragedy of it as fresh to her as if it were yesterday. The arbitrary nature of it is still unfathomable to her. They sat beside each other every day for six years in school. Now Helen is gone and Maura is still here. There's a responsibility that goes with that, there are duties that must be carried out. She sees herself as the custodian of her friend's legacy.

After Helen died, her jewellery was divided up between the

girls. It was Maura who divvied it out, Hugh had asked her to do it.

'Maybe there's something you'd like to keep back for yourself?' she'd asked him. 'As a memento.' And he'd said, 'God no, sure what would I be doing with any of her jewellery?' He had never thought to ask her whether she might like something as a keepsake. So Maura just divided the jewellery out between the two girls.

One rainy Monday afternoon after she picked them up from school they spilled it all out on to the bedspread and they raked through it with their eager little fingers. The pearl necklace, that was what Helen got for her twenty-first. The aquamarine earrings, Helen's mother had given her those for her wedding. The gold lockets and the charm bracelets, they were childhood trinkets. The lapis lazuli pendant and the tourmaline choker, presents from Hugh over the years. The engagement ring went to Addie, and Della got the wedding ring.

'Do you think that's why Della got married and I didn't?'

'Oh Addie! Don't be so fatalistic! What makes you think you won't get married yet?'

Ever the optimist, that's what they love about Maura. She believes in them, she wants the best for them.

'There's a lovely man in your future, Addie, I'm absolutely certain of it. It's just taking him a while to appear on the horizon.'

That was just after she'd broken up with David, when Maura had said that. Addie found herself thinking about it more and more now, it was as if she was testing it for strength, like a creaking floorboard you're about to step on to.

With her dancing black eyes and her sharp little face, it's always hard not to find yourself going along with Maura. The certainty of her, it's as if she can see things nobody else can see.

'There are plenty more fish in the sea,' she had said. 'Next time, forget the mackerel, go for the salmon!'

The girls inherited Helen's money of course. All that money she'd been left by her own parents in their wills, it passed on to Hugh when she died but he was too proud to touch it. So it was salted away for Addie and Della. Eventually it bought them both a roof over their heads.

There was some silver too, a canteen of cutlery that Helen's parents had been given as a wedding present. Hugh encouraged Della to take that with her when she moved out. Helen's christening mug, Addie had that on a shelf in her kitchen, she stored stray boxes of matches in it. She wasn't sure what else you would do with it.

Addie took no comfort from any of these things she had of her mother's. They were hard things all of them, just bits of metal and glass. You could take them out and look at them, you could polish them and buff them, but there was nothing of her mum in them. They were as impersonal as stones.

That's why the relics of the saints are so precious to people. Addie understands why people flock to see them. She's seen the pictures on the television, thousands of people queuing up for hours upon hours just to lay a hand on an old box with a fragment of bone inside it, or a clutch of dead hair.

Addie wishes she had a relic of her mother. She wishes she had a tooth or a lock of hair, something that might still harbour some essence of her. A swatch of fabric from a piece of clothing maybe, something that had touched her skin, something that she had sweated or bled into. If Addie had such a thing she would put it under her pillow. She would reach her hand in there during the night, finding comfort in the touch of it.

It was early evening before she got around to watching the DVD. They'd spent the day out on Howth Head, winding their way along the cliff paths, down on to one beach and then another, the dog crashing over the stones into the water. The headland, the lighthouse, the weaving road down into the village. They had stopped to buy fish on the pier, slipping into a pub for a pint of Guinness and a pack of crisps before straggling slowly back to the car. A hot bath, and now Addie was sitting on the floor in front of the TV. Her hair was still wet and she had a towel draped over her shoulders. Bruno was in the kitchen making the birthday dinner. A smell of garlic and aniseed. Searing butter. The sound of hot liquid being poured into a colander.

Addie pointed the remote at the TV and switched it to DVD mode.

The screen went blue.

She pressed play.

A plain black screen, there was a date written across the middle in clean white print. *8th January 1974*. Addie's fourth birthday.

Cross-legged on the carpet, she sat staring at the screen. Her heart was still.

The date faded away. A burst of noise as the picture

emerged. A wandering camera, it swung across some kitchen cabinets, coming down to hover over a row of little faces. Half a dozen little girls in party dresses were lined up at the kitchen table like skittles. The camera jolted and the little girls turned to look to the right of the picture, their eyes huge and bright.

Addie sat in the glow of the television, an expression of wonder on her face.

The camera roved over to the right, and she saw herself. She was standing on a kitchen chair, leaning eagerly over the table. Her hair was in two high bunches, feathery tufts growing out of either side of her head. Her chubby hands planted flat on the table, she was jumping up and down on her hind legs like a donkey.

Steady, Addie, steady, shouted someone. You're going to come off your chair.

Suddenly the lights went out, the faces became shadows. Eyes and teeth flashing in the darkness, shifting shapes. A male voice began to sing a booming happy birthday. Happy birthday to you. The little girls joined in, the camera wobbling along the row to capture their chirruping little faces. A woman's voice rose above them in an exaggerated soprano. Maura, thought Addie, it could only be Maura. You could hear her but you couldn't see her.

The camera had reached the empty doorway, a cake lit by four candles appeared out of the darkness. You saw the candles first, only afterwards did you notice the disembodied face floating above them. The flickering light threw shadows up over her like splashes. Her eyes were dancing as she sang along.

The camera stayed with her as she moved gingerly forward. Coming up behind Addie, she raised her elbows out to the side, making a hoop of her arms. Carefully, she lowered the hoop over Addie's bobbing head, setting the cake down in front of her on the table. She bent down so her face was next to Addie's and she whispered a prompt. The next thing Addie was huffing the candles out, there was a little cheer and the lights came back on.

Addie watched her four-year-old self proudly survey the table, her cheeks bright dabs of pink under the harsh overhead light. She watched as the camera waved around the kitchen. Her mother was cutting the cake now, distributing thick slices on thin paper plates that were buckling under their weight. Her hair was long and tawny, she had it pinned up in a messy bun on top of her head. Every so often she would push out her bottom lip to blow away a rogue curl that kept falling in front of her eyes. She was wearing a high-necked Victorian blouse, her mouth a wide red bow. She leaned back against the kitchen cupboards, a cigarette in her hand. Hugh was beside her, it took Addie a second to recognise him. An extravagant lock of hair swept across his forehead, he had a cigarette in his hand too. As Addie watched them, her mum leaned her head down on Hugh's shoulder for a moment. Then the picture abruptly ended and the screen went black.

When Bruno came in from the kitchen he found her crying. She was still sitting on the floor facing the television. Her back was straight, she had her legs crossed in front of her like a yogi, but her shoulders were shaking as she cried.

Addie had never seen a moving picture of her mother before. Photographs yes, but a moving picture is different. A moving picture is real in a way a photograph could never be. After all these years, to see her brought back to life again, it was a physical shock. Addie hadn't been expecting it.

When Bruno found her she was heaving with sobs, the air coming out of her in shuddering gasps. Jesus, he said, what's wrong? He rushed over and crouched down on the floor beside her, the tea towel still in his hand. He started to rub her back, up and down with the flat of his hand, in an effort to calm her.

Her face resting in her hands, she was shaking her head from side to side as if she was trying to shake the shock out of her. She was crying so much that it was hard to make out what it was that she was saying. Bruno leaned in towards her as he tried to decipher it.

'I don't remember her,' she was saying. She was sobbing bitterly into her hands. Bruno rubbed her back. He was still struggling to understand what had happened.

'I thought I had some memories of her, but now that I see her I know I don't, I must have made them up.'

She looked up at Bruno, her eyes red and confused.

'I don't know why I'm so upset. It's just that she's different from how I remembered her.'

She laughed at herself as she wiped her nose with the sleeve of her jumper.

'I'm sorry,' she said. 'I don't know why I'm so upset. I suppose it's just that I wasn't expecting it. It took me by surprise, that's all.'

'You don't need to explain,' said Bruno, 'there's no need to explain.'

'You're lucky,' she said to him afterwards. After they'd eaten the fish, after they'd cleared the plates away. They were talking about it calmly now, Addie was over the shock of it.

'You're lucky,' she said, 'you have a lifetime of memories of your mum.'

'Yes,' he said. But his face was so sad. 'Sometimes it seems to me there are too many memories of her. The end especially is very vivid to me. I sometimes wish I could forget the end.'

Chapter 34

Hugh has this way of sighing when he talks about his patients. He will suck in his breath and let it out again in a long weary sigh, before he even says anything. As if he knows there's only one way all of this can end, as if he can hardly muster the energy to explain it to you.

That sigh, that's exactly what Addie's doctor did when he sat her down to tell her the results of her scan. That was how she knew. She knew what he was going to say before he even opened his mouth.

He had asked her was there anyone she wanted to phone. He suggested that maybe she would like to have somebody with her.

She heard herself saying no, no, there was nobody she wanted to phone.

He sighed again, tracing the edges of her file with his finger. He didn't open the folder, he just traced the perimeter of it. His nails were well cared for, she noticed, he had beautifully manicured hands.

'The news is not good,' he said. At last, he looked up at her. 'But I think you knew that.'

She nodded. And it seemed to her that she did know. It seemed to her in that moment that she'd always known. She nodded, ignoring the tears that were welling up in her eyes.

He spoke in short, pithy sentences. She found herself agreeing with everything he said.

He was just drawing a diagram for her on the inside cover of the file when his mobile phone rang. It took him a moment to get the phone out of his pocket. When he did, he squinted at the screen. Then he glanced up at Addie, holding his index finger up in the air as he answered the call.

'Doherty.'

He had an air of boredom about him, a languid demeanour. His sun-splotched face spoke of Sundays on the golf course. Holidays in the Algarve. He had a fountain pen in the breast pocket of his suit jacket. It unsettled Addie, was he not worried that it might run?

'That leaves us one theatre down next week.'

He shifted his gaze to Addie, raising his eyes up to heaven in a gesture of complicity. She found herself smiling back at him sympathetically.

'Do I have a full list on Monday?'

As he listened he worried his teeth with his tongue. Addie watched him, intrigued. He had the exact same mannerisms as Hugh, they could have been brought up in the same house.

'For God's sake,' he was saying, 'we'll be weeks catching up.'

He was tipping his chair back, like a schoolboy. Abruptly he let the front legs come crashing back down as he disconnected the call.

'You'll have to excuse me,' he said, tucking the phone into his jacket pocket. 'I need to pop outside for a minute.'

He asked her was she OK to wait, would she like one of the nurses to come in and wait with her.

'No,' she said. 'No, I'm grand, thanks.'

Even as she was saying it, it seemed like a silly thing to say.

If you'd seen her there, she would have seemed like a woman in a painting, she was so still. She was sitting with her feet planted on the floor, her hands limp in her lap, her face lifted up to the light coming in the window.

She looked out the window at the big shifting sky. She looked at the soothing shape of the mountains. The quivering trees. The rude green of the golf course. The women in their knee-length trousers and their visors, their golf carts shaped like stooping vultures.

She looked at all of these things and thought, nothing. She was processing the words she had just heard. Groups of words, whole sentences. Words like untreatable. Not feasible. Worst case scenario.

She heard the pop of a golf ball, like something bursting. She heard the TV in the next room, the unnatural patterns in the newsreader's voice. A creak from the window frame, it was groaning in the sunlight. Footsteps in the corridor outside, she heard them approach and then she heard them move away again. She heard all of these things and thought nothing of them.

The sky was starting to make her feel dizzy, it was moving too fast. The trees were unsettling her, a chaotic pattern to their rustling. Only the mountains could still her, the solid dusky blue of them, their smooth rolling gradient. As long as she looked at the mountains she felt all right.

They had wanted her to call someone but she didn't want to. All she wanted was to go home.

Afterwards, she made her way back down the corridor towards the lift. As she walked, she was conscious of the extraordinary ease of her movements, of her body and her mind working together as a finely tuned instrument, as if she was floating through space. She pressed the button for the lift, watching as the digital display showed its progress down through three floors. When the doors opened she stepped in. She stood with her back to the mirror, watching as the doors closed. One floor down, she waited for the doors to open again, then she stepped out into the hospital lobby.

She remembered to take her parking ticket out of her handbag, slipping it into the slot in the machine at the front door. She found the correct coins in her pocket and fed them in. She watched the reading on the machine count down the parking fee until it reached zero. She waited for her ticket to re-emerge. Taking it in her hand she tucked it carefully into the pocket of her coat. She stepped outside, pausing for a moment in the set-down area as she tried to remember where she'd parked her car. Oh yes, over by the tree.

She opened the passenger door first, tossing her handbag on to the seat. Then she walked round to the driver's door and lowered herself in. The radio came on when she started the engine, she leaned over to turn it off. She followed the arrows on the ground towards the exit, pausing at the barrier to feed her ticket in. The barrier went up and Addie drove out of the hospital.

The traffic was thin and she was home in less than ten minutes. She opened the door, throwing her keys on to the hall table. She took off her coat and hung it up. Then she stepped into the living room.

Lola was lying on her mat behind the door. When Addie came into the room she raised her head expectantly. She started swishing her tail backwards and forwards along the floor.

Addie got down on her knees. Letting herself fall to the side, she curled herself around the dog. She wrapped her arms around the dog's hot little body and nuzzled her face into the back of her neck. She breathed in the compost heap smell of her.

There are no words to describe what she felt.

The words only came in instalments. It seemed that her mind could only assimilate them morsel by morsel, like an equation that needs to be broken up into several pieces before you can work it out.

She processed the things they'd said, arriving at their meaning painstakingly slowly. They mean I'm not going to get better, she thought, they mean I'm going to die. The others will go on without me. Lola will still be here, Bruno will be here. Hugh and Della, and Simon and the girls, their

336

lives will go on. But mine is going to end. I won't be here any more.

The enormity of it was measured by the number of times it went through her head, by the frequency of it. In the same way that you measure the proximity of a storm by the space between the lightning and the thunderclaps. By that measurement, this storm was near.

Chapter 35

She tried explaining it to Della.

'Do you remember when we were kids and we used to toss a coin? To do something really horrible, we'd toss a coin. Or if there was a bunch of us we'd pull straws.'

Della was crying, she hadn't stopped crying since Addie had told her.

Addie was trying to comfort her. 'It's OK,' she kept saying, 'it's OK.' Until Della wailed, 'Would you stop saying that? It's not OK.'

'No,' said Addie quietly, 'I suppose you're right. It's not okay.'

She tried talking Della through it.

'Do you remember that feeling? We used to pull straws and whoever lost would have to climb over the wall into the bad lady's garden. You knew someone had to lose, you knew it could be you. But it never really sunk in. Not until that moment when you were left holding the short straw. And everyone was standing there looking at you, they were all standing there holding their long straws and they were looking at you with this awful pity on their faces.'

Della had tears rolling down her face as she listened. Addie felt strangely removed, she might just as well have been watching someone cry on TV. She wasn't sure she'd ever seen Della cry before.

'Anyway,' said Addie. 'That's what it's like. It's a lonely feeling.'

'Hugh,' said Della all of a sudden, her eyes huge and haunted. 'Does Hugh know?'

Addie shook her head.

'Oh Jesus, Ad. How are we going to tell him?'

'Don't worry, I'll tell him. It's up to me to tell him.'

'And what about Bruno?'

Addie shook her head vigorously.

'Not yet. Not until after the inauguration.'

Addie was in charge now, she had to be. For the first time in her life, she was the leader, she was the one who had to lead the way. It was a good feeling. She felt strong like never before. She knew she was going to be able to do it.

'Are you not angry about any of this?' said Della. Her eyes were all red, her forehead furrowed, as if she was trying to understand it. 'I can't believe you're not angry.'

'Maybe I would be,' said Addie, 'if there was anything I could do about it. But there doesn't seem to be. So what's the point?'

*

Della was angry, she was in a rage.

As soon as Addie left she raced back through the house and out the back door as if she was going to vomit. She staggered down towards the bottom of the garden. When she got there she didn't know what to do with herself. She couldn't believe this was happening to her. It was like a nightmare. She wanted more than anything for it not to be happening.

She sat down on the brick edging of the flower bed, buried her face in her hands and howled. The noise came from deep within her chest, a terrible moaning sound. She had her fists tightly balled, her nails digging into the fleshy palms of her hands. She cried dry, retching tears as her mind hurtled through a dark tunnel, realisation after awful realisation jumping out at her like neon signs in the dark.

Her life would never be the same again. She would be left alone in the family with Hugh, she would have to live out the rest of her life as Hugh's only daughter. She would have to live with his grief, she would be the only one left to take care of him in his old age.

Her tears were wet now, they were wet and real. She could feel them forming in her heart, hot globs of them rolling up through her throat, coming down her face so fast that she couldn't wipe them away.

Who would she be without Addie? Less glamorous, without Addie to compare herself to. Less wild, without Addie to be shocked by her. Less interesting, less loved. Less, less, less.

Without Addie, her life would be impossible. How could Addie just die? How could that happen? She couldn't imagine the sequence of events, she couldn't put it together. This was all about Addie, that thought occurred to her now. This was Addie's tragedy. The rest of them would mourn her and they would miss her but their lives would go on. It was Addie who was going to die. Della's heart broke for her.

At least it's not one of the children, she realised with a shudder of relief. Imagine if it was one of the children, even Addie wouldn't want that to happen. But then fear gripped a hold of her. If this could happen to Addie what was there to say that one of the children wouldn't be next?

Her mind was racing through it all so fast now that she couldn't keep up. She had no way of knowing where it was all going to end. She rested her forehead down on her knees and wept.

When Addie told Hugh he looked at her as if she was mad.

'What on earth are you *talking* about, child?'

Addie spoke to him very gently.

'They're sure, Hugh, they told me they're absolutely sure.'

His face was screwed up in disdain, his chin drawn back into his polo neck in a gesture of disbelief.

'Do you even *know* what you're saying, Adeline? Do you have any idea what it is that you're *saying*?'

Addie said nothing.

'You see,' he said, as if he'd proven his point. 'This is all some kind of a misunderstanding. We'll have it cleared up in no time.'

'It's not a misunderstanding, Hugh, you have to listen to me.'

'Who was it that you went to?'

'Dermot Doherty.'

He gave a snort, breathing a harrumph of air out of his nostrils.

'Oh Christ, Doherty. And he was the one who told you this?'

'Yes,' she said. 'He was the one who gave me the diagnosis.'

'What diagnosis?' he roared. 'Jesus, child, you don't realise what it is you're talking about. You can't just *say* things like that, you can't just toss around these words as if they don't mean anything.'

'Hugh,' she said, gently. 'You're shouting at me.'

'Of course I'm shouting at you! I'm trying to get some sense out of you.'

So quietly that you could hardly hear her, Addie pleaded with him.

'Please, Hugh. Stop shouting at me. I haven't done anything wrong.'

She left him rifling through the drawers of his desk for his address book. Muttering to himself, a stream-of-consciousness rant.

'My own daughter,' he was saying. 'How do you think this makes me look? My own bloody daughter.'

He was down on his hands and knees now, wrenching open the bottom drawer of the desk. He didn't even notice Addie slipping out of the room.

'How do you think this makes me look? That I didn't even notice! Christ, this takes the bloody biscuit.'

With a grunt he fell upon the address book, heaved himself

up on to the chair and started flicking through the pages. Dennehy, Devane, Doherty. He pounded the number into the phone but it went straight to voicemail. He hung up without leaving a message. Next he rang the hospital switch and asked for Doherty's rooms. A delay as he was transferred through to another voicemail, this time the voice of the private secretary. She began to take him through the opening hours of the clinic. He looked at his watch and saw that it was already half past seven. He hung up the phone in disgust. He tried ringing Della's mobile but it rang out. He tried it once more and once more it rang out.

He started leafing frantically through the address book again. He was looking for the name of a guy he'd met at a conference in Philadelphia, was it Bristol where that guy was based? An Irish guy, he'd mentioned he was trialling a new treatment. But could Hugh remember his name?

Letting the address book fall out of his fingers on to the desk, he flopped back in his chair as if he'd been punched. A dazed expression on his face, his hair was wild, his eyes milky as he tried to process what was happening to him. He was still holding the receiver in his left hand, a faint beeping sound coming out of it. He slammed it back on to its cradle.

When Simon came home he couldn't find Della anywhere.

He went looking for her all over the house. None of the kids knew where she was, they couldn't say when they'd last seen her. They'd taken advantage of her absence and were all sitting up on top of the double bed eating cream crackers and watching *Sabrina*. The crumbs were everywhere.

The back door was wide open. Simon stepped out on to the dark patio, an irrational fear rising in him.

'Della,' he called out. The sound of his own voice spreading through the darkness only made him more nervous.

He walked down towards the back of the garden. With every step he was becoming more afraid of what he might find there.

'Della!'

She was hunched down on the ground behind one of the flower beds, a small dark shadow. She hadn't even heard him approaching.

'Della, what on earth's the matter?'

She raised her head and looked at him as if she was seeing a ghost. Her skin was splattered and blotchy in the moonlight, her face a deathly white.

'It's Addie,' she said, her voice cracking as she spoke. 'It's Addie, Simon, she's sick.'

And Simon got down on his knees beside her and he said who, he kept asking who's she seeing, who's the oncologist, who's the radiologist.

'Would you stop asking me that, I don't know!' screamed Della. 'Does it make any difference who she's seeing? I don't see how it makes any difference.'

'No,' said Simon, leaning his forehead against hers. 'You're right. It probably doesn't make any difference.'

Chapter 36

What possessed Addie now was a strange sense of calm. You could almost call it elation.

Everything seemed very clear to her all of a sudden. It was as if she was flying over the sea on a clear day. On a cloudy day the water looks opaque, you might as well be flying over mountains, or fields. It might be a grey sea or a blue sea, it might be a murky green but all you can make out is the surface of the water, there's no indication of anything underneath. But on a sunny day, on a sunny day the water is illuminated, you can see right through to the bottom. You can see black patches of rock and coral, you can see a shoal of fish sliding through the water. You can see the dark stencil shape of the plane you're travelling in, there it is moving steadily over the surface, the waves rippling through it.

That was the kind of clarity Addie had now. Her life was lit up from above and she could see it all clearly. A state of mind she had always longed for but never once achieved, not until now.

When Bruno woke up she pretended she was still asleep.

The whole time he was pottering around the bedroom getting dressed, she lay on her tummy, her face pressed into the pillow, her eyes shut. She was wide awake, listening to everything. She heard the cupboard door opening and closing, she heard Bruno picking up his boots and carrying them out of the room, she heard the soft pad of his socks on the floor, the hem of his jeans scraping along the floorboards. When he moved out into the kitchen she tracked the sound of the water bubbling in the kettle, the sound of him pouring dry food into Lola's bowl.

Even while he was out of the room, she didn't dare to open her eyes. She lay there suspended in time, listening to his day getting under way. Before he left he came back into the room. She was lying on her back now. He leaned down to kiss her and she turned over on to her side, she gave a sleepy groan. Even to her, it didn't seem very convincing.

'See you later,' she called after him as he went out of the room again. Her voice was spluttering and husky, the first spoken words of the day.

'Absolutely,' he said as he went out the door. 'And don't forget, we have a date with history!'

It was hard, not telling him, last night had been hard. Every minute that went by she had to concentrate so hard on not telling him, she had to concentrate on behaving normally. It wasn't his grief that she was dreading, she knew that couldn't be helped. What she feared most was an overreaction. She couldn't bear it if everyone freaked out. What she wanted more than anything now was calm.

She swung her legs over the edge of the bed and sat there for a moment, stretching her arms up over her head and arching her back. With the stretch, her nightdress was drawn up over her thighs, revealing the clutch of hair between her legs. It was distasteful to her, that tuft of hair, the shameful earthiness of it.

She stood up and moved towards the door, catching a glimpse of herself in the mirror on the back of the open cupboard door. The nightdress was a bit indecent, it only just about skimmed the cheeks of her bum. The straps were too loose, the bodice was hanging low, revealing a bulge of breast under each armpit. Ripe, that was the word that occurred to her, she looked young and ripe. It was incongruous, it was out of step with her situation.

She pulled her robe from the back of the door and wrapped herself up in it, tying the belt defiantly around her waist.

She was humming cheerily to herself as she made her way into the kitchen, unaware of what it was that she was humming.

Lola was standing there waiting for her, her tail swaying expectantly. Addie gave her a cursory petting, more like a pat on the back. Then she straightened up again, going over to switch on the coffee machine. She couldn't bear to think about Lola yet.

With her coffee cup in her hand, she found herself wandering around the apartment. Like a museum visitor, she floated from room to room. She looked over her desk, it looked like a sweet shop. The jars of pens and pencils all in a row, the neat little pots of brightly coloured ink. A half-finished ink drawing of a swimming pool spread out on the surface of a piece of dappled watercolour paper.

She wandered into the bathroom next, and stood there with her back against the sink. There was a lone black swim-suit hanging from a hook beside the bath. The fabric was perished in places, Addie could see that from here. The back of the suit was threadbare, the white elastic showing through.

Hopefully it will see me out, thought Addie. And she was relieved that she wouldn't have to trawl town for a new swimsuit. It had been getting harder and harder to find a decent swimsuit recently, it was all bikinis in the shops these days.

She scanned the bottles of cosmetics at the end of the bath. The conditioners and the shampoos, the glass vial of bath foam, she found herself measuring them. She was gauging what was left in them.

She had found herself doing this on holidays sometimes. Embarking on a manic effort to squeeze the last drop of suncream out of the tube rather than buy a new one on the last day. She had sometimes found herself cutting open a tube of moisturiser with nail scissors, or digging with her tooth-brush into the mouth of the toothpaste tube to prise out enough paste for one last brushing. The satisfaction of eking things out, that was a good feeling. She allowed herself to indulge it now.

The teabags in the kitchen cupboard, she found herself peering in and taking stock of them. The coffee, the cereals, the dried pasta. Sure she'd hardly need to do any more shopping. If she was careful, she might never have to set foot in a supermarket again.

She was still humming to herself. She realised with a smile what it was that she was humming, and she started to sing along.

'Well now everything dies baby that's a fact
But maybe everything that dies someday comes back.'

This was happening to her more and more now, she would find Bruce Springsteen playing out in her head. Sometimes she would even find herself singing a few lines out loud. Indoctrination, that's what she'd been subjected to. She was slightly embarrassed to find that it was working, it seemed to her a sign of a weak character. Like finding yourself lapsing into a foreign accent.

She looked down at her plain grey robe. A soft wool jersey, she had chosen it because it was comfortable. Her pale legs were sticking out the bottom, her toenails as always unpainted.

She felt bad about that now, she wished she'd made more of an effort with herself. She thought about her wardrobe, all those corduroy jeans and V-neck sweaters, all those leggings and T-shirts. She ran a hand through her cropped hair, wishing it was long so she could pin it up.

Suddenly, a tremendous desire took hold of her. She wanted to doll herself up, she wanted to spend the whole day getting ready for him. She pictured herself sitting at a dressing table somewhere, carefully applying red lipstick. She imagined what it would be like to squeeze herself into a tight dress, she imagined wearing suspender stockings and high heels. She would be waiting for him at the door when he came home. Already she could feel a current running through her, already she was pressing herself up against him, she could feel his hand sliding down her back. Taking him by the arm, she turned and moved away from him, pulling him behind her like a girl in a perfume ad.

'Put your make-up on fix your hair up pretty
And meet me tonight in Atlantic City.'

A flood of regret for all the things she'd never done, it hit her like a slap. She was filled with remorse for this life of hers that had been only half lived.

She decided to spend the morning alone, just herself and the little dog. She turned her phone off and left it plugged into its charger on the hall table. She took a tenner out of her purse and stuffed it into the pocket of her coat along with some dog bags and her keys.

For no reason whatsoever, she found herself walking along the canal rather than the beach. A day religious in its beauty, the branches of the trees were bare black stencils against a bright white sky. The reeds along the banks a pale whispery gold. The canal water was still and dark, the reflections of the trees stretching way down into its depths.

Addie had a moment, maybe two, to take it all in before Lola broke the peace. She went tearing down the grass verge and launched herself into the water, a big bellyflop of a dive. A man on the opposite towpath stopped and laughed out loud. Addie's heart swelled with pride.

There was a heron on the far bank, Addie only noticed him now. He was standing among the reeds, his body perfectly balanced on one skinny leg. His black eye glinting, he was watching Lola's approach.

The man on the far side was watching too. He was standing with his hands in his pockets, a slow smile on his face. There were some winos gathered on a bench further along the towpath, they'd all stopped what they were doing to watch the show. Lola had quite an audience as she chugged through the water towards the heron.

Addie watched it all unfold, but even as she was watching it she was thinking about Della. Poor Della was probably at home right now, leaving yet another message on Addie's voicemail. She might even be sitting outside Addie's door wondering where she was. Hugh would be pounding the phones, he'd be ringing round every one of his colleagues, demanding second and third opinions, lining up more scans and more blood tests. Addie was exhausted even thinking about it. And Bruno, Bruno would be sitting happily at his desk in the library. Poor Bruno, he was blissfully unaware of what was about to befall him.

She thought about all of these things and yet she wasn't unhappy. If anything she was more conscious of the big empty sky above her. The damp ground beneath her feet. The silence here, in the middle of the city. She was savouring this stolen time. She felt like she was mitching from school, the pleasure of your freedom heightened by your awareness of the school day rolling on without you.

Lola was almost within reach of the heron now, one leap and she would be upon him. He waited another unbearable

351

second, his magnificent body utterly motionless. Still he waited, as the dog scrambled to gain purchase on the muddy verge. Then slowly, so slowly, he raised up his wings. One great thundering beat and he was airborne. Lola was just dragging herself out of the water, she was springing up into the air after him, her bedraggled little body leaping higher and higher with every spring. The heron made a wide turn, coming back low over the canal, his shadow moving along the water below him. A triumphant fly-by, he soared over Lola's head in cool jubilation.

The winos were all laughing. The man in the suit chuckled, then he turned away and continued on along the towpath. Poor Lola stood staring after the heron. She looked baffled, she couldn't understand how she had been cheated out of her victory. She stared after him for a minute and then she seemed to forget what it was that she was staring at. She shook herself off and plunged cheerfully back into the canal.

Addie waited for her on the bank, registering with surprise this moment of pure, inappropriate happiness.

'Amid gathering clouds,' said Obama.

A freezing cold morning in Washington, the images on the screen were bleached by the cold, they were like black and white pictures that had been retouched. The red tie, the mustard yellow coat that she wore, all vivid blotches of colour on a sepia background.

'Chartreuse,' said Addie. 'The colour of her coat. It's not mustard, it's chartreuse. Believe me, this is one of my specialist topics.'

She was relieved that she'd got this far without telling him. A feeling like pride, she had accomplished what she'd set out to do. She'd made it over the line. All of a sudden it seemed easy not to tell him. As if she'd staggered to the end of a marathon only to find that she could just as soon keep on running.

She was caressing her secret like a smooth stone. She had it safely concealed in her closed hand. She had only to open her fingers and it would be revealed. A small movement but one which seemed impossible now to carry out.

She sat cross-legged on the couch. She was conscious of the way her head sat on top of her body. She was aware of the way she was holding her arms, the set of her shoulders. The dog was on the floor below her, looking up at her with steady eyes. Bruno was on the couch beside her, transfixed by what was happening on the screen.

She sat there and she turned her secret over and over in her head, she could think of nothing else. Now that her deadline had passed, every moment seemed like a deception. The joy he was feeling, the delight he was taking in this day, it was all in her gift. She could pull it out from under him at any moment. A horrible feeling, she was like an assassin waiting to pounce.

All of a sudden it was inconceivable to her to go any further without telling him.

Chapter 37

Bruno sat in the corridor outside the doctor's consulting rooms.

Eight o'clock in the morning and already he'd been waiting there for nearly an hour. The secretary kept popping out to tell him that he wouldn't be seen without an appointment. 'There's no question of you being seen,' she said, a steely note creeping into her voice. 'That's what I'm trying to explain to you. I'm afraid you're wasting your time.'

Bruno was at his most courteous. 'I appreciate that, ma'am,' he kept saying, 'but I think I'll just sit here and wait for him all the same.'

Every so often a patient would come out and shut the door quietly behind them. A few minutes would pass and then another one would come along to knock on the door, a deep rich voice calling out to them to come on in. The secretary would appear with a new armful of files. A short rap on the door before turning the door handle and she would disappear inside. Giving Bruno a wary glance as she went.

He has to come out some time, Bruno was thinking. Unless he climbs out of the window, he'll have to come out the door.

It was just a question of waiting.

For Bruno the shock of it was physical.

Not since his cocaine days had he felt like this. His head was pounding, his stomach churning like he'd just stepped off a rollercoaster. He was exhausted and yet he was wired at the same time.

He hadn't slept a wink. He had waited until she was asleep and then he had crept out to the living room again. He had turned on his laptop and started surfing the web. And what he had found there was horrifying, it made terrifying reading. He'd never heard of this thing before, he didn't know things like this even existed any more.

There was a chart of survival rates. Twenty per cent after one year. After three years, five per cent. Median survival from diagnosis, three to six months. Bruno knew that Addie had been through all this before him, he was as certain as he could be that she'd already followed this very same trail. He imagined he could see her footsteps ahead of him in the snow.

Virtually without symptoms, it said on all the websites. Notoriously difficult to diagnose. By the time it's discovered it's generally too late for treatment.

'Oh, how terrible,' said his sister, her voice straining to understand. Five in the morning in Ireland, midnight back in

355

the US, he had phoned her against his better judgement. He was perched on the arm of the couch in his T-shirt and his boxers, his bare toes curled under a cushion. The glow of the laptop screen was the only light in the room. He was whispering so as not to wake Addie.

'What a terrible thing,' said Eileen. 'I remember her so well! She's the younger one, right? Oh, she was the sweetest little thing. Not like the older one! The older one was a piece of work.'

It had been a mistake to ring. As soon as he heard her voice he had known it. She had been alarmed by the call. No, she hadn't been asleep! Even as she was saying it he could hear her struggling to make the lie sound convincing. He could hear the relief in her voice when he told her he was all right. He could hear her breath settling down, he could almost hear what she was thinking. This was somebody else's tragedy, not theirs.

In fairness to her, how could she possibly understand? As far as she knew, this was just a midlife crisis he was having, it was just a holiday romance. A girl he'd only known for a couple of months, a girl who would soon be a thing of the past. That's all Addie would ever be to his sisters, he could see that now. And a thought flitted across his mind, just a shadow of a thought. He would never be able to go back.

He could picture Eileen standing in the hallway, shivering in her nightdress. The phone cradled between her shoulder and her ear. Summoning the energy to be there for him when he needed her. He knew she would be longing to be back in her bed.

'Isn't there anything they can do?' she had asked.

'No,' Bruno had said, 'I'm afraid there doesn't appear to be.'

It was hard to believe, in this day and age, that there were still things that couldn't be fixed.

'What about the States?' he had said to Addie after she first told him. 'What about stem cells?'

But she'd just kept shaking her head.

'I don't really mind,' she had said. 'That's what I want you to try to understand. It's good that it's me it's happening to. I don't mind as much as someone else would.'

At that moment, Bruno would have done anything for her. Anything she'd asked of him, he would have tried to do it. But the one thing she had asked was something he wasn't capable of doing. He could not understand it, he could not make himself understand. It made no sense to him.

'I know it's very selfish of me,' she had said. 'It's much worse for all of you, I know that.'

Her voice was clear and steady as she spoke.

'You see,' she said, 'I never thought I could be this happy. That's all that matters to me, that we've been so happy.'

Even now, he could hear her saying it. He could hear the lightness in her tone, the cheerful delivery. He knew that she meant what she was saying. But still he couldn't accept it.

He had the feeling that he'd just lost a monumental argument, that he'd taken one side in a great debate about the meaning of life, and that he had lost without quite understanding why.

Two hours he'd been waiting now. Ten patients had been and gone. Ten trips back and forth by the receptionist, ten files

357

delivered. Bruno was just contemplating a dash to the coffee machine when he heard a commotion out at the front desk. The next thing Hugh came barging round the corner.

He looked crazy, his hair standing up on end, huge dark circles under his eyes. He looked like a mad scientist who'd been up all night in his laboratory. He stopped short in the middle of the corridor when he saw Bruno. A startled look on his face, it was as if he was trying to work out where he'd seen him before.

Bruno stood up to meet him. They squared off against each other for a moment, like love rivals.

'He won't see me,' said Bruno. 'I've been here for almost two hours already. They keep saying he won't see me.'

'The hell he won't!' said Hugh, and he made straight for the closed door. Without so much as a knock, he had wrestled it open, he was storming into the room with Bruno trailing after him.

The doctor looked up when they came in, a bored expression on his face. The patient who was sitting in front of him swung round to see what was going on, she looked terrified.

Hugh stood there in the middle of the room, his feet planted wide apart, like a bull about to charge. Bruno fell in beside him, trying not to look too ineffective by comparison.

'Hugh,' said Doherty evenly, his eyes drifting over towards his patient in silent apology.

'Dermot. I've been trying to reach you for two days! Did you not get any of my messages?'

'Ah yes, I'm sorry about that.' He waved his hand about dismissively on his limp wrist. 'I was out of town, I was at a conference. I'm afraid I left my mobile behind.'

He had this slow demeanour, as if every movement was an effort.

'Look,' he drawled, 'give me a moment would you, we were just finishing up here.'

Bruno was about to turn to leave the room when he noticed that Hugh was going nowhere, he was firmly standing his ground. Reluctantly Bruno stayed put.

Doherty had no choice but to wrap up the consultation. His patient jumped to her feet. Clutching her handbag and casting a fearful look at Hugh, she scurried out of the room.

'Now, gentlemen,' said Doherty, gesturing to the two empty chairs in front of his desk. 'Won't you please sit down.'

Hugh didn't budge.

'What did you think you were doing?' he roared. 'Seeing my daughter without telling me!'

'You're upset,' said Doherty evenly.

'Of course I'm bloody upset, Dermot. I've just been told my daughter has an adenocarcinoma. And nobody had the bloody courtesy to ring me to tell me about it!'

Doherty held both his hands out flat in front of him and brought them slowly down in a pacifying gesture.

'Would you calm down, Hugh, I didn't even know she was your daughter until I came in this morning. How on earth was I to know she was your daughter?'

Hugh could picture the rush to pull the file. He would have stabbed at the button on the intercom. 'Get me Adeline Murphy's file, would you? I need to have a look at it.'

Hugh had taken a step closer to the desk. He was glaring down at Doherty menacingly.

'Is that the way we do things now? We give a young girl a

diagnosis of terminal cancer without making sure she has someone with her?'

Doherty looked up at him like a disrespectful pupil. His voice was deep and eminently reasonable.

'We asked her if she wanted to call someone. For God's sake, Hugh, what do you take us for? She didn't want to call anyone, we had to respect her wishes. She's hardly a girl, for Chrissake, she's a forty-year-old woman.'

Thirty-nine, thought Bruno. It seemed like an important detail to him but he didn't say anything. He wouldn't have been able to get a word in anyway.

'You broke off the consultation to discuss hospital politics! You were talking about ward closures and nursing shortages while you were giving her the prognosis!'

Doherty raised his eyebrows. His voice, when it came out, was almost a yawn.

'I hardly think you're in a position, Hugh, to be lecturing anybody about doctor–patient etiquette.'

'You bastard!'

Before Bruno knew what had happened, Hugh had launched himself across the desk. Doherty gave a little yelp and flipped back his chair to escape the attack. Bruno had to spring forward to get a grip on Hugh, it took all his strength to hold him back.

'You bloody bastard,' he was saying, spitting the words out through his teeth. 'You miserable bloody bastard.'

Doherty was leaning his chair right back against the wall now, looking almost amused by the whole thing.

Bruno dragged Hugh backwards out of the room. The last image he had before they fell out into the corridor was of

Doherty straightening his tie as he brought his chair back down to rest on all four legs again.

Bruno watched Hugh as he weaved his way through the rows of cars towards the taxi rank. He had his head hanging down, the bald patch at the back clearly visible. He made a piteous sight.

Bruno had offered to walk him home but he'd mumbled something about an appointment. He had seemed in a hurry to get away.

The fight was gone out of him now, he'd been forced into a retreat. That loping walk of his, he was for all the world like a giant predator, returning home from a day's hunting without a kill.

The man was a law unto himself. He was everything Addie had said and worse. He was a nightmare. Obviously, he was a nightmare. And yet, despite all his flaws, it seemed to Bruno there was something heroic about Hugh.

Bruno couldn't recall when he had last admired someone so much.

Chapter 38

Hugh stood at the gates of the Four Courts and studied his watch.

He was a full hour early. He decided to go down to the canteen and treat himself to a second breakfast. He was quite hungry actually, he hadn't noticed that until now. He'd been in such a rush to get out of the house, he hadn't eaten properly. He queued up with a tray at the counter, placing an order for two fried eggs, two rashers and two sausages. Some toast and a pot of tea.

'I'll bring them down to you.'

A young man standing behind him in the queue kept stealing glances over at Hugh for some reason. Hugh was aware he was being watched, he tried to ignore it. He shuffled along the counter, piling cutlery and napkins on to his tray. He helped himself to some pats of butter, a miniature pot of marmalade with a cheerful gingham lid. He slid the tray on towards the till, offering it up for the scrutiny of the checkout lady.

'That marmalade is two euro.'

'Pardon me, what was that you said?'

'The marmalade, you have to pay two euro for it.'

For a moment he contemplated putting the marmalade back. It seemed to be what was expected of him. But he badly wanted it. He could taste it already, the delicious gloopy tang of it on the buttery toast.

'Yes,' he said, holding out a twenty-euro note. 'Yes, that's all right.'

The man beside him was watching the whole exchange. For some reason Hugh had the feeling that he was being judged. He picked up his tray and carried it to the furthest corner of the room. He sat down at a four-person table, his back to the wall, where he could keep his eye on everything. Too late, he realised that he should have bought himself a newspaper. They had a stack of them up beside the till. But he wasn't prepared to go back up and get one now.

The man who'd been watching him had joined a middle-aged couple at a table in the middle of the room. They were having coffee and scones, the man made no secret of the fact that he was watching Hugh. He was leaning in towards the others but his eyes were fixed on Hugh as he was talking.

There was something familiar about them. Hugh was just trying to place them when his breakfast arrived. A lady in a plastic shower cap set the plate down in front of him. He noticed with distaste that she was wearing a rubber glove.

'Mind that plate,' she said. 'It's hot.'

Without thinking he put his hand out to touch it, scalding the tip of his middle finger. He laid a paper napkin out on his lap, picked up his knife and fork and tucked into his food.

How long has it been since I've treated myself to a fry, he was thinking. Well, I'm not going to have it spoiled on me now just because some oddball is staring at me. Probably a patient, he was thinking, it's impossible to remember them all.

He cut into a sausage, dipping it into the yolk of his egg with childish pleasure before popping it in his mouth.

They were leaving now, thank God, they were struggling to their feet. The younger man was helping the older pair to gather up their coats.

Hugh kept on eating his breakfast, monitoring their movements out of the corner of his field of vision. It looked like they were coming over this way. Definitely one of them must have been a patient, they were probably coming over to thank him. He'd have to rush them through it or his breakfast would get cold.

'Mary,' the younger man was saying. He was tugging at her arm, trying to stop her. 'Just leave it, would you?'

'I'll only be a minute,' she said, coming round to stand in front of Hugh's table.

It was only then that Hugh recognised her.

'There's just one thing I'd love to know,' she said to him.

Her eyes were small and beady, her face dry and lined. The way she looked at him, it nearly stopped his heart. Nobody had ever looked at him like that before, with such pure and unadulterated contempt.

'Have you ever stopped to think,' she said, 'how you would feel . . .'

For the rest of his days he would remember the way she said it. The way she put the stress on that one particular word.

'. . . how you would feel if it was *your* daughter.'

Immediately, they saw the physical change in him. You noticed it as soon as you saw him coming through the leaded glass door. It was if the air had been let out of him. He looked deflated. He looked old.

He collapsed on to a chair opposite them. He had a leather satchel with him but he didn't open it, he just laid it down on the table in front of him. He didn't say a word to either of them, he just sat there with his helpless little satchel before him. His overcoat was folded over his left arm. He had the appearance of a man waiting for a train at the end of a very long day.

'Good morning, Hugh!' said the solicitor in a deliberately buoyant tone. The barrister echoed the greeting, his voice deep and theatrical. He was wearing his wig and gown. It gave him an added layer of drama, to have his costume on him. The solicitor looked a bit drab next to him, like a plain old female bird. A young junior counsel stood anxiously by the wall. Say nothing, she'd been told. There's no telling what would set him off.

They all waited for a response but there was no indication that Hugh had heard them. There was no answer from him. He just balanced there on the small upholstered chair, a slight trace of a frown on his face, as if he was trying to remember something.

The two lawyers looked at each other nervously. For a moment, neither of them quite knew what to do.

'Well, Hugh,' said the solicitor at last. 'There's a few things on the list ahead of us but it looks like we should get on some time this morning. The plaintiff will be the first up.'

Hugh looked through him. He was wearing a strange expression, like he was asleep and the two men sitting across the table from him were just people in his dream.

The solicitor looked down at the stack of papers in front of him and started shuffling through them, looking for something.

'We'll just take a quick run through things,' he said, glancing up at Hugh. 'Just to make sure we're all on the same page.'

He looked across to the barrister for support. But the barrister had leaned back into his chair. He had his robe spread out under him, his pinstriped legs stretched out into the corridor. He was watching Hugh with an expression of detached amusement, his eyebrows slightly raised as he waited to see what was going to happen next.

The double doors flapped and a gust of wind came through. The next thing a huge round man with a red face was standing beside the table. He had a suit on that looked like a shell he didn't quite fit into, his body squirming its way out of it.

'McGovern versus Murphy?'

The barrister sat up with a jolt.

'Court five?'

'Yes,' said the solicitor. 'Yes, yes, that's us.'

'The judge is ready for you.'

'Oh, very good. Yes, very good. We'll be with him directly.'

The solicitor was on his feet now, bundling his papers into a small suitcase he had on the floor beside him.

'We're in luck,' he said unconvincingly, looking up at Hugh.

'Show time!' said the barrister. And as he jumped up he wrapped his gown across his chest and pushed out his ribs. A primal gesture, he might as well have beaten on his chest with his fists.

Hugh looked from one to the other of them, a dark shadow passing over his face.

Before they knew what was happening he was on his feet and mumbling a garbled apology. He had his satchel clutched to his chest, his coat still slung over his arm. He stood there for a moment, as if he was waiting for the door of a train to open. The next thing he was on the move. Without another word, he navigated his way round the tipstaff, pushing through the double doors and out of sight.

They tried to catch up with him.

They dashed out after him, the three of them, the young junior counsel struggling to run in her high heels. They stood out on the street looking this way and that but there was no sign of him anywhere.

They tried calling him on his mobile to no avail. They tried for an adjournment but the judge was having none of it. In the end, they were forced to go ahead without him. Hamlet without the prince, whispered the barrister to the solicitor as they took their seats at the front of the court-room.

The insurance company made one last push to settle but the family dug their heels in. They wanted their day in court.

As witness after witness was called, as experts arrived from England to testify, still there was no sign of Hugh. Message after message was left on his answering machine, but not a word back. Three days it dragged on for, each one worse than the last.

The outcome was a foregone conclusion.

Chapter 39

The doctors said three months and three months it was, almost to the day.

Time is a funny thing, when you put it like that. You'd think it was rigid, you'd think it was something that can only be measured out in equal segments, one minute inevitably following the other at an unforgiving pace. But that's not the way it works. Time can be elastic too, it can be anything you want it to be.

The doctors said three months and it seemed like such a short time when they said it like that. But what went into those three months, that was the thing that defied all logic! Addie and Bruno managed to squeeze a whole marriage into that skinny little sliver of time.

The marriage ceremony was held in the register office on Grand Canal Street. You were supposed to give them three months' notice, Addie smiled when she heard that. You had to get a document from the courts to secure an exemption. You had to show you had a valid reason why the standard notification period posed a difficulty for you.

'That we can do,' said Addie cheerfully.

She had planned the wedding herself, right down to the last detail. The silver satin dress she bought in a second-hand shop, she spray-painted a pair of her old shoes to match. No fancy car, no photographer, no flowers, no fuss. She booked Danny's place for a late lunch, she ordered steak and chips for everyone. A stack of meringues as a cake. She told one of the waitresses she'd pay her extra to sing and play the guitar.

'Oh, I see,' said Della, 'it's a crazy wedding you're having.'

But Addie just laughed. That was the good thing about her situation, she could do anything she wanted to. The freedom of it! She felt like the strings that had been holding her down all her life had been severed. She was floating above the ground now, blowing along like a leaf caught on a gust of wind.

She gave the kids the job of smuggling Lola into the register office. She was absolutely determined that Lola be there.

'She's the closest thing I have to a baby,' she told them, and they all nodded solemnly.

They decided Lola needed a disguise. They dressed her up in a sunhat and a velvet wrap that they draped around her shoulders like a cloak. Then they manhandled her into a cloth carrier bag that they slung over Elsa's shoulder. All you could see were Lola's frightened eyes peering out from under the brim of the hat.

'Straight out of *ET*,' said Hugh when he saw her. And the kids crumpled into a noisy heap of giggles.

Tess sat Lola beside her on the bench, keeping her arm around her to hold her steady. She fed her a stream of dog biscuits from her pocket. The registrar was very cool, she pretended not to notice.

Afterwards they all strolled round the corner to Danny's. They drank champagne from stubby little wine glasses and Bruno read out the messages that had been sent by his sisters. There was a strict ban on speeches but Maura stood up anyway and proposed a toast. Nobody else attempted to speak, not even Hugh, who was surprisingly quiet. He kept patting Addie's arm, his eyes glistening behind his glasses with what looked alarmingly like tears.

After lunch the waitress settled herself and her guitar on to a high stool by the bar.

'First dance,' said the little girls, starting up a chant. 'First dance, first dance.'

Bruno stood up and held his hand out to Addie with a flourish. The kids were all clapping as she was dragged to her feet. She followed Bruno over to a tiny patch of floor space between the table and the coffee machine. Still holding Bruno's hand she leaned over and whispered something in the waitress's ear.

By special request of the bride, announced the waitress. And she started to sing, in a clear sweet voice.

'I beg your pardon,
I never promised you a rose garden.'

Bruno threw his head back and laughed, spinning Addie round by her waist in a tight little circle. They were both of them singing along as they danced.

'Along with the sunshine,
There's gotta be a little rain sometimes . . . '

The little girls were up dancing now, waltzing awkwardly along the narrow aisle in pairs, crashing into the tables as they went.

' . . . so smile for a while and let's be jolly:
Love shouldn't be so melancholy.
Come along share the good times while we can . . . '

Hugh and Maura sat side by side in quiet solidarity. They looked for all the world like an old married couple. Simon was watching the girls nervously, afraid they were about to break something. Della was staring at Addie and Bruno in horror, following them with her huge round eyes as they moved about the room.

'They're mad,' she said quietly to herself, 'they're completely bloody mad.'

Addie and Bruno were whirling around the room, lost in their own private joke. Della jumped up and ran to the loo in a flood of tears.

Before they left, Addie asked Danny to take a group photo.

In the photograph, they're all standing outside under the

shadow of the awning. Addie and Bruno are in the centre of the group with the little girls spread out in front of them. Hugh and Maura are standing to one side. Hugh has his arm draped awkwardly around Maura's shoulders, pulling her into the picture. Simon and Della are on the far side, Simon's hands firmly planted on Lisa's shoulders. Tess and Stella are both craning their heads back to look at Addie. Elsa is crouching down to hold Lola still.

Afterwards, Della will study that photograph time and time again, searching for any evidence of what it was they were going through. She will scrutinise their faces one by one, looking for an indication that there was something wrong. She will stare at her own face, looking back in time for some visual evidence of her agony. But there's nothing there, it's quite eerie. It's as if the photograph failed to capture anything at all.

In the picture you see Hugh standing tall, his head held high with his old air of defiance, his glasses reflecting the light. Maura is leaning in under his embrace, as jaunty as ever. Simon is at ease with himself, his shoulders thrown back, his child held square in front of him like a shield. Della has adopted a frozen smile. She looks as if she's been placed in this group by mistake. They could all be strangers to her.

Bruno is standing proudly in the centre of the picture, his arm around Addie's waist. He's looking straight at the camera, a patient air about him. And Addie, Addie looks like she doesn't have a care in the world!

*

For their honeymoon they drove down to the south coast. Bruno had found the hotel on the internet. A stone building set into the cliffs, it had an infinity pool looking out over the sea.

'How did you find it?' asked Addie. 'It couldn't be more perfect.'

Outside the window the view was clear right to the other side of the bay. You could pick out the mobile homes on the far headland, you could see the fluorescent yellow and pink buoys rolling in the water, the mustard-coloured lichen on the rocks below the hotel.

They were sitting in matching armchairs facing out of the window. They were drinking champagne out of thin flutes, both of them bundled up in huge white hotel bathrobes. Addie had her feet perched up on the coffee table in front of her. For once, she'd painted her toenails.

'I feel like a character in an F. Scott Fitzgerald novel. I feel like some beautiful tragic person in a Swiss sanatorium.'

He turned and looked at her and his eyes were so sad.

'Oh Bruno. Please don't look at me like that.'

She turned her head to look out the window. She took a sip of her champagne.

'You'll marry again,' she said gently.

He shook his head. 'I won't.'

She had her eyes fixed on the sea as she spoke. Her tone was matter-of-fact.

'Oh, you will. You'll marry again. I'd like you to, it would be the greatest compliment you could pay me. Della says people who've had one good marriage always get married again.'

She turned to face him.

'It makes sense,' she said. 'It's because they know how to be happy.'

When she turned back to the window the view had disappeared. All you could see was thick white cloud across everything, like a curtain. You could hear the sea, you knew it was there. You just couldn't see it.

'You're forgetting,' Bruno was saying, 'I've also had a number of unhappy marriages.'

'Oh, don't be worrying about that,' she said. 'We've managed to break that cycle.'

That night they ate seafood in the hotel restaurant, they said no to coffee and dessert, they were in bed by nine. They left the bedroom window open so they could listen to the sound of the waves crashing endlessly down on to the sand as they slept.

During the day they walked the beach.

'God, I miss Lola,' said Addie. 'I feel so disloyal walking on a beach without her. We should have brought her with us.'

'Oh, I'm sure she's having a good time with Hugh.'

'What would you give to be a fly on the wall?'

'Poor Lola,' said Bruno with a little shake of his head.

'Poor Hugh,' said Addie, laughing.

'I bet they're getting on like a house on fire.'

Addie hooked her arm into his, she looked up at him hopefully.

'Bruno,' she said. 'Do you think there's any chance that Hugh might get attached to her?'

And by the look on her face, he knew what it was that she was asking him, he knew what she was hoping for.

'Stranger things have happened,' he said, squeezing her hand.

And she nodded happily.

'It's nice to think of them together.'

They stopped walking. They had reached the end of the beach. The clouds had parted and the sun was out, the spray from the waves dancing in the sunlight. They turned to face the sea.

'Let's swim!' she said all of a sudden.

'Are you crazy?' said Bruno. 'It's April!'

But she was already pulling off her runners. She was dragging her jumper over her head. The next thing she was standing there before him in her vest and knickers.

'Come on! Quick, while the sun is out.'

Looking at her there, it was hard to believe there was anything wrong with her.

Bruno struggled out of his clothes, piling them up beside hers on a rock. Hopping along on the balls of his feet, he followed her across the damp sand towards the water.

He went in up to his knees, his arms out either side of him. He flapped them up and down, as if he was hoping he might rise up and hover above the water. She was ahead of him. She was already in beyond her hips.

'Just so you know,' he shouted, 'I don't think we should be doing this.'

She turned from the waist, the wind blowing her hair across her face.

'What are you so worried about?' she called back. 'That it might kill me?'

And with that she plunged her shoulders down under the water. He took a great leap and dived in after her.

They both came up gasping. Laughing and spluttering, swimming like crazy to keep the blood flowing. Bruno swam one way, she swam the other. Then they turned and came back towards each other.

'It's heaven!' she shouted. She was lying on her back, looking up at the sky. 'I love it!'

She flipped over on to her front again, swimming up to where Bruno was standing chest deep in the water. She draped her arms around his shoulders. She wrapped her legs around his hips and pressing her pelvis into his she sat up out of the sea. She was almost weightless.

'Would you look at us,' she said, throwing her head back and laughing a dirty laugh. 'Straight out of a honeymoon brochure.'

And she bent her head down to kiss him, her wet hair whipping his face, her arms closing tighter around his neck. The kiss could only have lasted a few seconds. But for Bruno it would be frozen in time. He would carry that kiss with him always.

They broke their trip off a day early.

'Bruno,' said Addie as they finished breakfast one morning. 'I think I need to get home.'

And Bruno didn't ask her why. He just went back to their room and started packing up their things. He gathered up their walking boots and their raincoats and their jumpers and he threw them into the suitcase. He took the wet swimsuits off the hook on the back of the bathroom door and he sealed them inside a plastic bag before putting them into the case too. He tossed the little shampoo bottles into his toiletry bag, he checked under the bed and he looked inside the wardrobe to make sure they weren't leaving anything behind. Then he carried their suitcase out to reception and paid the bill. He left Addie sitting on a sofa inside the door while he went to bring the car round.

'You're a good husband,' she said as she sat in the car. 'I couldn't have got myself a better husband.'

But Bruno didn't reply. He waited until she had the car door closed, then he swung a tight circle and drove down the hill towards the village. The beach was on their right as they passed through, another moment and it was gone.

Chapter 40

When Addie got sick, it was Bruno who nursed her. Della sat for hours on end and read to her. Simon took charge of her medical care. He liaised with the doctors. He put in place a care plan and he ordered up a range of ominous accessories that would be needed further on down the line. Strangely shaped cushions appeared, some kind of a winch. An electric airbed. The others watched the arrival of these things in horrified silence. To everyone's surprise, Hugh deferred to Simon without so much as a murmur. He was just a foot soldier now, if anything he seemed relieved that someone else was in charge.

Hugh's job was to walk the dog.

'My nemesis,' he called her. 'My nemesis and I are going for a stroll.'

They were reluctant companions, Hugh and Lola, each of them equally reluctant. Every morning Hugh would arrive to collect her. And every morning Lola would have to be hauled out the door, her hind legs dragging along the ground behind her, her jaw rigid with her determination not to go. Nobody could tell if she didn't want to leave Addie or if it was just that she didn't want to go with Hugh.

'Don't worry,' he growled, once they were outside on the street. 'I don't like you much either.'

The other dog walkers kept asking after Addie. 'Oh, she's fine,' Hugh had said, the first time he was asked. 'She's just gone away for a while.'

Even as he was saying it he was aware that it was a strange thing to do, to lie about it. He was aware that he was digging a hole for himself that it might be awkward to get out of. And so it was. Now they all kept asking when she was coming back.

'Oh, not for a while,' he would say, turning to the dog for help.

She wouldn't cross the road for him. When they got up to the beach road, they were standing at the traffic lights and the lights went red and Hugh started to walk across but Lola wouldn't budge. He didn't want to drag her across, not with people watching.

So he leaned down and scooped her up in his arms, cursing her under his breath as he staggered across the road. The smell of her, he couldn't drop her quick enough when they got to the other side.

'Go on,' he roared, 'off you go.' And he gestured at the expanse of beach ahead of them. 'What are you waiting for?'

But the dog kept coming round in front of him, hopping up and down expectantly, her eyes on his. He had to stop walking so he wouldn't trip over her.

'I don't have a ball to throw for you, you stupid hound.'

He made shooing gestures with his arms. 'Go off and have a run, you stupid dog, isn't that what we're here for?'

There was a pleading tone to his voice that surprised him. But still she didn't get it. She was skibbling backwards as he walked towards her, studying his face. As if she expected him to produce a ball from his pocket.

'Go on now, you're being a nuisance.'

At last, she gave up on him. She started charging after some birds, whirling around in a triumphant arc as they scattered into the air. He was relieved that she'd found something else to do. And yet he couldn't escape the feeling that he'd let her down, that he was an inadequate dog walker.

He walked, looking down at the ground as he went, his hands clenched in his pockets. The pattern of the sand was interesting to him, it had deep heel marks etched into it, as if thousands of hooves had left their imprint. He couldn't imagine what had made that pattern, it must have been the water.

His left eye suddenly went into spasm. He squeezed the eye shut, wiping away a big drop of water with his finger. A drop of rain, it must have been. It must have fallen right down inside his glasses, plopping into the corner of his eye. The first drop of rain, there were more of them coming down now, big wet globs of rain. The sky was still blue, the rain seemed to be coming out of nowhere.

He ploughed on, his head hanging low as he walked. There were bird prints in the sand, he noticed now, thousands and thousands of them. Tiny three-pronged prints, as clearly defined as if they'd been marked out with a penknife. What birds did they belong to, he wondered. They must be tiny little things to make such delicate prints. He looked around him and saw only big white birds. Not seagulls, they didn't seem to be big enough to be seagulls, so what were they? He didn't have a notion. Nearly forty years he'd been living on this beach and the birds were still strangers to him. An odd realisation, it made him feel utterly at sea.

He looked around and saw the expanse of beach slanting away from him, the water curving around the sand like molten glass. And the dog, crashing through the shallows. She, at least, was at home here.

He became aware of an unbearable silence, of the quiet sky above him, and the empty beach all around. Suddenly he remembered the iPod Addie had given him for Christmas. It occurred to him in a flash that he had it in his pocket, he had slipped it in there with this very situation in mind. He had imagined himself striding along the strand like a character in an opera, the sky a blazing backdrop behind him.

He unravelled the wires and managed somehow to stuff the earphones into his ears. Holding the gadget in his left hand he started prodding at the dial with the middle finger of his right hand. Addie had shown him how to do this but he'd forgotten what she'd said. After some trial and error he managed to bring up the menu and with another stab he brought a list of artists up on the screen. One last stab and, miraculously, the music started flowing. He was flooded with a sense of achievement. He tucked the thing back into his pocket and began to stride out towards the water's edge.

The piece of music was familiar to him. He'd heard it before, but he couldn't identify it. A trill of wind instruments, a sense of anticipation. He pushed his shoulders back and puffed his chest out as he walked, he could feel his heart swelling in his breast.

A plucking of strings, he waited for the voice that he knew was coming.

'Belle nuit, ô nuit d'amour . . .'

He followed that beautiful voice in its rise and fall, his throat tightening with emotion as he listened. He was forced to stop walking. He stood and let the music wash over him.

'Le temps fuit et sans retour
Emporte nos tendresses.'

There were other women's voices too, they separated and came together again. He had a curious notion that it was his wife and his daughters who were singing, he had a sense of them all around him, the women in his life.

And before he realised what was happening, he was crying. He was crying openly, he didn't care who saw him. He was crying for the wife he'd loved and lost, for the daughter he loved so much and would now lose. And for the daughter he'd never been able to love enough, the one who would be with him until the end.

There was a pattern to it all, he could see that now, there was a pattern he'd failed to see. Suddenly it seemed to him that he had never understood anything until now. He had stumbled through his life without seeing anything around him. And now that he could see it, he felt as if his heart would break.

He had defined himself by what he was not. And it was very clear to him now. He wasn't a good person. Almost deliberately, he had contrived not to be a good person.

How long since he had cried? Not since his wife had died. Had he cried even then? He had no recollection of it. But he cried now. He stood there at the edge of the water, and he howled in pain. The rain was coming down hard and he was getting drenched but he hardly noticed. His glasses were streaked, he could see nothing through them. He wrenched them off and stuffed them into his pocket, wiping his eyes with the sleeve of his coat. The music had finished and he could hear his own sobbing. A pathetic sound, it made him cry all the more. He held his face up to the sky and he let the rain beat down on him. The water was streaming down his face along with his tears.

He would never know how long he stood there, it could have been a minute or it could have been an hour. He might have stood there for ever, if he hadn't begun to notice something. The water was moving towards him, he could actually see it coming in around his feet. The sea was pooling into the ripples of the sand, it was as if it was advancing. Little tiny waves rippling through the shallows. They were coming his way.

He moved back one step and watched with fascination as the water moved with him. He moved back again and again it followed him. He noticed the birds now, they were gathered along the edge of the sand, little birds pecking away at the tide. He wondered why they were all gathering there? The dog was standing beside him, her head held stock still as she watched what he was watching. As if she was trying to figure it out as well.

He looked to his left and right but it was all a blur, he couldn't see a thing through the rain. Then it occurred to him that he'd taken his glasses off, that was why he couldn't see! He took them out of his pocket and tried to dry them on his sleeve. When he put them back on the glass was all streaked and cloudy. But at least he could see.

They were stranded.

They were standing on a spit of sand, perhaps a hundred yards wide, a couple of hundred yards long. Himself and the little dog in the middle. Around the edges, a fringe of tiny birds. And all around them, the sea.

He turned to face the shore. He could see the Martello tower, he could make out the long grey line of the promenade, and above it the houses along the Strand Road. Between here and there, an expanse of grey water.

He wasn't frightened at first, he was just furious with himself. 'Of all the stupid bloody ...' He didn't even finish the sentence. 'Of all the bloody idiots ...'

He was angry with the dog. 'Could you not have warned me? Could you not have barked or something? You stupid bloody hound, useless, that's what you are.' And Lola just stood there and looked at him, she looked like she was pleading for some reassurance but he didn't have any to give her.

He had no phone with him, he knew that straight away. He wondered for a moment did the iPod have any kind of communication mechanism on it but he discounted that thought. By a process of elimination, he arrived at the only course of action available to him. He would have to walk. It couldn't be that deep. He was soaked through anyway, it wouldn't make much of a difference. And the dog could swim. The dog could swim, couldn't she?

He stepped boldly off the sand bar, striding forward into the shallows. It took a moment for the water to seep into his shoes but when it did it was surprisingly warm, it was almost comforting. The dog was splashing along beside him, maybe this wouldn't be such a big deal after all. It was a bit of an adventure, that was all. Already he was imagining himself telling the story later, he would provide them all with a bit of entertainment, he would offer it up. He would let them have their money's worth. It would be a good diversion.

The water was up past his ankles now, the fabric of his trouser legs plastered to his skin. His feet were numb. The dog was in as far as her belly, much deeper and she would have to start swimming.

The rain had stopped, thank God, but it was getting colder, the light was going down. How long would it take to get dark? He didn't know. It wouldn't be much fun if it got dark.

He was making slow progress as the water got deeper. His coat was heavy at the bottom, it was dragging him back. You had to push your way through, it was surprisingly hard work. He concentrated on his technique. Big steps, he used his hips to charge the weight of the water. He turned round and saw the little dog chugging along behind him.

The iPod! He thought of it just in the nick of time. The water hadn't got into his pockets yet. He took it out, congratulating himself already on his foresight. He clutched it in his hand, holding it high up above the water as he walked.

It seemed like he wasn't making any progress, the promenade

looked as far away as ever. He looked behind him to measure how far he'd come, but the sandbank had disappeared. He was surprised by how dark it was getting, the water back there looked almost black, the sky a slate grey.

He was wading up to his waist in the water now, his body convulsing with the cold. He was holding his arms up above his head as he walked, as if he was carrying an invisible rifle. He tried not to think about what would happen if the water got any deeper. Would he be able to swim? He wasn't so sure. Not with all these clothes on, he didn't see how he would be able to swim.

This is how people die. Only now did that occur to him. Every week, you read about people drowning, you read about these things in the paper and you can't imagine for the life of you how it actually happens. But this is how it happens.

He couldn't die. What an inconvenience that would be for everyone, along with everything else that was going on.

It was almost pitch dark now. The lights were coming on in all the houses along the front, he could even make out his own house, a dark space sandwiched between its cheerfully lit neighbours. The tower was a flat shape against the sky, the trees and shrubs inky black. He could see the promenade up ahead of him, it was just a dark outline, shadowy people walking up and down. If he called out they might even be able to hear him. He knew he wouldn't call out.

How absurd! He found himself almost laughing at his situation. At the possibility that he might die here, within sight of his own house. Within earshot of dozens of people. What a ridiculous way to go. He could imagine people reading about it in the *Irish Times*, he could imagine their horror.

There would be a tinge of mirth. He thought about the tragi-comic figure he would cut in death and he shuddered at the thought.

That's what he was thinking when he stumbled. His foot hit on something under the water, a rock perhaps, and he fell forward. He thought he was going all the way down. In his panic, he thought he was going under. But he landed on his knees, his chin just above the surface, his hands desperately pushing at the water to keep himself up. The iPod was gone, he realised, he had let it go as he fell.

It didn't matter. Things had taken on a new dimension now, the iPod didn't matter. Somehow, he struggled to his feet again, gasping with the shock and the cold.

He had to get on now, he knew that. He had to focus all of his energies on moving forward. He was so cold, there was a real danger of hypothermia, it was essential that he keep moving. His coat was so heavy, it was weighing him down. With considerable difficulty he managed to pull it off him. Letting it fall back into the water, he struggled on without it.

He lifted his head up and fixed his eyes on the dark outline of the promenade. He held it in his sights like a target. Somebody up there had spotted him. There was somebody standing on the rocks, gesticulating wildly at him, but he couldn't hear what the person was saying. How embarrassing, he thought, how hideously bloody embarrassing.

The water was shallower now, there was no question about it. Suddenly he was finding it much easier going.

Up ahead of him he could see a whirling light. A squad car, two reflective jackets making their way steadily to the edge of the promenade.

Hugh trudged onward through the lapping shallows. The water was only up to his ankles now. Only moments ago, his situation had seemed life-threatening. Now it was ridiculous. He was miserable with humiliation, dreading his arrival. He was almost tempted to turn round and go back. As he reached the bottom of the steps one of the Guards was hovering above him. He reached his hand down to help Hugh up.

There was quite a crowd gathered up on the promenade to watch. The dog walkers and the joggers and the kids out playing football, they had all stopped to see the show. Hugh climbed the steps ever so slowly. His wet clothes clung to him like seaweed, his shoes were soggy. He had his head bowed down, praying that he would be allowed to pass in silence.

Behind him on the beach, a gangly sign stood high above the water on rusted stilts. A sign that had been there for years and years but Hugh had never once noticed it.

DANGER, it said.

PERSONS GOING 200 METRES BEYOND THIS NOTICE ARE IN DANGER OF BEING STRANDED BY INCOMING TIDE.

The Guards tried to persuade him to go to the hospital. He had a job convincing them it wasn't necessary. He glared at them, trying to muster all his professional command, in spite of the puddle of sea water spreading out at his feet.

'I'm a doctor myself,' he said in a gruff voice. 'Take my word for it, Guard, all I need is a hot shower.'

Reluctantly, they let him go. They stood and watched him as he squelched his way across the road. He was still in their sights as he climbed the steps of his house, pausing at the top to pat his hip pockets in vain for his keys. They watched as he bent down to retrieve the spare key from a crack in the stone steps. Only when the door opened did they turn away and head for their car.

As soon as Hugh closed the door behind him he peeled off his wet clothes. Climbing the stairs stark naked, he dumped the sodden bundle into the bath. He turned on the shower jets full blast and stood on the bathroom mat, waiting for the water to run hot.

And it was only then that he remembered the dog.

Chapter 41

The one thing that everybody was agreed on was that there
was no need to tell Addie.

'Not on your life,' said Della, when Hugh arrived at her
door. 'Under no circumstances must she be told.'

And Hugh nodded. His big head was lolling on his neck,
his eyes were desperately locked on to Della's face. She'd never
seen him like this before. It was as if the last piece of stuffing
had been knocked out of him. For the first time in her life,
Della took pity on him. She brought him in and made him a
mug of tea.

'I can't believe she would drown,' she said. She was thinking out loud. 'It doesn't make any sense. Lola the swimming
dog.'

Hugh sat in abject silence, his head hanging down.

'Look, Hugh,' she said, 'let's have a bit of perspective here.
It was only a dog.'

And he nodded miserably.

'In the grand scheme of things, it's probably for the best. The dog would have been pining for Addie, she would have been miserable without her.'

Still Hugh said nothing. He was grey in the face, his expression desolate. He looked old and tired.

'Addie's so sick now, she won't even notice that Lola's gone.'

Hugh was staring down into the mug of tea. He hadn't even taken a sip of it. Slowly, he brought his head up to look at her.

'Oh Della,' he said. 'How on earth are we going to manage without her?'

The evenings were brighter now, it was light up until nearly nine o'clock. Springtime, the magnolia tree in Della's front garden was in full bloom, its pink flowers opening out slowly like big clawed hands. For the rest of her life Della would take her cue from the magnolia tree. As soon as those cruel pink fists started to unfurl she would know it was time to start counting down the days.

She was finding it harder and harder to sit with Addie now. Bruno found it difficult too. She knew that without him saying it, she noticed him taking breaks. Hugh was the only one who seemed to be able to stay with her endlessly. He seemed to have an infinite capacity to sit in that sad space.

Della would find herself fussing around in the kitchen, she would find herself putting things away in the kitchen cupboards and emptying the dishwasher. Or standing out on the balcony with Bruno, smoking cigarettes, one after the other.

She would have to force herself to go back into the room. When she did go in, she would sit on the far side of the bed so she didn't have to look at Addie's face.

'You won't always have that image of her in your head,' said the nurse. 'It'll fade with time, I promise you. You'll remember her the way she was before.'

But Della didn't believe her. She knew she would never get the image of Addie's emaciated face out of her head. It was horrific to her. She was horrified by how long it was taking. She could never have imagined that it would take this long.

There was a time there, was it only a week ago? When she had prayed for it to last for ever. She'd been sitting in the window of Addie's room, reading to her as the daylight faded. She had been reluctant to turn on the lamp for fear it would break the spell. She couldn't tell whether Addie was awake or asleep but she kept on reading anyway. And it was then that she wished, she wished it with all her heart, that this time could last for ever.

That was only a week ago.

Now Della wanted it to be over. There was a pointlessness to it at this stage. It was like a book you already know the ending of. She felt like skipping the last few pages and going straight to the end.

Every so often the nurse would pull a chair up to Addie's bed. She would sit on the edge of the seat, her forearms draped over her knees, her head cocked slightly to the side. With a faint smile, she would watch Addie's face, studying her expression for any indication of pain.

'Bruno,' said Addie. 'Are you there?'

'She's awake,' said the nurse, poking her head into the kitchen. 'She's asking for you.'

Bruno came and sat into the nurse's chair, leaning down with his elbows on the edge of the bed, letting his hand rest on the covers over her thigh.

'Bruno,' said Addie, turning her head on the pillow so she was facing him. 'I was just thinking.'

She paused. It was taking her a long time to get the words out. He had to lean in to hear what it was that she was saying.

'I was thinking,' she said.

Her voice trailed off. It seemed to Bruno for a moment that she had forgotten what it was that she was going to say. But then she started again. It was such an effort for her to speak. The words fell out of her with her laboured breath. It was hard to listen to.

'I was thinking,' she said. 'How rude it is of me.'

She frowned.

'To abandon you here. With my family!'

She shook her head in self-reproach.

'Unforgivably rude.'

Her chest collapsed with the relief of having said it. She closed her eyes. Bruno lowered his head down, letting the side of his face rest on her belly. She moved her arm so it was cradling the back of his head. When the nurse came back in, it looked to her as if Addie was the one who was comforting him.

*

Addie kept waking up agitated. It was the same thing on her mind every time, always the same anxiety.

She had to pack, she needed to sort out her things. What she would take with her and what she would leave behind. She would have to clean out the apartment, she should change the sheets. How would she remember to put out the bin? She had to remember to put out the green bin.

She would start working it all through in her mind. Piecing it together slowly, it was painstaking work. The morphine was slowing her down, she was aware of that. It was taking her so long to figure things out.

Hugh leaned over and patted her gently on the hand. His voice sounded strange.

'Don't be silly, Addie,' he said, 'there's no need for packing.'

And she smiled at him as it dawned on her. It was such a relief every time. There was nothing she had to do, that's what she had to keep reminding herself. There was nothing left for her to do.

Bruno had given her a box set of *The Blue Planet* for Christmas, it was playing out on a large-screen TV he'd set up in the corner of the bedroom. He had the volume on it turned off. All you could hear was the great heaving breath of the airbed, like a sea swell. The curtains were closed and the room was bathed in shifting blue light. It was for all the world like being underwater.

Addie lay there, surrounded by all those lovely silent fish.

'Remember the mermaid?' she said suddenly. Her voice was surprisingly clear.

Hugh leaned in to her, giving a little snort.

'That bloody mermaid,' he said. 'How could I ever forget?'

Bruno was standing out on the balcony, staring up at the sky. He was smoking a cigarette. He knew he shouldn't, but what the hell.

It was pitch dark, it seemed to be darker than usual tonight. Bruno craned his head back to see if he could find the moon, but there was no sign of it anywhere. There were no stars in the sky either.

He was searching for something up there, looking for some kind of an answer.

'There's a man up there,' that's what his father had said to him.

Forty years ago, it must be nearly forty years now, his father had woken him up and brought him out into the garden. A sticky summer night, Bruno can still remember how he lay down flat on his back on the damp grass. He can still sense the large mass of his father's body lying right next to him.

'Look,' his father had said, pointing straight up at the moon. 'Tonight, for the first time in history, there's a man up there.'

And Bruno had tried to imagine it but he couldn't. He remembers lying there on the grass and trying and trying and trying to picture it but he just couldn't.

*

Time seemed to be moving so slowly.

Like when you're watching a movie and you keep falling asleep. Every time you open your eyes, it's the same scene.

Hugh was still sitting beside her in his chair, his book open on his lap, his hand resting between the pages. The door was ajar, slanted back into the corridor, the light out there a patch of yellow. She could hear a tumble of voices. Then they moved away.

Now Hugh was speaking, his voice floating around on the air.

'I'm sorry, Addie,' he was saying. 'I'm so very, very sorry.'

And she was confused, she didn't understand what he was apologising for.

She knew she should try to ask him. But she couldn't. It was as if she was in a dream. She couldn't make herself speak no matter how hard she tried.

When Della and the girls arrived they found Bruno lying on the balcony deck, staring up into the sky.

'Jesus, Bruno, are you all right?'

Bruno jerked his head up. They were all lined up at the door, Della and the four girls. They were staring down at him in amazement.

'Quick,' he said, 'you're missing it,' and he laid his head back down on the decking.

The girls rushed out on to the balcony, their faces craned back to look up into the sky.

A shaft of ghostly green light pierced the darkness, moving in a wide arc across the sky.

'Wow!'

'Omigod!'

'It's amazing.'

Bruno's voice came up out of the ground, the sound of it strangely flattened.

'You can see it better from down here.'

They all scrambled to lie down. There wasn't much room on the deck, they had to squash in together like sardines.

'Come on, Della, try it.'

'I can see just grand from here.'

'Come on, Mum, it's amazing.'

So Della lay down on the ground too. She squeezed herself in beside Tess, making a pillow for herself with her arms.

'Holy God!' she said. 'It's beautiful!'

'What is it?'

'Some kind of light show,' said Della. 'It looks like it's coming from the theatre.'

'But what's it for?'

'It's not for anything, darling, it's just for us to enjoy.'

They lay there on the wooden deck, the six of them lined up in a row like an angler's catch. Through the gaps in the wooden decking you could see the still dark water of the basin below them. Above them, the sky was seething with shifting green lights, the magic of it reflected in their eyes.

Addie could hear them all out there, she could hear their voices clearly outside the window.

The Northern Lights, she heard someone say. It was one of

398

the girls, it sounded like Stella. So that's what they were watching, they were watching the Northern Lights. Addie was so glad that Bruno had finally got his wish.

There was silence inside the room but she knew that Hugh was there. He was sitting between her and the window. It was so dark in the room that she couldn't see him. But she knew he was there.

She could hear Lola's breathing, she had a sense of her down on the floor beside the bed. She would only have to reach her hand down and she would be able to touch her. She didn't even have to reach down, she knew that Lola knew she was here.

She had a song running through her head, it occurred to her with interest that it was a song that she'd never even liked. She couldn't remember all the words, just the one line that kept looping in her head.

'*Brother Louie, Louie, Louie.*'

She couldn't remember the next bit.

A disco in Majorca. Rope-soled espadrilles on the hard dancefloor. Sunburned shoulders.

'*Brother Louie, Louie, Louie.*'

An absurd song. She did not want this song in her head. She tried to listen to the sounds in the room again. She heard Hugh shifting in his chair. She heard his book fall to the floor. She heard the dog breathing out through her nose, a long deep release of air, a long pause before the next breath.

She had images in her mind as if she was seeing them through the window of a moving car. Pale sky. Birds' nests in bare trees. A little gloved hand in a big gloved hand.

Sensations.

A shudder of cold water. Breathing out bubbles. A cherry-red swimsuit.

Outside, she heard Bruno saying something but she couldn't make out what it was. She heard the girls laughing.

And it was then that the most extraordinary thing occurred to her. A moment of absolute clarity, she knew it without a shadow of a doubt.

This is how it ends.

This Is How It Ends

Like our page, share your love,
and join the discussion

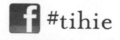 #tihie